COLLECTED WORKS OF
THOMAS LOVE PEACOCK

CONTENTS

NIGHTMARE ABBEY

There's a dark lantern of the spirit,
Which none see by but those who bear it,
That makes them in the dark see visions
And hag themselves with apparitions,
Find racks for their own minds, and vaunt
Of their own misery and want.

                                    BUTLER.

LONDON:

1818.

MATTHEW. Oh! it's your only fine humour, sir. Your true melancholy
breeds your perfect fine wit, sir. I am melancholy myself, divers
times, sir; and then do I no more but take pen and paper presently,
and overflow you half a score or a dozen of sonnets at a sitting.
STEPHEN. Truly, sir, and I love such things out of measure.
MATTHEW. Why, I pray you, sir, make use of my study: it's at your
service.
STEPHEN. I thank you, sir, I shall be bold, I warrant you. Have you a
stool there, to be melancholy upon?
BEN JONSON, *Every Man in his Humour*, Act 3, Sc. I

Ay esleu gazouiller et siffler oye, comme dit le commun
proverbe, entre les cygnes, plutoust que d'estre entre tant de gentils
poëtes et faconds orateurs mut du tout estimé.

RABELAIS, *Prol. L.* 5

13

CHAPTER I

Nightmare Abbey, a venerable family-mansion, in a highly picturesque state of semi-dilapidation, pleasantly situated on a strip of dry land between the sea and the fens, at the verge of the county of Lincoln, had the honour to be the seat of Christopher Glowry, Esquire. This gentleman was naturally of an atrabilarious temperament, and much troubled with those phantoms of indigestion which are commonly called *blue devils*. He had been deceived in an early friendship: he had been crossed in love; and had offered his hand, from pique, to a lady, who accepted it from interest, and who, in so doing, violently tore asunder the bonds of a tried and youthful attachment. Her vanity was gratified by being the mistress of a very extensive, if not very lively, establishment; but all the springs of her sympathies were frozen. Riches she possessed, but that which enriches them, the participation of affection, was wanting. All that they could purchase for her became indifferent to her, because that which they could not purchase, and which was more valuable than themselves, she had, for their sake, thrown away. She discovered, when it was too late, that she had mistaken the means for the end—that riches, rightly used, are instruments of happiness, but are not in themselves happiness. In this wilful blight of her affections, she found them valueless as means: they had been the end to which she had immolated all her affections, and were now the only end that remained to her. She did not confess this to herself as a principle of action, but it operated through the medium of unconscious self-deception, and terminated in inveterate avarice. She laid on external things the blame of her mind's internal disorder, and thus became by degrees an accomplished scold. She often went her daily rounds through a series of deserted apartments, every creature in the house vanishing at the creak of her shoe, much more at the sound of her voice, to which the nature of things affords no simile; for, as far as the voice of woman, when attuned by gentleness and love, transcends all other sounds in harmony, so far does it surpass all others in discord, when stretched into unnatural shrillness by anger and impatience.

Mr Glowry used to say that his house was no better than a spacious kennel, for every one in it led the life of a dog. Disappointed both in love and in friendship, and looking upon human learning as vanity, he had come to a conclusion that there was but one good thing in the world, *videlicet*, a good dinner; and this his parsimonious lady seldom suffered him to enjoy: but, one morning, like Sir Leoline in Christabel, 'he woke and found his lady dead,' and remained a very consulate widower, with one small child.

This only son and heir Mr Glowry had christened Scythrop, from the name of a maternal ancestor, who had hanged himself one rainy day in a fit of *toedium vitae*, and had been eulogised by a coroner's jury in the comprehensive phrase of *felo de se*; on which account, Mr Glowry held his memory in high honour, and made a punchbowl of his skull.

When Scythrop grew up, he was sent, as usual, to a public school, where a little learning was painfully beaten into him, and from thence to the university, where it was carefully taken out of him; and he was sent home like a well-threshed ear of corn, with nothing in his head: having finished his education to the high satisfaction of the master and fellows of his college, who had, in testimony of their approbation, presented him with a silver fish-slice, on which his name figured at the head of a laudatory inscription in some semi-barbarous dialect of Anglo-Saxonised Latin.

His fellow-students, however, who drove tandem and random in great perfection, and were connoisseurs in good inns, had taught him to drink deep ere he departed. He had passed much of his time with these choice spirits, and had seen the rays of the midnight lamp tremble on many a lengthening file of empty bottles. He passed his vacations sometimes at Nightmare Abbey, sometimes in London, at the house of his uncle, Mr Hilary, a very cheerful and elastic gentleman, who had married the sister of the melancholy Mr Glowry. The company that frequented his house was the gayest of the gay. Scythrop danced with the ladies and drank with the gentlemen, and was pronounced by both a very accomplished charming fellow, and an honour to the university.

At the house of Mr Hilary, Scythrop first saw the beautiful Miss Emily Girouette. He fell in love; which is nothing new. He was favourably received; which is nothing strange. Mr Glowry and Mr Girouette had a meeting on the occasion, and quarrelled about the terms of the bargain; which is neither new nor strange. The lovers were torn asunder, weeping and vowing everlasting constancy; and, in three weeks after this tragical event, the lady was led a smiling bride to the altar, by the Honourable Mr Lackwit; which is neither strange nor new.

Scythrop received this intelligence at Nightmare Abbey, and was half distracted on the occasion. It was his first disappointment, and preyed deeply on his sensitive spirit. His father, to comfort him, read him a Commentary on Ecclesiastes, which he had himself composed, and which demonstrated incontrovertibly that all is vanity. He insisted particularly on the text, 'One man among a thousand have I found, but a woman amongst all those have I not found.'

'How could he expect it,' said Scythrop, 'when the whole thousand were locked up in his seraglio? His experience is no precedent for a free state of society like that in which we live.'

'Locked up or at large,' said Mr Glowry, 'the result is the same: their minds are always locked up, and vanity and interest keep the key. I speak feelingly, Scythrop.'

'I am sorry for it, sir,' said Scythrop. 'But how is it that their minds are locked up? The fault is in their artificial education, which studiously models them into mere musical dolls, to be set out for sale in the great toy-shop of society.'

'To be sure,' said Mr Glowry, 'their education is not so well finished as yours has been; and your idea of a musical doll is good. I bought one myself, but it was confoundedly out of tune; but, whatever be the cause, Scythrop, the effect is certainly this, that one is pretty nearly as good as another, as far as any judgment can be formed of them before marriage. It is only after marriage that they show their true qualities, as I know by bitter experience. Marriage is, therefore, a lottery, and the less choice and selection a man bestows on his ticket the better; for, if he has incurred considerable pains and expense to obtain a lucky number, and his lucky number proves a blank, he experiences not a simple, but a complicated disappointment; the loss of labour and money being superadded to the disappointment of drawing a blank, which, constituting simply and entirely the grievance of him who has chosen his ticket at random, is, from its simplicity, the more endurable.' This very excellent reasoning was thrown away upon Scythrop, who retired to his tower as dismal and disconsolate as before.

The tower which Scythrop inhabited stood at the south-eastern angle of the Abbey; and, on the southern side, the foot of the tower opened on a terrace, which was called the garden, though nothing grew on it but ivy, and a few amphibious weeds. The south-western tower, which was ruinous and full of owls, might, with equal propriety, have been called the aviary. This terrace or garden, or terrace-garden, or garden-terrace (the reader may name it *ad libitum*), took in an oblique view of the open sea, and fronted a long tract of level sea-coast, and a fine monotony of fens and windmills.

The reader will judge, from what we have said, that this building was a sort of castellated abbey; and it will, probably, occur to him to inquire if it had been one of the strong-holds of the ancient church militant. Whether this was the case, or how far it had been indebted to the taste of Mr Glowry's ancestors for any transmutations from its original state, are, unfortunately, circumstances not within the pale of our knowledge.

The north-western tower contained the apartments of Mr Glowry. The moat at its base, and the fens beyond, comprised the whole of his prospect. This moat surrounded the Abbey, and was in immediate contact with the walls on every side but the south.

The north-eastern tower was appropriated to the domestics, whom Mr Glowry always chose by one of two criterions,—a long face, or a dismal name. His butler was Raven; his steward was Crow; his valet was Skellet. Mr Glowry maintained that the valet was of French extraction, and that his name was Squelette. His grooms were Mattocks and Graves. On one occasion, being in want of a footman, he received a letter from a person signing himself Diggory Deathshead, and lost no time in securing this acquisition; but on Diggory's arrival, Mr Glowry was horror-struck by the sight of a round ruddy face, and a pair of laughing eyes. Deathshead was always grinning,—not a ghastly smile, but the grin of a comic mask; and disturbed the echoes of the hall with so much unhallowed laughter, that Mr Glowry gave him his discharge. Diggory, however, had staid long enough to make conquests of all the old gentleman's maids, and left him a flourishing colony of young Deathsheads to join chorus with the owls, that had before been the exclusive choristers of Nightmare Abbey.

The main body of the building was divided into rooms of state, spacious apartments for feasting, and numerous bed-rooms for visitors, who, however, were few and far between.

Family interests compelled Mr Glowry to receive occasional visits from Mr and Mrs Hilary, who paid them from the same motive; and, as the lively gentleman on these occasions found few conductors for his exuberant gaiety, he became like a double-charged electric jar, which often exploded in some burst of outrageous merriment to the signal discomposure of Mr Glowry's nerves.

Another occasional visitor, much more to Mr Glowry's taste, was Mr Flosky,[1] a very lachrymose and morbid gentleman, of some note in the literary world, but in his own estimation of much more merit than name. The part of his character which recommended him to Mr Glowry, was his very fine sense of the grim and the tearful. No one could relate a dismal story with so many minutiæ of supererogatory wretchedness. No one could call up a *raw-head and bloody-bones* with so many adjuncts and circumstances of ghastliness. Mystery was his mental element. He lived in the midst of that visionary world in which nothing is but what is not. He dreamed with his eyes open, and saw ghosts dancing round him at noontide. He had been in his youth an enthusiast for liberty, and had hailed the dawn of the French Revolution as the promise of a day that was to banish war and slavery, and every form of vice and misery, from the face of the earth. Because all this was not done, he deduced that nothing was done; and from this deduction, according to his system of logic, he drew a conclusion that worse than nothing was done; that the overthrow of the feudal fortresses of tyranny and superstition was the greatest calamity that had ever befallen mankind; and that their only hope now was to rake the rubbish together, and rebuild it without any of those loopholes by which the light had originally crept in. To qualify himself for a coadjutor in this laudable task, he plunged into the central opacity of Kantian metaphysics, and lay *perdu* several years in transcendental darkness, till the common daylight of common sense became intolerable to his eyes. He called the sun an *ignis fatuus*; and exhorted all who would listen to his friendly voice, which were about as many as called 'God save King Richard,' to shelter themselves from its delusive radiance in the obscure haunt of Old Philosophy. This word Old had great charms for him. The good old times were always on his lips; meaning the days when polemic theology was in its prime, and rival prelates beat the drum ecclesiastic with Herculean vigour, till the one wound up his series of syllogisms with the very orthodox conclusion of roasting the other.

But the dearest friend of Mr Glowry, and his most welcome guest, was Mr Toobad, the Manichaean Millenarian. The twelfth verse of the twelfth chapter of Revelations was always in his mouth: 'Woe to the inhabiters of the earth and of the sea! for the devil is come among you, having great wrath, because he knoweth that he hath but a short time.' He maintained that the supreme dominion of the world was, for wise purposes, given over for a while to the Evil Principle; and that this precise period of time, commonly called the enlightened age, was the point of his plenitude of power. He used to add that by and by he would be cast down, and a high and happy order of things succeed; but he never omitted the saving clause, 'Not in our time'; which last words were always echoed in doleful response by the sympathetic Mr Glowry.

Another and very frequent visitor, was the Reverend Mr Larynx, the vicar of Claydyke, a village about ten miles distant;—a good-natured accommodating divine, who was always most obligingly ready to take a dinner and a bed at the house of any country gentleman in distress for a companion. Nothing came amiss to him,—a game at billiards, at chess, at draughts, at backgammon, at piquet, or at all-fours in a *tête-à-tête*,—or any game on the cards, round, square, or triangular, in a party of any number exceeding two. He would even dance among friends, rather than that a lady, even if she were on the wrong side of thirty, should sit still for want of a partner. For a ride, a walk, or a sail, in the morning,—a song after dinner, a ghost story after supper,—a bottle of port with the squire, or a cup of green tea with his lady,—for all or any of these, or for any thing else that was agreeable to any one else, consistently with the dye of his coat, the Reverend Mr Larynx was at all times equally ready. When at Nightmare Abbey, he would condole with Mr Glowry,—drink Madeira with Scythrop,—crack jokes with Mr Hilary,—hand Mrs Hilary to the piano, take charge of her fan and gloves, and turn over her music with surprising dexterity,—quote Revelations with Mr Toobad,—and lament the good old times of feudal darkness with the transcendental Mr Flosky.

* * * * *

CHAPTER II

Shortly after the disastrous termination of Scythrop's passion for Miss Emily Girouette, Mr Glowry found himself, much against his will, involved in a lawsuit, which compelled him to dance attendance on the High Court of Chancery. Scythrop was left alone at Nightmare Abbey. He was a burnt child, and dreaded the fire of female eyes. He wandered about the ample pile, or along the garden-terrace, with 'his cogitative faculties immersed in cogibundity of cogitation.' The terrace terminated at the south-western tower, which, as we have said, was ruinous and full of owls. Here would Scythrop take his evening seat, on a fallen fragment of mossy stone, with his back resting against the ruined wall,—a thick canopy of ivy, with an owl in it, over his head,—and the Sorrows of Werter in his hand. He had some taste for romance reading before he went to the university, where, we must confess, in justice to his college, he was cured of the love of reading in all its shapes; and the cure would have been radical, if disappointment in love, and total solitude, had not conspired to bring on a relapse. He began to devour romances and German tragedies, and, by the recommendation of Mr Flosky, to pore over ponderous tomes of transcendental philosophy, which reconciled him to the labour of studying them by their mystical jargon and necromantic imagery. In the congenial solitude of Nightmare Abbey, the distempered ideas of metaphysical romance and romantic metaphysics had ample time and space to germinate into a fertile crop of chimeras, which rapidly shot up into vigorous and abundant vegetation.

He now became troubled with the *passion for reforming the world*.[2] He built many castles in the air, and peopled them with secret tribunals, and bands of illuminati, who were always the imaginary instruments of his projected regeneration of the human species. As he intended to institute a perfect republic, he invested himself with absolute sovereignty over these mystical dispensers of liberty. He slept with Horrid Mysteries under his pillow, and dreamed of venerable eleutherarchs and ghastly confederates holding midnight conventions in subterranean caves. He passed whole mornings in his study, immersed in gloomy reverie, stalking about the room in his nightcap, which he pulled over his eyes like a cowl, and folding his striped calico dressing-gown about him like the mantle of a conspirator.

'Action,' thus he soliloquised, 'is the result of opinion, and to new-model opinion would be to new-model society. Knowledge is power; it is in the hands of a few, who employ it to mislead the many, for their own selfish purposes of aggrandisement and appropriation. What if it were in the hands of a few who should employ it to lead the many? What if it were universal, and the multitude were enlightened? No. The many must be always in leading-strings; but let them have wise and honest conductors. A few to think, and many to act; that is the only basis of perfect society. So thought the ancient philosophers: they had their esoterical and exoterical doctrines. So thinks the sublime Kant, who delivers his oracles in language which none but the initiated can comprehend. Such were the views of those secret associations of illuminati, which were the terror of superstition and tyranny, and which, carefully selecting wisdom and genius from the great wilderness of society, as the bee selects honey from the flowers of the thorn and the nettle, bound all human excellence in a chain, which, if it had not been prematurely broken, would have commanded opinion, and regenerated the world.'

Scythrop proceeded to meditate on the practicability of reviving a confederation of regenerators. To get a clear view of his own ideas, and to feel the pulse of the wisdom and genius of the age, he wrote and published a treatise, in which his meanings were carefully wrapt up in the monk's hood of transcendental technology, but filled with hints of matter deep and dangerous, which he thought would set the whole nation in a ferment; and he awaited the result in awful expectation, as a miner who has fired a train awaits the explosion of a rock. However, he listened and heard nothing; for the explosion, if any ensued, was not sufficiently loud to shake a single leaf of the ivy on the towers of Nightmare Abbey; and some months afterwards he received a letter from his bookseller, informing him that only seven copies had been sold, and concluding with a polite request for the balance.

Scythrop did not despair. 'Seven copies,' he thought, 'have been sold. Seven is a mystical number, and the omen is good. Let me find the seven purchasers of my seven copies, and they shall be the seven golden candlesticks with which I will illuminate the world.'

Scythrop had a certain portion of mechanical genius, which his romantic projects tended to develope. He constructed models of cells and recesses, sliding panels and secret passages, that would have baffled the skill of the Parisian police. He took the opportunity of his father's absence to smuggle a dumb carpenter into the Abbey, and between them they gave reality to one of these models in Scythrop's tower. Scythrop foresaw that a great leader of human regeneration would be involved in fearful dilemmas, and determined, for the benefit of mankind in general, to adopt all possible precautions for the preservation of himself.

The servants, even the women, had been tutored into silence. Profound stillness reigned throughout and around the Abbey, except when the occasional shutting of a door would peal in long reverberations through the galleries, or the heavy tread of the pensive butler would wake the hollow echoes of the hall. Scythrop stalked about like the grand inquisitor, and the servants flitted past him like familiars. In his evening meditations on the terrace, under the ivy of the ruined tower, the only sounds that came to his ear were the rustling of the wind in the ivy, the plaintive voices of the feathered choristers, the owls, the occasional striking of the Abbey clock, and the monotonous dash of the sea on its low and level shore. In the mean time, he drank Madeira, and laid deep schemes for a thorough repair of the crazy fabric of human nature.

* * * * *

CHAPTER III

Mr Glowry returned from London with the loss of his lawsuit. Justice was with him, but the law was against him. He found Scythrop in a mood most sympathetically tragic; and they vied with each other in enlivening their cups by lamenting the depravity of this degenerate age, and occasionally interspersing divers grim jokes about graves, worms, and epitaphs. Mr Glowry's friends, whom we have mentioned in the first chapter, availed themselves of his return to pay him a simultaneous visit. At the same time arrived Scythrop's friend and fellow-collegian, the Honourable Mr Listless. Mr Glowry had discovered this fashionable young gentleman in London, 'stretched on the rack of a too easy chair,' and devoured with a gloomy and misanthropical *nil curo*, and had pressed him so earnestly to take the benefit of the pure country air, at Nightmare Abbey, that Mr Listless, finding it would give him more trouble to refuse than to comply, summoned his French valet, Fatout, and told him he was going to Lincolnshire. On this simple hint, Fatout went to work, and the imperials were packed, and the post-chariot was at the door, without the Honourable Mr Listless having said or thought another syllable on the subject.

Mr and Mrs Hilary brought with them an orphan niece, a daughter of Mr Glowry's youngest sister, who had made a runaway love-match with an Irish officer. The lady's fortune disappeared in the first year: love, by a natural consequence, disappeared in the second: the Irishman himself, by a still more natural consequence, disappeared in the third. Mr Glowry had allowed his sister an annuity, and she had lived in retirement with her only daughter, whom, at her death, which had recently happened, she commended to the care of Mrs Hilary.

Miss Marionetta Celestina O'Carroll was a very blooming and accomplished young lady. Being a compound of the *Allegro Vivace* of the O'Carrolls, and of the *Andante Doloroso* of the Glowries, she exhibited in her own character all the diversities of an April sky. Her hair was light-brown; her eyes hazel, and sparkling with a mild but fluctuating light; her features regular; her lips full, and of equal size; and her person surpassingly graceful. She was a proficient in music. Her conversation was sprightly, but always on subjects light in their nature and limited in their interest: for moral sympathies, in any general sense, had no place in her mind. She had some coquetry, and more caprice, liking and disliking almost in the same moment; pursuing an object with earnestness while it seemed unattainable, and rejecting it when in her power as not worth the trouble of possession.

Whether she was touched with a *penchant* for her cousin Scythrop, or was merely curious to see what effect the tender passion would have on so *outré* a person, she had not been three days in the Abbey before she threw out all the lures of her beauty and accomplishments to make a prize of his heart. Scythrop proved an easy conquest. The image of Miss Emily Girouette was already sufficiently dimmed by the power of philosophy and the exercise of reason: for to these influences, or to any influence but the true one, are usually ascribed the mental cures performed by the great physician Time. Scythrop's romantic dreams had indeed given him many *pure anticipated cognitions* of combinations of beauty and intelligence, which, he had some misgivings, were not exactly realised in his cousin Marionetta; but, in spite of these misgivings, he soon became distractedly in love; which, when the young lady clearly perceived, she altered her tactics, and assumed as much coldness and reserve as she had before shown ardent and ingenuous attachment. Scythrop was confounded at the sudden change; but, instead of falling at her feet and requesting an explanation, he retreated to his tower, muffled himself in his nightcap, seated himself in the president's chair of his imaginary secret tribunal, summoned Marionetta with all terrible formalities, frightened her out of her wits, disclosed himself, and clasped the beautiful penitent to his bosom.

While he was acting this reverie—in the moment in which the awful president of the secret tribunal was throwing back his cowl and his mantle, and discovering himself to the lovely culprit as her adoring and magnanimous lover, the door of the study opened, and the real Marionetta appeared.

The motives which had led her to the tower were a little penitence, a little concern, a little affection, and a little fear as to what the sudden secession of Scythrop, occasioned by her sudden change of manner, might portend. She had tapped several times unheard, and of course unanswered; and at length, timidly and cautiously opening the door, she discovered him standing up before a black velvet chair, which was mounted on an old oak table, in the act of throwing open his striped calico dressing-gown, and flinging away his nightcap—which is what the French call an imposing attitude.

Each stood a few moments fixed in their respective places—the lady in astonishment, and the gentleman in confusion. Marionetta was the first to break silence. 'For heaven's sake,' said she, 'my dear Scythrop, what is the matter?'

'For heaven's sake, indeed!' said Scythrop, springing from the table; 'for your sake, Marionetta, and you are my heaven,—distraction is the matter. I adore you, Marionetta, and your cruelty drives me mad.' He threw himself at her knees, devoured her hand with kisses, and breathed a thousand vows in the most passionate language of romance.

Marionetta listened a long time in silence, till her lover had exhausted his eloquence and paused for a reply. She then said, with a very arch look, 'I prithee deliver thyself like a man of this world.' The levity of this quotation, and of the manner in which it was delivered, jarred so discordantly on the high-wrought enthusiasm of the romantic inamorato, that he sprang upon his feet, and beat his forehead with his clenched fist. The young lady was terrified; and, deeming it expedient to soothe him, took one of his hands in hers, placed the other hand on his shoulder, looked up in his face with a winning seriousness, and said, in the tenderest possible tone, 'What would you have, Scythrop?'

Scythrop was in heaven again. 'What would I have? What but you, Marionetta? You, for the companion of my studies, the partner of my thoughts, the auxiliary of my great designs for the emancipation of mankind.'

'I am afraid I should be but a poor auxiliary, Scythrop. What would you have me do?'

'Do as Rosalia does with Carlos, divine Marionetta. Let us each open a vein in the other's arm, mix our blood in a bowl, and drink it as a sacrament of love. Then we shall see visions of transcendental illumination, and soar on the wings of ideas into the space of pure intelligence.'

Marionetta could not reply; she had not so strong a stomach as Rosalia, and turned sick at the proposition. She disengaged herself suddenly from Scythrop, sprang through the door of the tower, and fled with precipitation along the corridors. Scythrop pursued her, crying, 'Stop, stop, Marionetta—my life, my love!' and was gaining rapidly on her flight, when, at an ill-omened corner, where two corridors ended in an angle, at the head of a staircase, he came into sudden and violent contact with Mr Toobad, and they both plunged together to the foot of the stairs, like two billiard-balls into one pocket. This gave the young lady time to escape, and enclose herself in her chamber; while Mr Toobad, rising slowly, and rubbing his knees and shoulders, said, 'You see, my dear Scythrop, in this little incident, one of the innumerable proofs of the temporary supremacy of the devil; for what but a systematic design and concurrent contrivance of evil could have made the angles of time and place coincide in our unfortunate persons at the head of this accursed staircase?'

'Nothing else, certainly,' said Scythrop: 'you are perfectly in the right, Mr Toobad. Evil, and mischief, and misery, and confusion, and vanity, and vexation of spirit, and death, and disease, and assassination, and war, and poverty, and pestilence, and famine, and avarice, and selfishness, and rancour, and jealousy, and spleen, and malevolence, and the disappointments of philanthropy, and the faithlessness of friendship, and the crosses of love—all prove the accuracy of your views, and the truth of your system; and it is not impossible that the infernal interruption of this fall downstairs may throw a colour of evil on the whole of my future existence.'

'My dear boy,' said Mr Toobad, 'you have a fine eye for consequences.'

So saying, he embraced Scythrop, who retired, with a disconsolate step, to dress for dinner; while Mr Toobad stalked across the hall, repeating, 'Woe to the inhabiters of the earth, and of the sea, for the devil is come among you, having great wrath.'

* * * * *

CHAPTER IV

The flight of Marionetta, and the pursuit of Scythrop, had been witnessed by Mr Glowry, who, in consequence, narrowly observed his son and his niece in the evening; and, concluding from their manner, that there was a better understanding between them than he wished to see, he determined on obtaining the next morning from Scythrop a full and satisfactory explanation. He, therefore, shortly after breakfast, entered Scythrop's tower, with a very grave face, and said, without ceremony or preface, 'So, sir, you are in love with your cousin.'

Scythrop, with as little hesitation, answered, 'Yes, sir.'

'That is candid, at least; and she is in love with you.'

'I wish she were, sir.'

'You know she is, sir.'

'Indeed, sir, I do not.'

'But you hope she is.'

'I do, from my soul.'

'Now that is very provoking, Scythrop, and very disappointing: I could not have supposed that you, Scythrop Glowry, of Nightmare Abbey, would have been infatuated with such a dancing, laughing, singing, thoughtless, careless, merry-hearted thing, as Marionetta—in all respects the reverse of you and me. It is very disappointing, Scythrop. And do you know, sir, that Marionetta has no fortune?'

'It is the more reason, sir, that her husband should have one.'

'The more reason for her; but not for you. My wife had no fortune, and I had no consolation in my calamity. And do you reflect, sir, what an enormous slice this lawsuit has cut out of our family estate? we who used to be the greatest landed proprietors in Lincolnshire.'

'To be sure, sir, we had more acres of fen than any man on this coast: but what are fens to love? What are dykes and windmills to Marionetta?'

'And what, sir, is love to a windmill? Not grist, I am certain: besides, sir, I have made a choice for you. I have made a choice for you, Scythrop. Beauty, genius, accomplishments, and a great fortune into the bargain. Such a lovely, serious creature, in a fine state of high dissatisfaction with the world, and every thing in it. Such a delightful surprise I had prepared for you. Sir, I have pledged my honour to the contract—the honour of the Glowries of Nightmare Abbey: and now, sir, what is to be done?'

'Indeed, sir, I cannot say. I claim, on this occasion, that liberty of action which is the co-natal prerogative of every rational being.'

'Liberty of action, sir? there is no such thing as liberty of action. We are all slaves and puppets of a blind and unpathetic necessity.'

'Very true, sir; but liberty of action, between individuals, consists in their being differently influenced, or modified, by the same universal necessity; so that the results are unconsentaneous, and their respective necessitated volitions clash and fly off in a tangent.'

'Your logic is good, sir: but you are aware, too, that one individual may be a medium of adhibiting to another a mode or form of necessity, which may have more or less influence in the production of consentaneity; and, therefore, sir, if you do not comply with my wishes in this instance (you have had your own way in every thing else), I shall be under the necessity of disinheriting you, though I shall do it with tears in my eyes.' Having said these words, he vanished suddenly, in the dread of Scythrop's logic.

Mr Glowry immediately sought Mrs Hilary, and communicated to her his views of the case in point. Mrs Hilary, as the phrase is, was as fond of Marionetta as if she had been her own child: but—there is always a *but* on these occasions—she could do nothing for her in the way of fortune, as she had two hopeful sons, who were finishing their education at Brazen-nose, and who would not like to encounter any diminution of their prospects, when they should be brought out of the house of mental bondage—i.e. the university—to the land flowing with milk and honey—i.e. the west end of London.

Mrs Hilary hinted to Marionetta, that propriety, and delicacy, and decorum, and dignity, &c. &c. &c.,[3] would require them to leave the Abbey immediately. Marionetta listened in silent submission, for she knew that her inheritance was passive obedience; but, when Scythrop, who had watched the opportunity of Mrs Hilary's departure, entered, and, without speaking a word, threw himself at her feet in a paroxysm of grief, the young lady, in equal silence and sorrow, threw her arms round his neck and burst into tears. A very tender scene ensued, which the sympathetic susceptibilities of the soft-hearted reader can more accurately imagine than we can delineate. But when Marionetta hinted that she was to leave the Abbey immediately, Scythrop snatched from its repository his ancestor's skull, filled it with Madeira, and presenting himself before Mr Glowry, threatened to drink off the contents if Mr Glowry did not immediately promise that Marionetta should not be taken from the Abbey without her own consent. Mr Glowry, who took the Madeira to be some deadly brewage, gave the required promise in dismal panic. Scythrop returned to Marionetta with a joyful heart, and drank the Madeira by the way.

Mr Glowry, during his residence in London, had come to an agreement with his friend Mr Toobad, that a match between Scythrop and Mr Toobad's daughter would be a very desirable occurrence. She was finishing her education in a German convent, but Mr Toobad described her as being fully impressed with the truth of his Ahrimanic philosophy,[4] and being altogether as gloomy and antithalian a young lady as Mr Glowry himself could desire for the future mistress of Nightmare Abbey. She had a great fortune in her own right, which was not, as we have seen, without its weight in inducing Mr Glowry to set his heart upon her as his daughter-in-law that was to be; he was therefore very much disturbed by Scythrop's untoward attachment to Marionetta. He condoled on the occasion with

Mr Toobad; who said, that he had been too long accustomed to the intermeddling of the devil in all his affairs, to be astonished at this new trace of his cloven claw; but that he hoped to outwit him yet, for he was sure there could be no comparison between his daughter and Marionetta in the mind of any one who had a proper perception of the fact, that, the world being a great theatre of evil, seriousness and solemnity are the characteristics of wisdom, and laughter and merriment make a human being no better than a baboon. Mr Glowry comforted himself with this view of the subject, and urged Mr Toobad to expedite his daughter's return from Germany. Mr Toobad said he was in daily expectation of her arrival in London, and would set off immediately to meet her, that he might lose no time in bringing her to Nightmare Abbey. 'Then,' he added, 'we shall see whether Thalia or Melpomene—whether the Allegra or the Penserosa—will carry off the symbol of victory.'—'There can be no doubt,' said Mr Glowry, 'which way the scale will incline, or Scythrop is no true scion of the venerable stem of the Glowries.'

* * * * *

CHAPTER V

Marionetta felt secure of Scythrop's heart; and notwithstanding the difficulties that surrounded her, she could not debar herself from the pleasure of tormenting her lover, whom she kept in a perpetual fever. Sometimes she would meet him with the most unqualified affection; sometimes with the most chilling indifference; rousing him to anger by artificial coldness—softening him to love by eloquent tenderness—or inflaming him to jealousy by coquetting with the Honourable Mr Listless, who seemed, under her magical influence, to burst into sudden life, like the bud of the evening primrose. Sometimes she would sit by the piano, and listen with becoming attention to Scythrop's pathetic remonstrances; but, in the most impassioned part of his oratory, she would convert all his ideas into a chaos, by striking up some Rondo Allegro, and saying, 'Is it not pretty?' Scythrop would begin to storm; and she would answer him with,

'Zitti, zitti, piano, piano,
Non facciamo confusione,'

or some similar *facezia*, till he would start away from her, and enclose himself in his tower, in an agony of agitation, vowing to renounce her, and her whole sex, for ever; and returning to her presence at the summons of the billet, which she never failed to send with many expressions of penitence and promises of amendment. Scythrop's schemes for regenerating the world, and detecting his seven golden candle-sticks, went on very slowly in this fever of his spirit.

34

Things proceeded in this train for several days; and Mr Glowry began to be uneasy at receiving no intelligence from Mr Toobad; when one evening the latter rushed into the library, where the family and the visitors were assembled, vociferating, 'The devil is come among you, having great wrath!' He then drew Mr Glowry aside into another apartment, and after remaining some time together, they re-entered the library with faces of great dismay, but did not condescend to explain to any one the cause of their discomfiture.

The next morning, early, Mr Toobad departed. Mr Glowry sighed and groaned all day, and said not a word to any one. Scythrop had quarrelled, as usual, with Marionetta, and was enclosed in his tower, in a fit of morbid sensibility. Marionetta was comforting herself at the piano, with singing the airs of *Nina pazza per amore*; and the Honourable Mr Listless was listening to the harmony, as he lay supine on the sofa, with a book in his hand, into which he peeped at intervals. The Reverend Mr Larynx approached the sofa, and proposed a game at billiards.

THE HONOURABLE MR LISTLESS

Billiards! Really I should be very happy; but, in my present exhausted state, the exertion is too much for me. I do not know when I have been equal to such an effort. *(He rang the bell for his valet. Fatout entered.)* Fatout! when did I play at billiards last?

FATOUT

De fourteen December de last year, Monsieur. *(Fatout bowed and retired.)*

THE HONOURABLE MR LISTLESS

So it was. Seven months ago. You see, Mr Larynx; you see, sir. My nerves, Miss O'Carroll, my nerves are shattered. I have been advised to try Bath. Some of the faculty recommend Cheltenham. I think of trying both, as the seasons don't clash. The season, you know, Mr Larynx—the season, Miss O'Carroll—the season is every thing.

MARIONETTA

And health is something. *N'est-ce pas*, Mr Larynx?

THE REVEREND MR LARYNX

Most assuredly, Miss O'Carroll. For, however reasoners may dispute about the *summum bonum*, none of them will deny that a very good dinner is a very good thing: and what is a good dinner without a good appetite? and whence is a good appetite but from good health? Now, Cheltenham, Mr Listless, is famous for good appetites.

THE HONOURABLE MR LISTLESS

The best piece of logic I ever heard, Mr Larynx; the very best, I assure you. I have thought very seriously of Cheltenham: very seriously and profoundly. I thought of it—let me see—when did I think of it? *(He rang again, and Fatout reappeared.)* Fatout! when did I think of going to Cheltenham, and did not go?

FATOUT

De Juillet twenty-von, de last summer, Monsieur. *(Fatout retired.)*

THE HONOURABLE MR LISTLESS

So it was. An invaluable fellow that, Mr Larynx—invaluable, Miss O'Carroll.

MARIONETTA

So I should judge, indeed. He seems to serve you as a walking memory, and to be a living chronicle, not of your actions only, but of your thoughts.

THE HONOURABLE MR LISTLESS

An excellent definition of the fellow, Miss O'Carroll,—excellent, upon my honour. Ha! ha! he! Heigho! Laughter is pleasant, but the exertion is too much for me.

A parcel was brought in for Mr Listless; it had been sent express. Fatout was summoned to unpack it; and it proved to contain a new novel, and a new poem, both of which had long been anxiously expected by the whole host of fashionable readers; and the last number of a popular Review, of which the editor and his coadjutors were in high favour at court, and enjoyed ample pensions[5] for their services to church and state. As Fatout left the room, Mr Flosky entered, and curiously inspected the literary arrivals.

MR FLOSKY

(*Turning over the leaves.*) 'Devilman, a novel.' Hm. Hatred—revenge—misanthropy—and quotations from the Bible. Hm. This is the morbid anatomy of black bile.—'Paul Jones, a poem.' Hm. I see how it is. Paul Jones, an amiable enthusiast—disappointed in his affections—turns pirate from ennui and magnanimity—cuts various masculine throats, wins various feminine hearts—is hanged at the yard-arm! The catastrophe is very awkward, and very unpoetical.—'The Downing Street Review.' Hm. First article—An Ode to the Red Book, by Roderick Sackbut, Esquire. Hm. His own poem reviewed by himself. Hm—m—m.

(*Mr Flosky proceeded in silence to look over the other articles of the review;
Marionetta inspected the novel, and Mr Listless the poem.*)

THE REVEREND MR LARYNX

For a young man of fashion and family, Mr Listless, you seem to be of a very studious turn.

THE HONOURABLE MR LISTLESS

Studious! You are pleased to be facetious, Mr Larynx. I hope you do not suspect me of being studious. I have finished my education. But there are some fashionable books that one must read, because they are ingredients of the talk of the day; otherwise, I am no fonder of books than I dare say you yourself are, Mr Larynx.

THE REVEREND MR LARYNX

Why, sir, I cannot say that I am indeed particularly fond of books; yet neither can I say that I never do read. A tale or a poem, now and then, to a circle of ladies over their work, is no very heterodox employment of the vocal energy. And I must say, for myself, that few men have a more Job-like endurance of the eternally recurring questions and answers that interweave themselves, on these occasions, with the crisis of an adventure, and heighten the distress of a tragedy.

THE HONOURABLE MR LISTLESS

And very often make the distress when the author has omitted it.

MARIONETTA

I shall try your patience some rainy morning, Mr Larynx; and Mr Listless shall recommend us the very newest new book, that every body reads.

THE HONOURABLE MR LISTLESS

You shall receive it, Miss O'Carroll, with all the gloss of novelty; fresh as a ripe green-gage in all the downiness of its bloom. A mail-coach copy from Edinburgh, forwarded express from London.

MR FLOSKY

This rage for novelty is the bane of literature. Except my works and those of my particular friends, nothing is good that is not as old as Jeremy Taylor: and, *entre nous*, the best parts of my friends' books were either written or suggested by myself.

THE HONOURABLE MR LISTLESS

Sir, I reverence you. But I must say, modern books are very consolatory and congenial to my feelings. There is, as it were, a delightful north-east wind, an intellectual blight breathing through them; a delicious misanthropy and discontent, that demonstrates the nullity of virtue and energy, and puts me in good humour with myself and my sofa.

MR FLOSKY

Very true, sir. Modern literature is a north-east wind—a blight of the human soul. I take credit to myself for having helped to make it so. The way to produce fine fruit is to blight the flower. You call this a paradox. Marry, so be it. Ponder thereon.

The conversation was interrupted by the re-appearance of Mr Toobad, covered with mud. He just showed himself at the door, muttered 'The devil is come among you!' and vanished. The road which connected Nightmare Abbey with the civilised world, was artificially raised above the level of the fens, and ran through them in a straight line as far as the eye could reach, with a ditch on each side, of which the water was rendered invisible by the aquatic vegetation that covered the surface. Into one of these ditches the sudden action of a shy horse, which took fright at a windmill, had precipitated the travelling chariot of Mr Toobad, who had been reduced to the necessity of scrambling in dismal plight through the window. One of the wheels was found to be broken; and Mr Toobad, leaving the postilion to get the chariot as well as he could to Claydyke for the purpose of cleaning and repairing, had walked back to Nightmare Abbey, followed by his servant with the imperial, and repeating all the way his favourite quotation from the Revelations.

* * * * *

CHAPTER VI

Mr Toobad had found his daughter Celinda in London, and after the first joy of meeting was over, told her he had a husband ready for her. The young lady replied, very gravely, that she should take the liberty to choose for herself. Mr Toobad said he saw the devil was determined to interfere with all his projects, but he was resolved on his own part, not to have on his conscience the crime of passive obedience and non-resistance to Lucifer, and therefore she should marry the person he had chosen for her. Miss Toobad replied, *très posément*, she assuredly would not. 'Celinda, Celinda,' said Mr Toobad, 'you most assuredly shall.'—'Have I not a fortune in my own right, sir?' said Celinda. 'The more is the pity,' said Mr Toobad: 'but I can find means, miss; I can find means. There are more ways than one of breaking in obstinate girls.' They parted for the night with the expression of opposite resolutions, and in the morning the young lady's chamber was found empty, and what was become of her Mr Toobad had no clue to conjecture. He continued to investigate town and country in search of her; visiting and revisiting Nightmare Abbey at intervals, to consult with his friend, Mr Glowry. Mr Glowry agreed with Mr Toobad that this was a very flagrant instance of filial disobedience and rebellion; and Mr Toobad declared, that when he discovered the fugitive, she should find that 'the devil was come unto her, having great wrath.'

In the evening, the whole party met, as usual, in the library. Marionetta sat at the harp; the Honourable Mr Listless sat by her and turned over her music, though the exertion was almost too much for him. The Reverend Mr Larynx relieved him occasionally in this delightful labour. Scythrop, tormented by the demon Jealousy, sat in the corner biting his lips and fingers. Marionetta looked at him every now and then with a smile of most provoking good humour, which he pretended not to see, and which only the more exasperated his troubled spirit. He took down a volume of Dante, and pretended to be deeply interested in the Purgatorio, though he knew not a word he was reading, as Marionetta was well aware; who, tripping across the room, peeped into his book, and said to him, 'I see you are in the middle of Purgatory.'—'I am in the middle of hell,' said Scythrop furiously. 'Are you?' said she; 'then come across the room, and I will sing you the finale of Don Giovanni.'

'Let me alone,' said Scythrop. Marionetta looked at him with a deprecating smile, and said, 'You unjust, cross creature, you.'—'Let me alone,' said Scythrop, but much less emphatically than at first, and by no means wishing to be taken at his word. Marionetta left him immediately, and returning to the harp, said, just loud enough for Scythrop to hear— 'Did you ever read Dante, Mr Listless? Scythrop is reading Dante, and is just now in Purgatory.'—'And I' said the Honourable Mr Listless, 'am not reading Dante, and am just now in Paradise,' bowing to Marionetta.

MARIONETTA

You are very gallant, Mr Listless; and I dare say you are very fond of reading Dante.

THE HONOURABLE MR LISTLESS

I don't know how it is, but Dante never came in my way till lately. I never had him in my collection, and if I had had him I should not have read him. But I find he is growing fashionable, and I am afraid I must read him some wet morning.

MARIONETTA

No, read him some evening, by all means. Were you ever in love, Mr Listless?

THE HONOURABLE MR LISTLESS

I assure you, Miss O'Carroll, never—till I came to Nightmare Abbey. I dare say it is very pleasant; but it seems to give so much trouble that I fear the exertion would be too much for me.

MARIONETTA

Shall I teach you a compendious method of courtship, that will give you no trouble whatever?

THE HONOURABLE MR LISTLESS

You will confer on me an inexpressible obligation. I am all impatience to learn it.

MARIONETTA

Sit with your back to the lady and read Dante; only be sure to begin in the middle, and turn over three or four pages at once—backwards as well as forwards, and she will immediately perceive that you are desperately in love with her—desperately.

(The Honourable Mr Listless sitting between Scythrop and Marionetta, and fixing all his attention on the beautiful speaker, did not observe Scythrop, who was doing as she described.)

THE HONOURABLE MR LISTLESS

You are pleased to be facetious, Miss O'Carroll. The lady would infallibly conclude that I was the greatest brute in town.

MARIONETTA

Far from it. She would say, perhaps, some people have odd methods of showing their affection.

THE HONOURABLE MR LISTLESS

But I should think, with submission—

MR FLOSKY (joining them from another part of the room)

Did I not hear Mr Listless observe that Dante is becoming fashionable?

THE HONOURABLE MR LISTLESS

I did hazard a remark to that effect, Mr Flosky, though I speak on such subjects with a consciousness of my own nothingness, in the presence of so great a man as Mr Flosky. I know not what is the colour of Dante's devils, but as he is certainly becoming fashionable I conclude they are blue; for the blue devils, as it seems to me, Mr Flosky, constitute the fundamental feature of fashionable literature.

MR FLOSKY

The blue are, indeed, the staple commodity; but as they will not always be commanded, the black, red, and grey may be admitted as substitutes. Tea, late dinners, and the French Revolution, have played the devil, Mr Listless, and brought the devil into play.

MR TOOBAD (starting up)

Having great wrath.

MR FLOSKY

This is no play upon words, but the sober sadness of veritable fact.

THE HONOURABLE MR LISTLESS

Tea, late dinners, and the French Revolution. I cannot exactly see the connection of ideas.

MR FLOSKY

I should be sorry if you could; I pity the man who can see the connection of his own ideas. Still more do I pity him, the connection of whose ideas any other person can see. Sir, the great evil is, that there is too much common-place light in our moral and political literature; and light is a great enemy to mystery, and mystery is a great friend to enthusiasm. Now the enthusiasm for abstract truth is an exceedingly fine thing, as long as the truth, which is the object of the enthusiasm, is so completely abstract as to be altogether out of the reach of the human faculties; and, in that sense, I have myself an enthusiasm for truth, but in no other, for the pleasure of metaphysical investigation lies in the means, not in the end; and if the end could be found, the pleasure of the means would cease. The mind, to be kept in health, must be kept in exercise. The proper exercise of the mind is elaborate reasoning. Analytical reasoning is a base and mechanical process, which takes to pieces and examines, bit by bit, the rude material of knowledge, and extracts therefrom a few hard and obstinate things called facts, every thing in the shape of which I cordially hate. But synthetical reasoning, setting up as its goal some unattainable abstraction, like an imaginary quantity in algebra, and commencing its course with taking for granted some two assertions which cannot be proved, from the union of these two assumed truths produces a third assumption, and so on in infinite series, to the unspeakable benefit of the human intellect. The beauty of this process is, that at every step it strikes out into two branches, in a compound ratio of ramification; so that you are perfectly sure of losing your way, and keeping your mind in perfect health, by the perpetual exercise of an interminable quest; and for these reasons I have christened my eldest son Emanuel Kant Flosky.

THE REVEREND MR LARYNX

Nothing can be more luminous.

THE HONOURABLE MR LISTLESS

And what has all that to do with Dante, and the blue devils?

MR HILARY

Not much, I should think, with Dante, but a great deal with the blue devils.

MR FLOSKY

It is very certain, and much to be rejoiced at, that our literature is hag-ridden. Tea has shattered our nerves; late dinners make us slaves of indigestion; the French Revolution has made us shrink from the name of philosophy, and has destroyed, in the more refined part of the community (of which number I am one), all enthusiasm for political liberty. That part of the *reading public* which shuns the solid food of reason for the light diet of fiction, requires a perpetual adhibition of *sauce piquante* to the palate of its depraved imagination. It lived upon ghosts, goblins, and skeletons (I and my friend Mr Sackbut served up a few of the best), till even the devil himself, though magnified to the size of Mount Athos, became too base, common, and popular, for its surfeited appetite. The ghosts have therefore been laid, and the devil has been cast into outer darkness, and now the delight of our spirits is to dwell on all the vices and blackest passions of our nature, tricked out in a masquerade dress of heroism and disappointed benevolence; the whole secret of which lies in forming combinations that contradict all our experience, and affixing the purple shred of some particular virtue to that precise character, in which we should be most certain not to find it in the living world; and making this single virtue not only redeem all the real and manifest vices of the character, but make them actually pass for necessary adjuncts, and indispensable accompaniments and characteristics of the said virtue.

MR TOOBAD

That is, because the devil is come among us, and finds it for his interest to destroy all our perceptions of the distinctions of right and wrong.

MARIONETTA

I do not precisely enter into your meaning, Mr Flosky, and should be glad if you would make it a little more plain to me.

MR FLOSKY

One or two examples will do it, Miss O'Carroll. If I were to take all the mean and sordid qualities of a money-dealing Jew, and tack on to them, as with a nail, the quality of extreme benevolence, I should have a very decent hero for a modern novel; and should contribute my quota to the fashionable method of administering a mass of vice, under a thin and unnatural covering of virtue, like a spider wrapt in a bit of gold leaf, and administered as a wholesome pill. On the same principle, if a man knocks me down, and takes my purse and watch by main force, I turn him to account, and set him forth in a tragedy as a dashing young fellow, disinherited for his romantic generosity, and full of a most amiable hatred of the world in general, and his own country in particular, and of a most enlightened and chivalrous affection for himself: then, with the addition of a wild girl to fall in love with him, and a series of adventures in which they break all the Ten Commandments in succession (always, you will observe, for some sublime motive, which must be carefully analysed in its progress), I have as amiable a pair of tragic characters as ever issued from that new region of the belles lettres, which I have called the Morbid Anatomy of Black Bile, and which is greatly to be admired and rejoiced at, as affording a fine scope for the exhibition of mental power.

MR HILARY

Which is about as well employed as the power of a hothouse would be in forcing up a nettle to the size of an elm. If we go on in this way, we shall have a new art of poetry, of which one of the first rules will be: To remember to forget that there are any such things as sunshine and music in the world.

THE HONOURABLE MR LISTLESS

It seems to be the case with us at present, or we should not have interrupted Miss O'Carroll's music with this exceedingly dry conversation.

MR FLOSKY

I should be most happy if Miss O'Carroll would remind us that there are yet both music and sunshine—

THE HONOURABLE MR LISTLESS

In the voice and the smile of beauty. May I entreat the favour of— *(turning over the pages of music.)*
All were silent, and Marionetta sung:

Why are thy looks so blank, grey friar?
Why are thy looks so blue?
Thou seem'st more pale and lank, grey friar,
Than thou wast used to do:—
Say, what has made thee rue?

Thy form was plump, and a light did shine
In thy round and ruby face,
Which showed an outward visible sign
Of an inward spiritual grace:—
Say, what has changed thy case?

Yet will I tell thee true, grey friar,
I very well can see,
That, if thy looks are blue, grey friar,
'Tis all for love of me,—
'Tis all for love of me.

But breathe not thy vows to me, grey friar,
Oh, breathe them not, I pray;
For ill beseems in a reverend friar,
The love of a mortal may;
And I needs must say thee nay.

But, could'st thou think my heart to move
With that pale and silent scowl?
Know, he who would win a maiden's love,
Whether clad in cap or cowl,
Must be more of a lark than an owl.

Scythrop immediately replaced Dante on the shelf, and joined the circle round the beautiful singer. Marionetta gave him a smile of approbation that fully restored his complacency, and they continued on the best possible terms during the remainder of the evening. The Honourable Mr Listless turned over the leaves with double alacrity, saying, 'You are severe upon invalids, Miss O'Carroll: to escape your satire, I must try to be sprightly, though the exertion is too much for me.'

* * * * *

CHAPTER VII

A new visitor arrived at the Abbey, in the person of Mr Asterias, the ichthyologist. This gentleman had passed his life in seeking the living wonders of the deep through the four quarters of the world; he had a cabinet of stuffed and dried fishes, of shells, sea-weeds, corals, and madrepores, that was the admiration and envy of the Royal Society. He had penetrated into the watery den of the Sepia Octopus, disturbed the conjugal happiness of that turtle-dove of the ocean, and come off victorious in a sanguinary conflict. He had been becalmed in the tropical seas, and had watched, in eager expectation, though unhappily always in vain, to see the colossal polypus rise from the water, and entwine its enormous arms round the masts and the rigging. He maintained the origin of all things from water, and insisted that the polypodes were the first of animated things, and that, from their round bodies and many-shooting arms, the Hindoos had taken their gods, the most ancient of deities. But the chief object of his ambition, the end and aim of his researches, was to discover a triton and a mermaid, the existence of which he most potently and implicitly believed, and was prepared to demonstrate, *à priori, à posteriori, à fortiori*, synthetically and analytically, syllogistically and inductively, by arguments deduced both from acknowledged facts and plausible hypotheses. A report that a mermaid had been seen 'sleeking her soft alluring locks' on the sea-coast of Lincolnshire, had brought him in great haste from London, to pay a long-promised and often-postponed visit to his old acquaintance, Mr Glowry.

Mr Asterias was accompanied by his son, to whom he had given the name of Aquarius—flattering himself that he would, in the process of time, become a constellation among the stars of ichthyological science. What charitable female had lent him the mould in which this son was cast, no one pretended to know; and, as he never dropped the most distant allusion to Aquarius's mother, some of the wags of London maintained that he had received the favours of a mermaid, and that the scientific perquisitions which kept him always prowling about the sea-shore, were directed by the less philosophical motive of regaining his lost love.

Mr Asterias perlustrated the sea-coast for several days, and reaped disappointment, but not despair. One night, shortly after his arrival, he was sitting in one of the windows of the library, looking towards the sea, when his attention was attracted by a figure which was moving near the edge of the surf, and which was dimly visible through the moonless summer night. Its motions were irregular, like those of a person in a state of indecision. It had extremely long hair, which floated in the wind. Whatever else it might be, it certainly was not a fisherman. It might be a lady; but it was neither Mrs Hilary nor Miss O'Carroll, for they were both in the library. It might be one of the female servants; but it had too much grace, and too striking an air of habitual liberty, to render it probable. Besides, what should one of the female servants be doing there at this hour, moving to and fro, as it seemed, without any visible purpose? It could scarcely be a stranger; for Claydyke, the nearest village, was ten miles distant; and what female would come ten miles across the fens, for no purpose but to hover over the surf under the walls of Nightmare Abbey? Might it not be a mermaid? It was possibly a mermaid. It was probably a mermaid. It was very probably a mermaid. Nay, what else could it be but a mermaid? It certainly was a mermaid. Mr Asterias stole out of the library on tiptoe, with his finger on his lips, having beckoned Aquarius to follow him.

The rest of the party was in great surprise at Mr Asterias's movement, and some of them approached the window to see if the locality would tend to elucidate the mystery. Presently they saw him and Aquarius cautiously stealing along on the other side of the moat, but they saw nothing more; and Mr Asterias returning, told them, with accents of great disappointment, that he had had a glimpse of a mermaid, but she had eluded him in the darkness, and was gone, he presumed, to sup with some enamoured triton, in a submarine grotto.

'But, seriously, Mr Asterias,' said the Honourable Mr Listless, 'do you positively believe there are such things as mermaids?'

MR ASTERIAS

Most assuredly; and tritons too.

THE HONOURABLE MR LISTLESS

What! things that are half human and half fish?

MR ASTERIAS

Precisely. They are the oran-outangs of the sea. But I am persuaded that there are also complete sea men, differing in no respect from us, but that they are stupid, and covered with scales; for, though our organisation seems to exclude us essentially from the class of amphibious animals, yet anatomists well know that the *foramen ovale* may remain open in an adult, and that respiration is, in that case, not necessary to life: and how can it be otherwise explained that the Indian divers, employed in the pearl fishery, pass whole hours under the water; and that the famous Swedish gardener of Troningholm lived a day and a half under the ice without being drowned? A nereid, or mermaid, was taken in the year 1403 in a Dutch lake, and was in every respect like a French woman, except that she did not speak. Towards the end of the seventeenth century, an English ship, a hundred and fifty leagues from land, in the Greenland seas, discovered a flotilla of sixty or seventy little skiffs, in each of which was a triton, or sea man: at the approach of the English vessel the whole of them, seized with simultaneous fear, disappeared, skiffs and all, under the water, as if they had been a human variety of the nautilus. The illustrious Don Feijoo has preserved an authentic and well-attested story of a young Spaniard, named Francis de la Vega, who, bathing with some of his friends in June, 1674, suddenly dived under the sea and rose no more. His friends thought him drowned; they were plebeians and pious Catholics; but a philosopher might very legitimately have drawn the same conclusion.

THE REVEREND MR LARYNX

Nothing could be more logical.

MR ASTERIAS

Five years afterwards, some fishermen near Cadiz found in their nets a triton, or sea man; they spoke to him in several languages—

THE REVEREND MR LARYNX

They were very learned fishermen.

MR HILARY

They had the gift of tongues by especial favour of their brother fisherman, Saint Peter.

THE HONOURABLE MR LISTLESS

Is Saint Peter the tutelar saint of Cadiz?

(None of the company could answer this question, and
MR ASTERIAS proceeded.)

They spoke to him in several languages, but he was as mute as a fish. They handed him over to some holy friars, who exorcised him; but the devil was mute too. After some days he pronounced the name Lierganes. A monk took him to that village. His mother and brothers recognised and embraced him; but he was as insensible to their caresses as any other fish would have been. He had some scales on his body, which dropped off by degrees; but his skin was as hard and rough as shagreen. He stayed at home nine years, without recovering his speech or his reason: he then disappeared again; and one of his old acquaintance, some years after, saw him pop his head out of the water near the coast of the Asturias. These facts were certified by his brothers, and by Don Gaspardo de la Riba Aguero, Knight of Saint James, who lived near Lierganes, and often had the pleasure of our triton's company to dinner.—Pliny mentions an embassy of the Olyssiponians to Tiberius, to give him intelligence of a triton which had been heard playing on its shell in a certain cave; with several other authenticated facts on the subject of tritons and nereids.

THE HONOURABLE MR LISTLESS

You astonish me. I have been much on the sea-shore, in the season, but I do not think I ever saw a mermaid. *(He rang, and summoned Fatout, who made his appearance half-seas-over.)* Fatout! did I ever see a mermaid?

FATOUT

Mermaid! mer-r-m-m-aid! Ah! merry maid! Oui, monsieur! Yes, sir, very many. I vish dere vas von or two here in de kitchen—ma foi! Dey be all as melancholic as so many tombstone.

THE HONOURABLE MR LISTLESS

I mean, Fatout, an odd kind of human fish.

FATOUT

De odd fish! Ah, oui! I understand de phrase: ve have seen nothing else since ve left town—ma foi!

THE HONOURABLE MR LISTLESS

You seem to have a cup too much, sir.

FATOUT

Non, monsieur: de cup too little. De fen be very unwholesome, and I drink-a-de ponch vid Raven de butler, to keep out de bad air.

THE HONOURABLE MR LISTLESS

Fatout! I insist on your being sober.

FATOUT

Oui, monsieur; I vil be as sober as de révérendissime père Jean. I should be ver glad of de merry maid; but de butler be de odd fish, and he swim in de bowl de ponch. Ah! ah! I do recollect de leetle-a song:— 'About fair maids, and about fair maids, and about my merry maids all.' *(Fatout reeled out, singing.)*

THE HONOURABLE MR LISTLESS

I am overwhelmed: I never saw the rascal in such a condition before. But will you allow me, Mr Asterias, to inquire into the *cui bono* of all the pains and expense you have incurred to discover a mermaid? The *cui bono*, sir, is the question I always take the liberty to ask when I see any one taking much trouble for any object. I am myself a sort of Signor Pococurante, and should like to know if there be any thing better or pleasanter, than the state of existing and doing nothing?

MR ASTERIAS

I have made many voyages, Mr Listless, to remote and barren shores: I have travelled over desert and inhospitable lands: I have defied danger— I have endured fatigue—I have submitted to privation. In the midst of these I have experienced pleasures which I would not at any time have exchanged for that of existing and doing nothing. I have known many evils, but I have never known the worst of all, which, as it seems to me, are those which are comprehended in the inexhaustible varieties of *ennui*:

spleen, chagrin, vapours, blue devils, time-killing, discontent, misanthropy, and all their interminable train of fretfulness, querulousness, suspicions, jealousies, and fears, which have alike infected society, and the literature of society; and which would make an arctic ocean of the human mind, if the more humane pursuits of philosophy and science did not keep alive the better feelings and more valuable energies of our nature.

THE HONOURABLE MR LISTLESS

You are pleased to be severe upon our fashionable belles lettres.

MR ASTERIAS

Surely not without reason, when pirates, highwaymen, and other varieties of the extensive genus Marauder, are the only *beau idéal* of the active, as splenetic and railing misanthropy is of the speculative energy. A gloomy brow and a tragical voice seem to have been of late the characteristics of fashionable manners: and a morbid, withering, deadly, antisocial sirocco, loaded with moral and political despair, breathes through all the groves and valleys of the modern Parnassus; while science moves on in the calm dignity of its course, affording to youth delights equally pure and vivid—to maturity, calm and grateful occupation—to old age, the most pleasing recollections and inexhaustible materials of agreeable and salutary reflection; and, while its votary enjoys the disinterested pleasure of enlarging the intellect and increasing the comforts of society, he is himself independent of the caprices of human intercourse and the accidents of human fortune. Nature is his great and inexhaustible treasure. His days are always too short for his enjoyment: *ennui*, is a stranger to his door. At peace with the world and with his own mind, he suffices to himself, makes all around him happy, and the close of his pleasing and beneficial existence is the evening of a beautiful day.[6]

THE HONOURABLE MR LISTLESS

Really I should like very well to lead such a life myself, but the exertion would be too much for me. Besides, I have been at college. I contrive to get through my day by sinking the morning in bed, and killing the evening in company; dressing and dining in the intermediate space, and stopping the chinks and crevices of the few vacant moments that remain with a little easy reading. And that amiable discontent and antisociality which you reprobate in our present drawing-room-table literature, I find, I do assure you, a very fine mental tonic, which reconciles me to my favourite pursuit of doing nothing, by showing me that nobody is worth doing any thing for.

MARIONETTA

But is there not in such compositions a kind of unconscious self-detection, which seems to carry their own antidote with them? For surely no one who cordially and truly either hates or despises the world will publish a volume every three months to say so.

MR FLOSKY

There is a secret in all this, which I will elucidate with a dusky remark. According to Berkeley, the *esse* of things is *percipi*. They exist as they are perceived. But, leaving for the present, as far as relates to the material world, the materialists, hyloists, and antihyloists, to settle this point among them, which is indeed

A subtle question, raised among
Those out o' their wits, and those i' the wrong:

for only we transcendentalists are in the right: we may very safely assert that the *esse* of happiness is *percipi*. It exists as it is perceived. 'It is the mind that maketh well or ill.' The elements of pleasure and pain are every where. The degree of happiness that any circumstances or objects can confer on us depends on the mental disposition with which we approach them. If you consider what is meant by the common phrases, a happy disposition and a discontented temper, you will perceive that the truth for which I am contending is universally admitted.

(Mr Flosky suddenly stopped: he found himself unintentionally trespassing within the limits of common sense.)

MR HILARY

It is very true; a happy disposition finds materials of enjoyment every where. In the city, or the country—in society, or in solitude—in the theatre, or the forest—in the hum of the multitude, or in the silence of the mountains, are alike materials of reflection and elements of pleasure. It is one mode of pleasure to listen to the music of 'Don Giovanni,' in a theatre glittering with light, and crowded with elegance and beauty: it is another to glide at sunset over the bosom of a lonely lake, where no sound disturbs the silence but the motion of the boat through the waters. A happy disposition derives pleasure from both, a discontented temper from neither, but is always busy in detecting deficiencies, and feeding dissatisfaction with comparisons. The one gathers all the flowers, the other all the nettles, in its path. The one has the faculty of enjoying every thing, the other of enjoying nothing. The one realises all the pleasure of the present good; the other converts it into pain, by pining after something better, which is only better because it is not present, and which, if it were present, would not be enjoyed. These morbid spirits are in life what professed critics are in literature; they see nothing but faults, because they are predetermined to shut their eyes to beauties. The critic does his utmost to blight genius in its infancy; that which rises in spite of him he will not see; and then he complains of the decline of literature. In like manner, these cankers of society complain of human nature and society, when they have wilfully debarred themselves from all the good they contain, and done their utmost to blight their own happiness and that of all around them. Misanthropy is sometimes the product of disappointed benevolence; but it is more frequently the offspring of overweening and mortified vanity, quarrelling with the world for not being better treated than it deserves.

SCYTHROP (to Marionetta)

These remarks are rather uncharitable. There is great good in human nature, but it is at present ill-conditioned. Ardent spirits cannot but be dissatisfied with things as they are; and, according to their views of the probabilities of amelioration, they will rush into the extremes of either hope or despair—of which the first is enthusiasm, and the second misanthropy; but their sources in this case are the same, as the Severn and the Wye run in different directions, and both rise in Plinlimmon.

MARIONETTA

'And there is salmon in both;' for the resemblance is about as close as that between Macedon and Monmouth.

* * * * *

CHAPTER VIII

Marionetta observed the next day a remarkable perturbation in Scythrop, for which she could not imagine any probable cause. She was willing to believe at first that it had some transient and trifling source, and would pass off in a day or two; but, contrary to this expectation, it daily increased. She was well aware that Scythrop had a strong tendency to the love of mystery, for its own sake; that is to say, he would employ mystery to serve a purpose, but would first choose his purpose by its capability of mystery. He seemed now to have more mystery on his hands than the laws of the system allowed, and to wear his coat of darkness with an air of great discomfort. All her little playful arts lost by degrees much of their power either to irritate or to soothe; and the first perception of her diminished influence produced in her an immediate depression of spirits, and a consequent sadness of demeanour, that rendered her very interesting to Mr Glowry; who, duly considering the improbability of accomplishing his wishes with respect to Miss Toobad (which improbability naturally increased in the diurnal ratio of that young lady's absence), began to reconcile himself by degrees to the idea of Marionetta being his daughter.

Marionetta made many ineffectual attempts to extract from Scythrop the secret of his mystery; and, in despair of drawing it from himself, began to form hopes that she might find a clue to it from Mr Flosky, who was Scythrop's dearest friend, and was more frequently than any other person admitted to his solitary tower. Mr Flosky, however, had ceased to be visible in a morning. He was engaged in the composition of a dismal ballad; and, Marionetta's uneasiness overcoming her scruples of decorum, she determined to seek him in the apartment which he had chosen for his study. She tapped at the door, and at the sound 'Come in,' entered the apartment. It was noon, and the sun was shining in full splendour, much to the annoyance of Mr Flosky, who had obviated the inconvenience by closing the shutters, and drawing the window-curtains. He was sitting at his table by the light of a solitary candle, with a pen in one hand, and a muffineer in the other, with which he occasionally sprinkled salt on the wick, to make it burn blue. He sate with 'his eye in a fine frenzy rolling,' and turned his inspired gaze on Marionetta as if she had been the ghastly ladie of a magical vision; then placed his hand before his eyes, with an appearance of manifest pain—shook his head—withdrew his hand—rubbed his eyes, like a waking man—and said, in a tone of ruefulness most jeremitaylorically pathetic, 'To what am I to attribute this very unexpected pleasure, my dear Miss O'Carroll?'

MARIONETTA

I must apologise for intruding on you, Mr Flosky; but the interest which I—you—take in my cousin Scythrop—

MR FLOSKY

Pardon me, Miss O'Carroll; I do not take any interest in any person or thing on the face of the earth; which sentiment, if you analyse it, you will find to be the quintessence of the most refined philanthropy.

MARIONETTA

I will take it for granted that it is so, Mr Flosky; I am not conversant with metaphysical subtleties, but—

MR FLOSKY

Subtleties! my dear Miss O'Carroll. I am sorry to find you participating in the vulgar error of the *reading public*, to whom an unusual collocation of words, involving a juxtaposition of antiperistatical ideas, immediately suggests the notion of hyperoxysophistical paradoxology.

MARIONETTA

Indeed, Mr Flosky, it suggests no such notion to me. I have sought you for the purpose of obtaining information.

MR FLOSKY (shaking his head)

No one ever sought me for such a purpose before.

MARIONETTA

I think, Mr Flosky—that is, I believe—that is, I fancy—that is, I imagine—

MR FLOSKY

The [Greek: toytesti], the *id est*, the *cioè*, the *c'est à dire*, the *that is*, my dear Miss O'Carroll, is not applicable in this case—if you will permit me to take the liberty of saying so. Think is not synonymous with believe— for belief, in many most important particulars, results from the total absence, the absolute negation of thought, and is thereby the sane and orthodox condition of mind; and thought and belief are both essentially different from fancy, and fancy, again, is distinct from imagination. This distinction between fancy and imagination is one of the most abstruse and important points of metaphysics. I have written seven hundred pages of promise to elucidate it, which promise I shall keep as faithfully as the bank will its promise to pay.

MARIONETTA

I assure you, Mr Flosky, I care no more about metaphysics than I do about the bank; and, if you will condescend to talk to a simple girl in intelligible terms—

MR FLOSKY

Say not condescend! Know you not that you talk to the most humble of men, to one who has buckled on the armour of sanctity, and clothed himself with humility as with a garment?

MARIONETTA

My cousin Scythrop has of late had an air of mystery about him, which gives me great uneasiness.

MR FLOSKY

That is strange: nothing is so becoming to a man as an air of mystery. Mystery is the very key-stone of all that is beautiful in poetry, all that is sacred in faith, and all that is recondite in transcendental psychology. I am writing a ballad which is all mystery; it is 'such stuff as dreams are made of,' and is, indeed, stuff made of a dream; for, last night I fell asleep as usual over my book, and had a vision of pure reason. I composed five hundred lines in my sleep; so that, having had a dream of a ballad, I am now officiating as my own Peter Quince, and making a ballad of my dream, and it shall be called Bottom's Dream, because it has no bottom.

MARIONETTA

I see, Mr Flosky, you think my intrusion unseasonable, and are inclined to punish it, by talking nonsense to me. *(Mr Flosky gave a start at the word nonsense, which almost overturned the table.)* I assure you, I would not have intruded if I had not been very much interested in the question I wish to ask you.—*(Mr Flosky listened in sullen dignity.)*—My cousin Scythrop seems to have some secret preying on his mind.—*(Mr Flosky was silent.)*—He seems very unhappy—Mr Flosky.—Perhaps you are acquainted with the cause.—*(Mr Flosky was still silent.)*—I only wish to know—Mr Flosky—if it is any thing—that could be remedied by any thing—that any one—of whom I know any thing—could do.

MR FLOSKY (after a pause)

There are various ways of getting at secrets. The most approved methods, as recommended both theoretically and practically in philosophical novels, are eavesdropping at key-holes, picking the locks of chests and desks, peeping into letters, steaming wafers, and insinuating hot wire under sealing wax; none of which methods I hold it lawful to practise.

MARIONETTA

Surely, Mr Flosky, you cannot suspect me of wishing to adopt or encourage such base and contemptible arts.

MR FLOSKY

Yet are they recommended, and with well-strung reasons, by writers of gravity and note, as simple and easy methods of studying character, and gratifying that laudable curiosity which aims at the knowledge of man.

MARIONETTA

I am as ignorant of this morality which you do not approve, as of the metaphysics which you do: I should be glad to know by your means, what is the matter with my cousin; I do not like to see him unhappy, and I suppose there is some reason for it.

MR FLOSKY

Now I should rather suppose there is no reason for it: it is the fashion to be unhappy. To have a reason for being so would be exceedingly common-place: to be so without any is the province of genius: the art of being miserable for misery's sake, has been brought to great perfection in our days; and the ancient Odyssey, which held forth a shining example of the endurance of real misfortune, will give place to a modern one, setting

64

out a more instructive picture of querulous impatience under imaginary evils.

MARIONETTA

Will you oblige me, Mr Flosky, by giving me a plain answer to a plain question?

MR FLOSKY

It is impossible, my dear Miss O'Carroll. I never gave a plain answer to a question in my life.

MARIONETTA

Do you, or do you not, know what is the matter with my cousin?

MR FLOSKY

To say that I do not know, would be to say that I am ignorant of something; and God forbid, that a transcendental metaphysician, who has pure anticipated cognitions of every thing, and carries the whole science of geometry in his head without ever having looked into Euclid, should fall into so empirical an error as to declare himself ignorant of any thing: to say that I do know, would be to pretend to positive and circumstantial knowledge touching present matter of fact, which, when you consider the nature of evidence, and the various lights in which the same thing may be seen—

MARIONETTA

I see, Mr Flosky, that either you have no information, or are determined not to impart it; and I beg your pardon for having given you this unnecessary trouble.

MR FLOSKY

My dear Miss O'Carroll, it would have given me great pleasure to have said any thing that would have given you pleasure; but if any person living could make report of having obtained any information on any subject from Ferdinando Flosky, my transcendental reputation would be ruined for ever.

* * * * *

CHAPTER IX

Scythrop grew every day more reserved, mysterious, and distrait; and gradually lengthened the duration of his diurnal seclusions in his tower. Marionetta thought she perceived in all this very manifest symptoms of a warm love cooling.

It was seldom that she found herself alone with him in the morning, and, on these occasions, if she was silent in the hope of his speaking first, not a syllable would he utter; if she spoke to him indirectly, he assented monosyllabically; if she questioned him, his answers were brief, constrained, and evasive. Still, though her spirits were depressed, her playfulness had not so totally forsaken her, but that it illuminated at intervals the gloom of Nightmare Abbey; and if, on any occasion, she observed in Scythrop tokens of unextinguished or returning passion, her love of tormenting her lover immediately got the better both of her grief and her sympathy, though not of her curiosity, which Scythrop seemed determined not to satisfy. This playfulness, however, was in a great measure artificial, and usually vanished with the irritable Strephon, to whose annoyance it had been exerted. The Genius Loci, the *tutela* of Nightmare Abbey, the spirit of black melancholy, began to set his seal on her pallescent countenance. Scythrop perceived the change, found his tender sympathies awakened, and did his utmost to comfort the afflicted damsel, assuring her that his seeming inattention had only proceeded from his being involved in a profound meditation on a very hopeful scheme for the regeneration of human society. Marionetta called him ungrateful, cruel, cold-hearted, and accompanied her reproaches with many sobs and tears; poor Scythrop growing every moment more soft and submissive—till, at length, he threw himself at her feet, and declared that no competition of beauty, however dazzling, genius, however transcendent, talents, however cultivated, or philosophy, however enlightened, should ever make him renounce his divine Marionetta.

'Competition!' thought Marionetta, and suddenly, with an air of the most freezing indifference, she said, 'You are perfectly at liberty, sir, to do as you please; I beg you will follow your own plans, without any reference to me.'

Scythrop was confounded. What was become of all her passion and her tears? Still kneeling, he kissed her hand with rueful timidity, and said, in most pathetic accents, 'Do you not love me, Marionetta?'

'No,' said Marionetta, with a look of cold composure: 'No.' Scythrop still looked up incredulously. 'No, I tell you.'

'Oh! very well, madam,' said Scythrop, rising, 'if that is the case, there are those in the world—'

'To be sure there are, sir;—and do you suppose I do not see through your designs, you ungenerous monster?'

'My designs? Marionetta!'

'Yes, your designs, Scythrop. You have come here to cast me off, and artfully contrive that it should appear to be my doing, and not yours, thinking to quiet your tender conscience with this pitiful stratagem. But do not suppose that you are of so much consequence to me: do not suppose it: you are of no consequence to me at all—none at all: therefore, leave me: I renounce you: leave me; why do you not leave me?'

Scythrop endeavoured to remonstrate, but without success. She reiterated her injunctions to him to leave her, till, in the simplicity of his spirit, he was preparing to comply. When he had nearly reached the door, Marionetta said, 'Farewell.' Scythrop looked back. 'Farewell, Scythrop,' she repeated, 'you will never see me again.'

'Never see you again, Marionetta?'

'I shall go from hence to-morrow, perhaps to-day; and before we meet again, one of us will be married, and we might as well be dead, you know, Scythrop.'

The sudden change of her voice in the last few words, and the burst of tears that accompanied them, acted like electricity on the tender-hearted youth; and, in another instant, a complete reconciliation was accomplished without the intervention of words.

There are, indeed, some learned casuists, who maintain that love has no language, and that all the misunderstandings and dissensions of lovers arise from the fatal habit of employing words on a subject to which words are inapplicable; that love, beginning with looks, that is to say, with the physiognomical expression of congenial mental dispositions, tends through a regular gradation of signs and symbols of affection, to that consummation which is most devoutly to be wished; and that it neither is necessary that there should be, nor probable that there would be, a single word spoken from first to last between two sympathetic spirits, were it not that the arbitrary institutions of society have raised, at every step of this very simple process, so many complicated impediments and barriers in the shape of settlements and ceremonies, parents and guardians, lawyers, Jew-brokers, and parsons, that many an adventurous knight (who, in order to obtain the conquest of the Hesperian fruit, is obliged to fight his way through all these monsters), is either repulsed at the onset, or vanquished before the achievement of his enterprise: and such a quantity of unnatural talking is rendered inevitably necessary through all the stages of the progression, that the tender and volatile spirit of love often takes flight on the pinions of some of the [Greek: epea pteroenta], or *winged words* which are pressed into his service in despite of himself.

At this conjuncture, Mr Glowry entered, and sitting down near them, said, 'I see how it is; and, as we are all sure to be miserable do what we may, there is no need of taking pains to make one another more so; therefore, with God's blessing and mine, there'—joining their hands as he spoke.

Scythrop was not exactly prepared for this decisive step; but he could only stammer out, 'Really, sir, you are too good;' and Mr Glowry departed to bring Mr Hilary to ratify the act.

Now, whatever truth there may be in the theory of love and language, of which we have so recently spoken, certain it is, that during Mr Glowry's absence, which lasted half an hour, not a single word was said by either Scythrop or Marionetta.

Mr Glowry returned with Mr Hilary, who was delighted at the prospect of so advantageous an establishment for his orphan niece, of whom he considered himself in some manner the guardian, and nothing remained, as Mr Glowry observed, but to fix the day.

Marionetta blushed, and was silent. Scythrop was also silent for a time, and at length hesitatingly said, 'My deal sir, your goodness overpowers me; but really you are so precipitate.'

Now, this remark, if the young lady had made it, would, whether she thought it or not—for sincerity is a thing of no account on these occasions, nor indeed on any other, according to Mr Flosky—this remark, if the young lady had made it, would have been perfectly *comme il faut*; but, being made by the young gentleman, it was *toute autre chose*, and was, indeed, in the eyes of his mistress, a most heinous and irremissible offence. Marionetta was angry, very angry, but she concealed her anger, and said, calmly and coldly, 'Certainly, you are much too precipitate, Mr Glowry. I assure you, sir, I have by no means made up my mind; and, indeed, as far as I know it, it inclines the other way; but it will be quite time enough to think of these matters seven years hence. Before surprise permitted reply, the young lady had locked herself up in her own apartment.

'Why, Scythrop,' said Mr Glowry, elongating his face exceedingly, 'the devil is come among us sure enough, as Mr Toobad observes: I thought you and Marionetta were both of a mind.'

'So we are, I believe, sir,' said Scythrop, gloomily, and stalked away to his tower.

'Mr Glowry,' said Mr Hilary, 'I do not very well understand all this.'

'Whims, brother Hilary,' said Mr Glowry; 'some little foolish love quarrel, nothing more. Whims, freaks, April showers. They will be blown over by to-morrow.'

'If not,' said Mr Hilary, 'these April showers have made us April fools.'

'Ah!' said Mr Glowry, 'you are a happy man, and in all your afflictions you can console yourself with a joke, let it be ever so bad, provided you crack it yourself. I should be very happy to laugh with you, if it would give you any satisfaction; but, really, at present, my heart is so sad, that I find it impossible to levy a contribution on my muscles.'

* * * * *

CHAPTER X

On the evening on which Mr Asterias had caught a glimpse of a female figure on the sea-shore, which he had translated into the visual sign of his interior cognition of a mermaid, Scythrop, retiring to his tower, found his study preoccupied. A stranger, muffled in a cloak, was sitting at his table. Scythrop paused in surprise. The stranger rose at his entrance, and looked at him intently a few minutes, in silence. The eyes of the stranger alone were visible. All the rest of the figure was muffled and mantled in the folds of a black cloak, which was raised, by the right hand, to the level of the eyes. This scrutiny being completed, the stranger, dropping the cloak, said, 'I see, by your physiognomy, that you may be trusted;' and revealed to the astonished Scythrop a female form and countenance of dazzling grace and beauty, with long flowing hair of raven blackness, and large black eyes of almost oppressive brilliancy, which strikingly contrasted with a complexion of snowy whiteness. Her dress was extremely elegant, but had an appearance of foreign fashion, as if both the lady and her mantua-maker were of 'a far countree.'

'I guess 'twas frightful there to see
A lady so richly clad as she,
Beautiful exceedingly.'

For, if it be terrible to one young lady to find another under a tree at midnight, it must, *à fortiori*, be much more terrible to a young gentleman to find a young lady in his study at that hour. If the logical consecutiveness of this conclusion be not manifest to my readers, I am sorry for their dulness, and must refer them, for more ample elucidation, to a treatise which Mr Flosky intends to write, on the Categories of Relation, which comprehend Substance and Accident, Cause and Effect, Action and Reaction.

Scythrop, therefore, either was or ought to have been frightened; at all events, he was astonished; and astonishment, though not in itself fear, is nevertheless a good stage towards it, and is, indeed, as it were, the halfway house between respect and terror, according to Mr Burke's graduated scale of the sublime.[7]

'You are surprised,' said the lady; 'yet why should you be surprised? If you had met me in a drawing-room, and I had been introduced to you by an old woman, it would have been a matter of course: can the division of two or three walls, and the absence of an unimportant personage, make the same object essentially different in the perception of a philosopher?'

'Certainly not,' said Scythrop; 'but when any class of objects has habitually presented itself to our perceptions in invariable conjunction with particular relations, then, on the sudden appearance of one object of the class divested of those accompaniments, the essential difference of the relation is, by an involuntary process, transferred to the object itself, which thus offers itself to our perceptions with all the strangeness of novelty.'

'You are a philosopher,' said the lady, 'and a lover of liberty. You are the author of a treatise, called "Philosophical Gas; or, a Project for a General Illumination of the Human Mind."'

'I am,' said Scythrop, delighted at this first blossom of his renown.

'I am a stranger in this country,' said the lady; 'I have been but a few days in it, yet I find myself immediately under the necessity of seeking refuge from an atrocious persecution. I had no friend to whom I could apply; and, in the midst of my difficulties, accident threw your pamphlet in my way. I saw that I had, at least, one kindred mind in this nation, and determined to apply to you.'

'And what would you have me do?' said Scythrop, more and more amazed, and not a little perplexed.

'I would have you,' said the young lady, 'assist me in finding some place of retreat, where I can remain concealed from the indefatigable search that is being made for me. I have been so nearly caught once or twice already, that I cannot confide any longer in my own ingenuity.'

Doubtless, thought Scythrop, this is one of my golden candle-sticks. 'I have constructed,' said he, 'in this tower, an entrance to a small suite of unknown apartments in the main building, which I defy any creature living to detect. If you would like to remain there a day or two, till I can find you a more suitable concealment, you may rely on the honour of a transcendental eleutherarch.'

'I rely on myself,' said the lady. 'I act as I please, go where I please, and let the world say what it will. I am rich enough to set it at defiance. It is the tyrant of the poor and the feeble, but the slave of those who are above the reach of its injury.'

Scythrop ventured to inquire the name of his fair *protégée*. 'What is a name?' said the lady: 'any name will serve the purpose of distinction. Call me Stella. I see by your looks,' she added, 'that you think all this very strange. When you know me better, your surprise will cease. I submit not to be an accomplice in my sex's slavery. I am, like yourself, a lover of freedom, and I carry my theory into practice. *They alone are subject to blind authority who have no reliance on their own strength.*'

Stella took possession of the recondite apartments. Scythrop intended to find her another asylum; but from day to day he postponed his intention, and by degrees forgot it. The young lady reminded him of it from day to day, till she also forgot it. Scythrop was anxious to learn her history; but she would add nothing to what she had already communicated, that she was shunning an atrocious persecution. Scythrop thought of Lord C. and the Alien Act, and said, 'As you will not tell your name, I suppose it is in the green bag.' Stella, not understanding what he meant, was silent; and Scythrop, translating silence into acquiescence, concluded that he was sheltering an *illuminée* whom Lord S. suspected of an intention to take the Tower, and set fire to the Bank: exploits, at least, as likely to be accomplished by the hands and eyes of a young beauty, as by a drunken cobbler and doctor, armed with a pamphlet and an old stocking.

Stella, in her conversations with Scythrop, displayed a highly cultivated and energetic mind, full of impassioned schemes of liberty, and impatience of masculine usurpation. She had a lively sense of all the oppressions that are done under the sun; and the vivid pictures which her imagination presented to her of the numberless scenes of injustice and misery which are being acted at every moment in every part of the inhabited world, gave an habitual seriousness to her physiognomy, that made it seem as if a smile had never once hovered on her lips. She was intimately conversant with the German language and literature; and Scythrop listened with delight to her repetitions of her favourite passages from Schiller and Goethe, and to her encomiums on the sublime Spartacus Weishaupt, the immortal founder of the sect of the Illuminati. Scythrop found that his soul had a greater capacity of love than the image of Marionetta had filled. The form of Stella took possession of every vacant corner of the cavity, and by degrees displaced that of Marionetta from many of the outworks of the citadel; though the latter still held possession of the *keep*. He judged, from his new friend calling herself Stella, that, if it were not her real name, she was an admirer of the principles of the German play from which she had taken it, and took an opportunity of leading the conversation to that subject; but to his great surprise, the lady spoke very ardently of the singleness and exclusiveness of love, and declared that the reign of affection was one and indivisible; that it might be transferred, but could not be participated. 'If I ever love,' said she, 'I shall do so without limit or restriction. I shall hold all difficulties light, all sacrifices cheap, all obstacles gossamer. But for love so total, I shall claim a return as absolute. I will have no rival: whether more or less favoured will be of little moment. I will be neither first nor second—I will be alone. The heart which I shall possess I will possess entirely, or entirely renounce.'

Scythrop did not dare to mention the name of Marionetta; he trembled lest some unlucky accident should reveal it to Stella, though he scarcely knew what result to wish or anticipate, and lived in the double fever of a perpetual dilemma. He could not dissemble to himself that he was in love, at the same time, with two damsels of minds and habits as remote as the antipodes. The scale of predilection always inclined to the fair one who happened to be present; but the absent was never effectually outweighed, though the degrees of exaltation and depression varied according to accidental variations in the outward and visible signs of the inward and spiritual graces of his respective charmers. Passing and repassing several times a day from the company of the one to that of the other, he was like a shuttlecock between two battledores, changing its direction as rapidly as the oscillations of a pendulum, receiving many a hard knock on the cork of a sensitive heart, and flying from point to point on the feathers of a super-sublimated head. This was an awful state of things. He had now as much mystery about him as any romantic transcendentalist or transcendental romancer could desire. He had his esoterical and his exoterical love. He could not endure the thought of losing either of them, but he trembled when he imagined the possibility that some fatal discovery might deprive him of both. The old proverb concerning two strings to a bow gave him some gleams of comfort; but that concerning two stools occurred to him more frequently, and covered his forehead with a cold perspiration. With Stella, he could indulge freely in all his romantic and philosophical visions. He could build castles in the air, and she would pile towers and turrets on the imaginary edifices. With Marionetta it was otherwise: she knew nothing of the world and society beyond the sphere of her own experience. Her life was all music and sunshine, and she wondered what any one could see to complain of in such a pleasant state of things. She loved Scythrop, she hardly knew why; indeed she was not always sure that she loved him at all: she felt her fondness increase or diminish in an inverse ratio to his. When she had manoeuvred him into a fever of passionate love, she often felt and always assumed indifference: if she found that her coldness was contagious, and that Scythrop either was, or pretended to be, as indifferent as herself, she would become doubly kind, and raise him again to that elevation from which she had previously thrown him down. Thus, when his love was flowing, hers was ebbing: when his was ebbing, hers was flowing. Now and then there were moments of level tide, when reciprocal affection seemed to promise imperturbable harmony; but Scythrop could scarcely resign his spirit to the pleasing illusion, before the pinnace of the lover's affections was caught in some eddy of the lady's caprice, and he was whirled away from the shore of his hopes, without rudder or compass, into an ocean of mists and storms. It resulted, from this system of conduct, that all that passed between Scythrop and Marionetta, consisted in making and unmaking love. He had no opportunity to take measure of her understanding by conversations on general subjects, and on his favourite designs; and, being left in this respect to the exercise of indefinite conjecture, he took it for granted, as most lovers would do in similar circumstances, that she had great natural talents, which she wasted at present on trifles: but coquetry would end with marriage, and leave room for philosophy to exert its influence on her mind. Stella had no coquetry, no disguise: she was an enthusiast in subjects of general interest; and her conduct to Scythrop was always uniform, or rather showed a regular progression of partiality which seemed fast ripening into love.

* * * * *

CHAPTER XI

Scythrop, attending one day the summons to dinner, found in the drawing-room his friend Mr Cypress the poet, whom he had known at college, and who was a great favourite of Mr Glowry. Mr Cypress said, he was on the point of leaving England, but could not think of doing so without a farewell-look at Nightmare Abbey and his respected friends, the moody Mr Glowry and the mysterious Mr Scythrop, the sublime Mr Flosky and the pathetic Mr Listless; to all of whom, and the morbid hospitality of the melancholy dwelling in which they were then assembled, he assured them he should always look back with as much affection as his lacerated spirit could feel for any thing. The sympathetic condolence of their respective replies was cut short by Raven's announcement of 'dinner on table.'

The conversation that took place when the wine was in circulation, and the ladies were withdrawn, we shall report with our usual scrupulous fidelity.

MR GLOWRY

You are leaving England, Mr Cypress. There is a delightful melancholy in saying farewell to an old acquaintance, when the chances are twenty to one against ever meeting again. A smiling bumper to a sad parting, and let us all be unhappy together.

MR CYPRESS (filling a bumper)

This is the only social habit that the disappointed spirit never unlearns.

THE REVEREND MR LARYNX (filling)

It is the only piece of academical learning that the finished educatee retains.

MR FLOSKY (filling)

It is the only objective fact which the sceptic can realise.

SCYTHROP (filling)

It is the only styptic for a bleeding heart.

THE HONOURABLE MR LISTLESS (filling)

It is the only trouble that is very well worth taking.

MR ASTERIAS (filling)

It is the only key of conversational truth.

MR TOOBAD (filling)

It is the only antidote to the great wrath of the devil.

MR HILARY (filling)

It is the only symbol of perfect life. The inscription 'HIC NON BIBITUR' will suit nothing but a tombstone.

MR GLOWRY

You will see many fine old ruins, Mr Cypress; crumbling pillars, and mossy walls—many a one-legged Venus and headless Minerva—many a Neptune buried in sand—many a Jupiter turned topsy-turvy—many a perforated Bacchus doing duty as a water-pipe—many reminiscences of the ancient world, which I hope was better worth living in than the modern; though, for myself, I care not a straw more for one than the other, and would not go twenty miles to see any thing that either could show.

MR CYPRESS

It is something to seek, Mr Glowry. The mind is restless, and must persist in seeking, though to find is to be disappointed. Do you feel no aspirations towards the countries of Socrates and Cicero? No wish to wander among the venerable remains of the greatness that has passed for ever?

MR GLOWRY

Not a grain.

SCYTHROP

It is, indeed, much the same as if a lover should dig up the buried form of his mistress, and gaze upon relics which are any thing but herself, to wander among a few mouldy ruins, that are only imperfect indexes to lost volumes of glory, and meet at every step the more melancholy ruins of human nature—a degenerate race of stupid and shrivelled slaves, grovelling in the lowest depths of servility and superstition.

THE HONOURABLE MR LISTLESS

It is the fashion to go abroad. I have thought of it myself, but am hardly equal to the exertion. To be sure, a little eccentricity and originality are allowable in some cases; and the most eccentric and original of all characters is an Englishman who stays at home.

SCYTHROP

I should have no pleasure in visiting countries that are past all hope of regeneration. There is great hope of our own; and it seems to me that an Englishman, who, either by his station in society, or by his genius, or (as in your instance, Mr Cypress,) by both, has the power of essentially serving his country in its arduous struggle with its domestic enemies, yet forsakes his country, which is still so rich in hope, to dwell in others which are only fertile in the ruins of memory, does what none of those ancients, whose fragmentary memorials you venerate, would have done in similar circumstances.

MR CYPRESS

Sir, I have quarrelled with my wife; and a man who has quarrelled with his wife is absolved from all duty to his country. I have written an ode to tell the people as much, and they may take it as they list.

SCYTHROP

Do you suppose, if Brutus had quarrelled with his wife, he would have given it as a reason to Cassius for having nothing to do with his enterprise? Or would Cassius have been satisfied with such an excuse?

MR FLOSKY

Brutus was a senator; so is our dear friend: but the cases are different. Brutus had some hope of political good: Mr Cypress has none. How should he, after what we have seen in France?

SCYTHROP

A Frenchman is born in harness, ready saddled, bitted, and bridled, for any tyrant to ride. He will fawn under his rider one moment, and throw him and kick him to death the next; but another adventurer springs on his back, and by dint of whip and spur on he goes as before. We may, without much vanity, hope better of ourselves.

MR CYPRESS

I have no hope for myself or for others. Our life is a false nature; it is not in the harmony of things; it is an all-blasting upas, whose root is earth, and whose leaves are the skies which rain their poison-dews upon mankind. We wither from our youth; we gasp with unslaked thirst for unattainable good; lured from the first to the last by phantoms—love, fame, ambition, avarice—all idle, and all ill—one meteor of many names, that vanishes in the smoke of death.[8]

MR FLOSKY

A most delightful speech, Mr Cypress. A most amiable and instructive philosophy. You have only to impress its truth on the minds of all living men, and life will then, indeed, be the desert and the solitude; and I must do you, myself, and our mutual friends, the justice to observe, that let society only give fair play at one and the same time, as I flatter myself it is inclined to do, to your system of morals, and my system of metaphysics, and Scythrop's system of politics, and Mr Listless's system of manners, and Mr Toobad's system of religion, and the result will be as fine a mental chaos as even the immortal Kant himself could ever have hoped to see; in the prospect of which I rejoice.

MR HILARY

'Certainly, ancient, it is not a thing to rejoice at:' I am one of those who cannot see the good that is to result from all this mystifying and blue-devilling of society. The contrast it presents to the cheerful and solid wisdom of antiquity is too forcible not to strike any one who has the least knowledge of classical literature. To represent vice and misery as the necessary accompaniments of genius, is as mischievous as it is false, and the feeling is as unclassical as the language in which it is usually expressed.

MR TOOBAD

It is our calamity. The devil has come among us, and has begun by taking possession of all the cleverest fellows. Yet, forsooth, this is the enlightened age. Marry, how? Did our ancestors go peeping about with dark lanterns, and do we walk at our ease in broad sunshine? Where is the manifestation of our light? By what symptoms do you recognise it? What are its signs, its tokens, its symptoms, its symbols, its categories, its conditions? What is it, and why? How, where, when is it to be seen, felt, and understood? What do we see by it which our ancestors saw not, and which at the same time is worth seeing? We see a hundred men hanged, where they saw one. We see five hundred transported, where they saw one. We see five thousand in the workhouse, where they saw one. We see scores of Bible Societies, where they saw none. We see paper, where they saw gold. We see men in stays, where they saw men in armour. We see painted faces, where they saw healthy ones. We see children perishing in manufactories, where they saw them flourishing in the fields. We see prisons, where they saw castles. We see masters, where they saw representatives. In short, they saw true men, where we see false knaves. They saw Milton, and we see Mr Sackbut.

MR FLOSKY

The false knave, sir, is my honest friend; therefore, I beseech you, let him be countenanced. God forbid but a knave should have some countenance at his friend's request.

MR TOOBAD

'Good men and true' was their common term, like the chalos chagathos of the Athenians. It is so long since men have been either good or true, that it is to be questioned which is most obsolete, the fact or the phraseology.

MR CYPRESS

There is no worth nor beauty but in the mind's idea. Love sows the wind and reaps the whirlwind.[9] Confusion, thrice confounded, is the portion of him who rests even for an instant on that most brittle of reeds—the affection of a human being. The sum of our social destiny is to inflict or to endure.[10]

MR HILARY

Rather to bear and forbear, Mr Cypress—a maxim which you perhaps despise. Ideal beauty is not the mind's creation: it is real beauty, refined and purified in the mind's alembic, from the alloy which always more or less accompanies it in our mixed and imperfect nature. But still the gold exists in a very ample degree. To expect too much is a disease in the expectant, for which human nature is not responsible; and, in the common name of humanity, I protest against these false and mischievous ravings. To rail against humanity for not being abstract perfection, and against human love for not realising all the splendid visions of the poets of chivalry, is to rail at the summer for not being all sunshine, and at the rose for not being always in bloom.

MR CYPRESS

Human love! Love is not an inhabitant of the earth. We worship him as the Athenians did their unknown God: but broken hearts are the martyrs of his faith, and the eye shall never see the form which phantasy paints, and which passion pursues through paths of delusive beauty, among flowers whose odours are agonies, and trees whose gums are poison.[11]

MR HILARY

You talk like a Rosicrucian, who will love nothing but a sylph, who does not believe in the existence of a sylph, and who yet quarrels with the whole universe for not containing a sylph.

MR CYPRESS

The mind is diseased of its own beauty, and fevers into false creation. The forms which the sculptor's soul has seized exist only in himself.[12]

MR FLOSKY

Permit me to discept. They are the mediums of common forms combined and arranged into a common standard. The ideal beauty of the Helen of Zeuxis was the combined medium of the real beauty of the virgins of Crotona.

MR HILARY

But to make ideal beauty the shadow in the water, and, like the dog in the fable, to throw away the substance in catching at the shadow, is scarcely the characteristic of wisdom, whatever it may be of genius. To reconcile man as he is to the world as it is, to preserve and improve all that is good, and destroy or alleviate all that is evil, in physical and moral nature—have been the hope and aim of the greatest teachers and ornaments of our species. I will say, too, that the highest wisdom and the highest genius have been invariably accompanied with cheerfulness. We have sufficient proofs on record that Shakspeare and Socrates were the most festive of companions. But now the little wisdom and genius we have seem to be entering into a conspiracy against cheerfulness.

MR TOOBAD

How can we be cheerful with the devil among us!

THE HONOURABLE MR LISTLESS

How can we be cheerful when our nerves are shattered?

MR FLOSKY

How can we be cheerful when we are surrounded by a *reading public*, that is growing too wise for its betters?

SCYTHROP

How can we be cheerful when our great general designs are crossed every moment by our little particular passions?

MR CYPRESS

How can we be cheerful in the midst of disappointment and despair?

MR GLOWRY

Let us all be unhappy together.

MR HILARY

Let us sing a catch.

MR GLOWRY

No: a nice tragical ballad. The Norfolk Tragedy to the tune of the Hundredth Psalm.

MR HILARY

I say a catch.

MR GLOWRY

I say no. A song from Mr Cypress.

ALL

A song from Mr Cypress.

MR CYPRESS sung—

There is a fever of the spirit,
The brand of Cain's unresting doom,
Which in the lone dark souls that bear it
Glows like the lamp in Tullia's tomb:
Unlike that lamp, its subtle fire
Burns, blasts, consumes its cell, the heart,
Till, one by one, hope, joy, desire,
Like dreams of shadowy smoke depart.

When hope, love, life itself, are only
Dust—spectral memories—dead and cold—
The unfed fire burns bright and lonely,
Like that undying lamp of old:
And by that drear illumination,
Till time its clay-built home has rent,
Thought broods on feeling's desolation—
The soul is its own monument.

MR GLOWRY

Admirable. Let us all be unhappy together.

MR HILARY

Now, I say again, a catch.

THE REVEREND MR LARYNX

I am for you.

ME HILARY

'Seamen three.'

THE REVEREND MR LARYNX

Agreed. I'll be Harry Gill, with the voice of three. Begin

MR HILARY AND THE REVEREND MR LARYNX

Seamen three! I What men be ye?
Gotham's three wise men we be.
Whither in your bowl so free?
To rake the moon from out the sea.
The bowl goes trim. The moon doth shine.
And our ballast is old wine;
And your ballast is old wine.

Who art thou, so fast adrift?
I am he they call Old Care.
Here on board we will thee lift.
No: I may not enter there.
Wherefore so? 'Tis Jove's decree,
In a bowl Care may not be;
In a bowl Care may not be.

Pear ye not the waves that roll?
No: in charmed bowl we swim.
What the charm that floats the bowl?
Water may not pass the brim.
The bowl goes trim. The moon doth shine.
And our ballast is old wine;
And your ballast is old wine.

This catch was so well executed by the spirit and science of Mr Hilary, and the deep tri-une voice of the reverend gentleman, that the whole party, in spite of themselves, caught the contagion, and joined in chorus at the conclusion, each raising a bumper to his lips:

The bowl goes trim: the moon doth shine:
And our ballast is old wine.

Mr Cypress, having his ballast on board, stepped, the same evening, into his bowl, or travelling chariot, and departed to rake seas and rivers, lakes and canals, for the moon of ideal beauty.

* * * * *

CHAPTER XII

It was the custom of the Honourable Mr Listless, on adjourning from the bottle to the ladies, to retire for a few moments to make a second toilette, that he might present himself in becoming taste. Fatout, attending as usual, appeared with a countenance of great dismay, and informed his master that he had just ascertained that the abbey was haunted. Mrs Hilary's *gentlewoman*, for whom Fatout had lately conceived a *tendresse*, had been, as she expressed it, 'fritted out of her seventeen senses' the preceding night, as she was retiring to her bedchamber, by a ghastly figure which she had met stalking along one of the galleries, wrapped in a white shroud, with a bloody turban on its head. She had fainted away with fear; and, when she recovered, she found herself in the dark, and the figure was gone. '*Sacre—cochon—bleu!*' exclaimed Fatout, giving very deliberate emphasis to every portion of his terrible oath—'I vould not meet de *revenant*, de ghost—*non*—not for all de *bowl-de-ponch* in de vorld.'

'Fatout,' said the Honourable Mr Listless, 'did I ever see a ghost?'

'*Jamais*, monsieur, never.'

'Then I hope I never shall, for, in the present shattered state of my nerves, I am afraid it would be too much for me. There—loosen the lace of my stays a little, for really this plebeian practice of eating—Not too loose—consider my shape. That will do. And I desire that you bring me no more stories of ghosts; for, though I do not believe in such things, yet, when one is awake in the night, one is apt, if one thinks of them, to have fancies that give one a kind of a chill, particularly if one opens one's eyes suddenly on one's dressing gown, hanging in the moonlight, between the bed and the window.'

The Honourable Mr Listless, though he had prohibited Fatout from bringing him any more stories of ghosts, could not help thinking of that which Fatout had already brought; and, as it was uppermost in his mind, when he descended to the tea and coffee cups, and the rest of the company in the library, he almost involuntarily asked Mr Flosky, whom he looked up to as a most oraculous personage, whether any story of any ghost that had ever appeared to any one, was entitled to any degree of belief?

MR FLOSKY

By far the greater number, to a very great degree.

THE HONOURABLE MR LISTLESS

Really, that is very alarming!

MR FLOSKY

Sunt geminoe somni portoe. There are two gates through which ghosts find their way to the upper air: fraud and self-delusion. In the latter case, a ghost is a *deceptio visûs*, an ocular spectrum, an idea with the force of a sensation. I have seen many ghosts myself. I dare say there are few in this company who have not seen a ghost.

THE HONOURABLE MR LISTLESS

I am happy to say, I never have, for one.

THE REVEREND MR LARYNX

We have such high authority for ghosts, that it is rank scepticism to disbelieve them. Job saw a ghost, which came for the express purpose of asking a question, and did not wait for an answer.

THE HONOURABLE MR LISTLESS

Because Job was too frightened to give one.

THE REVEREND MR LARYNX

Spectres appeared to the Egyptians during the darkness with which Moses covered Egypt. The witch of Endor raised the ghost of Samuel. Moses and Elias appeared on Mount Tabor. An evil spirit was sent into the army of Sennacherib, and exterminated it in a single night.

MR TOOBAD

Saying, The devil is come among you, having great wrath.

MR FLOSKY

Saint Macarius interrogated a skull, which was found in the desert, and made it relate, in presence of several witnesses, what was going forward in hell. Saint Martin of Tours, being jealous of a pretended martyr, who was the rival saint of his neighbourhood, called up his ghost, and made him confess that he was damned. Saint Germain, being on his travels, turned out of an inn a large party of ghosts, who had every night taken possession of the *table d'hôte*, and consumed a copious supper.

MR HILARY

Jolly ghosts, and no doubt all friars. A similar party took possession of the cellar of M. Swebach, the painter, in Paris, drank his wine, and threw the empty bottles at his head.

THE REVEREND MR LARYNX

An atrocious act.

MR FLOSKY

Pausanias relates, that the neighing of horses and the tumult of combatants were heard every night on the field of Marathon: that those who went purposely to hear these sounds suffered severely for their curiosity; but those who heard them by accident passed with impunity.

THE REVEREND MR LARYNX

I once saw a ghost myself, in my study, which is the last place where any one but a ghost would look for me. I had not been into it for three months, and was going to consult Tillotson, when, on opening the door, I saw a venerable figure in a flannel dressing gown, sitting in my armchair, and reading my Jeremy Taylor. It vanished in a moment, and so did I; and what it was or what it wanted I have never been able to ascertain.

MR FLOSKY

It was an idea with the force of a sensation. It is seldom that ghosts appeal to two senses at once; but, when I was in Devonshire, the following story was well attested to me. A young woman, whose lover was at sea, returning one evening over some solitary fields, saw her lover sitting on a stile over which she was to pass. Her first emotions were surprise and joy, but there was a paleness and seriousness in his face that made them give place to alarm. She advanced towards him, and he said to her, in a solemn voice, 'The eye that hath seen me shall see me no more. Thine eye is upon me, but I am not.' And with these words he vanished; and on that very day and hour, as it afterwards appeared, he had perished by shipwreck.

The whole party now drew round in a circle, and each related some ghostly anecdote, heedless of the flight of time, till, in a pause of the conversation, they heard the hollow tongue of midnight sounding twelve.

MR HILARY

All these anecdotes admit of solution on psychological principles. It is more easy for a soldier, a philosopher, or even a saint, to be frightened at his own shadow, than for a dead man to come out of his grave. Medical writers cite a thousand singular examples of the force of imagination. Persons of feeble, nervous, melancholy temperament, exhausted by fever, by labour, or by spare diet, will readily conjure up, in the magic ring of their own phantasy, spectres, gorgons, chimaeras, and all the objects of their hatred and their love. We are most of us like Don Quixote, to whom a windmill was a giant, and Dulcinea a magnificent princess: all more or less the dupes of our own imagination, though we do not all go so far as to see ghosts, or to fancy ourselves pipkins and teapots.

MR FLOSKY

I can safely say I have seen too many ghosts myself to believe in their external existence. I have seen all kinds of ghosts: black spirits and white, red spirits and grey. Some in the shapes of venerable old men, who have met me in my rambles at noon; some of beautiful young women, who have peeped through my curtains at midnight.

THE HONOURABLE MR LISTLESS

And have proved, I doubt not, 'palpable to feeling as to sight.'

MR FLOSKY

By no means, sir. You reflect upon my purity. Myself and my friends, particularly my friend Mr Sackbut, are famous for our purity. No, sir, genuine untangible ghosts. I live in a world of ghosts. I see a ghost at this moment.

Mr Flosky fixed his eyes on a door at the farther end of the library. The company looked in the same direction. The door silently opened, and a ghastly figure, shrouded in white drapery, with the semblance of a bloody turban on its head, entered and stalked slowly up the apartment. Mr Flosky, familiar as he was with ghosts, was not prepared for this apparition, and made the best of his way out at the opposite door. Mrs Hilary and Marionetta followed, screaming. The Honourable Mr Listless, by two turns of his body, rolled first off the sofa and then under it. The Reverend Mr Larynx leaped up and fled with so much precipitation, that he overturned the table on the foot of Mr Glowry. Mr Glowry roared with pain hi the ear of Mr Toobad. Mr Toobad's alarm so bewildered his senses, that, missing the door, he threw up one of the windows, jumped out in his panic, and plunged over head and ears in the moat. Mr Asterias and his son, who were on the watch for their mermaid, were attracted by the splashing, threw a net over him, and dragged him to land.

Scythrop and Mr Hilary meanwhile had hastened to his assistance, and, on arriving at the edge of the moat, followed by several servants with ropes and torches, found Mr Asterias and Aquarius busy in endeavouring to extricate Mr Toobad from the net, who was entangled in the meshes, and floundering with rage. Scythrop was lost in amazement; but Mr Hilary saw, at one view, all the circumstances of the adventure, and burst into an immoderate fit of laughter; on recovering from which, he said to Mr Asterias, 'You have caught an odd fish, indeed.' Mr Toobad was highly exasperated at this unseasonable pleasantry; but Mr Hilary softened his anger, by producing a knife, and cutting the Gordian knot of his reticular envelopment. 'You see,' said Mr Toobad, 'you see, gentlemen, in my unfortunate person proof upon proof of the present dominion of the devil in the affairs of this world; and I have no doubt but that the apparition of this night was Apollyon himself in disguise, sent for the express purpose of terrifying me into this complication of misadventures. The devil is come among you, having great wrath, because he knoweth that he hath but a short time.'

* * * * *

CHAPTER XIII

Mr Glowry was much surprised, on occasionally visiting Scythrop's tower, to find the door always locked, and to be kept sometimes waiting many minutes for admission: during which he invariably heard a heavy rolling sound like that of a ponderous mangle, or of a waggon on a weighing-bridge, or of theatrical thunder.

He took little notice of this for some time; at length his curiosity was excited, and, one day, instead of knocking at the door, as usual, the instant he reached it, he applied his ear to the key-hole, and like Bottom, in the Midsummer Night's Dream, 'spied a voice,' which he guessed to be of the feminine gender, and knew to be not Scythrop's, whose deeper tones he distinguished at intervals. Having attempted in vain to catch a syllable of the discourse, he knocked violently at the door, and roared for immediate admission. The voices ceased, the accustomed rolling sound was heard, the door opened, and Scythrop was discovered alone. Mr Glowry looked round to every corner of the apartment, and then said, 'Where is the lady?'

'The lady, sir?' said Scythrop.

'Yes, sir, the lady.'

'Sir, I do not understand you.'

'You don't, sir?'

'No, indeed, sir. There is no lady here.'

'But, sir, this is not the only apartment in the tower, and I make no doubt there is a lady up stairs.'

'You are welcome to search, sir.'

'Yes, and while I am searching, she will slip out from some lurking place, and make her escape.'

'You may lock this door, sir, and take the key with you.'

'But there is the terrace door: she has escaped by the terrace.'

'The terrace, sir, has no other outlet, and the walls are too high for a lady to jump down.'

'Well, sir, give me the key.'

Mr Glowry took the key, searched every nook of the tower, and returned.

'You are a fox, Scythrop; you are an exceedingly cunning fox, with that demure visage of yours. What was that lumbering sound I heard before you opened the door?'

'Sound, sir?'

'Yes, sir, sound.'

'My dear sir, I am not aware of any sound, except my great table, which I moved on rising to let you in.'

'The table!—let me see that. No, sir; not a tenth part heavy enough, not a tenth part.'

'But, sir, you do not consider the laws of acoustics: a whisper becomes a peal of thunder in the focus of reverberation. Allow me to explain this: sounds striking on concave surfaces are reflected from them, and, after reflection, converge to points which are the foci of these surfaces. It follows, therefore, that the ear may be so placed in one, as that it shall hear a sound better than when situated nearer to the point of the first impulse: again, in the case of two concave surfaces placed opposite to each other—'

'Nonsense, sir. Don't tell me of foci. Pray, sir, will concave surfaces produce two voices when nobody speaks? I heard two voices, and one was feminine; feminine, sir: what say you to that?'

'Oh, sir, I perceive your mistake: I am writing a tragedy, and was acting over a scene to myself. To convince you, I will give you a specimen; but you must first understand the plot. It is a tragedy on the German model.

The Great Mogul is in exile, and has taken lodgings at Kensington, with his only daughter, the Princess Rantrorina, who takes in needlework, and keeps a day school. *The princess is discovered hemming a set of shirts for the parson of the parish: they are to be marked with a large R. Enter to her the Great Mogul. A pause, during which they look at each other expressively. The princess changes colour several times. The Mogul takes snuff in great agitation. Several grains are heard to fall on the stage. His heart is seen to beat through his upper benjamin.*—THE MOGUL *(with a mournful look at his left shoe).* 'My shoe-string is broken.'— THE PRINCESS *(after an interval of melancholy reflection).* 'I know it.' THE MOGUL. 'My second shoe-string! The first broke when I lost my empire: the second has broken to-day. When will my poor heart break?'—THE PRINCESS. 'Shoe-strings, hearts, and empires! Mysterious sympathy!'

'Nonsense, sir,' interrupted Mr Glowry. 'That is not at all like the voice I heard.'

'But, sir,' said Scythrop, 'a key-hole may be so constructed as to act like an acoustic tube, and an acoustic tube, sir, will modify sound in a very remarkable manner. Consider the construction of the ear, and the nature and causes of sound. The external part of the ear is a cartilaginous funnel.'

'It wo'n't do, Scythrop. There is a girl concealed in this tower, and find her I will. There are such things as sliding panels and secret closets.'—He sounded round the room with his cane, but detected no hollowness.—'I have heard, sir,' he continued, 'that during my absence, two years ago, you had a dumb carpenter closeted with you day after day. I did not dream that you were laying contrivances for carrying on secret intrigues. Young men will have their way: I had my way when I was a young man: but, sir, when your cousin Marionetta—'

Scythrop now saw that the affair was growing serious. To have clapped his hand upon his father's mouth, to have entreated him to be silent, would, in the first place, not have made him so; and, in the second, would have shown a dread of being overheard by somebody. His only resource, therefore, was to try to drown Mr Glowry's voice; and, having no other subject, he continued his description of the ear, raising his voice continually as Mr Glowry raised his.

'When your cousin Marionetta,' said Mr Glowry, 'whom you profess to love—whom you profess to love, sir—'

'The internal canal of the ear,' said Scythrop, 'is partly bony and partly cartilaginous. This internal canal is—'

'Is actually in the house, sir; and, when you are so shortly to be—as I expect—'

'Closed at the further end by the *membrana tympani*—'

'Joined together in holy matrimony—'

'Under which is carried a branch of the fifth pair of nerves—'

'I say, sir, when you are so shortly to be married to your cousin Marionetta—'

'The *cavitas tympani*—'

A loud noise was heard behind the book-case, which, to the astonishment of Mr Glowry, opened in the middle, and the massy compartments, with all their weight of books, receding from each other in the manner of a theatrical scene, with a heavy rolling sound (which Mr Glowry immediately recognised to be the same which had excited his curiosity,) disclosed an interior apartment, in the entrance of which stood the beautiful Stella, who, stepping forward, exclaimed, 'Married! Is he going to be married? The profligate!'

'Really, madam,' said Mr Glowry, 'I do not know what he is going to do, or what I am going to do, or what any one is going to do; for all this is incomprehensible.'

'I can explain it all,' said Scythrop, 'in a most satisfactory manner, if you will but have the goodness to leave us alone.'

'Pray, sir, to which act of the tragedy of the Great Mogul does this incident belong?'

'I entreat you, my dear sir, leave us alone.'

Stella threw herself into a chair, and burst into a tempest of tears. Scythrop sat down by her, and took her hand. She snatched her hand away, and turned her back upon him. He rose, sat down on the other side, and took her other hand. She snatched it away, and turned from him again. Scythrop continued entreating Mr Glowry to leave them alone; but the old gentleman was obstinate, and would not go.

'I suppose, after all,' said Mr Glowry maliciously, 'it is only a phænomenon in acoustics, and this young lady is a reflection of sound from concave surfaces.'

Some one tapped at the door: Mr Glowry opened it, and Mr Hilary entered. He had been seeking Mr Glowry, and had traced him to Scythrop's tower. He stood a few moments in silent surprise, and then addressed himself to Mr Glowry for an explanation.

'The explanation,' said Mr Glowry, 'is very satisfactory. The Great Mogul has taken lodgings at Kensington, and the external part of the ear is a cartilaginous funnel.'

'Mr Glowry, that is no explanation.'

'Mr Hilary, it is all I know about the matter.'

'Sir, this pleasantry is very unseasonable. I perceive that my niece is sported with in a most unjustifiable manner, and I shall see if she will be more successful in obtaining an intelligible answer.' And he departed in search of Marionetta.

Scythrop was now in a hopeless predicament. Mr Hilary made a hue and cry in the abbey, and summoned his wife and Marionetta to Scythrop's apartment. The ladies, not knowing what was the matter, hastened in great consternation. Mr Toobad saw them sweeping along the corridor, and judging from their manner that the devil had manifested his wrath in some new shape, followed from pure curiosity.

Scythrop meanwhile vainly endeavoured to get rid of Mr Glowry and to pacify Stella. The latter attempted to escape from the tower, declaring she would leave the abbey immediately, and he should never see her or hear of her more. Scythrop held her hand and detained her by force, till Mr Hilary reappeared with Mrs Hilary and Marionetta. Marionetta, seeing Scythrop grasping the hand of a strange beauty, fainted away in the arms of her aunt. Scythrop flew to her assistance; and Stella with redoubled anger sprang towards the door, but was intercepted in her intended flight by being caught in the arms of Mr Toobad, who exclaimed—'Celinda!'

'Papa!' said the young lady disconsolately.

'The devil is come among you,' said Mr Toobad, 'how came my daughter here?'

'Your daughter!' exclaimed Mr Glowry.

'Your daughter!' exclaimed Scythrop, and Mr and Mrs Hilary.

'Yes,' said Mr Toobad, 'my daughter Celinda.'

Marionetta opened her eyes and fixed them on Celinda; Celinda in return fixed hers on Marionetta. They were at remote points of the apartment. Scythrop was equidistant from both of them, central and motionless, like Mahomet's coffin.

'Mr Glowry,' said Mr Toobad, 'can you tell by what means my daughter came here?'

'I know no more,' said Mr Glowry, 'than the Great Mogul.'

'Mr Scythrop,' said Mr Toobad, 'how came my daughter here?'

'I did not know, sir, that the lady was your daughter.'

'But how came she here?'

'By spontaneous locomotion,' said Scythrop, sullenly.

'Celinda,' said Mr Toobad, 'what does all this mean?'

'I really do not know, sir.'

'This is most unaccountable. When I told you in London that I had chosen a husband for you, you thought proper to run away from him; and now, to all appearance, you have run away to him.'

'How, sir! was that your choice?'

'Precisely; and if he is yours too we shall be both of a mind, for the first time in our lives.'

'He is not my choice, sir. This lady has a prior claim: I renounce him.'

'And I renounce him,' said Marionetta.

Scythrop knew not what to do. He could not attempt to conciliate the one without irreparably offending the other; and he was so fond of both, that the idea of depriving himself for ever of the society of either was intolerable to him: he therefore retreated into his stronghold, mystery; maintained an impenetrable silence; and contented himself with stealing occasionally a deprecating glance at each of the objects of his idolatry. Mr Toobad and Mr Hilary, in the mean time, were each insisting on an explanation from Mr Glowry, who they thought had been playing a double game on this occasion. Mr Glowry was vainly endeavouring to persuade them of his innocence in the whole transaction. Mrs Hilary was endeavouring to mediate between her husband and brother. The Honourable Mr Listless, the Reverend Mr Larynx, Mr Flosky, Mr Asterias, and Aquarius, were attracted by the tumult to the scene of action, and were appealed to severally and conjointly by the respective disputants. Multitudinous questions, and answers *en masse*, composed a *charivari*, to which the genius of Rossini alone could have given a suitable accompaniment, and which was only terminated by Mrs Hilary and Mr Toobad retreating with the captive damsels. The whole party followed, with the exception of Scythrop, who threw himself into his arm-chair, crossed his left foot over his right knee, placed the hollow of his left hand on the interior ancle of his left leg, rested his right elbow on the elbow of the chair, placed the ball of his right thumb against his right temple, curved the forefinger along the upper part of his forehead, rested the point of the middle finger on the bridge of his nose, and the points of the two others on the lower part of the palm, fixed his eyes intently on the veins in the back of his left hand, and sat in this position like the immoveable Theseus, who, as is well known to many who have not been at college, and to some few who have, *sedet, oeternumque sedebit.*[13] We hope the admirers of the *minutiæ* in poetry and romance will appreciate this accurate description of a pensive attitude.

* * * * *

CHAPTER XIV

Scythrop was still in this position when Raven entered to announce that dinner was on table.

'I cannot come,' said Scythrop.

Raven sighed. 'Something is the matter,' said Raven: 'but man is born to trouble.'

'Leave me,' said Scythrop: 'go, and croak elsewhere.'

'Thus it is,' said Raven. 'Five-and-twenty years have I lived in Nightmare Abbey, and now all the reward of my affection is—Go, and croak elsewhere. I have danced you on my knee, and fed you with marrow.'

'Good Raven,' said Scythrop, 'I entreat you to leave me.'

'Shall I bring your dinner here?' said Raven. 'A boiled fowl and a glass of Madeira are prescribed by the faculty in cases of low spirits. But you had better join the party: it is very much reduced already.'

'Reduced! how?'

'The Honourable Mr Listless is gone. He declared that, what with family quarrels in the morning, and ghosts at night, he could get neither sleep nor peace; and that the agitation was too much for his nerves: though Mr Glowry assured him that the ghost was only poor Crow walking in his sleep, and that the shroud and bloody turban were a sheet and a red nightcap.'

'Well, sir?'

'The Reverend Mr Larynx has been called off on duty, to marry or bury (I don't know which) some unfortunate person or persons, at Claydyke: but man is born to trouble!'

'Is that all?'

'No. Mr Toobad is gone too, and a strange lady with him.'

'Gone!'

'Gone. And Mr and Mrs Hilary, and Miss O'Carroll: they are all gone. There is nobody left but Mr Asterias and his son, and they are going to-night.'

'Then I have lost them both.'

'Won't you come to dinner?'

'No.'

'Shall I bring your dinner here?'

'Yes.'

'What will you have?'

'A pint of port and a pistol.'[14]

'A pistol!'

'And a pint of port. I will make my exit like Werter. Go. Stay. Did Miss O'Carroll say any thing?'

'No.'

'Did Miss Toobad say any thing?'

'The strange lady? No.'

'Did either of them cry?'

'No.'

'What did they do?'

'Nothing.'

'What did Mr Toobad say?'

'He said, fifty times over, the devil was come among us.'

'And they are gone?'

'Yes; and the dinner is getting cold. There is a time for every thing under the sun. You may as well dine first, and be miserable afterwards.'

'True, Raven. There is something in that. I will take your advice: therefore, bring me—'

'The port and the pistol?'

'No; the boiled fowl and Madeira.'

Scythrop had dined, and was sipping his Madeira alone, immersed in melancholy musing, when Mr Glowry entered, followed by Raven, who, having placed an additional glass and set a chair for Mr Glowry, withdrew. Mr Glowry sat down opposite Scythrop. After a pause, during which each filled and drank in silence, Mr Glowry said, 'So, sir, you have played your cards well. I proposed Miss Toobad to you: you refused her. Mr Toobad proposed you to her: she refused you. You fell in love with Marionetta, and were going to poison yourself, because, from pure fatherly regard to your temporal interests, I withheld my consent. When, at length, I offered you my consent, you told me I was too precipitate. And, after all, I find you and Miss Toobad living together in the same tower, and behaving in every respect like two plighted lovers. Now, sir, if there be any rational solution of all this absurdity, I shall be very much obliged to you for a small glimmering of information.'

'The solution, sir, is of little moment; but I will leave it in writing for your satisfaction. The crisis of my fate is come: the world is a stage, and my direction is *exit*.'

'Do not talk so, sir;—do not talk so, Scythrop. What would you have?'

'I would have my love.'

'And pray, sir, who is your love?'

'Celinda—Marionetta—either—both.'

'Both! That may do very well in a German tragedy; and the Great Mogul might have found it very feasible in his lodgings at Kensington; but it will not do in Lincolnshire. Will you have Miss Toobad?'

'Yes.'

'And renounce Marionetta?'

'No.'

'But you must renounce one.'

'I cannot.'

'And you cannot have both. What is to be done?'

'I must shoot myself.'

'Don't talk so, Scythrop. Be rational, my dear Scythrop. Consider, and make a cool, calm choice, and I will exert myself in your behalf.'

'Why should I choose, sir? Both have renounced *me*: I have no hope of either.'

'Tell me which you will have, and I will plead your cause irresistibly.'

'Well, sir,—I will have—no, sir, I cannot renounce either. I cannot choose either. I am doomed to be the victim of eternal disappointments; and I have no resource but a pistol.'

'Scythrop—Scythrop;—if one of them should come to you—what then?'

'That, sir, might alter the case: but that cannot be.'

'It can be, Scythrop; it will be: I promise you it will be. Have but a little patience—but a week's patience; and it shall be.'

'A week, sir, is an age: but, to oblige you, as a last act of filial duty, I will live another week. It is now Thursday evening, twenty-five minutes past seven. At this hour and minute, on Thursday next, love and fate shall smile on me, or I will drink my last pint of port in this world.'

Mr Glowry ordered his travelling chariot, and departed from the abbey.

* * * * *

CHAPTER XV

The day after Mr Glowry's departure was one of incessant rain, and Scythrop repented of the promise he had given. The next day was one of bright sunshine: he sat on the terrace, read a tragedy of Sophocles, and was not sorry, when Raven announced dinner, to find himself alive. On the third evening, the wind blew, and the rain beat, and the owl flapped against his windows; and he put a new flint in his pistol. On the fourth day, the sun shone again; and he locked the pistol up in a drawer, where he left it undisturbed, till the morning of the eventful Thursday, when he ascended the turret with a telescope, and spied anxiously along the road that crossed the fens from Claydyke: but nothing appeared on it. He watched in this manner from ten A.M. till Raven summoned him to dinner at five; when he stationed Crow at the telescope, and descended to his own funeral-feast. He left open the communications between the tower and turret, and called aloud at intervals to Crow,—'Crow, Crow, is any thing coming?' Crow answered, 'The wind blows, and the windmills turn, but I see nothing coming;' and, at every answer, Scythrop found the necessity of raising his spirits with a bumper. After dinner, he gave Raven his watch to set by the abbey clock. Raven brought it, Scythrop placed it on the table, and Raven departed. Scythrop called again to Crow; and Crow, who had fallen asleep, answered mechanically, 'I see nothing coming.' Scythrop laid his pistol between his watch and his bottle. The hour-hand passed the VII.—the minute-hand moved on;—it was within three minutes of the appointed time. Scythrop called again to Crow: Crow answered as before. Scythrop rang the bell: Raven appeared.

'Raven,' said Scythrop, 'the clock is too fast.'

'No, indeed,' said Raven, who knew nothing of Scythrop's intentions; 'if any thing, it is too slow.'

'Villain!' said Scythrop, pointing the pistol at him; 'it is too fast.'

'Yes—yes—too fast, I meant,' said Raven, in manifest fear.

'How much too fast?' said Scythrop.

'As much as you please,' said Raven.

'How much, I say?' said Scythrop, pointing the pistol again.

'An hour, a full hour, sir,' said the terrified butler.

'Put back my watch,' said Scythrop.

Raven, with trembling hand, was putting back the watch, when the rattle of wheels was heard in the court; and Scythrop, springing down the stairs by three steps together, was at the door in sufficient time to have handed either of the young ladies from the carriage, if she had happened to be in it; but Mr Glowry was alone.

'I rejoice to see you,' said Mr Glowry; 'I was fearful of being too late, for I waited till the last moment in the hope of accomplishing my promise; but all my endeavours have been vain, as these letters will show.'

Scythrop impatiently broke the seals. The contents were these:

Almost a stranger in England, I fled from parental tyranny, and the dread of an arbitrary marriage, to the protection of a stranger and a philosopher, whom I expected to find something better than, or at least something different from, the rest of his worthless species. Could I, after what has occurred, have expected nothing more from you than the common-place impertinence of sending your father to treat with me, and with mine, for me? I should be a little moved in your favour, if I could believe you capable of carrying into effect the resolutions which your father says you have taken, in the event of my proving inflexible; though I doubt not you will execute them, as far as relates to the pint of wine, twice over, at least. I wish you much happiness with Miss O'Carroll. I shall always cherish a grateful recollection of

108

Nightmare Abbey, for having been the means of introducing me to a true transcendentalist; and, though he is a little older than myself, which is all one in Germany, I shall very soon have the pleasure of subscribing myself

CELINDA FLOSKY

I hope, my dear cousin, that you will not be angry with me, but that you will always think of me as a sincere friend, who will always feel interested in your welfare; I am sure you love Miss Toobad much better than me, and I wish you much happiness with her. Mr Listless assures me that people do not kill themselves for love now-a-days, though it is still the fashion to talk about it. I shall, in a very short time, change my name and situation, and shall always be happy to see you in Berkeley Square, when, to the unalterable designation of your affectionate cousin, I shall subjoin the signature of

MARIONETTA LISTLESS

Scythrop tore both the letters to atoms, and railed in good set terms against the fickleness of women.

'Calm yourself, my dear Scythrop,' said Mr Glowry; 'there are yet maidens in England.'

'Very true, sir,' said Scythrop.

'And the next time,' said Mr Glowry, 'have but one string to your bow.'

'Very good advice, sir,' said Scythrop.

'And, besides,' said Mr Glowry, 'the fatal time is past, for it is now almost eight.'

'Then that villain, Raven,' said Scythrop, 'deceived me when he said that the clock was too fast; but, as you observe very justly, the time has gone by, and I have just reflected that these repeated crosses in love qualify me to take a very advanced degree in misanthropy; and there is, therefore, good hope that I may make a figure in the world. But I shall ring for the rascal Raven, and admonish him.'

Raven appeared. Scythrop looked at him very fiercely two or three minutes; and Raven, still remembering the pistol, stood quaking in mute apprehension, till Scythrop, pointing significantly towards the dining-room, said, 'Bring some Madeira.'

THE END

NOTES

NIGHTMARE ABBEY
CHAPTER I

1   *Mr Flosky*: A corruption of Filosky, quasi Greek: philoschios], a lover, or sectator, of shadows.

CHAPTER II

2   *the passion for reforming the world*: See Forsyth's *Principles of Moral Science.*

CHAPTER IV

3   *decorum, and dignity, &c. &c. &c.*: We are not masters of the whole vocabulary. See any novel by any literary lady.

4   *his Ahrimanic philosophy*: Ahrimanes, in the Persian mythology, is the evil power, the prince of the kingdom of darkness. He is the rival of Oromazes, the prince of the kingdom of light. These two powers have divided and equal dominion. Sometimes one of the two has a temporary supremacy.—According to Mr Toobad, the present period would be the reign of Ahrimanes. Lord Byron seems to be of the same opinion, by the use he has made of Ahrimanes in 'Manfred'; where the great Alastor, or Greek: Kachos Daimôn], of Persia, is hailed king of the world by the Nemesis of Greece, in concert with three of the Scandinavian Valkyrae, under the name

of the Destinies; the astrological spirits of the alchemists of the middle ages; an elemental witch, transplanted from Denmark to the Alps; and a chorus of Dr Faustus's devils, who come in the last act for a soul. It is difficult to conceive where this heterogeneous mythological company could have originally met, except at a *table d'hôte*, like the six kings in 'Candide'.

CHAPTER V

5   *pensions*: 'PENSION. Pay given to a slave of state for treason to his country.'—JOHNSON'S *Dictionary*.

CHAPTER VII

6   *. . . of a beautiful day*: See Denys Montfort: *Histoire Naturelle des Mollusques; Vues Générales*, pp. 37, 38. (P.) The second half of this speech by Mr Asterias and the opening sentence of his previous speech are a paraphrase from Montfort, pp. 37-9.

CHAPTER X

7   *Mr Burke's graduated scale of the sublime*: There must be some mistake in this, for the whole honourable band of gentlemen-pensioners has resolved unanimously, that Mr Burke was a very sublime person, particularly after he had prostituted his own soul, and betrayed his country and mankind, for 1200*l.* a year: yet he does not appear to have been a very terrible personage, and certainly went off with a very small portion of human respect, though he contrived to excite, in a great degree, the astonishment of all honest men. Our immaculate laureate (who gives us to understand that, if he had not been purified by holy matrimony into a mystical type, he would have died a virgin,) is another sublime gentleman of the same genus: he

very much astonished some persons when he sold his birthright for a pot of sack; but not even his *Sosia* has a grain of respect for him, though, doubtless, he thinks his name very terrible to the enemy, when he flourishes his criticopoeticopolitical tomahawk, and sets up his Indian yell for the blood of his old friends: but, at best, he is a mere political scarecrow, a man of straw, ridiculous to all who know of what materials he is made; and to none more so, than to those who have stuffed him, and set him up, as the Priapus of the garden of the golden apples of corruption.

CHAPTER XI

8   . . . *vanishes in the smoke of death*: *Childe Harold*, canto 4. cxxiv. cxxvi.

9   . . . *and reaps the whirlwind*: *Childe Harold*, canto 4. cxxiii.

10   . . . *or to endure*: *Ibid.* canto 3. lxxi.

11   . . . *whose gums are poison*: *Ibid.* canto 4. cxxi. cxxxvi.

12   . . . *exist only in himself*: *Childe Harold*, canto 4. cxxii.

CHAPTER XIII

13   *sedet, oeternumque sedebit*: Sits, and will sit for ever.

CHAPTER XIV

14   *a pint of port and a pistol*: See *The Sorrows of Werter*, Letter 93.

HEADLONG HALL

All philosophers, who find
Some favourite system to their mind,
In every point to make it fit,
Will force all nature to submit.

PREFACE

To

"Headlong Hall" and the three novels published along with it in 1837.

* * * * *

ALL these little publications appeared originally without prefaces. I left them to speak for themselves; and I thought I might very fitly preserve my own impersonality, having never intruded on the personality of others, nor taken any liberties but with public conduct and public opinions. But an old friend assures me, that to publish a book without a preface is like entering a drawing-room without making a bow. In deference to this opinion, though I am not quite clear of its soundness, I make my prefatory bow at this eleventh hour.

"Headlong Hall" was written in 1815; "Nightmare Abbey" in 1817; "Maid Marian", with the exception of the last three chapters, in 1818; "Crotchet Castle" in 1830. I am desirous to note the intervals, because, at each of those periods, things were true, in great matters and in small, which are true no longer. "Headlong Hall" begins with the Holyhead Mail, and "Crotchet Castle" ends with a rotten borough. The Holyhead mail no longer keeps the same hours, nor stops at the Capel Cerig Inn, which the progress of improvement has thrown out of the road; and the rotten boroughs of 1830 have ceased to exist, though there are some very pretty pocket properties, which are their worthy successors. But the classes of tastes, feelings, and opinions, which were successively brought into play in these little tales, remain substantially the same. Perfectibilians, deteriorationists, statu-quo-ites, phrenologists, transcendentalists, political economists, theorists in all sciences, projectors in all arts, morbid visionaries, romantic enthusiasts, lovers of music, lovers of the picturesque, and lovers of good dinners, march, and will march for ever, *pari passu* with the march of mechanics, which some facetiously call the march of the intellect. The fastidious in old wine are a race that does not decay. Literary violators of the confidences of private life still gain a disreputable livelihood and an unenviable notoriety. Match-makers from interest, and the disappointed in love and in friendship, are varieties of which specimens are extant. The great principle of the Right of Might is as flourishing now as in the days of Maid Marian: the array of false pretensions, moral, political, and literary, is as imposing as ever: the rulers of the world still feel things in their effects, and never foresee them in their causes: and political mountebanks continue, and will continue, to puff nostrums and practise legerdemain under the eyes of the multitude: following, like the "learned friend" of Crotchet Castle, a course as tortuous as that of a river, but in a reverse process; beginning by being dark and deep, and ending by being transparent.

THE AUTHOR OF "HEADLONG HALL".
March 4, 1837.

CHAPTER I

THE MAIL

THE ambiguous light of a December morning, peeping through the windows of the Holyhead mail, dispelled the soft visions of the four insides, who had slept, or seemed to sleep, through the first seventy miles of the road, with as much comfort as may be supposed consistent with the jolting of the vehicle, and an occasional admonition to *remember the coachman*, thundered through the open door, accompanied by the gentle breath of Boreas, into the ears of the drowsy traveller.

A lively remark, that *the day was none of the finest*, having elicited a repartee of *quite the contrary*, the various knotty points of meteorology, which usually form the exordium of an English conversation, were successively discussed and exhausted; and, the ice being thus broken, the colloquy rambled to other topics, in the course of which it appeared, to the surprise of every one, that all four, though perfect strangers to each other, were actually bound to the same point, namely, Headlong Hall, the seat of the ancient and honourable family of the Headlongs, of the vale of Llanberris, in Caernarvonshire. This name may appear at first sight not to be truly Cambrian, like those of the Rices, and Prices, and Morgans, and Owens, and Williamses, and Evanses, and Parrys, and Joneses; but, nevertheless, the Headlongs claim to be not less genuine derivatives from the antique branch of Cadwallader than any of the last named multiramified families. They claim, indeed, by one account, superior antiquity to all of them, and even to Cadwallader himself, a tradition having been handed down in Headlong Hall for some few thousand years, that the founder of the family was preserved in the deluge on the summit of Snowdon, and took the name of Rhaiader, which signifies a *waterfall*, in consequence of his having accompanied the water in its descent or diminution, till he found himself comfortably seated on the rocks of Llanberris. But, in later days, when commercial bagmen began to scour the country, the ambiguity of the sound induced his descendants to drop the suspicious denomination of *Riders*, and translate the word into English; when, not being well pleased with the sound of the *thing*, they substituted that of the *quality*, and accordingly adopted the name *Headlong*, the appropriate epithet of waterfall.

I cannot tell how the truth may be:
I say the tale as 'twas said to me.

The present representative of this ancient and dignified house, Harry Headlong, Esquire, was, like all other Welsh squires, fond of shooting, hunting, racing, drinking, and other such innocent amusements, μειζονος δ' αλλου τινος, as Menander expresses it. But, unlike other Welsh squires, he had actually suffered certain phenomena, called books, to find their way into his house; and, by dint of lounging over them after dinner, on those occasions when he was compelled to take his bottle alone, he became seized with a violent passion to be thought a philosopher and a man of taste; and accordingly set off on an expedition to Oxford, to inquire for other varieties of the same genera, namely, men of taste and philosophers; but, being assured by a learned professor that there were no such things in the University, he proceeded to London, where, after beating up in several booksellers' shops, theatres, exhibition-rooms, and other resorts of literature and taste, he formed as extensive an acquaintance with philosophers and dilettanti as his utmost ambition could desire: and it now became his chief wish to have them all together in Headlong Hall, arguing, over his old Port and Burgundy, the various knotty points which had puzzled his pericranium. He had, therefore, sent them invitations in due form to pass their Christmas at Headlong Hall; which invitations the extensive fame of his kitchen fire had induced the greater part of them to accept; and four of the chosen guests had, from different parts of the metropolis, ensconced themselves in the four corners of the Holyhead mail.

These four persons were, Mr Foster[1], the perfectibilian; Mr Escot[2], the deteriorationist; Mr Jenkison[3], the statu-quo-ite; and the Reverend Doctor Gaster[4], who, though of course neither a philosopher nor a man of taste, had so won on the Squire's fancy, by a learned dissertation on the art of stuffing a turkey, that he concluded no Christmas party would be complete without him.

The conversation among these illuminati soon became animated; and Mr Foster, who, we must observe, was a thin gentleman, about thirty years of age, with an aquiline nose, black eyes, white teeth, and black hair—took occasion to panegyrize the vehicle in which they were then travelling, and observed what remarkable improvements had been made in the means of facilitating intercourse between distant parts of the kingdom: he held forth with great energy on the subject of roads and railways, canals and tunnels, manufactures and machinery: "In short," said he, "every thing we look on attests the progress of mankind in all the arts of life, and demonstrates their gradual advancement towards a state of unlimited perfection."

Mr Escot, who was somewhat younger than Mr Foster, but rather more pale and saturnine in his aspect, here took up the thread of the discourse, observing, that the proposition just advanced seemed to him perfectly contrary to the true state of the case: "for," said he, "these improvements, as you call them, appear to me only so many links in the great chain of corruption, which will soon fetter the whole human race in irreparable slavery and incurable wretchedness: your improvements proceed in a simple ratio, while the factitious wants and unnatural appetites they engender proceed in a compound one; and thus one generation acquires fifty wants, and fifty means of supplying them are invented, which each in its turn engenders two new ones; so that the next generation has a hundred, the next two hundred, the next four hundred, till every human being becomes such a helpless compound of perverted inclinations, that he is altogether at the mercy of external circumstances, loses all independence and singleness of character, and degenerates so rapidly from the primitive dignity of his sylvan origin, that it is scarcely possible to indulge in any other expectation, than that the whole species must at length be exterminated by its own infinite imbecility and vileness."

"Your opinions," said Mr Jenkison, a round-faced little gentleman of about forty-five, "seem to differ *toto cælo*. I have often debated the matter in my own mind, *pro* and *con*, and have at length arrived at this conclusion,—that there is not in the human race a tendency either to moral perfectibility or deterioration; but that the quantities of each are so exactly balanced by their reciprocal results, that the species, with respect to the sum of good and evil, knowledge and ignorance, happiness and misery, remains exactly and perpetually *in statu quo*."

"Surely," said Mr Foster, "you cannot maintain such a proposition in the face of evidence so luminous. Look at the progress of all the arts and sciences,—see chemistry, botany, astronomy—"

"Surely," said Mr Escot, "experience deposes against you. Look at the rapid growth of corruption, luxury, selfishness—"

"Really, gentlemen," said the Reverend Doctor Gaster, after clearing the husk in his throat with two or three hems, "this is a very sceptical, and, I must say, atheistical conversation, and I should have thought, out of respect to my cloth—"

Here the coach stopped, and the coachman, opening the door, vociferated—"Breakfast, gentlemen;" a sound which so gladdened the ears of the divine, that the alacrity with which he sprang from the vehicle superinduced a distortion of his ankle, and he was obliged to limp into the inn between Mr Escot and Mr Jenkison; the former observing, that he ought to look for nothing but evil, and, therefore, should not be surprised at this little accident; the latter remarking, that the comfort of a good breakfast, and the pain of a sprained ankle, pretty exactly balanced each other.

CHAPTER II

THE SQUIRE—THE BREAKFAST

SQUIRE HEADLONG, in the meanwhile, was quadripartite in his locality; that is to say, he was superintending the operations in four scenes of action—namely, the cellar, the library, the picture-gallery, and the dining-room,—preparing for the reception of his philosophical and dilettanti visitors. His myrmidon on this occasion was a little red-nosed butler, whom nature seemed to have cast in the genuine mould of an antique Silenus, and who waddled about the house after his master, wiping his forehead and panting for breath, while the latter bounced from room to room like a cracker, and was indefatigable in his requisitions for the proximity of his vinous Achates, whose advice and co-operation he deemed no less necessary in the library than in the cellar. Multitudes of packages had arrived, by land and water, from London, and Liverpool, and Chester, and Manchester, and Birmingham, and various parts of the mountains: books, wine, cheese, globes, mathematical instruments, turkeys, telescopes, hams, tongues, microscopes, quadrants, sextants, fiddles, flutes, tea, sugar, electrical machines, figs, spices, air-pumps, soda-water, chemical apparatus, eggs, French-horns, drawing books, palettes, oils and colours, bottled ale and porter, scenery for a private theatre, pickles and fish-sauce, patent lamps and chandeliers, barrels of oysters, sofas, chairs, tables, carpets, beds, looking-glasses, pictures, fruits and confections, nuts, oranges, lemons, packages of salt salmon, and jars of Portugal grapes. These, arriving with infinite rapidity, and in inexhaustible succession, had been deposited at random, as the convenience of the moment dictated,—sofas in the cellar, chandeliers in the kitchen, hampers of ale in the drawing-room, and fiddles and fish-sauce in the library. The servants, unpacking all these in furious haste, and flying with them from place to place, according to the tumultuous directions of Squire Headlong and the little fat butler who fumed at his heels, chafed, and crossed, and clashed, and tumbled over one another up stairs and down. All was bustle, uproar, and confusion; yet nothing seemed to advance: while the rage and impetuosity of the Squire continued fermenting to the highest degree of exasperation, which he signified, from time to time, by converting some newly unpacked article, such as a book, a bottle, a ham, or a fiddle, into a missile against the head of some unfortunate servant who did not seem to move in a ratio of velocity corresponding to the intensity of his master's desires.

In this state of eager preparation we shall leave the happy inhabitants of Headlong Hall, and return to the three philosophers and the unfortunate divine, whom we left limping with a sprained ankle, into the breakfast-room of the inn; where his two supporters deposited him safely in a large arm-chair, with his wounded leg comfortably stretched out on another. The morning being extremely cold, he contrived to be seated as near the fire as was consistent with his other object of having a perfect command of the table and its apparatus; which consisted not only of the ordinary comforts of tea and toast, but of a delicious supply of new-laid eggs, and a magnificent round of beef; against which Mr Escot immediately pointed all the artillery of his eloquence, declaring the use of animal food, conjointly with that of fire, to be one of the principal causes of the present degeneracy of mankind. "The natural and original man," said he, "lived in the woods: the roots and fruits of the earth supplied his simple nutriment: he had few desires, and no diseases. But, when he began to sacrifice victims on the altar of superstition, to pursue the goat and the deer, and, by the pernicious invention of fire, to pervert their flesh into food, luxury, disease, and premature death, were let loose upon the world.

Such is clearly the correct interpretation of the fable of Prometheus, which is the symbolical portraiture of that disastrous epoch, when man first applied fire to culinary purposes, and thereby surrendered his liver to the vulture of disease. From that period the stature of mankind has been in a state of gradual diminution, and I have not the least doubt that it will continue to grow *small by degrees, and lamentably less*, till the whole race will vanish imperceptibly from the face of the earth."

"I cannot agree," said Mr Foster, "in the consequences being so very disastrous. I admit, that in some respects the use of animal food retards, though it cannot materially inhibit, the perfectibility of the species. But the use of fire was indispensably necessary, as Æschylus and Virgil expressly assert, to give being to the various arts of life, which, in their rapid and interminable progress, will finally conduct every individual of the race to the philosophic pinnacle of pure and perfect felicity."

"In the controversy concerning animal and vegetable food," said Mr Jenkison, "there is much to be said on both sides; and, the question being in equipoise, I content myself with a mixed diet, and make a point of eating whatever is placed before me, provided it be good in its kind."

In this opinion his two brother philosophers practically coincided, though they both ran down the theory as highly detrimental to the best interests of man.

"I am really astonished," said the Reverend Doctor Gaster, gracefully picking off the supernal fragments of an egg he had just cracked, and clearing away a space at the top for the reception of a small piece of butter—"I am really astonished, gentlemen, at the very heterodox opinions I have heard you deliver: since nothing can be more obvious than that all animals were created solely and exclusively for the use of man."

"Even the tiger that devours him?" said Mr Escot.

"Certainly," said Doctor Gaster.

"How do you prove it?" said Mr Escot.

"It requires no proof," said Doctor Gaster: "it is a point of doctrine. It is written, therefore it is so."

"Nothing can be more logical," said Mr Jenkison. "It has been said," continued he, "that the ox was expressly made to be eaten by man: it may be said, by a parity of reasoning, that man was expressly made to be eaten by the tiger: but as wild oxen exist where there are no men, and men where there are no tigers, it would seem that in these instances they do not properly answer the ends of their creation."

"It is a mystery," said Doctor Gaster.

"Not to launch into the question of final causes," said Mr Escot, helping himself at the same time to a slice of beef, "concerning which I will candidly acknowledge I am as profoundly ignorant as the most dogmatical theologian possibly can be, I just wish to observe, that the pure and peaceful manners which Homer ascribes to the Lotophagi, and which at this day characterise many nations (the Hindoos, for example, who subsist exclusively on the fruits of the earth), depose very strongly in favour of a vegetable regimen."

"It may be said, on the contrary," said Mr Foster, "that animal food acts on the mind as manure does on flowers, forcing them into a degree of expansion they would not otherwise have attained. If we can imagine a philosophical auricula falling into a train of theoretical meditation on its original and natural nutriment, till it should work itself up into a profound abomination of bullock's blood, sugar-baker's scum, and other *unnatural* ingredients of that rich composition of soil which had brought it to perfection[1], and insist on being planted in common earth, it would have all the advantage of natural theory on its side that the most strenuous advocate of the vegetable system could desire; but it would soon discover the practical error of its retrograde experiment by its lamentable inferiority in strength and beauty to all the auriculas around it. I am afraid, in some instances at least, this analogy holds true with respect to mind. No one will make a comparison, in point of mental power, between the Hindoos and the ancient Greeks."

"The anatomy of the human stomach," said Mr Escot, "and the formation of the teeth, clearly place man in the class of frugivorous animals."

"Many anatomists," said Mr Foster, "are of a different opinion, and agree in discerning the characteristics of the carnivorous classes."

"I am no anatomist," said Mr Jenkison, "and cannot decide where doctors disagree; in the meantime, I conclude that man is omnivorous, and on that conclusion I act."

"Your conclusion is truly orthodox," said the Reverend Doctor Gaster: "indeed, the loaves and fishes are typical of a mixed diet; and the practice of the Church in all ages shows—"

"That it never loses sight of the loaves and fishes," said Mr Escot.

"It never loses sight of any point of sound doctrine," said the reverend doctor.

The coachman now informed them their time was elapsed; nor could all the pathetic remonstrances of the reverend divine, who declared he had not half breakfasted, succeed in gaining one minute from the inexorable Jehu.

"You will allow," said Mr Foster, as soon as they were again in motion, "that the wild man of the woods could not transport himself over two hundred miles of forest, with as much facility as one of these vehicles transports you and me through the heart of this cultivated country."

"I am certain," said Mr Escot, "that a wild man can travel an immense distance without fatigue; but what is the advantage of locomotion? The wild man is happy in one spot, and there he remains: the civilised man is wretched in every place he happens to be in, and then congratulates himself on being accommodated with a machine, that will whirl him to another, where he will be just as miserable as ever."

We shall now leave the mail-coach to find its way to Capel Cerig, the nearest point of the Holyhead road to the dwelling of Squire Headlong.

CHAPTER III

THE ARRIVALS

IN the midst of that scene of confusion thrice confounded, in which we left the inhabitants of Headlong Hall, arrived the lovely Caprioletta Headlong, the Squire's sister (whom he had sent for, from the residence of her maiden aunt at Caernarvon, to do the honours of his house), beaming like light on chaos, to arrange disorder and harmonise discord. The tempestuous spirit of her brother became instantaneously as smooth as the surface of the lake of Llanberris; and the little fat butler "plessed Cot, and St Tafit, and the peautiful tamsel," for being permitted to move about the house in his natural pace. In less than twenty-four hours after her arrival, everything was disposed in its proper station, and the Squire began to be all impatience for the appearance of his promised guests.

The first visitor with whom he had the felicity of shaking hands was Marmaduke Milestone, Esquire, who arrived with a portfolio under his arm. Mr Milestone[1] was a picturesque landscape gardener of the first celebrity, who was not without hopes of persuading Squire Headlong to put his romantic pleasure-grounds under a process of improvement, promising himself a signal triumph for his incomparable art in the difficult and, therefore, glorious achievement of polishing and trimming the rocks of Llanberris.

Next arrived a post-chaise from the inn at Capel Cerig, containing the Reverend Doctor Gaster. It appeared, that, when the mail-coach deposited its valuable cargo, early on the second morning, at the inn at Capel Cerig, there was only one post-chaise to be had; it was therefore determined that the reverend Doctor and the luggage should proceed in the chaise, and that the three philosophers should walk. When the reverend gentleman first seated himself in the chaise, the windows were down all round; but he allowed it to drive off under the idea that he could easily pull them up. This task, however, he had considerable difficulty in accomplishing, and when he had succeeded, it availed him little; for the frames and glasses had long since discontinued their ancient familiarity. He had, however, no alternative but to proceed, and to comfort himself, as he went, with some choice quotations from the book of Job. The road led along the edges of tremendous chasms, with torrents dashing in the bottom; so that, if his teeth had not chattered with cold, they would have done so with fear. The Squire shook him heartily by the hand, and congratulated him on his safe arrival at Headlong Hall. The Doctor returned the squeeze, and assured him that the congratulation was by no means misapplied.

Next came the three philosophers, highly delighted with their walk, and full of rapturous exclamations on the sublime beauties of the scenery.

The Doctor shrugged up his shoulders, and confessed he preferred the scenery of Putney and Kew, where a man could go comfortably to sleep in his chaise, without being in momentary terror of being hurled headlong down a precipice.

Mr Milestone observed, that there were great capabilities in the scenery, but it wanted shaving and polishing. If he could but have it under his care for a single twelvemonth, he assured them no one would be able to know it again.

Mr Jenkison thought the scenery was just what it ought to be, and required no alteration.

Mr Foster thought it could be improved, but doubted if that effect would be produced by the system of Mr Milestone.

Mr Escot did not think that any human being could improve it, but had no doubt of its having changed very considerably for the worse, since the days when the now barren rocks were covered with the immense forest of Snowdon, which must have contained a very fine race of wild men, not less than ten feet high.

The next arrival was that of Mr Cranium, and his lovely daughter Miss Cephalis Cranium, who flew to the arms of her dear friend Caprioletta, with all that warmth of friendship which young ladies usually assume towards each other in the presence of young gentlemen.[2]

Miss Cephalis blushed like a carnation at the sight of Mr Escot, and Mr Escot glowed like a corn-poppy at the sight of Miss Cephalis. It was at least obvious to all observers, that he could imagine the possibility of one change for the better, even in this terrestrial theatre of universal deterioration.

Mr Cranium's eyes wandered from Mr Escot to his daughter, and from his daughter to Mr Escot; and his complexion, in the course of the scrutiny, underwent several variations, from the dark red of the peony to the deep blue of the convolvulus.

Mr Escot had formerly been the received lover of Miss Cephalis, till he incurred the indignation of her father by laughing at a very profound craniological dissertation which the old gentleman delivered; nor had Mr Escot yet discovered the means of mollifying his wrath.

Mr Cranium carried in his own hands a bag, the contents of which were too precious to be intrusted to any one but himself; and earnestly entreated to be shown to the chamber appropriated for his reception, that he might deposit his treasure in safety. The little butler was accordingly summoned to conduct him to his *cubiculum*.

Next arrived a post-chaise, carrying four insides, whose extreme thinness enabled them to travel thus economically without experiencing the slightest inconvenience. These four personages were, two very profound critics, Mr Gall and Mr Treacle, who followed the trade of reviewers, but occasionally indulged themselves in the composition of bad poetry; and two very multitudinous versifiers, Mr Nightshade and Mr Mac Laurel, who followed the trade of poetry, but occasionally indulged themselves in the composition of bad criticism. Mr Nightshade and Mr

Mac Laurel were the two senior lieutenants of a very formidable corps of critics, of whom Timothy Treacle, Esquire, was captain, and Geoffrey Gall, Esquire, generalissimo.

The last arrivals were Mr Cornelius Chromatic, the most profound and scientific of all amateurs of the fiddle, with his two blooming daughters, Miss Tenorina and Miss Graziosa; Sir Patrick O'Prism, a dilettante painter of high renown, and his maiden aunt, Miss Philomela Poppyseed, an indefatigable compounder of novels, written for the express purpose of supporting every species of superstition and prejudice; and Mr Panscope, the chemical, botanical, geological, astronomical, mathematical, metaphysical, meteorological, anatomical, physiological, galvanistical, musical, pictorial, bibliographical, critical philosopher, who had run through the whole circle of the sciences, and understood them all equally well.

Mr Milestone was impatient to take a walk round the grounds, that he might examine how far the system of clumping and levelling could be carried advantageously into effect. The ladies retired to enjoy each other's society in the first happy moments of meeting: the Reverend Doctor Gaster sat by the library fire, in profound meditation over a volume of the "*Almanach des Gourmands*:" Mr Panscope sat in the opposite corner with a volume of Rees' Cyclopædia: Mr Cranium was busy upstairs: Mr Chromatic retreated to the music-room, where he fiddled through a book of solos before the ringing of the first dinner bell. The remainder of the party supported Mr Milestone's proposition; and, accordingly, Squire Headlong and Mr Milestone leading the van, they commenced their perambulation.

CHAPTER IV

THE GROUNDS

"I PERCEIVE," said Mr Milestone, after they had walked a few paces, "these grounds have never been touched by the finger of taste."

"The place is quite a wilderness," said Squire Headlong: "for, during the latter part of my father's life, while I was *finishing* my *education*, he troubled himself about nothing but the cellar, and suffered everything else to go to rack and ruin. A mere wilderness, as you see, even now in December; but in summer a complete nursery of briers, a forest of thistles, a plantation of nettles, without any live stock but goats, that have eaten up all the bark of the trees. Here you see is the pedestal of a statue, with only half a leg and four toes remaining: there were many here once. When I was a boy, I used to sit every day on the shoulders of Hercules: what became of *him* I have never been able to ascertain. Neptune has been lying these seven years in the dust-hole; Atlas had his head knocked off to fit him for propping a shed; and only the day before yesterday we fished Bacchus out of the horse-pond."

"My dear sir," said Mr Milestone, "accord me your permission to wave the wand of enchantment over your grounds. The rocks shall be blown up, the trees shall be cut down, the wilderness and all its goats shall vanish like mist. Pagodas and Chinese bridges, gravel walks and shrubberies, bowling-greens, canals, and clumps of larch, shall rise upon its ruins. One age, sir, has brought to light the treasures of ancient learning; a second has penetrated into the depths of metaphysics; a third has brought to perfection the science of astronomy; but it was reserved for the exclusive genius of the present times, to invent the noble art of picturesque gardening, which has given, as it were, a new tint to the complexion of nature, and a new outline to the physiognomy of the universe!"

"Give me leave," said Sir Patrick O'Prism, "to take an exception to that same. Your system of levelling, and trimming, and clipping, and docking, and clumping, and polishing, and cropping, and shaving, destroys all the beautiful intricacies of natural luxuriance, and all the graduated harmonies of light and shade, melting into one another, as you see them on that rock over yonder. I never saw one of your improved places, as you call them, and which are nothing but big bowling-greens, like sheets of green paper, with a parcel of round clumps scattered over them, like so many spots of ink, flicked at random out of a pen,[1] and a solitary animal here and there looking as if it were lost, that I did not think it was for all the world like Hounslow Heath, thinly sprinkled over with bushes and highwaymen."

"Sir," said Mr Milestone, "you will have the goodness to make a distinction between the picturesque and the beautiful."

"Will I?" said Sir Patrick, "och! but I won't. For what is beautiful? That what pleases the eye. And what pleases the eye? Tints variously broken and blended. Now, tints variously broken and blended constitute the picturesque."

"Allow me," said Mr Gall. "I distinguish the picturesque and the beautiful, and I add to them, in the laying out of grounds, a third and distinct character, which I call *unexpectedness*."

"Pray, sir," said Mr Milestone, "by what name do you distinguish this character, when a person walks round the grounds for the second time?"[2]

Mr Gall bit his lips, and inwardly vowed to revenge himself on Milestone, by cutting up his next publication.

A long controversy now ensued concerning the picturesque and the beautiful, highly edifying to Squire Headlong.

The three philosophers stopped, as they wound round a projecting point of rock, to contemplate a little boat which was gliding over the tranquil surface of the lake below.

"The blessings of civilisation," said Mr Foster, "extend themselves to the meanest individuals of the community. That boatman, singing as he sails along, is, I have no doubt, a very happy, and, comparatively to the men of his class some centuries back, a very enlightened and intelligent man."

"As a partisan of the system of the moral perfectibility of the human race," said Mr Escot,—who was always for considering things on a large scale, and whose thoughts immediately wandered from the lake to the ocean, from the little boat to a ship of the line,—"you will probably be able to point out to me the degree of improvement that you suppose to have taken place in the character of a sailor, from the days when Jason sailed through the Cyanean Symplegades, or Noah moored his ark on the summit of Ararat."

"If you talk to me," said Mr Foster, "of mythological personages, of course I cannot meet you on fair grounds."

"We will begin, if you please, then," said Mr Escot, "no further back than the battle of Salamis; and I will ask you if you think the mariners of England are, in any one respect, morally or intellectually, superior to those who then preserved the liberties of Greece, under the direction of Themistocles?"

"I will venture to assert," said Mr Foster, "that considered merely as sailors, which is the only fair mode of judging them, they are as far superior to the Athenians, as the structure of our ships is superior to that of theirs. Would not one English seventy-four, think you, have been sufficient to have sunk, burned, and put to flight, all the Persian and Grecian vessels in that memorable bay? Contemplate the progress of naval architecture, and the slow, but immense succession of concatenated intelligence, by which it has gradually attained its present stage of perfectibility. In this, as in all other branches of art and science, every generation possesses all the knowledge of the preceding, and adds to it its own discoveries in a progression to which there seems no limit. The skill requisite to direct these immense machines is proportionate to their magnitude and complicated mechanism; and, therefore, the English sailor, considered merely as a sailor, is vastly superior to the ancient Greek."

"You make a distinction, of course," said Mr Escot, "between scientific and moral perfectibility?"

"I conceive," said Mr Foster, "that men are virtuous in proportion as they are enlightened; and that, as every generation increases in knowledge, it also increases in virtue."

"I wish it were so," said Mr Escot; "but to me the very reverse appears to be the fact. The progress of knowledge is not general: it is confined to a chosen few of every age. How far these are better than their neighbours, we may examine by and bye. The mass of mankind is composed of beasts of burden, mere clods, and tools of their superiors. By enlarging and complicating your machines, you degrade, not exalt, the human animals you employ to direct them. When the boatswain of a seventy-four pipes all hands to the main tack, and flourishes his rope's end over the shoulders of the poor fellows who are tugging at the ropes, do you perceive so dignified, so gratifying a picture, as Ulysses exhorting his dear friends, his ΕΡΙΗΡΕΣ ῾ΕΤΑΙΡΟΙ, to ply their oars with energy? You will say, Ulysses was a fabulous character. But the economy of his vessel is drawn from nature. Every man on board has a character and a will of his own. He talks to them, argues with them, convinces them; and they obey him, because they love him, and know the reason of his orders. Now, as I have said before, all singleness of character is lost. We divide men into herds like cattle: an individual man, if you strip him of all that is extraneous to himself, is the most wretched and contemptible creature on the face of the earth. The sciences advance. True. A few years of study puts a modern mathematician in possession of more than

Newton knew, and leaves him at leisure to add new discoveries of his own. Agreed. But does this make him a Newton? Does it put him in possession of that range of intellect, that grasp of mind, from which the discoveries of Newton sprang? It is mental power that I look for: if you can demonstrate the increase of that, I will give up the field. Energy—independence—individuality—disinterested virtue—active benevolence—self-oblivion—universal philanthropy—these are the qualities I desire to find, and of which I contend that every succeeding age produces fewer examples. I repeat it; there is scarcely such a thing to be found as a single individual man; a few classes compose the whole frame of society, and when you know one of a class you know the whole of it. Give me the wild man of the woods; the original, unthinking, unscientific, unlogical savage: in him there is at least some good; but, in a civilised, sophisticated, cold-blooded, mechanical, calculating slave of Mammon and the world, there is none—absolutely none. Sir, if I fall into a river, an unsophisticated man will jump in and bring me out; but a philosopher will look on with the utmost calmness, and consider me in the light of a projectile, and, making a calculation of the degree of force with which I have impinged the surface, the resistance of the fluid, the velocity of the current, and the depth of the water in that particular place, he will ascertain with the greatest nicety in what part of the mud at the bottom I may probably be found, at any given distance of time from the moment of my first immersion."

Mr Foster was preparing to reply, when the first dinner-bell rang, and he immediately commenced a precipitate return towards the house; followed by his two companions, who both admitted that he was now leading the way to at least a temporary period of physical amelioration: "but, alas!" added Mr Escot, after a moment's reflection, "Epulæ NOCUERE repostæ!³"

138

CHAPTER V

THE DINNER

THE sun was now terminating his diurnal course, and the lights were glittering on the festal board. When the ladies had retired, and the Burgundy had taken two or three tours of the table, the following conversation took place:—

Squire Headlong. Push about the bottle: Mr Escot, it stands with you. No heeltaps. As to skylight, liberty-hall.

Mr Mac Laurel. Really, Squire Headlong, this is the vara nectar itsel. Ye hae saretainly discovered the tarrestrial paradise, but it flows wi' a better leecor than milk an' honey.

The Reverend Doctor Gaster. Hem! Mr Mac Laurel! there is a degree of profaneness in that observation, which I should not have looked for in so staunch a supporter of church and state. Milk and honey was the pure food of the antediluvian patriarchs, who knew not the use of the grape, happily for them.—(*Tossing off a bumper of Burgundy.*)

Mr Escot. Happy, indeed! The first inhabitants of the world knew not the use either of wine or animal food; it is, therefore, by no means incredible that they lived to the age of several centuries, free from war, and commerce, and arbitrary government, and every other species of desolating wickedness. But man was then a very different animal to what he now is: he had not the faculty of speech; he was not encumbered with clothes; he lived in the open air; his first step out of which, as Hamlet truly observes, is *into his grave*[1]. His first dwellings, of course, were the hollows of trees and rocks. In process of time he began to build: thence grew villages; thence grew cities. Luxury, oppression, poverty, misery, and disease kept pace with the progress of his pretended improvements, till, from a free, strong, healthy, peaceful animal, he has become a weak, distempered, cruel, carnivorous slave.

The Reverend Doctor Gaster. Your doctrine is orthodox, in so far as you assert that the original man was not encumbered with clothes, and that he lived in the open air; but, as to the faculty of speech, that, it is certain, he had, for the authority of Moses—

Mr Escot. Of course, sir, I do not presume to dissent from the very exalted authority of that most enlightened astronomer and profound cosmogonist, who had, moreover, the advantage of being inspired; but when I indulge myself with a ramble in the fields of speculation, and attempt to deduce what is probable and rational from the sources of analysis, experience, and comparison, I confess I am too often apt to lose sight of the doctrines of that great fountain of theological and geological philosophy.

Squire Headlong. Push about the bottle.

Mr Foster. Do you suppose the mere animal life of a wild man, living on acorns, and sleeping on the ground, comparable in felicity to that of a Newton, ranging through unlimited space, and penetrating into the arcana of universal motion—to that of a Locke, unravelling the labyrinth of mind—to that of a Lavoisier, detecting the minutest combinations of matter, and reducing all nature to its elements—to that of a Shakespeare, piercing and developing the springs of passion—or of a Milton, identifying himself, as it were, with the beings of an invisible world?

Mr Escot. You suppose extreme cases: but, on the score of happiness, what comparison can you make between the tranquil being of the wild man of the woods and the wretched and turbulent existence of Milton, the victim of persecution, poverty, blindness, and neglect? The records of literature demonstrate that Happiness and Intelligence are seldom sisters. Even if it were otherwise, it would prove nothing. The many are always sacrificed to the few. Where one man advances, hundreds retrograde; and the balance is always in favour of universal deterioration.

Mr Foster. Virtue is independent of external circumstances. The exalted understanding looks into the truth of things, and, in its own peaceful contemplations, rises superior to the world. No philosopher would resign his mental acquisitions for the purchase of any terrestrial good.

Mr Escot. In other words, no man whatever would resign his identity, which is nothing more than the consciousness of his perceptions, as the price of any acquisition. But every man, without exception, would willingly effect a very material change in his relative situation to other individuals. Unluckily for the rest of your argument, the understanding of literary people is for the most part *exalted*, as you express it, not so much by the love of truth and virtue, as by arrogance and self-sufficiency; and there is, perhaps, less disinterestedness, less liberality, less general benevolence, and more envy, hatred, and uncharitableness among them, than among any other description of men.

(The eye of Mr Escot, as he pronounced these words, rested very innocently and unintentionally on Mr Gall.)

Mr Gall. You allude, sir, I presume, to my review.

Mr Escot. Pardon me, sir. You will be convinced it is impossible I can allude to your review, when I assure you that I have never read a single page of it.

Mr Gall, Mr Treacle, Mr Nightshade, and Mr Mac Laurel. Never read our review! ! ! !

141

Mr Escot. Never. I look on periodical criticism in general to be a species of shop, where panegyric and defamation are sold, wholesale, retail, and for exportation. I am not inclined to be a purchaser of these commodities, or to encourage a trade which I consider pregnant with mischief.

Mr Mac Laurel. I can readily conceive, sir, ye wou'd na wullingly encoorage ony dealer in panegeeric: but, frae the manner in which ye speak o' the first creetics an' scholars o' the age, I shou'd think ye wou'd hae a leetle mair predilaction for deefamation.

Mr Escot. I have no predilection, sir, for defamation. I make a point of speaking the truth on all occasions; and it seldom happens that the truth can be spoken without some stricken deer pronouncing it a libel.

Mr Nightshade. You are perhaps, sir, an enemy to literature in general?

Mr Escot. If I were, sir, I should be a better friend to periodical critics.

Squire Headlong. Buz!

Mr Treacle. May I simply take the liberty to inquire into the basis of your objection?

Mr Escot. I conceive that periodical criticism disseminates superficial knowledge, and its perpetual adjunct, vanity; that it checks in the youthful mind the habit of thinking for itself; that it delivers partial opinions, and thereby misleads the judgment; that it is never conducted with a view to the general interests of literature, but to serve the interested ends of individuals, and the miserable purposes of party.

Mr Mac Laurel. Ye ken, sir, a mon mun leeve.

Mr Escot. While he can live honourably, naturally, justly, certainly: no longer.

Mr Mac Laurel. Every mon, sir, leeves according to his ain notions of honour an' justice: there is a wee defference amang the learned wi' respact to the defineetion o' the terms.

142

Mr Escot. I believe it is generally admitted that one of the ingredients of justice is disinterestedness.

Mr Mac Laurel. It is na admitted, sir, amang the pheelosophers of Edinbroo', that there is ony sic thing as desenterestedness in the warld, or that a mon can care for onything sae much as his ain sel: for ye mun observe, sir, every mon has his ain parteecular feelings of what is gude, an' beautifu', an' consentaneous to his ain indiveedual nature, an' desires to see every thing aboot him in that parteecular state which is maist conformable to his ain notions o' the moral an' poleetical fetness o' things. Twa men, sir, shall purchase a piece o' grund atween 'em, and ae mon shall cover his half wi' a park—

Mr Milestone. Beautifully laid out in lawns and clumps, with a belt of trees at the circumference, and an artificial lake in the centre.

Mr Mac Laurel. Exactly, sir: an' shall keep it a' for his ain sel: an' the other mon shall divide his half into leetle farms of twa or three acres—

Mr Escot. Like those of the Roman republic, and build a cottage on each of them, and cover his land with a simple, innocent, and smiling population, who shall owe, not only their happiness, but their existence, to his benevolence.

Mr Mac Laurel. Exactly, sir: an' ye will ca' the first mon selfish, an' the second desenterested; but the pheelosophical truth is semply this, that the ane is pleased wi' looking at trees, an' the other wi' seeing people happy an' comfortable. It is aunly a matter of indiveedual feeling. A paisant saves a mon's life for the same reason that a hero or a footpad cuts his thrapple: an' a pheelosopher delevers a mon frae a preson, for the same reason that a tailor or a prime meenester puts him into it: because it is conformable to his ain parteecular feelings o' the moral an' poleetical fetness o' things.

Squire Headlong. Wake the Reverend Doctor. Doctor, the bottle stands with you.

The Reverend Doctor Gaster. It is an error of which I am seldom guilty.

Mr Mac Laurel. Noo, ye ken, sir, every mon is the centre of his ain system, an' endaivours as much as possible to adapt every thing aroond him to his ain parteecular views.

Mr Escot. Thus, sir, I presume, it suits the particular views of a poet, at one time to take the part of the people against their oppressors, and at another, to take the part of the oppressors, against the people.

Mr Mac Laurel. Ye mun alloo, sir, that poetry is a sort of ware or commodity, that is brought into the public market wi' a' other descreptions of merchandise, an' that a mon is pairfectly justified in getting the best price he can for his article. Noo, there are three reasons for taking the part o' the people; the first is, when general leeberty an' public happiness are conformable to your ain parteecular feelings o' the moral an' poleetical fetness o' things: the second is, when they happen to be, as it were, in a state of exceetabeelity, an' ye think ye can get a gude price for your commodity, by flingin' in a leetle seasoning o' pheelanthropy an' republican speerit; the third is, when ye think ye can bully the menestry into gieing ye a place or a pansion to hau'd your din, an' in that case, ye point an attack against them within the pale o' the law; an' if they tak nae heed o' ye, ye open a stronger fire; an' the less heed they tak, the mair ye bawl; an' the mair factious ye grow, always within the pale o' the law, till they send a plenipotentiary to treat wi' ye for yoursel, an' then the mair popular ye happen to be, the better price ye fetch.

Squire Headlong. Off with your heeltaps.

Mr Cranium. I perfectly agree with Mr Mac Laurel in his definition of self-love and disinterestedness: every man's actions are determined by his peculiar views, and those views are determined by the organisation of his skull. A man in whom the organ of benevolence is not developed, cannot be benevolent: he in whom it is so, cannot be otherwise. The organ of self-love is prodigiously developed in the greater number of subjects that have fallen under my observation.

Mr Escot. Much less I presume, among savage than civilised men, who, *constant only to the love of self, and consistent only in their aim to deceive, are always actuated by the hope of personal advantage, or by the dread of personal punishment².*

Mr Cranium. Very probably.

Mr Escot. You have, of course, found very copious specimens of the organs of hypocrisy, destruction, and avarice.

Mr Cranium. Secretiveness, destructiveness, and covetiveness. You may add, if you please, that of constructiveness.

Mr Escot. Meaning, I presume, the organ of building; which I contend to be not a natural organ of the *featherless biped.*

Mr Cranium. Pardon me: it is here.——(*As he said these words, he produced a skull from his pocket, and placed it on the table to the great surprise of the company.*)——This was the skull of Sir Christopher Wren. You observe this protuberance——(*The skull was handed round the table.*)

Mr Escot. I contend that the original unsophisticated man was by no means constructive. He lived in the open air, under a tree.

The Reverend Doctor Gaster. The tree of life. Unquestionably. Till he had tasted the forbidden fruit.

Mr Jenkison. At which period, probably, the organ of constructiveness was added to his anatomy, as a punishment for his transgression.

Mr Escot. There could not have been a more severe one, since the propensity which has led him to building cities has proved the greatest curse of his existence.

Squire Headlong. (*taking the skull.*) *Memento mori.* Come, a bumper of Burgundy.

Mr Nightshade. A very classical application, Squire Headlong. The Romans were in the practice of adhibiting skulls at their banquets, and sometimes little skeletons of silver, as a silent admonition to the guests to enjoy life while it lasted.

The Reverend Doctor Gaster. Sound doctrine, Mr Nightshade.

Mr Escot. I question its soundness. The use of vinous spirit has a tremendous influence in the deterioration of the human race.

Mr Foster. I fear, indeed, it operates as a considerable check to the progress of the species towards moral and intellectual perfection. Yet many great men have been of opinion that it exalts the imagination, fires the genius, accelerates the flow of ideas, and imparts to dispositions naturally cold and deliberative that enthusiastic sublimation which is the source of greatness and energy.

Mr Nightshade. Laudibus arguitur vini vinosus Homerus.[3]

Mr Jenkison. I conceive the use of wine to be always pernicious in excess, but often useful in moderation: it certainly kills some, but it saves the lives of others: I find that an occasional glass, taken with judgment and caution, has a very salutary effect in maintaining that equilibrium of the system, which it is always my aim to preserve; and this calm and temperate use of wine was, no doubt, what Homer meant to inculcate, when he said: Παρ δε δεπας οινοιο, πιειν 'οτε θυμος ανωγοι.[4]

Squire Headlong. Good. Pass the bottle. (*Un morne silence*). Sir Christopher does not seem to have raised our spirits. Chromatic, favour us with a specimen of your vocal powers. Something in point.

Mr Chromatic, without further preface, immediately struck up the following

SONG

In his last binn SIR PETER lies,
    Who knew not what it was to frown:
Death took him mellow, by surprise,
    And in his cellar stopped him down.
Through all our land we could not boast
    A knight more gay, more prompt than he,
To rise and fill a bumper toast,
    And pass it round with THREE TIMES THREE.

None better knew the feast to sway,
 Or keep Mirth's boat in better trim;
For Nature had but little clay
 Like that of which she moulded him.
The meanest guest that graced his board
 Was there the freest of the free,
His bumper toast when PETER poured,
 And passed it round with THREE TIMES THREE.

He kept at true good humour's mark
 The social flow of pleasure's tide:
He never made a brow look dark,
 Nor caused a tear, but when he died.
No sorrow round his tomb should dwell:
 More pleased his gay old ghost would be,
For funeral song, and passing bell,
 To hear no sound but THREE TIMES THREE.

  (Hammering of knuckles and glasses and shouts of bravo!)

Mr Panscope. (Suddenly emerging from a deep reverie.) I have heard, with the most profound attention, every thing which the gentleman on the other side of the table has thought proper to advance on the subject of human deterioration; and I must take the liberty to remark, that it augurs a very considerable degree of presumption in any individual, to set himself up against the *authority* of so many great men, as may be marshalled in metaphysical phalanx under the opposite banners of the controversy; such as Aristotle, Plato, the scholiast on Aristophanes, St Chrysostom, St Jerome, St Athanasius, Orpheus, Pindar, Simonides, Gronovius, Hemsterhusius, Longinus, Sir Isaac Newton, Thomas Paine, Doctor Paley, the King of Prussia, the King of Poland, Cicero, Monsieur Gautier, Hippocrates, Machiavelli,

Milton, Colley Cibber, Bojardo, Gregory Nazianzenus, Locke, D'Alembert, Boccaccio, Daniel Defoe, Erasmus, Doctor Smollett, Zimmermann, Solomon, Confucius, Zoroaster, and Thomas-a-Kempis.

Mr Escot. I presume, sir, you are one of those who value an *authority* more than a reason.

Mr Panscope. The *authority*, sir, of all these great men, whose works, as well as the whole of the Encyclopædia Britannica, the entire series of the Monthly Review, the complete set of the Variorum Classics, and the Memoirs of the Academy of Inscriptions, I have read through from beginning to end, deposes, with irrefragable refutation, against your ratiocinative speculations, wherein you seem desirous, by the futile process of analytical dialectics, to subvert the pyramidal structure of synthetically deduced opinions, which have withstood the secular revolutions of physiological disquisition, and which I maintain to be transcendentally self-evident, categorically certain, and syllogistically demonstrable.

Squire Headlong. Bravo! Pass the bottle. The very best speech that ever was made.

Mr Escot. It has only the slight disadvantage of being unintelligible.

Mr Panscope. I am not obliged, sir, as Dr Johnson observed on a similar occasion, to furnish you with an understanding.

Mr Escot. I fear, sir, you would have some difficulty in furnishing me with such an article from your own stock.

Mr Panscope. 'Sdeath, sir, do you question my understanding?

Mr Escot. I only question, sir, where I expect a reply; which, from things that have no existence, I am not visionary enough to anticipate.

Mr Panscope. I beg leave to observe, sir, that my language was perfectly perspicuous, and etymologically correct; and, I conceive, I have demonstrated what I shall now take the liberty to say in plain terms, that all your opinions are extremely absurd.

Mr Escot. I should be sorry, sir, to advance any opinion that you would not think absurd.

Mr Panscope. Death and fury, sir—

Mr Escot. Say no more, sir. That apology is quite sufficient.

Mr Panscope. Apology, sir?

Mr Escot. Even so, sir. You have lost your temper, which I consider equivalent to a confession that you have the worst of the argument.

Mr Panscope. Lightning and devils! sir—

Squire Headlong. No civil war!—Temperance, in the name of Bacchus!—A glee! a glee! *Music has charms to bend the knotted oak.* Sir Patrick, you'll join?

Sir Patrick O'Prism. Troth, with all my heart; for, by my soul, I'm bothered completely.

Squire Headlong. Agreed, then; you, and I, and Chromatic. Bumpers! Come, strike up.

Squire Headlong, Mr Chromatic, and Sir Patrick O'Prism, each holding a bumper, immediately vociferated the following

GLEE

A heeltap! a heeltap! I never could bear it!
So fill me a bumper, a bumper of claret!
Let the bottle pass freely, don't shirk it nor spare it,
For a heeltap! a heeltap! I never could bear it!

No skylight! no twilight! while Bacchus rules o'er us:
No thinking! no shrinking! all drinking in chorus:
Let us moisten our clay, since 'tis thirsty and porous:
No thinking! no shrinking! all drinking in chorus!

GRAND CHORUS

By Squire Headlong, Mr Chromatic, Sir Patrick O'Prism, Mr Panscope, Mr Jenkison, Mr Gall, Mr Treacle, Mr Nightshade, Mr Mac Laurel, Mr Cranium, Mr Milestone, and the Reverend Dr Gaster.

A heeltap! a heeltap! I never could bear it!
So fill me a bumper, a bumper of claret!
Let the bottle pass freely, don't shirk it nor spare it,
For a heeltap! a heeltap! I never could bear it!

'ΟΜΑΔΟΣ ΚΑΙ ΔΟΥΠΟΣ ΟΡΩΡΕΙ'

The little butler now waddled in with a summons from the ladies to tea and coffee. The squire was unwilling to leave his Burgundy. Mr Escot strenuously urged the necessity of immediate adjournment, observing, that the longer they continued drinking the worse they should be. Mr Foster seconded the motion, declaring the transition from the bottle to female society to be an indisputable amelioration of the state of the sensitive man. Mr Jenkison allowed the squire and his two brother philosophers to settle the point between them, concluding that he was just as well in one place as another. The question of adjournment was then put, and carried by a large majority.

CHAPTER VI

THE EVENING

MR PANSCOPE, highly irritated by the cool contempt with which Mr Escot had treated him, sate sipping his coffee and meditating revenge. He was not long in discovering the passion of his antagonist for the beautiful Cephalis, for whom he had himself a species of predilection; and it was also obvious to him, that there was some lurking anger in the mind of her father, unfavourable to the hopes of his rival. The stimulus of revenge, superadded to that of preconceived inclination, determined him, after due deliberation, to *cut out* Mr Escot in the young lady's favour. The practicability of this design he did not trouble himself to investigate; for the havoc he had made in the hearts of some silly girls, who were extremely vulnerable to flattery, and who, not understanding a word he said, considered him a *prodigious clever man*, had impressed him with an unhesitating idea of his own irresistibility. He had not only the requisites already specified for fascinating female vanity, he could likewise fiddle with tolerable dexterity, though by no means so *quick* as Mr Chromatic (for our readers are of course aware that rapidity of execution, not delicacy of expression, constitutes the scientific perfection of modern music), and could warble a fashionable love-ditty with considerable affectation of feeling: besides this, he was always extremely well dressed, and was heir-apparent to an estate of ten thousand a-year. The influence which the latter consideration might have on the minds of the majority of his female acquaintance, whose morals had been formed by the novels of such writers as Miss Philomela Poppyseed, did not once enter into his calculation of his own personal attractions. Relying, therefore, on past success, he determined *to appeal to his fortune*, and already, in imagination, considered himself sole lord and master of the affections of the beautiful Cephalis.

Mr Escot and Mr Foster were the only two of the party who had entered the library (to which the ladies had retired, and which was interior to the music-room) in a state of perfect sobriety. Mr Escot had placed himself next to the beautiful Cephalis: Mr Cranium had laid aside much of the terror of his frown; the short craniological conversation, which had passed between him and Mr Escot, had softened his heart in his favour; and the copious libations of Burgundy in which he had indulged had smoothed his brow into unusual serenity.

Mr Foster placed himself near the lovely Caprioletta, whose artless and innocent conversation had already made an impression on his susceptible spirit.

The Reverend Doctor Gaster seated himself in the corner of a sofa near Miss Philomela Poppyseed. Miss Philomela detailed to him the plan of a very moral and aristocratical novel she was preparing for the press, and continued holding forth, with her eyes half shut, till a long-drawn nasal tone from the reverend divine compelled her suddenly to open them in all the indignation of surprise. The cessation of the hum of her voice awakened the reverend gentleman, who, lifting up first one eyelid, then the other, articulated, or rather murmured, "Admirably planned, indeed!"

"I have not quite finished, sir," said Miss Philomela, bridling. "Will you have the goodness to inform me where I left off?"

The doctor hummed a while, and at length answered: "I think you had just laid it down as a position, that a thousand a-year is an indispensable ingredient in the passion of love, and that no man, who is not so far gifted by *nature*, can reasonably presume to feel that passion himself, or be correctly the object of it with a well-educated female."

"That, sir," said Miss Philomela, highly incensed, "is the fundamental principle which I lay down in the first chapter, and which the whole four volumes, of which I detailed to you the outline, are intended to set in a strong practical light."

"Bless me!" said the doctor, "what a nap I must have had!"

Miss Philomela flung away to the side of her dear friends Gall and Treacle, under whose fostering patronage she had been puffed into an extensive reputation, much to the advantage of the young ladies of the age, whom she taught to consider themselves as a sort of commodity, to be put up at public auction, and knocked down to the highest bidder. Mr Nightshade and Mr Mac Laurel joined the trio; and it was secretly resolved, that Miss Philomela should furnish them with a portion of her manuscripts, and that Messieurs Gall & Co. should devote the following morning to cutting and drying a critique on a work calculated to prove so extensively beneficial, that Mr Gall protested he really *envied* the writer.

While this amiable and enlightened quintetto were busily employed in flattering one another, Mr Cranium retired to complete the preparations he had begun in the morning for a lecture, with which he intended, on some future evening, to favour the company: Sir Patrick O'Prism walked out into the grounds to study the effect of moonlight on the snow-clad mountains: Mr Foster and Mr Escot continued to make love, and Mr Panscope to digest his plan of attack on the heart of Miss Cephalis: Mr Jenkison sate by the fire, reading *Much Ado about Nothing*: the Reverend Doctor Gaster was still enjoying the benefit of Miss Philomela's opiate, and serenading the company from his solitary corner: Mr Chromatic was reading music, and occasionally humming a note: and Mr Milestone had produced his portfolio for the edification and amusement of Miss Tenorina, Miss Graziosa, and Squire Headlong, to whom he was pointing out the various beauties of his plan for Lord Littlebrain's park.

Mr Milestone. This, you perceive, is the natural state of one part of the grounds. Here is a wood, never yet touched by the finger of taste;

thick, intricate, and gloomy. Here is a little stream, dashing from stone to stone, and overshadowed with these untrimmed boughs.

Miss Tenorina. The sweet romantic spot! How beautifully the birds must sing there on a summer evening!

Miss Graziosa. Dear sister! how can you endure the horrid thicket?

Mr Milestone. You are right, Miss Graziosa: your taste is correct—perfectly *en règle.* Now, here is the same place corrected—trimmed—polished—decorated—adorned. Here sweeps a plantation, in that beautiful regular curve: there winds a gravel walk: here are parts of the old wood, left in these majestic circular clumps, disposed at equal distances with wonderful symmetry: there are some single shrubs scattered in elegant profusion: here a Portugal laurel, there a juniper; here a laurustinus, there a spruce fir; here a larch, there a lilac; here a rhododendron, there an arbutus. The stream, you see, is become a canal: the banks are perfectly smooth and green, sloping to the water's edge: and there is Lord Littlebrain, rowing in an elegant boat.

Squire Headlong. Magical, faith!

Mr Milestone. Here is another part of the grounds in its natural state. Here is a large rock, with the mountain-ash rooted in its fissures, overgrown, as you see, with ivy and moss; and from this part of it bursts a little fountain, that runs bubbling down its rugged sides.

Miss Tenorina. O how beautiful! How I should love the melody of that miniature cascade!

Mr Milestone. Beautiful, Miss Tenorina! Hideous. Base, common, and popular. Such a thing as you may see anywhere, in wild and mountainous districts. Now, observe the metamorphosis. Here is the same rock, cut into the shape of a giant. In one hand he holds a horn, through which that little fountain is thrown to a prodigious elevation. In the other is a ponderous stone, so exactly balanced as to be apparently ready to fall on the head of any person who may happen to be beneath[1]: and there is Lord Littlebrain walking under it.

154

Squire Headlong. Miraculous, by Mahomet!

Mr Milestone. This is the summit of a hill, covered, as you perceive, with wood, and with those mossy stones scattered at random under the trees.

Miss Tenorina. What a delightful spot to read in, on a summer's day! The air must be so pure, and the wind must sound so divinely in the tops of those old pines!

Mr Milestone. Bad taste, Miss Tenorina. Bad taste, I assure you. Here is the spot improved. The trees are cut down: the stones are cleared away: this is an octagonal pavilion, exactly on the centre of the summit: and there you see Lord Littlebrain, on the top of the pavilion, enjoying the prospect with a telescope.

Squire Headlong. Glorious, egad!

Mr Milestone. Here is a rugged mountainous road, leading through impervious shades: the ass and the four goats characterise a wild uncultured scene. Here, as you perceive, it is totally changed into a beautiful gravel-road, gracefully curving through a belt of limes: and there is Lord Littlebrain driving four-in-hand.

Squire Headlong. Egregious, by Jupiter!

Mr Milestone. Here is Littlebrain Castle, a Gothic, moss-grown structure, half bosomed in trees. Near the casement of that turret is an owl peeping from the ivy.

Squire Headlong. And devilish wise he looks.

Mr Milestone. Here is the new house, without a tree near it, standing in the midst of an undulating lawn: a white, polished, angular building, reflected to a nicety in this waveless lake: and there you see Lord Littlebrain looking out of the window.

Squire Headlong. And devilish wise he looks too. You shall cut me a giant before you go.

Mr Milestone. Good. I'll order down my little corps of pioneers.

During this conversation, a hot dispute had arisen between Messieurs Gall and Nightshade; the latter pertinaciously insisting on having his new poem reviewed by Treacle, who he knew would extol it most loftily, and not by Gall, whose sarcastic commendation he held in superlative horror. The remonstrances of Squire Headlong silenced the disputants, but did not mollify the inflexible Gall, nor appease the irritated Nightshade, who secretly resolved that, on his return to London, he would beat his drum in Grub Street, form a mastigophoric corps of his own, and hoist the standard of determined opposition against this critical Napoleon.

Sir Patrick O'Prism now entered, and, after some rapturous exclamations on the effect of the mountain-moonlight, entreated that one of the young ladies would favour him with a song. Miss Tenorina and Miss Graziosa now enchanted the company with some very scientific compositions, which, as usual, excited admiration and astonishment in every one, without a single particle of genuine pleasure. The beautiful Cephalis being then summoned to take her station at the harp, sang with feeling and simplicity the following air:—

LOVE AND OPPORTUNITY

Oh! who art thou, so swiftly flying?
　　My name is Love, the child replied:
Swifter I pass than south-winds sighing,
　　Or streams, through summer vales that glide.
And who art thou, his flight pursuing?
　　'Tis cold Neglect whom now you see:
The little god you there are viewing,
　　Will die, if once he's touched by me.

Oh! who art thou so fast proceeding,
　　Ne'er glancing back thine eyes of flame?
Marked but by few, through earth I'm speeding,

And Opportunity's my name.
What form is that, which scowls beside thee?
    Repentance is the form you see:
Learn then, the fate may yet betide thee:
    She seizes them who seize not me.[2]

The little butler now appeared with a summons to supper, shortly after which the party dispersed for the night.

CHAPTER VII

THE WALK

IT was an old custom in Headlong Hall to have breakfast ready at eight, and continue it till two; that the various guests might rise at their own hour, breakfast when they came down, and employ the morning as they thought proper; the squire only expecting that they should punctually assemble at dinner. During the whole of this period, the little butler stood sentinel at a side-table near the fire, copiously furnished with all the apparatus of tea, coffee, chocolate, milk, cream, eggs, rolls, toast, muffins, bread, butter, potted beef, cold fowl and partridge, ham, tongue, and anchovy. The Reverend Doctor Gaster found himself rather *queasy* in the morning, therefore preferred breakfasting in bed, on a mug of buttered ale and an anchovy toast. The three philosophers made their appearance at eight, and enjoyed *les prémices des dépouilles*. Mr Foster proposed that, as it was a fine frosty morning, and they were all good pedestrians, they should take a walk to Tremadoc, to see the improvements carrying on in that vicinity. This being readily acceded to, they began their walk.

After their departure, appeared Squire Headlong and Mr Milestone, who agreed, over their muffin and partridge, to walk together to a ruined tower, within the precincts of the squire's grounds, which Mr Milestone thought he could improve.

The other guests dropped in by ones and twos, and made their respective arrangements for the morning. Mr Panscope took a little ramble with Mr Cranium, in the course of which, the former professed a great enthusiasm for the science of craniology, and a great deal of love for the beautiful Cephalis, adding a few words about his expectations; the old gentleman was unable to withstand this triple battery, and it was accordingly determined—after the manner of the heroic age, in which it was deemed superfluous to consult the opinions and feelings of the lady, as to the manner in which she should be disposed of—that the lovely Miss Cranium should be made the happy bride of the accomplished Mr Panscope. We shall leave them for the present to settle preliminaries, while we accompany the three philosophers in their walk to Tremadoc.

The vale contracted as they advanced, and, when they had passed the termination of the lake, their road wound along a narrow and romantic pass, through the middle of which an impetuous torrent dashed over vast fragments of stone. The pass was bordered on both sides by perpendicular rocks, broken into the wildest forms of fantastic magnificence.

"These are, indeed," said Mr Escot, "*confracti mundi rudera*[1]: yet they must be feeble images of the valleys of the Andes, where the philosophic eye may contemplate, in their utmost extent, the effects of that tremendous convulsion which destroyed the perpendicularity of the poles, and inundated this globe with that torrent of physical evil, from which the greater torrent of moral evil has issued, that will continue to roll on, with an expansive power and an accelerated impetus, till the whole human race shall be swept away in its vortex."

"The precession of the equinoxes," said Mr Foster, "will gradually ameliorate the physical state of our planet, till the ecliptic shall again coincide with the equator, and the equal diffusion of light and heat over the whole surface of the earth typify the equal and happy existence of man, who will then have attained the final step of pure and perfect intelligence."

"It is by no means clear," said Mr Jenkison, "that the axis of the earth was ever perpendicular to the plane of its orbit, or that it ever will be so. Explosion and convulsion are necessary to the maintenance of either hypothesis: for La Place has demonstrated, that the precession of the equinoxes is only a secular equation of a very long period, which, of course, proves nothing either on one side or the other."

They now emerged, by a winding ascent, from the vale of Llanberris, and after some little time arrived at Bedd Gelert. Proceeding through the sublimely romantic pass of Aberglaslynn, their road led along the edge of Traeth Mawr, a vast arm of the sea, which they then beheld in all the magnificence of the flowing tide. Another five miles brought them to the embankment, which has since been completed, and which, by connecting the two counties of Meirionnydd and Caernarvon, excludes the sea from an extensive tract. The embankment, which was carried on at the same time from both the opposite coasts, was then very nearly meeting in the centre. They walked to the extremity of that part of it which was thrown out from the Caernarvonshire shore. The tide was now ebbing: it had filled the vast basin within, forming a lake about five miles in length and more than one in breadth. As they looked upwards with their backs to the open sea, they beheld a scene which no other in this country can parallel, and which the admirers of the magnificence of nature will ever remember with regret, whatever consolation may be derived from the probable utility of the works which have excluded the waters from their ancient receptacle. Vast rocks and precipices, intersected with little torrents, formed the barrier on the left: on the right, the triple summit of Moëlwyn reared its majestic boundary: in the depth was that sea of mountains, the wild and stormy outline of the Snowdonian chain, with the giant Wyddfa towering in the midst. The mountain-frame remains unchanged, unchangeable: but the liquid mirror it enclosed is gone.

The tide ebbed with rapidity: the waters within, retained by the embankment, poured through its two points an impetuous cataract, curling and boiling in innumerable eddies, and making a tumultuous melody admirably in unison with the surrounding scene. The three philosophers looked on in silence; and at length unwillingly turned away, and proceeded to the little town of Tremadoc, which is built on land recovered in a similar manner from the sea. After inspecting the manufactories, and refreshing themselves at the inn on a cold saddle of mutton and a bottle of sherry, they retraced their steps towards Headlong Hall, commenting as they went on the various objects they had seen.

Mr Escot. I regret that time did not allow us to see the caves on the sea-shore. There is one of which the depth is said to be unknown. There is a tradition in the country, that an adventurous fiddler once resolved to explore it; that he entered, and never returned; but that the subterranean sound of a fiddle was heard at a farm-house seven miles inland. It is, therefore, concluded that he lost his way in the labyrinth of caverns, supposed to exist under the rocky soil of this part of the country.

Mr Jenkison. A supposition that must always remain in force, unless a second fiddler, equally adventurous and more successful, should return with an accurate report of the true state of the fact.

Mr Foster. What think you of the little colony we have just been inspecting; a city, as it were, in its cradle?

Mr Escot. With all the weakness of infancy, and all the vices of maturer age. I confess, the sight of those manufactories, which have suddenly sprung up, like fungous excrescences, in the bosom of these wild and desolate scenes, impressed me with as much horror and amazement as the sudden appearance of the stocking manufactory struck into the mind of Rousseau, when, in a lonely valley of the Alps, he had just congratulated himself on finding a spot where man had never been.

Mr Foster. The manufacturing system is not yet purified from some evils which necessarily attend it, but which I conceive are greatly overbalanced by their concomitant advantages. Contemplate the vast sum of human industry to which this system so essentially contributes: seas covered with vessels, ports resounding with life, profound researches, scientific inventions, complicated mechanism, canals carried over deep valleys, and through the bosoms of hills:

employment and existence thus given to innumerable families, and the multiplied comforts and conveniences of life diffused over the whole community.

Mr Escot. You present to me a complicated picture of artificial life, and require me to admire it. Seas covered with vessels: every one of which contains two or three tyrants, and from fifty to a thousand slaves, ignorant, gross, perverted, and active only in mischief. Ports resounding with life: in other words, with noise and drunkenness, the mingled din of avarice, intemperance, and prostitution. Profound researches, scientific inventions: to what end? To contract the sum of human wants? to teach the art of living on a little? to disseminate independence, liberty, and health? No; to multiply factitious desires, to stimulate depraved appetites, to invent unnatural wants, to heap up incense on the shrine of luxury, and accumulate expedients of selfish and ruinous profusion. Complicated machinery: behold its blessings. Twenty years ago, at the door of every cottage sate the good woman with her spinning-wheel: the children, if not more profitably employed than in gathering heath and sticks, at least laid in a stock of health and strength to sustain the labours of maturer years. Where is the spinning-wheel now, and every simple and insulated occupation of the industrious cottager? Wherever this boasted machinery is established, the children of the poor are death-doomed from their cradles. Look for one moment at midnight into a cotton-mill, amidst the smell of oil, the smoke of lamps, the rattling of wheels, the dizzy and complicated motions of diabolical mechanism: contemplate the little human machines that keep play with the revolutions of the iron work, robbed at that hour of their natural rest, as of air and exercise by day: observe their pale and ghastly features, more ghastly in that baleful and malignant light, and tell me if you do not fancy yourself on the threshold of Virgil's hell, where

Continuo auditæ voces, vagitus et ingens,
Infantumque animæ flentes, in limine primo,
Quos *dulcis vitæ exsortes,* et ab ubere raptos,
Abstulit atra dies, et FUNERE MERSIT ACERBO!

As Mr Escot said this, a little rosy-cheeked girl, with a basket of heath on her head, came tripping down the side of one of the rocks on the left. The force of contrast struck even on the phlegmatic spirit of Mr Jenkison, and he almost inclined for a moment to the doctrine of deterioration. Mr Escot continued:

Mr Escot. Nor is the lot of the parents more enviable. Sedentary victims of unhealthy toil, they have neither the corporeal energy of the savage, nor the mental acquisitions of the civilised man. Mind, indeed, they have none, and scarcely animal life. They are mere automata, component parts of the enormous machines which administer to the pampered appetites of the few, who consider themselves the most valuable portion of a state, because they consume in indolence the fruits of the earth, and contribute nothing to the benefit of the community.

Mr Jenkison. That these are evils cannot be denied; but they have their counterbalancing advantages. That a man should pass the day in a furnace and the night in a cellar, is bad for the individual, but good for others who enjoy the benefit of his labour.

Mr Escot. By what right do they so?

Mr Jenkison. By the right of all property and all possession: *le droit du plus fort.*

Mr Escot. Do you justify that principle?

Mr Jenkison. I neither justify nor condemn it. It is practically recognised in all societies; and, though it is certainly the source of enormous evil, I conceive it is also the source of abundant good, or it would not have so many supporters.

Mr Escot. That is by no means a consequence. Do we not every day see men supporting the most enormous evils, which they know to be so with respect to others, and which in reality are so with respect to themselves, though an erroneous view of their own miserable self-interest induces them to think otherwise?

Mr Jenkison. Good and evil exist only as they are perceived. I cannot therefore understand, how that which a man perceives to be good can be in reality an evil to him: indeed, the word *reality* only signifies *strong belief.*

Mr Escot. The views of such a man I contend are false. If he could be made to see the truth—

Mr Jenkison. He sees his own truth. Truth is that which a man *troweth.* Where there is no man there is no truth. Thus the truth of one is not the truth of another.[2]

Mr Foster. I am aware of the etymology; but I contend that there is an universal and immutable truth, deducible from the nature of things.

Mr Jenkison. By whom deducible? Philosophers have investigated the nature of things for centuries, yet no two of them will agree in *trowing* the same conclusion.

Mr Foster. The progress of philosophical investigation, and the rapidly increasing accuracy of human knowledge, approximate by degrees the diversities of opinion; so that, in process of time, moral science will be susceptible of mathematical demonstration; and, clear and indisputable principles being universally recognised, the coincidence of deduction will necessarily follow.

Mr Escot. Possibly when the inroads of luxury and disease shall have exterminated nine hundred and ninety-nine thousand nine hundred and ninety-nine of every million of the human race, the remaining fractional units may congregate into one point, and come to something like the same conclusion.

Mr Jenkison. I doubt it much. I conceive, if only we three were survivors of the whole system of terrestrial being, we should never agree in our decisions as to the cause of the calamity.

Mr Escot. Be that as it may, I think you must at least assent to the following positions: that the many are sacrificed to the few; that ninety-nine in a hundred are occupied in a perpetual struggle for the preservation of a perilous and precarious existence, while the remaining one wallows in all the redundancies of luxury that can be wrung from their labours and privations; that luxury and liberty are incompatible; and that every new want you invent for civilised man is a new instrument of torture for him who cannot indulge it.

They had now regained the shores of the lake, when the conversation was suddenly interrupted by a tremendous explosion, followed by a violent splashing of water, and various sounds of tumult and confusion, which induced them to quicken their pace towards the spot whence they proceeded.

CHAPTER VIII

THE TOWER

IN all the thoughts, words, and actions of Squire Headlong, there was a remarkable alacrity of progression, which almost annihilated the interval between conception and execution. He was utterly regardless of obstacles, and seemed to have expunged their very name from his vocabulary. His designs were never nipped in their infancy by the contemplation of those trivial difficulties which often turn awry the current of enterprise; and, though the rapidity of his movements was sometimes arrested by a more formidable barrier, either naturally existing in the pursuit he had undertaken, or created by his own impetuosity, he seldom failed to succeed either in knocking it down or cutting his way through it. He had little idea of gradation: he saw no interval between the first step and the last, but pounced upon his object with the impetus of a mountain cataract. This rapidity of movement, indeed, subjected him to some disasters which cooler spirits would have escaped. He was an excellent sportsman, and almost always killed his game; but now and then he killed his dog.[1] Rocks, streams, hedges, gates, and ditches, were objects of no account in his estimation; though a dislocated shoulder, several severe bruises, and two or three narrow escapes for his neck, might have been expected to teach him a certain degree of caution in effecting his transitions. He was so singularly alert in climbing precipices and traversing torrents, that, when he went out on a shooting party, he was very soon left to continue his sport alone, for he was sure to dash up or down some nearly perpendicular path, where no one else had either ability or inclination to follow. He had a pleasure boat on the lake, which he steered with amazing dexterity; but as he always indulged himself in the utmost possible latitude of sail, he was occasionally upset by a sudden gust, and was indebted to his skill in the art of swimming for the opportunity of tempering with a copious libation of wine the unnatural frigidity introduced into his stomach by the extraordinary intrusion of water, an element which he had religiously determined should never pass his lips, but of which, on these occasions, he was sometimes compelled to swallow no inconsiderable quantity. This circumstance alone, of the various disasters that befell him, occasioned him any permanent affliction, and he accordingly noted the day in his pocket-book as a *dies nefastus*, with this simple abstract, and brief chronicle of the calamity: *Mem. Swallowed two or three pints of water*: without any notice whatever of the concomitant circumstances. These days, of which there were several, were set apart in Headlong Hall for the purpose of anniversary expiation; and, as often as the day returned on which the squire had swallowed water, he not only made a point of swallowing a treble allowance of wine himself, but imposed a heavy mulct on every one of his servants who should be detected in a state of sobriety after sunset: but their conduct on these occasions was so uniformly exemplary, that no instance of the infliction of the penalty appears on record.

The squire and Mr Milestone, as we have already said, had set out immediately after breakfast to examine the capabilities of the scenery. The object that most attracted Mr Milestone's admiration was a ruined tower on a projecting point of rock, almost totally overgrown with ivy. This ivy, Mr Milestone observed, required trimming and clearing in various parts: a little pointing and polishing was also necessary for the dilapidated walls: and the whole effect would be materially increased by a plantation of spruce fir, interspersed with cypress and juniper, the present rugged and broken ascent from the land side being first converted into a beautiful slope, which might be easily effected by blowing up a part of the rock with gunpowder, laying on a quantity of fine mould, and covering the whole with an elegant stratum of turf.

Squire Headlong caught with avidity at this suggestion; and, as he had always a store of gunpowder in the house, for the accommodation of himself and his shooting visitors, and for the supply of a small battery of cannon, which he kept for his private amusement, he insisted on commencing operations immediately. Accordingly, he bounded back to the house, and very speedily returned, accompanied by the little butler, and half a dozen servants and labourers, with pickaxes and gunpowder, a hanging stove and a poker, together with a basket of cold meat and two or three bottles of Madeira: for the Squire thought, with many others, that a copious supply of provision is a very necessary ingredient in all rural amusements.

Mr Milestone superintended the proceedings. The rock was excavated, the powder introduced, the apertures strongly blockaded with fragments of stone: a long train was laid to a spot which Mr Milestone fixed on as sufficiently remote from the possibility of harm: the Squire seized the poker, and, after flourishing it in the air with a degree of dexterity which induced the rest of the party to leave him in solitary possession of an extensive circumference, applied the end of it to the train; and the rapidly communicated ignition ran hissing along the surface of the soil.

At this critical moment, Mr Cranium and Mr Panscope appeared at the top of the tower, which, unseeing and unseen, they had ascended on the opposite side to that where the Squire and Mr Milestone were conducting their operations. Their sudden appearance a little dismayed the Squire, who, however, comforted himself with the reflection, that the tower was perfectly safe, or at least was intended to be so, and that his friends were in no probable danger but of a knock on the head from a flying fragment of stone.

The succession of these thoughts in the mind of the Squire was commensurate in rapidity to the progress of the ignition, which having reached its extremity, the explosion took place, and the shattered rock was hurled into the air in the midst of fire and smoke.

Mr Milestone had properly calculated the force of the explosion; for the tower remained untouched: but the Squire, in his consolatory reflections, had omitted the consideration of the influence of sudden fear, which had so violent an effect on Mr Cranium, who was just commencing a speech concerning the very fine prospect from the top of the tower, that, cutting short the thread of his observations, he bounded, under the elastic influence of terror, several feet into the air. His ascent being unluckily a little out of the perpendicular, he descended with a proportionate curve from the apex of his projection, and alighted not on the wall of the tower, but in an ivy-bush by its side, which, giving way beneath him, transferred him to a tuft of hazel at its base, which, after upholding him an instant, consigned him to the boughs of an ash that had rooted itself in a fissure about half way down the rock, which finally transmitted him to the waters below.

Squire Headlong anxiously watched the tower as the smoke which at first enveloped it rolled away; but when this shadowy curtain was withdrawn, and Mr Panscope was discovered, *solus*, in a tragical attitude, his apprehensions became boundless, and he concluded that the unlucky collision of a flying fragment of rock had indeed emancipated the spirit of the craniologist from its terrestrial bondage.

Mr Escot had considerably outstripped his companions, and arrived at the scene of the disaster just as Mr Cranium, being utterly destitute of natatorial skill, was in imminent danger of final submersion. The deteriorationist, who had cultivated this valuable art with great success, immediately plunged in to his assistance, and brought him alive and in safety to a shelving part of the shore. Their landing was hailed with a view-holla from the delighted Squire, who, shaking them both heartily by the hand, and making ten thousand lame apologies to Mr Cranium, concluded by asking, in a pathetic tone, *How much water he had swallowed?* and without waiting for his answer, filled a large tumbler with Madeira, and insisted on his tossing it off, which was no sooner said than done. Mr Jenkison and Mr Foster now made their appearance. Mr Panscope descended the tower, which he vowed never again to approach within a quarter of a mile. The tumbler of Madeira was replenished, and handed round to recruit the spirits of the party, which now began to move towards Headlong Hall, the Squire capering for joy in the van, and the little fat butler waddling in the rear.

The Squire took care that Mr Cranium should be seated next to him at dinner, and plied him so hard with Madeira to prevent him, as he said, from taking cold, that long before the ladies sent in their summons to coffee, every organ in his brain was in a complete state of revolution, and the Squire was under the necessity of ringing for three or four servants to carry him to bed, observing, with a smile of great satisfaction, that he was in a very excellent way for escaping any ill consequences that might have resulted from his accident.

The beautiful Cephalis, being thus freed from his *surveillance*, was enabled, during the course of the evening, to develop to his preserver the full extent of her gratitude.

CHAPTER IX

THE SEXTON

MR ESCOT passed a sleepless night, the ordinary effect of love, according to some amatory poets, who seem to have composed their whining ditties for the benevolent purpose of bestowing on others that gentle slumber of which they so pathetically lament the privation. The deteriorationist entered into a profound moral soliloquy, in which he first examined *whether a philosopher ought to be in love?* Having decided this point affirmatively against Plato and Lucretius, he next examined, *whether that passion ought to have the effect of keeping a philosopher awake?* Having decided this negatively, he resolved to go to sleep immediately: not being able to accomplish this to his satisfaction, he tossed and tumbled, like Achilles or Orlando, first on one side, then on the other; repeated to himself several hundred lines of poetry; counted a thousand; began again, and counted another thousand: in vain: the beautiful Cephalis was the predominant image in all his soliloquies, in all his repetitions: even in the numerical process from which he sought relief, he did but associate the idea of number with that of his dear tormentor, till she appeared to his mind's eye in a thousand similitudes, distinct, not different. These thousand images, indeed, were but one; and yet the one was a thousand, a sort of uni-multiplex phantasma, which will be very intelligible to some understandings.

He arose with the first peep of day, and sallied forth to enjoy the balmy breeze of morning, which any but a lover might have thought too cool; for it was an intense frost, the sun had not risen, and the wind was rather fresh from north-east and by north. But a lover, who, like Ladurlad in the Curse of Kehama, always has, or at least is supposed to have, "a fire in his heart and a fire in his brain," feels a wintry breeze from N.E. and by N. steal over his cheek like the south over a bank of violets; therefore, on walked the philosopher, with his coat unbuttoned and his hat in his hand, careless of whither he went, till he found himself near the enclosure of a little mountain chapel. Passing through the wicket, and stepping over two or three graves, he stood on a rustic tombstone, and peeped through the chapel window, examining the interior with as much curiosity as if he had "forgotten what the inside of a church was made of," which, it is rather to be feared, was the case. Before him and beneath him were the font, the altar, and the grave; which gave rise to a train of moral reflections on the three great epochs in the course of the *featherless biped*,—birth, marriage, and death. The middle stage of the process arrested his attention; and his imagination placed before him several figures, which he thought, with the addition of his own, would make a very picturesque group; the beautiful Cephalis, "arrayed in her bridal apparel of white;" her friend Caprioletta officiating as bridemaid; Mr Cranium giving her away; and, last, not least, the Reverend Doctor Gaster, intoning the marriage ceremony with the regular orthodox allowance of nasal recitative. Whilst he was feasting his eyes on this imaginary picture, the demon of mistrust insinuated himself into the storehouse of his conceptions, and, removing his figure from the group, substituted that of Mr Panscope, which gave such a violent shock to his feelings, that he suddenly exclaimed, with an extraordinary elevation of voice, Οιμοι κακοδαιμων, και τρις κακοδαιμων, και τετρακις, και πεντακις, και δωδεκακις, και μυριακις! [h] to the great terror of the sexton, who was just entering the churchyard, and, not knowing from whence the voice proceeded, *pensa que fut un diableteau*. The sight of the philosopher dispelled his apprehensions, when, growing suddenly valiant, he immediately addressed him:—

172

"Cot pless your honour, I should n't have thought of meeting any pody here at this time of the morning, except, look you, it was the tevil—who, to pe sure, toes not often come upon consecrated cround—put for all that, I think I have seen him now and then, in former tays, when old Nanny Llwyd of Llyn-isa was living—Cot teliver us! a terriple old witch to pe sure she was—I tid n't much like tigging her crave—put I prought two cocks with me—the tevil hates cocks—and tied them py the leg on two tombstones—and I tug, and the cocks crowed, and the tevil kept at a tistance. To pe sure now, if I had n't peen very prave py nature—as I ought to pe truly—for my father was Owen Ap-Llwyd Ap-Gryffydd Ap-Shenkin Ap-Williams Ap-Thomas Ap-Morgan Ap-Parry Ap-Evan Ap-Rhys, a coot preacher and a lover of *cwrw*²—I should have thought just now pefore I saw your honour, that the foice I heard was the tevil's calling Nanny Llwyd—Cot pless us! to pe sure she should have been puried in the middle of the river, where the tevil can't come, as your honour fery well knows."

"I am perfectly aware of it," said Mr Escot.

"True, true," continued the sexton; "put to pe sure, Owen Thomas of Morfa-Bach will have it that one summer evening—when he went over to Cwm Cynfael in Meirionnydd, apout some cattles he wanted to puy—he saw a strange figure—pless us!—with five horns!—Cot save us! sitting on Hugh Llwyd's pulpit, which, your honour fery well knows, is a pig rock in the middle of the river—"

"Of course he was mistaken," said Mr Escot.

"To pe sure he was," said the sexton. "For there is no toubt put the tevil, when Owen Thomas saw him, must have peen sitting on a piece of rock in a straight line from him on the other side of the river, where he used to sit, look you, for a whole summer's tay, while Hugh Llwyd was on his pulpit, and there they used to talk across the water! for Hugh Llwyd, please your honour, never raised the tevil except when he was safe in the middle of the river, which proves that Owen Thomas, in his fright, did n't pay proper attention to the exact spot where the tevil was."

The sexton concluded his speech with an approving smile at his own sagacity, in so luminously expounding the nature of Owen Thomas's mistake.

"I perceive," said Mr Escot, "you have a very deep insight into things, and can, therefore, perhaps, facilitate the resolution of a question, concerning which, though I have little doubt on the subject, I am desirous of obtaining the most extensive and accurate information."

The sexton scratched his head, the language of Mr Escot not being to his apprehension quite so luminous as his own.

"You have been sexton here," continued Mr Escot, in the language of Hamlet, "man and boy, forty years."

The sexton turned pale. The period Mr Escot named was so nearly the true one, that he began to suspect the personage before him of being rather too familiar with Hugh Llwyd's sable visitor. Recovering himself a little, he said, "Why, thereapouts, sure enough."

"During this period, you have of course dug up many bones of the people of ancient times."

"Pones! Cot pless you, yes! pones as old as the 'orlt."

"Perhaps you can show me a few."

The sexton grinned horribly a ghastly smile. "Will you take your Pible oath you ton't want them to raise the tevil with?"

"Willingly," said Mr Escot, smiling; "I have an abstruse reason for the inquiry."

"Why, if you have an *obtuse* reason," said the sexton, who thought this a good opportunity to show that he could pronounce hard words as well as other people; "if you have an *obtuse* reason, that alters the case."

So saying he lead the way to the bone-house, from which he began to throw out various bones and skulls of more than common dimensions, and amongst them a skull of very extraordinary magnitude, which he swore by St David was the skull of Cadwallader.

"How do you know this to be his skull?" said Mr Escot.

"He was the piggest man that ever lived, and he was puried here; and this is the piggest skull I ever found: you see now—"

"Nothing can be more logical," said Mr Escot. "My good friend will you allow me to take this skull away with me?"

"St Winifred pless us!" exclaimed the sexton, "would you have me haunted py his chost for taking his plessed pones out of consecrated cround? Would you have him come in the tead of the night, and fly away with the roof of my house? Would you have all the crop of my carden come to nothing? for, look you, his epitaph says,

"He that my pones shall ill pestow,
Leek in his cround shall never crow."

"You will ill bestow them," said Mr Escot, "in confounding them with those of the sons of little men, the degenerate dwarfs of later generations; you will well bestow them in giving them to me: for I will have this illustrious skull bound with a silver rim, and filled with mantling wine, with this inscription, NUNC TANDEM: signifying that that pernicious liquor has at length found its proper receptacle; for, when the wine is in, the brain is out."

Saying these words, he put a dollar into the hands of the sexton, who instantly stood spellbound by the talismanic influence of the coin, while Mr Escot walked off in triumph with the skull of Cadwallader.

CHAPTER X

THE SKULL

WHEN Mr Escot entered the breakfast-room he found the majority of the party assembled, and the little butler very active at his station. Several of the ladies shrieked at the sight of the skull; and Miss Tenorina, starting up in great haste and terror, caused the subversion of a cup of chocolate, which a servant was handing to the Reverend Doctor Gaster, into the nape of the neck of Sir Patrick O'Prism. Sir Patrick, rising impetuously, *to clap an extinguisher*, as he expressed himself, *on the farthing rushlight of the rascal's life*, pushed over the chair of Marmaduke Milestone, Esquire, who, catching for support at the first thing that came in his way, which happened unluckily to be the corner of the table-cloth, drew it instantaneously with him to the floor, involving plates, cups and saucers, in one promiscuous ruin. But, as the principal *matériel* of the breakfast apparatus was on the little butler's side-table, the confusion occasioned by this accident was happily greater than the damage. Miss Tenorina was so agitated that she was obliged to retire: Miss Graziosa accompanied her through pure sisterly affection and sympathy, not without a lingering look at Sir Patrick, who likewise retired to change his coat, but was very expeditious in returning to resume his attack on the cold partridge. The broken cups were cleared away, the cloth relaid, and the array of the table restored with wonderful celerity.

Mr Escot was a little surprised at the scene of confusion which signalised his entrance; but, perfectly unconscious that it originated with the skull of Cadwallader, he advanced to seat himself at the table by the side of the beautiful Cephalis, first placing the skull in a corner, out of the reach of Mr Cranium, who sate eyeing it with lively curiosity, and after several efforts to restrain his impatience, exclaimed, "You seem to have found a rarity."

"A rarity indeed," said Mr Escot, cracking an egg as he spoke; "no less than the genuine and indubitable skull of Cadwallader."

"The skull of Cadwallader!" vociferated Mr Cranium; "O treasure of treasures!"

Mr Escot then detailed by what means he had become possessed of it, which gave birth to various remarks from the other individuals of the party: after which, rising from table, and taking the skull again in his hand,

"This skull," said he, "is the skull of a hero, παλαι κατατεθνειωτος[1], and sufficiently demonstrates a point, concerning which I never myself entertained a doubt, that the human race is undergoing a gradual process of diminution, in length, breadth, and thickness. Observe this skull. Even the skull of our reverend friend, which is the largest and thickest in the company, is not more than half its size. The frame this skull belonged to could scarcely have been less than nine feet high. Such is the lamentable progress of degeneracy and decay. In the course of ages, a boot of the present generation would form an ample chateau for a large family of our remote posterity. The mind, too, participates in the contraction of the body. Poets and philosophers of all ages and nations have lamented this too visible process of physical and moral deterioration. 'The sons of little men', says Ossian. 'Οιοι νυν βροτοι εισιν,' says Homer: 'such men as live in these degenerate days.' 'All things,' says Virgil, 'have a retrocessive tendency, and grow worse and worse by the inevitable doom of fate.'[2] 'We live in the ninth age,' says Juvenal, 'an age worse than the age of iron; nature has no metal sufficiently pernicious to give a denomination to its wickedness.'[3] 'Our fathers,' says Horace, 'worse than our grandfathers, have given birth to us, their more vicious progeny, who, in our turn, shall become the parents of a still viler generation.'[4] You all know the fable of the buried Pict, who bit off the end of a pickaxe, with which sacrilegious hands were breaking open his grave, and called out with a voice like subterranean thunder, *I perceive the degeneracy of your race by the smallness of your little finger!* videlicet, the pickaxe. This, to be sure, is a fiction; but it shows the prevalent opinion, the feeling, the conviction, of absolute, universal, irremediable deterioration."

"I should be sorry," said Mr Foster, "that such an opinion should become universal, independently of my conviction of its fallacy. Its general admission would tend, in a great measure, to produce the very evils it appears to lament. What could be its effect, but to check the ardour of investigation, to extinguish the zeal of philanthropy, to freeze the current of enterprising hope, to bury in the torpor of scepticism and in the stagnation of despair, every better faculty of the human mind, which will necessarily become retrograde in ceasing to be progressive?"

"I am inclined to think, on the contrary," said Mr Escot, "that the deterioration of man is accelerated by his blindness—in many respects wilful blindness—to the truth of the fact itself, and to the causes which produce it; that there is no hope whatever of ameliorating his condition but in a total and radical change of the whole scheme of human life, and that the advocates of his indefinite perfectibility are in reality the greatest enemies to the practical possibility of their own system, by so strenuously labouring to impress on his attention that he is going on in a good way, while he is really in a deplorably bad one."

"I admit," said Mr Foster, "there are many things that may, and therefore will, be changed for the better."

"Not on the present system," said Mr Escot, "in which every change is for the worse."

"In matters of taste I am sure it is," said Mr Gall: "there is, in fact, no such thing as good taste left in the world."

"Oh, Mr Gall!" said Miss Philomela Poppyseed, "I thought my novel—"

178

"My paintings," said Sir Patrick O'Prism—

"My ode," said Mr Mac Laurel—

"My ballad," said Mr Nightshade—

"My plan for Lord Littlebrain's park," said Marmaduke Milestone, Esquire—

"My essay," said Mr Treacle—

"My sonata," said Mr Chromatic—

"My claret," said Squire Headlong—

"My lectures," said Mr Cranium—

"Vanity of vanities," said the Reverend Doctor Gaster, turning down an empty egg-shell; "all is vanity and vexation of spirit."

CHAPTER XI

THE ANNIVERSARY

AMONG the *dies albâ cretâ notandos*, which the beau monde of the Cambrian mountains was in the habit of remembering with the greatest pleasure, and anticipating with the most lively satisfaction, was the Christmas ball which the ancient family of the Headlongs had been accustomed to give from time immemorial. Tradition attributed the honour of its foundation to Headlong Ap-Headlong Ap-Breakneck Ap-Headlong Ap-Cataract Ap-Pistyll Ap-Rhaidr[1] Ap-Headlong, who lived about the time of the Trojan war. Certain it is, at least, that a grand chorus was always sung after supper in honour of this illustrious ancestor of the squire. This ball was, indeed, an æra in the lives of all the beauty and fashion of Caernarvon, Meirionnydd, and Anglesea, and, like the Greek Olympiads and the Roman consulates, served as the main pillar of memory, round which all the events of the year were suspended and entwined. Thus, in recalling to mind any circumstance imperfectly recollected, the principal point to be ascertained was, whether it had occurred in the year of the first, second, third, or fourth ball of Headlong Ap-Breakneck, or Headlong Ap-Torrent, or Headlong Ap-Hurricane; and, this being satisfactorily established, the remainder followed of course in the natural order of its ancient association.

This eventful anniversary being arrived, every chariot, coach, barouche and barouchette, landau and landaulet, chaise, curricle, buggy, whiskey, and tilbury, of the three counties, was in motion: not a horse was left idle within five miles of any gentleman's seat, from the high-mettled hunter to the heath-cropping galloway. The ferrymen of the Menai were at their stations before daybreak, taking a double allowance of rum and *cwrw* to strengthen them for the fatigues of the day. The ivied towers of Caernarvon, the romantic woods of Tan-y-bwlch, the heathy hills of Kernioggau, the sandy shores of Tremadoc, the mountain recesses of Bedd-Gelert, and the lonely lakes of Capel-Cerig, re-echoed to the voices of the delighted ostlers and postillions, who reaped on this happy day their wintry harvest. Landlords and landladies, waiters, chambermaids, and toll-gate keepers, roused themselves from the torpidity which the last solitary tourist, flying with the yellow leaves on the wings of the autumnal wind, had left them to enjoy till the returning spring: the bustle of August was renewed on all the mountain roads, and, in the meanwhile, Squire Headlong and his little fat butler carried most energetically into effect the lessons of the *savant* in the Court of Quintessence, *qui par engin mirificque jectoit les maisons par les fenestres*[2].

It was the custom for the guests to assemble at dinner on the day of the ball, and depart on the following morning after breakfast. Sleep during this interval was out of the question: the ancient harp of Cambria suspended the celebration of the noble race of Shenkin, and the songs of Hoel and Cyveilioc, to ring to the profaner but more lively modulation of *Voulez vous danser, Mademoiselle?* in conjunction with the symphonious scraping of fiddles, the tinkling of triangles, and the beating of tambourines. Comus and Momus were the deities of the night; and Bacchus of course was not forgotten by the male part of the assembly (with them, indeed, a ball was invariably a scene of *"tipsy dance and jollity"*): the servants flew about with wine and negus, and the little butler was indefatigable with his corkscrew, which is reported on one occasion to have grown so hot under the influence of perpetual friction that it actually set fire to the cork.

The company assembled. The dinner, which on this occasion was a secondary object, was despatched with uncommon celerity. When the cloth was removed, and the bottle had taken its first round, Mr Cranium stood up and addressed the company.

"Ladies and gentlemen," said he, "the golden key of mental phænomena, which has lain buried for ages in the deepest vein of the mine of physiological research, is now, by a happy combination of practical and speculative investigations, grasped, if I may so express myself, firmly and inexcusably, in the hands of physiognomical empiricism." The Cambrian visitors listened with profound attention, not comprehending a single syllable he said, but concluding he would finish his speech by proposing the health of Squire Headlong. The gentlemen accordingly tossed off their heeltaps, and Mr Cranium proceeded: "Ardently desirous, to the extent of my feeble capacity, of disseminating as much as possible, the inexhaustible treasures to which this golden key admits the humblest votary of philosophical truth, I invite you, when you have sufficiently restored, replenished, refreshed, and exhilarated that osteosarchæ-matosplanchnochondroneuromuelous, or to employ a more intelligible term, osseocarnisanguineoviscericartilaginonervomedullary, *compages*, or shell, the body, which at once envelopes and developes that mysterious and inestimable kernel, the desiderative, determinative, ratiocinative, imaginative, inquisitive, appetitive, comparative, reminiscent, congeries of ideas and notions, simple and compound, comprised in the comprehensive denomination of mind, to take a peep with me into the mechanical arcana of the anatomico-metaphysical universe. Being not in the least dubitative of your spontaneous compliance, I proceed," added he, suddenly changing his tone, "to get everything ready in the library." Saying these words, he vanished.

The Welsh squires now imagined they had caught a glimpse of his meaning, and set him down in their minds for a sort of gentleman conjuror, who intended to amuse them before the ball with some tricks of legerdemain. Under this impression, they became very impatient to follow him, as they had made up their minds not to be drunk before supper. The ladies, too, were extremely curious to witness an exhibition

182

which had been announced in so singular a preamble; and the squire, having previously insisted on every gentleman tossing off a half-pint bumper, adjourned the whole party to the library, where they were not a little surprised to discover Mr Cranium seated, in a pensive attitude, at a large table, decorated with a copious variety of skulls.

Some of the ladies were so much shocked at this extraordinary display, that a scene of great confusion ensued. Fans were very actively exercised, and water was strenuously called for by some of the most officious of the gentlemen; on which the little butler entered with a large allowance of liquid, which bore, indeed, the name of *water*, but was in reality a very powerful spirit. This was the only species of water which the little butler had ever heard called for in Headlong Hall. The mistake was not attended with any evil effects: for the fluid was no sooner applied to the lips of the fainting fair ones, than it resuscitated them with an expedition truly miraculous.

Order was at length restored; the audience took their seats, and the craniological orator held forth in the following terms:

CHAPTER XII

THE LECTURE

"PHYSIOLOGISTS have been much puzzled to account for the varieties of moral character in men, as well as for the remarkable similarity of habit and disposition in all the individual animals of every other respective species. A few brief sentences, perspicuously worded, and scientifically arranged, will enumerate all the characteristics of a lion, or a tiger, or a wolf, or a bear, or a squirrel, or a goat, or a horse, or an ass, or a rat, or a cat, or a hog, or a dog; and whatever is physiologically predicted of any individual lion, tiger, wolf, bear, squirrel, goat, horse, ass, hog, or dog, will be found to hold true of all lions, tigers, wolves, bears, squirrels, goats, horses, asses, hogs, and dogs, whatsoever. Now, in man, the very reverse of this appears to be the case; for he has so few distinct and characteristic marks which hold true of all his species, that philosophers in all ages have found it a task of infinite difficulty to give him a definition. Hence one has defined him to be a *featherless biped*, a definition which is equally applicable to an unfledged fowl: another to be *an animal which forms opinions*, than which nothing can be more inaccurate, for a very small number of the species form opinions, and the remainder take them upon trust, without investigation or inquiry.

"Again, man has been defined to be *an animal that carries a stick*: an attribute which undoubtedly belongs to man only, but not to all men always; though it uniformly characterises some of the graver and more imposing varieties, such as physicians, oran-outangs, and lords in waiting.

"We cannot define man to be a reasoning animal, for we do not dispute that idiots are men; to say nothing of that very numerous description of persons who consider themselves reasoning animals, and are so denominated by the ironical courtesy of the world, who labour, nevertheless, under a very gross delusion in that essential particular.

"It appears to me that man may be correctly defined an animal, which, without any peculiar or distinguishing faculty of its own, is, as it were, a bundle or compound of faculties of other animals, by a distinct enumeration of which any individual of the species may be satisfactorily described. This is manifest, even in the ordinary language of conversation, when, in summing up, for example, the qualities of an accomplished courtier, we say he has the vanity of a peacock, the cunning of a fox, the treachery of an hyæna, the cold-heartedness of a cat, and the servility of a jackal. That this is perfectly consentaneous to scientific truth, will appear in the further progress of these observations.

"Every particular faculty of the mind has its corresponding organ in the brain. In proportion as any particular faculty or propensity acquires paramount activity in any individual, these organs develope themselves, and their development becomes externally obvious by corresponding lumps and bumps, exuberances and protuberances, on the osseous compages of the occiput and sinciput. In all animals but man, the same organ is equally developed in every individual of the species: for instance, that of migration in the swallow, that of destruction in the tiger, that of architecture in the beaver, and that of parental affection in the bear. The human brain, however, consists, as I have said, of a bundle or compound of all the faculties of all other animals; and from the greater development of one or more of these, in the infinite varieties of combination, result all the peculiarities of individual character.

"Here is the skull of a beaver, and that of Sir Christopher Wren. You observe, in both these specimens, the prodigious development of the organ of constructiveness.

"Here is the skull of a bullfinch, and that of an eminent fiddler. You may compare the organ of music.

"Here is the skull of a tiger. You observe the organ of carnage. Here is the skull of a fox. You observe the organ of plunder. Here is the skull of a peacock. You observe the organ of vanity. Here is the skull of an illustrious robber, who, after a long and triumphant process of depredation and murder, was suddenly checked in his career by means of a certain quality inherent in preparations of hemp, which, for the sake of perspicuity, I shall call *suspensiveness*. Here is the skull of a conqueror, who, after over-running several kingdoms, burning a number of cities, and causing the deaths of two or three millions of men, women, and children, was entombed with all the pageantry of public lamentation, and figured as the hero of several thousand odes and a round dozen of epics; while the poor highwayman was twice executed—

'At the gallows first, and after in a ballad,
Sung to a villainous tune.'

"You observe, in both these skulls, the combined development of the organs of carnage, plunder, and vanity, which I have separately pointed out in the tiger, the fox, and the peacock. The greater enlargement of the organ of vanity in the hero is the only criterion by which I can distinguish them from each other. Born with the same faculties, and the same propensities, these two men were formed by nature to run the same career: the different combinations of external circumstances decided the differences of their destinies.

"Here is the skull of a Newfoundland dog. You observe the organ of benevolence, and that of attachment. Here is a human skull, in which you may observe a very striking negation of both these organs; and an equally striking development of those of destruction, cunning, avarice, and self-love. This was one of the most illustrious statesmen that ever flourished in the page of history.

186

"Here is the skull of a turnspit, which, after a wretched life of *dirty work*, was turned out of doors to die on a dunghill. I have been induced to preserve it, in consequence of its remarkable similarity to this, which belonged to a courtly poet, who having grown grey in flattering the great, was cast off in the same manner to perish by the same catastrophe."

After these, and several other illustrations, during which the skulls were handed round for the inspection of the company, Mr Cranium proceeded thus:—

"It is obvious, from what I have said, that no man can hope for worldly honour or advancement, who is not placed in such a relation to external circumstances as may be consentaneous to his peculiar cerebral organs; and I would advise every parent, who has the welfare of his son at heart, to procure as extensive a collection as possible of the skulls of animals, and, before determining on the choice of a profession, to compare with the utmost nicety their bumps and protuberances with those of the skull of his son. If the development of the organ of destruction point out a similarity between the youth and the tiger, let him be brought to some profession (whether that of a butcher, a soldier, or a physician, may be regulated by circumstances) in which he may be furnished with a licence to kill: as, without such licence, the indulgence of his natural propensity may lead to the untimely rescission of his vital thread, 'with edge of penny cord and vile reproach.' If he show an analogy with the jackal, let all possible influence be used to procure him a place at court, where he will infallibly thrive. If his skull bear a marked resemblance to that of a magpie, it cannot be doubted that he will prove an admirable lawyer; and if with this advantageous conformation be combined any similitude to that of an owl, very confident hopes may be formed of his becoming a judge."

A furious flourish of music was now heard from the ball-room, the squire having secretly dispatched the little butler to order it to strike up, by way of a hint to Mr Cranium to finish his harangue. The company took the hint and adjourned tumultuously, having just understood as much of the lecture as furnished them with amusement for the ensuing twelvemonth, in feeling the skulls of all their acquaintance.

CHAPTER XIII

THE BALL

THE ball-room was adorned with great taste and elegance, under the direction of Miss Caprioletta and her friend Miss Cephalis, who were themselves its most beautiful ornaments, even though romantic Meirion, the pre-eminent in loveliness, sent many of its loveliest daughters to grace the festive scene. Numberless were the solicitations of the dazzled swains of Cambria for the honour of the two first dances with the one or the other of these fascinating friends; but little availed, on this occasion, the pedigree lineally traced from Caractacus or King Arthur; their two philosophical lovers, neither of whom could have given the least account of his great-great-grandfather, had engaged them many days before. Mr Panscope chafed and fretted like Llugwy in his bed of rocks, when the object of his adoration stood up with his rival: but he consoled himself with a lively damsel from the vale of Edeirnion, having first compelled Miss Cephalis to promise him her hand for the fourth set.

The ball was accordingly opened by Miss Caprioletta and Mr Foster, which gave rise to much speculation among the Welsh gentry, as to who this Mr Foster could be; some of the more learned among them secretly resolving to investigate most profoundly the antiquity of the name of Foster, and ascertain what right a person so denominated could have to open the most illustrious of all possible balls with the lovely Caprioletta Headlong, the only sister of Harry Headlong, Esquire, of Headlong Hall, in the Vale of Llanberris, the only surviving male representative of the antediluvian family of Headlong Ap-Rhaiader.

When the first two dances were ended, Mr Escot, who did not choose to dance with any one but his adorable Cephalis, looking round for a convenient seat, discovered Mr Jenkison in a corner by the side of the Reverend Doctor Gaster, who was keeping excellent time with his nose to the lively melody of the harp and fiddle. Mr Escot seated himself by the side of Mr Jenkison, and inquired if he took no part in the amusement of the night?

Mr Jenkison. No. The universal cheerfulness of the company induces me to rise; the trouble of such violent exercise induces me to sit still. Did I see a young lady in want of a partner, gallantry would incite me to offer myself as her devoted knight for half an hour: but, as I perceive there are enough without me, that motive is null. I have been weighing these points *pro* and *con*, and remain *in statu quo*.

Mr Escot. I have danced, contrary to my system, as I have done many other things since I have been here, from a motive that you will easily guess. (*Mr Jenkison smiled.*) I have great objections to dancing. The wild and original man is a calm and contemplative animal. The stings of natural appetite alone rouse him to action. He satisfies his hunger with roots and fruits, unvitiated by the malignant adhibition of fire, and all its diabolical processes of elixion and assation; he slakes his thirst in the mountain-stream, συμμίσγεται τη επιτυχούση, and returns to his peaceful state of meditative repose.

Mr Jenkison. Like the metaphysical statue of Condillac.

Mr Escot. With all its senses and purely natural faculties developed, certainly. Imagine this tranquil and passionless being, occupied in his first meditation on the simple question of *Where am I? Whence do I come? And what is the end of my existence?* Then suddenly place before him a chandelier, a fiddler, and a magnificent beau in silk stockings and pumps, bounding, skipping, swinging, capering, and throwing himself into ten thousand attitudes, till his face glows with fever, and distils with perspiration: the first impulse excited in his mind by such an apparition will be that of violent fear, which, by the reiterated perception of its harmlessness, will subside into simple astonishment. Then let any genius, sufficiently powerful to impress on his mind all the terms of the communication, impart to him, that after a long process of ages, when his race shall have attained what some people think proper to denominate a very advanced stage of perfectibility, the most favoured and distinguished of the community shall meet by hundreds, to grin, and labour, and gesticulate, like the phantasma before him, from sunset to sunrise, while all nature is at rest, and that they shall consider this a happy and pleasurable mode of existence, and furnishing the most delightful of all possible contrasts to what they will call his vegetative state: would he not groan from his inmost soul for the lamentable condition of his posterity?

Mr Jenkison. I know not what your wild and original man might think of the matter in the abstract; but comparatively, I conceive, he would be better pleased with the vision of such a scene as this, than with that of a party of Indians (who would have all the advantage of being nearly as wild as himself), dancing their infernal war-dance round a midnight fire in a North American forest.

Mr Escot. Not if you should impart to him the true nature of both, by laying open to his view the springs of action in both parties.

Mr Jenkison. To do this with effect, you must make him a profound metaphysician, and thus transfer him at once from his wild and original state to a very advanced stage of intellectual progression; whether that progression be towards good or evil, I leave you and our friend Foster to settle between you.

Mr Escot. I wish to make no change in his habits and feelings, but to give him, hypothetically, so much mental illumination, as will enable him to take a clear view of two distinct stages of the deterioration of his posterity, that he may be enabled to compare them with each other, and with his own more happy condition. The Indian, dancing round the midnight fire, is very far deteriorated; but the magnificent beau, dancing to the light of chandeliers, is infinitely more so. The Indian is a hunter: he makes great use of fire, and subsists almost entirely on animal food. The malevolent passions that spring from these pernicious habits involve him in perpetual war. He is, therefore, necessitated, for his own preservation, to keep all the energies of his nature in constant activity: to this end his midnight war-dance is very powerfully subservient, and, though in itself a frightful spectacle, is at least justifiable on the iron plea of necessity.

Mr Jenkison. On the same iron plea, the modern system of dancing is more justifiable. The Indian dances to prepare himself for killing his enemy: but while the beaux and belles of our assemblies dance, they are in the very act of killing theirs—TIME!—a more inveterate and formidable foe than any the Indian has to contend with; for, however completely and ingeniously killed, he is sure to rise again, "with twenty mortal murders on his crown," leading his army of blue devils, with ennui in the van, and vapours in the rear.

Mr Escot. Your observation militates on my side of the question; and it is a strong argument in favour of the Indian, that he has no such enemy to kill.

Mr Jenkison. There is certainly a great deal to be said against dancing: there is also a great deal to be said in its favour. The first side of the question I leave for the present to you: on the latter, I may venture to allege that no amusement seems more natural and more congenial to youth than this. It has the advantage of bringing young persons of both sexes together, in a manner which its publicity renders perfectly unexceptionable, enabling them to see and know each other better than, perhaps, any other mode of general association. *Tête-à-têtes* are dangerous things. Small family parties are too much under mutual observation. A ball-room appears to me almost the only scene uniting that degree of rational and innocent liberty of intercourse, which it is desirable to promote as much as possible between young persons, with that scrupulous attention to the delicacy and propriety of female conduct, which I consider the fundamental basis of all our most valuable social relations.

Mr Escot. There would be some plausibility in your argument, if it were not the very essence of this species of intercourse to exhibit them to each other under false colours. Here all is show, and varnish, and hypocrisy, and coquetry; they dress up their moral character for the evening at the same toilet where they manufacture their shapes and faces. Ill-temper lies buried under a studied accumulation of smiles. Envy, hatred, and malice, retreat from the countenance, to entrench themselves more deeply in the heart. Treachery lurks under the flowers of courtesy. Ignorance and folly take refuge in that unmeaning gabble which it would be profanation to call language, and which even those whom long experience in "the dreary intercourse of daily life" has screwed up to such a pitch of stoical endurance that they can listen to it by the hour, have branded with the ignominious appellation of "*small talk.*" Small indeed!— the absolute minimum of the infinitely little.

Mr Jenkison. Go on. I have said all I intended to say on the favourable side. I shall have great pleasure in hearing you balance the argument.

Mr Escot. I expect you to confess that I shall have more than balanced it. A ball-room is an epitome of all that is most worthless and unamiable in the great sphere of human life. Every petty and malignant passion is called into play. Coquetry is perpetually on the alert to captivate, caprice to mortify, and vanity to take offence. One amiable female is rendered miserable for the evening by seeing another, whom she intended to outshine, in a more attractive dress than her own; while the other omits no method of giving stings to her triumph, which she enjoys with all the secret arrogance of an oriental sultana. Another is compelled to dance with a *monster* she abhors. A third has set her heart on dancing with a particular partner, perhaps for the amiable motive of annoying one of her *dear friends*: not only he does not ask her, but she sees him dancing with that identical *dear friend*, whom from that moment she hates more cordially than ever. Perhaps, what is worse than all, she has set her heart on refusing some impertinent fop, who does not give her the opportunity.—As to the men, the case is very nearly the same with them. To be sure, they have the privilege of making the first advances, and are, therefore, less liable to have an odious partner forced upon them; though this sometimes happens, as I know by woeful experience: but it is seldom they can procure the very partner they prefer; and when they do, the absurd necessity of changing every two dances forces them away, and leaves them only the miserable alternative of taking up with something disagreeable perhaps in itself, and at all events rendered so by contrast, or of retreating into some solitary corner, to vent their spleen on the first idle coxcomb they can find.

Mr Jenkison. I hope that is not the motive which brings you to me.

Mr Escot. Clearly not. But the most afflicting consideration of all is, that these malignant and miserable feelings are masked under that uniform disguise of pretended benevolence, *that fine and delicate irony, called politeness, which gives so much ease and pliability to the mutual intercourse of civilised man, and enables him to assume the appearance of every virtue without the reality of one.*[1]

The second set of dances was now terminated, and Mr Escot flew off to reclaim the hand of the beautiful Cephalis, with whom he figured away with surprising alacrity, and probably felt at least as happy among the chandeliers and silk stockings, at which he had just been railing, as he would have been in an American forest, making one in an Indian ring, by the light of a blazing fire, even though his hand had been locked in that of the most beautiful *squaw* that ever listened to the roar of Niagara.

Squire Headlong was now beset by his maiden aunt, Miss Brindle-mew Grimalkin Phœbe Tabitha Ap-Headlong, on one side, and Sir Patrick O'Prism on the other; the former insisting that he should immediately procure her a partner; the latter earnestly requesting the same interference in behalf of Miss Philomela Poppyseed. The squire thought to emancipate himself from his two petitioners by making them dance with each other; but Sir Patrick vehemently pleading a prior engagement, the squire threw his eyes around till they alighted on Mr Jenkison and the Reverend Doctor Gaster; both of whom, after waking the latter, he pressed into the service. The doctor, arising with a strange kind of guttural sound, which was half a yawn and half a groan, was handed by the officious squire to Miss Philomela, who received him with sullen dignity: she had not yet forgotten his falling asleep during the first chapter of her novel, while she was condescending to detail to him the outlines of four superlative volumes. The doctor, on his part, had most completely forgotten it; and though he thought there was something in her physiognomy rather more forbidding than usual, he gave himself no concern about the cause, and had not the least suspicion that it was at all connected with himself. Miss Brindle-mew was very well contented with Mr Jenkison, and gave him two or three ogles, accompanied by a most risible distortion of the countenance which she intended for a captivating smile. As to Mr Jenkison, it was all one to him with whom he danced, or whether he danced or not: he was therefore just as well pleased as if he had been left alone in his corner; which is probably more than could have been said of any other human being under similar circumstances.

At the end of the third set, supper was announced; and the party, pairing off like turtles, adjourned to the supper-room. The squire was now the happiest of mortal men, and the little butler the most laborious. The centre of the largest table was decorated with a model of Snowdon, surmounted with an enormous artificial leek, the leaves of angelica, and the bulb of blancmange. A little way from the summit was a tarn, or mountain-pool, supplied through concealed tubes with an inexhaustible flow of milk-punch, which, dashing in cascades down the miniature rocks, fell into the more capacious lake below, washing the mimic foundations of Headlong Hall. The reverend doctor handed Miss Philomela to the chair most conveniently situated for enjoying this interesting scene, protesting he had never before been sufficiently impressed with the magnificence of that mountain, which he now perceived to be well worthy of all the fame it had obtained.

"Now, when they had eaten and were satisfied," Squire Headlong called on Mr Chromatic for a song; who, with the assistance of his two accomplished daughters, regaled the ears of the company with the following

TERZETTO[2]

Grey Twilight, from her shadowy hill,
    Discolours Nature's vernal bloom,
And sheds on grove, and field, and rill,
    One placid tint of deepening gloom.

The sailor sighs 'mid shoreless seas,
    Touched by the thought of friends afar,
As, fanned by ocean's flowing breeze,
    He gazes on the western star.

The wanderer hears, in pensive dream,
    The accents of the last farewell,
As, pausing by the mountain stream,
    He listens to the evening bell.

This terzetto was of course much applauded; Mr Milestone observing, that he thought the figure in the last verse would have been more picturesque, if it had been represented with its arms folded and its back against a tree; or leaning on its staff, with a cockle-shell in its hat, like a pilgrim of ancient times.

Mr Chromatic professed himself astonished that a gentleman of genuine modern taste, like Mr Milestone, should consider the words of a song of any consequence whatever, seeing that they were at the best only a species of pegs, for the more convenient suspension of crotchets and quavers. This remark drew on him a very severe reprimand from Mr Mac Laurel, who said to him, "Dinna ye ken, sir, that soond is a thing utterly worthless in itsel, and only effectual in agreeable excitements, as far as it is an aicho to sense? Is there ony soond mair meeserable an' peetifu' than the scrape o' a feddle, when it does na touch ony chord i' the human sensorium? Is there ony mair divine than the deep note o' a bagpipe, when it breathes the auncient meelodies o' leeberty an' love? It is true, there are peculiar trains o' feeling an' sentiment, which parteecular combinations o' meelody are calculated to excite; an' sae far music can produce its effect without words: but it does na follow, that, when ye put words to it, it becomes a matter of indeeference what they are; for a gude strain of impassioned poetry will greatly increase the effect, and a tessue o' nonsensical doggrel will destroy it a' thegither. Noo, as gude poetry can produce its effect without music, sae will gude music without poetry; and as gude music will be mair pooerfu' by itsel' than wi' bad poetry, sae will gude poetry than wi' bad music: but, when ye put gude music an' gude poetry thegither, ye produce the divinest compound o' sentimental harmony that can possibly find its way through the lug to the saul."

Mr Chromatic admitted that there was much justice in these observations, but still maintained the subserviency of poetry to music. Mr Mac Laurel as strenuously maintained the contrary; and a furious war of words was proceeding to perilous lengths, when the squire interposed his authority towards the reproduction of peace, which was forthwith

196

concluded, and all animosities drowned in a libation of milk-punch, the Reverend Doctor Gaster officiating as high priest on the occasion.

Mr Chromatic now requested Miss Caprioletta to favour the company with an air. The young lady immediately complied, and sung the following simple

BALLAD

"O Mary, my sister, thy sorrow give o'er,
I soon shall return, girl, and leave thee no more:
But with children so fair, and a husband so kind,
I shall feel less regret when I leave thee behind.

"I have made thee a bench for the door of thy cot,
And more would I give thee, but more I have not:
Sit and think of me there, in the warm summer day,
And give me three kisses, my labour to pay."

She gave him three kisses, and forth did he fare.
And long did he wander, and no one knew where;
And long from her cottage, through sunshine and rain,
She watched his return, but he came not again.

Her children grew up, and her husband grew grey;
She sate on the bench through the long summer day:
One evening, when twilight was deep on the shore,
There came an old soldier, and stood by the door.

In English he spoke, and none knew what he said,
But her oatcake and milk on the table she spread;
Then he sate to his supper, and blithely he sung,
And she knew the dear sounds of her own native tongue:

"O rich are the feasts in the Englishman's hall,
And the wine sparkles bright in the goblets of Gaul:
But their mingled attractions I well could withstand,
For the milk and the oatcake of Meirion's dear land."

"And art thou a Welchman, old soldier?" she cried.
"Many years have I wandered," the stranger replied:
"'Twixt Danube and Thames many rivers there be,
But the bright waves of Cynfael are fairest to me.

"I felled the grey oak, ere I hastened to roam,
And I fashioned a bench for the door of my home;
And well my dear sister my labour repaid,
Who gave me three kisses when first it was made.

"In the old English soldier thy brother appears:
Here is gold in abundance, the saving of years:
Give me oatcake and milk in return for my store,
And a seat by thy side on the bench at the door."

Various other songs succeeded, which, as we are not composing a song book, we shall lay aside for the present.

An old squire, who had not missed one of these anniversaries, during more than half a century, now stood up, and filling a half-pint bumper, pronounced, with a stentorian voice—"To the immortal memory of Headlong Ap-Rhaiader, and to the health of his noble descendant and worthy representative!" This example was followed by all the gentlemen present. The harp struck up a triumphal strain; and, the old squire already mentioned, vociferating the first stave, they sang, or rather roared, the following

CHORUS

Hail to the Headlong! the Headlong Ap-Headlong!
All hail to the Headlong, the Headlong Ap-Headlong!
    The Headlong Ap-Headlong
    Ap-Breakneck Ap-Headlong
Ap-Cataract Ap-Pistyll Ap-Rhaiader Ap-Headlong!

The bright bowl we steep in the name of the Headlong:
Let the youths pledge it deep to the Headlong Ap-Headlong,
    And the rosy-lipped lasses
    Touch the brim as it passes,
And kiss the red tide for the Headlong Ap-Headlong!

The loud harp resounds in the hall of the Headlong:
The light step rebounds in the hall of the Headlong:
    Where shall music invite us,
    Or beauty delight us,
If not in the hall of the Headlong Ap-Headlong?

Huzza! to the health of the Headlong Ap-Headlong!
Fill the bowl, fill in floods, to the health of the Headlong!
    Till the stream ruby-glowing,
    On all sides o'erflowing,
Shall fall in cascades to the health of the Headlong!
    The Headlong Ap-Headlong
    Ap-Breakneck Ap-Headlong
Ap-Cataract Ap-Pistyll Ap-Rhaiader Ap-Headlong!

Squire Headlong returned thanks with an appropriate libation, and
the company re-adjourned to the ballroom, where they kept it up till
sunrise, when the little butler summoned them to breakfast.

CHAPTER XIV

THE PROPOSALS

THE chorus which celebrated the antiquity of her lineage, had been ringing all night in the ears of Miss Brindle-mew Grimalkin Phœbe Tabitha Ap-Headlong, when, taking the squire aside, while the visitors were sipping their tea and coffee, "Nephew Harry," said she, "I have been noting your behaviour, during the several stages of the ball and supper; and, though I cannot tax you with any want of gallantry, for you are a very gallant young man, Nephew Harry, very gallant—I wish I could say as much for every one" (added she, throwing a spiteful look towards a distant corner, where Mr Jenkison was sitting with great *nonchalance*, and at the moment dipping a rusk in a cup of chocolate); "but I lament to perceive that you were at least as pleased with your lakes of milk-punch, and your bottles of Champagne and Burgundy, as with any of your delightful partners. Now, though I can readily excuse this degree of incombustibility in the descendant of a family so remarkable in all ages for personal beauty as ours, yet I lament it exceedingly, when I consider that, in conjunction with your present predilection for the easy life of a bachelor, it may possibly prove the means of causing our ancient genealogical tree, which has its roots, if I may so speak, in the foundations of the world, to terminate suddenly in a point: unless you feel yourself moved by my exhortations to follow the example of all your ancestors, by choosing yourself a fitting and suitable helpmate to immortalize the pedigree of Headlong Ap-Rhaiader."

"Egad!" said Squire Headlong, "that is very true, I'll marry directly. A good opportunity to fix on some one, now they are all here; and I'll pop the question without further ceremony."

"What think you," said the old lady, "of Miss Nanny Glen-Du, the lineal descendant of Llewelyn Ap-Yorwerth?"

"She won't do," said Squire Headlong.

"What say you, then," said the lady, "to Miss Williams, of Pontyglasrhydyrallt, the descendant of the ancient family of—?"

"I don't like her," said Squire Headlong; "and as to her ancient family, that is a matter of no consequence. I have antiquity enough for two. They are all moderns, people of yesterday, in comparison with us. What signify six or seven centuries, which are the most they can make up?"

"Why, to be sure," said the aunt, "on that view of the question, it is no consequence. What think you, then, of Miss Owen, of Nidd-y-Gygfraen? She will have six thousand a year."

"I would not have her," said Squire Headlong, "if she had fifty. I'll think of somebody presently. I should like to be married on the same day with Caprioletta."

"Caprioletta!" said Miss Brindle-mew; "without my being consulted."

"Consulted!" said the squire: "I was commissioned to tell you, but somehow or other I let it slip. However, she is going to be married to my friend Mr Foster, the philosopher."

"Oh!" said the maiden aunt, "that a daughter of our ancient family should marry a philosopher! It is enough to make the bones of all the Ap-Rhaiaders turn in their graves!"

"I happen to be more enlightened," said Squire Headlong, "than any of my ancestors were. Besides, it is Caprioletta's affair, not mine. I tell you, the matter is settled, fixed, determined; and so am I, to be married on the same day. I don't know, now I think of it, whom I can choose better than one of the daughters of my friend Chromatic."

"A Saxon!" said the aunt, turning up her nose, and was commencing a vehement remonstrance; but the squire, exclaiming "Music has charms!" flew over to Mr Chromatic, and, with a hearty slap on the shoulder, asked him "how he should like him for a son-in-law?" Mr Chromatic, rubbing his shoulder, and highly delighted with the proposal, answered, "Very much indeed:" but, proceeding to ascertain which of his daughters had captivated the squire, the squire demurred, and was unable to satisfy his curiosity. "I hope," said Mr Chromatic, "it may be Tenorina; for I imagine Graziosa has conceived a *penchant* for Sir Patrick O'Prism."—"Tenorina, exactly," said Squire Headlong; and became so impatient to bring the matter to a conclusion, that Mr Chromatic undertook to communicate with his daughter immediately. The young lady proved to be as ready as the squire, and the preliminaries were arranged in little more than five minutes.

Mr Chromatic's words, that he imagined his daughter Graziosa had conceived a *penchant* for Sir Patrick O'Prism, were not lost on the squire, who at once determined to have as many companions in the scrape as possible, and who, as soon as he could tear himself from Mrs Headlong elect, took three flying bounds across the room to the baronet, and said, "So, Sir Patrick, I find you and I are going to be married?"

"Are we?" said Sir Patrick: "then sure won't I wish you joy, and myself too? for this is the first I have heard of it."

"Well," said Squire Headlong, "I have made up my mind to it, and you must not disappoint me."

"To be sure I won't, if I can help it," said Sir Patrick; "and I am very much obliged to you for taking so much trouble off my hands. And pray, now, who is it that I am to be metamorphosing into Lady O'Prism?"

"Miss Graziosa Chromatic," said the squire.

"Och violet and vermilion!" said Sir Patrick; "though I never thought of it before, I dare say she will suit me as well as another: but then you must persuade the ould Orpheus to draw out a few *notes* of rather a more magical description than those he is so fond of scraping on his crazy violin."

"To be sure he shall," said the squire; and, immediately returning to Mr Chromatic, concluded the negotiation for Sir Patrick as expeditiously as he had done for himself.

The squire next addressed himself to Mr Escot: "Here are three couple of us going to throw off together, with the Reverend Doctor Gaster for whipper-in: now, I think you cannot do better than make the fourth with Miss Cephalis; and then, as my father-in-law that is to be would say, we shall compose a very harmonious octave."

"Indeed," said Mr Escot, "nothing would be more agreeable to both of us than such an arrangement: but the old gentleman, since I first knew him, has changed, like the rest of the world, very lamentably for the worse: now, we wish to bring him to reason, if possible, though we mean to dispense with his consent, if he should prove much longer refractory."

"I'll settle him," said Squire Headlong; and immediately posted up to Mr Cranium, informing him that four marriages were about to take place by way of a merry winding up of the Christmas festivities.

"Indeed!" said Mr Cranium; "and who are the parties?"

"In the first place," said the squire, "my sister and Mr Foster: in the second, Miss Graziosa Chromatic and Sir Patrick O'Prism: in the third, Miss Tenorina Chromatic and your humble servant: and in the fourth to which, by the by, your consent is wanted—"

"Oho!" said Mr Cranium.

"Your daughter," said Squire Headlong.

"And Mr Panscope?" said Mr Cranium.

"And Mr Escot," said Squire Headlong. "What would you have better? He has ten thousand virtues."

"So has Mr Panscope," said Mr Cranium; "he has ten thousand a year."

"Virtues?" said Squire Headlong.

"Pounds," said Mr Cranium.

"I have set my mind on Mr Escot," said the squire.

"I am much obliged to you," said Mr Cranium, "for dethroning me from my paternal authority."

"Who fished you out of the water?" said Squire Headlong.

"What is that to the purpose?" said Mr Cranium. "The whole process of the action was mechanical and necessary. The application of the poker necessitated the ignition of the powder: the ignition necessitated the explosion: the explosion necessitated my sudden fright, which necessitated my sudden jump, which, from a necessity equally powerful, was in a curvilinear ascent: the descent, being in a corresponding curve, and commencing at a point perpendicular to the extreme line of the edge of the tower, I was, by the necessity of gravitation, attracted, first, through the ivy, and secondly through the hazel, and thirdly through the ash, into the water beneath. The motive or impulse thus adhibited in the person of a drowning man, was as powerful on his material compages as the force of gravitation on mine; and he could no more help jumping into the water than I could help falling into it."

"All perfectly true," said Squire Headlong; "and, on the same principle, you make no distinction between the man who knocks you down and him who picks you up."

"I make this distinction," said Mr Cranium, "that I avoid the former as a machine containing a peculiar *cataballitive* quality, which I have found to be not consentaneous to my mode of pleasurable existence; but I attach no moral merit or demerit to either of them, as these terms are usually employed, seeing that they are equally creatures of necessity, and must act as they do from the nature of their organisation. I no more blame or praise a man for what is called vice or virtue, than I tax a tuft of hemlock with malevolence, or discover great philanthropy in a field of potatoes, seeing that the men and the plants are equally incapacitated, by their original internal organisation, and the combinations and modifications of external circumstances, from being any thing but what they are. *Quod victus fateare necesse est.*"

"Yet you destroy the hemlock," said Squire Headlong, "and cultivate the potato; that is my way, at least."

"I do," said Mr Cranium; "because I know that the farinaceous qualities of the potato will tend to preserve the great requisites of unity and coalescence in the various constituent portions of my animal republic; and that the hemlock, if gathered by mistake for parsley, chopped up small with butter, and eaten with a boiled chicken, would necessitate a great derangement, and perhaps a total decomposition, of my corporeal mechanism."

"Very well," said the squire; "then you are necessitated to like Mr Escot better than Mr Panscope?"

"That is a *non sequitur*," said Mr Cranium.

"Then this is a *sequitur*," said the squire: "your daughter and Mr Escot are necessitated to love one another; and, unless you feel necessitated to adhibit your consent, they will feel necessitated to dispense with it; since it does appear to moral and political economists to be essentially inherent in the eternal fitness of things."

Mr Cranium fell into a profound reverie: emerging from which, he said, looking Squire Headlong full in the face, "Do you think Mr Escot would give me that skull?"

"Skull!" said Squire Headlong.

"Yes," said Mr Cranium, "the skull of Cadwallader."

"To be sure he will," said the squire.

"Ascertain the point," said Mr Cranium.

"How can you doubt it?" said the squire.

"I simply know," said Mr Cranium, "that if it were once in my possession, I would not part with it for any acquisition on earth, much less for a wife. I have had one: and, as marriage has been compared to a pill, I can very safely assert that *one is a dose*; and my reason for thinking that he will not part with it is, that its extraordinary magnitude tends to support his system, as much as its very marked protuberances tend to support mine; and you know his own system is of all things the dearest to every man of liberal thinking and a philosophical tendency."

The Squire flew over to Mr Escot. "I told you," said he, "I would settle him: but there is a very hard condition attached to his compliance."

"I submit to it," said Mr Escot, "be it what it may."

"Nothing less," said Squire Headlong, "than the absolute and unconditional surrender of the skull of Cadwallader."

"I resign it," said Mr Escot.

"The skull is yours," said the squire, skipping over to Mr Cranium.

"I am perfectly satisfied," said Mr Cranium.

"The lady is yours," said the squire, skipping back to Mr Escot.

"I am the happiest man alive," said Mr Escot.

"Come," said the squire, "then there is an amelioration in the state of the sensitive man."

"A slight oscillation of good in the instance of a solitary individual," answered Mr Escot, "by no means affects the solidity of my opinions concerning the general deterioration of the civilised world; which when I can be induced to contemplate with feelings of satisfaction, I doubt not but that I may be persuaded *to be in love with tortures, and to think charitably of the rack*[1]."

Saying these words, he flew off as nimbly as Squire Headlong himself, to impart the happy intelligence to his beautiful Cephalis.

Mr Cranium now walked up to Mr Panscope, to condole with him on the disappointment of their mutual hopes. Mr Panscope begged him not to distress himself on the subject, observing, that the monotonous system of female education brought every individual of the sex to so remarkable an approximation of similarity, that no wise man would suffer himself to be annoyed by a loss so easily repaired; and that there was much truth, though not much elegance, in a remark which he had heard made on a similar occasion by a post-captain of his acquaintance, "that there never was a fish taken out of the sea, but left another as good behind."

206

Mr Cranium replied that no two individuals having all the organs of the skull similarly developed, the universal resemblance of which Mr Panscope had spoken could not possibly exist. Mr Panscope rejoined; and a long discussion ensued, concerning the comparative influence of natural organisation and artificial education, in which the beautiful Cephalis was totally lost sight of, and which ended, as most controversies do, by each party continuing firm in his own opinion, and professing his profound astonishment at the blindness and prejudices of the other.

In the meanwhile, a great confusion had arisen at the outer doors, the departure of the ball-visitors being impeded by a circumstance which the experience of ages had discovered no means to obviate. The grooms, coachmen, and postillions, were all drunk. It was proposed that the gentlemen should officiate in their places: but the gentlemen were almost all in the same condition. This was a fearful dilemma: but a very diligent investigation brought to light a few servants and a few gentlemen not above *half-seas-over*, and by an equitable distribution of these rarities, the greater part of the guests were enabled to set forward, with very nearly an even chance of not having their necks broken before they reached home.

CHAPTER XV

THE CONCLUSION

THE squire and his select party of philosophers and dilettanti were again left in peaceful possession of Headlong Hall: and, as the former made a point of never losing a moment in the accomplishment of a favourite object, he did not suffer many days to elapse, before the spiritual metamorphosis of eight into four was effected by the clerical dexterity of the Reverend Doctor Gaster.

Immediately after the ceremony, the whole party dispersed, the squire having first extracted from every one of his chosen guests a positive promise to re-assemble in August, when they would be better enabled, in its most appropriate season, to form a correct judgment of Cambrian hospitality.

Mr Jenkison shook hands at parting with his two brother philosophers. "According to your respective systems," said he, "I ought to congratulate *you* on a change for the better, which I do most cordially: and to condole with *you* on a change for the worse, though, when I consider whom you have chosen, I should violate every principle of probability in doing so."

"You will do well," said Mr Foster, "to follow our example. The extensive circle of general philanthropy, which, in the present advanced stage of human nature, comprehends in its circumference the destinies of the whole species, originated, and still proceeds, from that narrower circle of domestic affection, which first set limits to the empire of selfishness, and, by purifying the passions and enlarging the affections of mankind, has given to the views of benevolence an increasing and illimitable expansion, which will finally diffuse happiness and peace over the whole surface of the world."

"The affection," said Mr Escot, "of two congenial spirits, united not by legal bondage and superstitious imposture, but by mutual confidence and reciprocal virtues, is the only counterbalancing consolation in this scene of mischief and misery. But how rarely is this the case according to the present system of marriage! So far from being a central point of expansion to the great circle of universal benevolence, it serves only to concentrate the feelings of natural sympathy in the reflected selfishness of family interest, and to substitute for the *humani nihil alienum puto* of youthful philanthropy, the *charity begins at home* of maturer years. And what accession of individual happiness is acquired by this oblivion of the general good? Luxury, despotism, and avarice have so seized and entangled nine hundred and ninety-nine out of every thousand of the human race, that the matrimonial compact, which ought to be the most easy, the most free, and the most simple of all engagements, is become the most slavish and complicated,—a mere question of finance,—a system of bargain, and barter, and commerce, and trick, and chicanery, and dissimulation, and fraud. Is there one instance in ten thousand, in which the buds of first affection are not most cruelly and hopelessly blasted, by avarice, or ambition, or arbitrary power? Females, condemned during the whole flower of their youth to a worse than monastic celibacy, irrevocably debarred from the hope to which their first affections pointed, will, at a certain period of life, as the natural delicacy of taste and feeling is gradually worn away by the attrition of society, become willing to take up with any coxcomb or scoundrel, whom that merciless and mercenary gang of cold-blooded slaves and assassins, called, in the ordinary prostitution of language *friends*, may agree in designating as a *prudent choice*. Young men, on the other hand, are driven by the same vile superstitions from the company of the most amiable and modest of the opposite sex, to that of those miserable victims and outcasts of a world which dares to call itself virtuous, whom that very society whose pernicious institutions first caused their aberrations,—consigning them, without one tear of pity or one struggle of remorse, to penury, infamy, and disease,—condemns to bear the burden of its own atrocious absurdities! Thus, the youth of one sex is consumed in slavery, disappointment, and spleen; that of the other, in frantic folly and selfish intemperance: till at length, on the necks of a couple so enfeebled, so perverted, so distempered both in body and soul, society throws the yoke of marriage: that yoke which, once rivetted on the necks of its victims, clings to them like the poisoned garments of Nessus or Medea. What can be expected from these ill-assorted yoke-fellows, but that, like two ill-tempered hounds, coupled by a tyrannical sportsman, they should drag on their indissoluble fetter, snarling and growling, and pulling in different directions? What can be expected for their wretched offspring, but sickness and suffering, premature decrepitude, and untimely death? In this, as in every other institution of civilised society, avarice, luxury, and disease constitute the TRIANGULAR HARMONY of the life of man. Avarice conducts him to the abyss of toil and crime: luxury seizes on his ill-gotten spoil; and, while he revels in her enchantments, or groans beneath her tyranny, disease bursts upon him, and sweeps him from the earth."

"Your theory," said Mr Jenkison, "forms an admirable counterpoise to your example. As far as I am attracted by the one, I am repelled by the other. Thus, the scales of my philosophical balance remain eternally equiponderant, and I see no reason to say of either of them, OIXETAI ΕΙΣ ΑΙΔΑΟ[1]."

NOTES

Chapter 1

1 Foster, quasi Φωστηρ,—from φαος and τηρεω, lucem servo, conservo, observo, custodio,—one who watches over and guards the light; a sense in which the word is often used amongst us, when we speak of *fostering* a flame.

2 Escot, quasi ες σκοτον, *in tenebras*, scilicet, intuens; one who is always looking into the dark side of the question.

3 Jenkison: This name may be derived from αιεν εξ ισων, *semper ex æqualibus*—scilicet, mensuris omnia metiens: one who from equal measures divides and distributes all things: one who from equal measures can always produce arguments on both sides of a question, with so much nicety and exactness, as to keep the said question eternally pending, and the balance of the controversy perpetually in statu quo. By an aphæresis of the *a*, an elision of the second ε, and an easy and natural mutation of ξ into κ, the derivation of this name proceeds according to the strictest principles of etymology: αιεν εξ ισων—Ιεν εξ ισων—Ιεν εκ ισων—Ιεν 'κ ισων—Ιενκισων—Ienkison—Jenkison.

4 Gaster: scilicet Γαστηρ—Venter, et præterea nihil.

Chapter 2

1 See Emmerton on the Auricula.

Chapter 3

1   Mr Knight, in a note to the Landscape, having taken the liberty of laughing at a notable device of a celebrated *improver*, for giving greatness of character to a place, and showing an undivided extent of property, by placing the family arms on the neighbouring *milestones*, the improver retorted on him with a charge of misquotation, misrepresentation, and malice prepense. Mr Knight, in the preface to the second edition of his poem, quotes the improver's words:—"The market-house, or other public edifice, or even a *mere stone with distances*, may bear the arms of the family:" and adds:—"By a *mere stone with distances*, the author of the Landscape certainly thought he meant a *milestone*; but, if he did not, any other interpretation which he may think more advantageous to himself shall readily be adopted, as it will equally answer the purpose of the quotation." The improver, however, did not condescend to explain what he really meant by a *mere stone with distances*, though he strenuously maintained that he did *not* mean a *milestone*. His idea, therefore, stands on record, invested with all the sublimity that obscurity can confer.

2   "Il est constant qu'elles se baisent de meilleur cœur, et se caressent avec plus de grace devant les hommes, fières d'aiguiser impunément leur convoitise par l'image des faveurs qu'elles savent leur faire envier."—Rousseau, *Emile*, liv. 5.

Chapter 4

1   See Price on the Picturesque.

2   See Knight on Taste, and the Edinburgh Review, No. XIV.

3   Protracted banquets have been copious sources of evil.

Chapter 5

1   See Lord Monboddo's Ancient Metaphysics.
2   Drummond's Academical Questions.
3   Homer is proved to have been a lover of wine by the praises he bestows upon it.
4   A cup of wine at hand, to drink as inclination prompts.

Chapter 6

1   See Knight on Taste.
2   This stanza is imitated from Machiavelli's *Capitolo dell' Occasione*.

Chapter 7

1   Fragments of a demolished world.
2   Took's Diversions of Purley.

Chapter 8

1   Some readers will, perhaps, recollect the Archbishop of Prague, who also was an excellent sportsman, and who,

> Com' era scritto in certi suoi giornali,
> Ucciso avea con le sue proprie mani
> Un numero infinito d'animali:
> Cinquemila con quindici fagiani,
> Seimila lepri, ottantantrè cignali,
> E per disgrazia, ancor *tredici cani*, &c.

Chapter 9

1   Me miserable! and thrice miserable! and four times, and five times, and twelve times, and ten thousand times miserable!

2   Pronounced cooroo—the Welsh word for *ale*.

Chapter 10

1   Long since dead.

2   Georg. I. 199.

3   Sat. XIII. 28.

4   Carm. III. 6, 46.

Chapter 11

1   Pistyll, in Welch, signifies a cataract, and Rhaidr a cascade.

2   Rabelais.

Chapter 13

1   Rousseau, Discours sur les Sciences.

2   Imitated from a passage in the Purgatorio of Dante.

Chapter 14

1   Jeremy Taylor.

Chapter 15

1   *It descends to the shades*: or, in other words, *it goes to the devil.*

CROTCHET CASTLE

INTRODUCTION

Thomas Love Peacock was born at Weymouth in 1785. His first poem, "The Genius of the Thames," was in its second edition when he became one of the friends of Shelley. That was in 1812, when Shelley's age was twenty, Peacock's twenty-seven. The acquaintance strengthened, until Peacock became the friend in whose judgment Shelley put especial trust. There were many points of agreement. Peacock, at that time, shared, in a more practical way, Shelley's desire for root and branch reform; both wore poets, although not equally gifted, and both loved Plato and the Greek tragedians. In "Crotchet Castle" Peacock has expressed his own delight in Greek literature through the talk of the Reverend Dr. Folliott.

But Shelley's friendship for Peacock included a trust in him that was maintained by points of unlikeness. Peacock was shrewd and witty. He delighted in extravagance of a satire which usually said more than it meant, but always rested upon a foundation of good sense. Then also there was a touch of the poet to give grace to the utterances of a clear-headed man of the world. It was Peacock who gave its name to Shelley's poem of "Alastor, or the Spirit of Solitude," published in 1816. The "Spirit of Solitude" being treated as a spirit of evil, Peacock suggested calling it "Alastor," since the Greek [Greek text] means an evil genius.

Peacock's novels are unlike those of other men: they are the genuine expressions of an original and independent mind. His reading and his thinking ran together; there is free quotation, free play of wit and satire, grace of invention too, but always unconventional. The story is always pleasant, although always secondary to the play of thought for which it gives occasion. He quarrelled with verse, whimsically but in all seriousness, in an article on "The Four Ages of Poetry," contributed in 1820 to a short-lived journal, "Ollier's Literary Miscellany." The four ages were, he said, the iron age, the Bardic; the golden, the Homeric; the silver, the Virgilian; and the brass, in which he himself lived. "A poet in our time," he said, "is a semi-barbarian in a civilised community . . . The highest inspirations of poetry are resolvable into three ingredients: the rant of unregulated passion, the whining of exaggerated feeling, and the cant of factitious sentiment; and can, therefore, serve only to ripen a splendid lunatic like Alexander, a puling driveller like Werter, or a morbid dreamer like Wordsworth." In another part of this essay he says: "While the historian and the philosopher are advancing in and accelerating the progress of knowledge, the poet is wallowing in the rubbish of departed ignorance, and raking up the ashes of dead savages to find gewgaws and rattles for the grown babies of the age. Mr. Scott digs up the poacher and cattle-stealers of the ancient Border. Lord Byron cruises for thieves and pirates on the shores of the Morea and among the Greek islands. Mr. Southey wades through ponderous volumes of travels and old chronicles, from which he carefully selects all that is false, useless, and absurd, as being essentially poetical; and when he has a commonplace book full of monstrosities, strings them into an epic." And so forth; Peacock going on to characterise, in further illustration of his argument, Wordsworth, Coleridge, Moore, and Campbell. He did not refer to Shelley; and Shelley read his friend's whimsical attack on poetry with all good humour, proceeding to reply to it with a "Defence of Poetry," which would have appeared in the same journal, if the journal had survived. In this novel of "Crotchet Castle" there is the same good-humoured exaggeration in the treatment of "our learned friend"—Lord Brougham—to whom and to whose labours for the Diffusion of Useful Knowledge there are repeated allusions. In one case Peacock associates the labours of "our learned friend" for the general instruction of the masses with encouragement of robbery (page 172), and in another with body-snatching, or, worse,—murder for dissection (page 99). "The Lord deliver me from the learned friend!" says Dr. Folliott. Brougham's elevation to a peerage in November, 1830, as Lord Brougham and Vaux, is referred to on page 177, where he is called Sir Guy do Vaux. It is not to be forgotten, in the reading, that this story was written in 1831, the year before the passing of the Reform Bill. It ends with a scene suggested by the agricultural riots of that time. In the ninth chapter, again, there is a passage dealing with Sir Walter Scott after the fashion of the criticisms in the "Four Ages of Poetry." But this critical satire gave nobody pain. Always there was a ground-work of good sense, and the broad sweep of the satire was utterly unlike the nibbling censure of the men whose wit is tainted with ill-humour. We may see also that the poet's nature cannot be expelled. In this volume we should find the touch of a poet's hand in the tale itself when dealing with the adventures of Mr. Chainmail, while he stays at the Welsh mountain inn, if the story did not again and again break out into actual song, for it includes half-a-dozen little poems.

When Peacock wrote his attack on Poetry, he had, only two years before, produced a poem of his own—"Rhododaphne"—with a Greek fancy of the true and the false love daintily worked out. It was his chief work in verse, and gave much pleasure to a few, among them his friend Shelley. But he felt that, as the world went, he was not strong enough to help it by his singing, so he confined his writing to the novels, in which he could speak his mind in his own way, while doing his duty by his country in the East India House, where he obtained a post in 1818. From 1836 to 1856, when he retired on a pension, he was Examiner of India Correspondence. Peacock died in 1866, aged eighty-one.

H. M.

NOTE that in this tale Mac Quedy is Mac Q. E. D., son of a demonstration; Mr. Skionar, the transcendentalist, is named from Ski(as) onar, the dream of a shadow; and Mr. Philpot,—who loves rivers, is Phil(o)pot(amos).

CHAPTER I:

THE VILLA

Captain Jamy. I wad full fain hear some question 'tween you tway. HENRY V.

In one of those beautiful valleys, through which the Thames (not yet polluted by the tide, the scouring of cities, or even the minor defilement of the sandy streams of Surrey) rolls a clear flood through flowery meadows, under the shade of old beech woods, and the smooth mossy greensward of the chalk hills (which pour into it their tributary rivulets, as pure and pellucid as the fountain of Bandusium, or the wells of Scamander, by which the wives and daughters of the Trojans washed their splendid garments in the days of peace, before the coming of the Greeks); in one of those beautiful valleys, on a bold round-surfaced lawn, spotted with juniper, that opened itself in the bosom of an old wood, which rose with a steep, but not precipitous ascent, from the river to the summit of the hill, stood the castellated villa of a retired citizen. Ebenezer Mac Crotchet, Esquire, was the London-born offspring of a worthy native of the "north countrie," who had walked up to London on a commercial adventure, with all his surplus capital, not very neatly tied up in a not very clean handkerchief, suspended over his shoulder from the end of a hooked stick, extracted from the first hedge on his pilgrimage; and who, after having worked himself a step or two up the ladder of life, had won the virgin heart of the only daughter of a highly respectable merchant of

Duke's Place, with whom he inherited the honest fruits of a long series of ingenuous dealings.

Mr. Mac Crotchet had derived from his mother the instinct, and from his father the rational principle, of enriching himself at the expense of the rest of mankind, by all the recognised modes of accumulation on the windy side of the law. After passing many years in the Alley, watching the turn of the market, and playing many games almost as desperate as that of the soldier of Lucullus, the fear of losing what he had so righteously gained predominated over the sacred thirst of paper-money; his caution got the better of his instinct, or rather transferred it from the department of acquisition to that of conservation. His friend, Mr. Ramsbottom, the zodiacal mythologist, told him that he had done well to withdraw from the region of Uranus or Brahma, the Maker, to that of Saturn or Veeshnu, the Preserver, before he fell under the eye of Jupiter or Seva, the Destroyer, who might have struck him down at a blow.

It is said that a Scotchman, returning home after some years' residence in England, being asked what he thought of the English, answered: "They hanna ower muckle sense, but they are an unco braw people to live amang;" which would be a very good story, if it were not rendered apocryphal by the incredible circumstance of the Scotchman going back.

Mr. Mac Crotchet's experience had given him a just title to make, in his own person, the last-quoted observation, but he would have known better than to go back, even if himself, and not his father, had been the first comer of his line from the north. He had married an English Christian, and, having none of the Scotch accent, was ungracious enough to be ashamed of his blood. He was desirous to obliterate alike the Hebrew and Caledonian vestiges in his name, and signed himself E. M. Crotchet, which by degrees induced the majority of his neighbours to think that his name was Edward Matthew. The more effectually to sink the Mac, he christened his villa "Crotchet Castle," and determined to hand down to posterity the honours of Crotchet of Crotchet. He found it essential to his dignity to furnish himself with a coat of arms, which, after the proper ceremonies (payment being the principal), he obtained, videlicet: Crest, a crotchet rampant, in A sharp; Arms, three empty bladders, turgescent, to show how opinions are formed; three bags of gold, pendent, to show why they are maintained; three naked swords, tranchant, to show how they are administered; and three barbers' blocks, gaspant, to show how they are swallowed.

Mr. Crotchet was left a widower, with two children; and, after the death of his wife, so strong was his sense of the blessed comfort she had been to him, that he determined never to give any other woman an opportunity of obliterating the happy recollection.

He was not without a plausible pretence for styling his villa a castle, for, in its immediate vicinity, and within his own enclosed domain, were the manifest traces, on the brow of the hill, of a Roman station, or castellum, which was still called the "Castle" by the country people. The primitive mounds and trenches, merely overgrown with greensward, with a few patches of juniper and box on the vallum, and a solitary ancient beech surmounting the place of the praetorium, presented nearly the same depths, heights, slopes, and forms, which the Roman soldiers had originally given them. From this cartel Mr. Crotchet christened his villa. With his rustic neighbours he was, of course, immediately and necessarily a squire: Squire Crotchet of the Castle; and he seemed to himself to settle down as naturally into an English country gentleman, as if his parentage had been as innocent of both Scotland and Jerusalem, as his education was of Rome and Athens.

But as, though you expel nature with a pitch-fork, she will yet always come back; he could not become, like a true-born English squire, part and parcel of the barley-giving earth; he could not find in game-bagging, poacher-shooting, trespasser-pounding, footpath-stopping, common-enclosing, rack-renting, and all the other liberal pursuits and pastimes which make a country gentleman an ornament to the world and a blessing to the poor: he could not find in these valuable and amiable occupations, and in a corresponding range of ideas, nearly commensurate with that

223

of the great King Nebuchadnezzar when he was turned out to grass; he could not find in this great variety of useful action, and vast field of comprehensive thought, modes of filling up his time that accorded with his Caledonian instinct. The inborn love of disputation, which the excitements and engagements of a life of business had smothered, burst forth through the calmer surface of a rural life. He grew as fain as Captain Jamy, "to hear some argument betwixt ony tway," and being very hospitable in his establishment, and liberal in his invitations, a numerous detachment from the advanced guard of the "march of intellect," often marched down to Crotchet Castle.

When the fashionable season filled London with exhibitors of all descriptions, lecturers and else, Mr. Crotchet was in his glory; for, in addition to the perennial literati of the metropolis, he had the advantage of the visits of a number of hardy annuals, chiefly from the north, who, as the interval of their metropolitan flowering allowed, occasionally accompanied their London brethren in excursions to Crotchet Castle.

Amongst other things, he took very naturally to political economy, read all the books on the subject which were put forth by his own countrymen, attended all lectures thereon, and boxed the technology of the sublime science as expertly as an able seaman boxes the compass.

With this agreeable mania he had the satisfaction of biting his son, the hope of his name and race, who had borne off from Oxford the highest academical honours; and who, treading in his father's footsteps to honour and fortune, had, by means of a portion of the old gentleman's surplus capital, made himself a junior partner in the eminent loan-jobbing firm of Catchflat and Company. Here, in the days of paper prosperity, he applied his science-illumined genius to the blowing of bubbles, the bursting of which sent many a poor devil to the gaol, the workhouse, or the bottom of the river, but left young Crotchet rolling in riches.

These riches he had been on the point of doubling, by a marriage with the daughter of Mr. Touchandgo, the great banker, when, one foggy morning, Mr. Touchandgo and the contents of his till were suddenly reported absent; and as the fortune which the young gentleman had intended to marry was not forthcoming, this tender affair of the heart was nipped in the bud.

Miss Touchandgo did not meet the shock of separation quite so complacently as the young gentleman: for he lost only the lady, whereas she lost a fortune as well as a lover. Some jewels, which had glittered on her beautiful person as brilliantly as the bubble of her father's wealth had done in the eyes of his gudgeons, furnished her with a small portion of paper-currency; and this, added to the contents of a fairy purse of gold, which she found in her shoe on the eventful morning when Mr. Touchandgo melted into thin air, enabled her to retreat into North Wales, where she took up her lodging in a farm-house in Merionethshire, and boarded very comfortably for a trifling payment, and the additional consideration of teaching English, French, and music, to the little Ap-Llymrys. In the course of this occupation she acquired sufficient knowledge of Welsh to converse with the country people.

She climbed the mountains, and descended the dingles, with a foot which daily habit made by degrees almost as steady as a native's. She became the nymph of the scene; and if she sometimes pined in thought for her faithless Strephon, her melancholy was anything but green and yellow: it was as genuine white and red as occupation, mountain air, thyme-fed mutton, thick cream, and fat bacon could make it: to say nothing of an occasional glass of double X, which Ap-Llymry, who yielded to no man west of the Wrekin in brewage, never failed to press upon her at dinner and supper. He was also earnest, and sometimes successful, in the recommendation of his mead, and most pertinacious on winter nights in enforcing a trial of the virtues of his elder wine. The young lady's personal appearance, consequently, formed a very advantageous contrast to that of her quondam lover, whose physiognomy the intense anxieties of his bubble-blowing days, notwithstanding their triumphant result, had left blighted, sallowed, and crow's-footed, to a degree not far below that of the fallen spirit who, in the expressive language of German romance,

225

is described as "scathed by the ineradicable traces of the thunderbolts of Heaven;" so that, contemplating their relative geological positions, the poor deserted damsel was flourishing on slate, while her rich and false young knight was pining on chalk.

Squire Crotchet had also one daughter, whom he had christened Lemma, and who, as likely to be endowed with a very ample fortune was, of course, an object very tempting to many young soldiers of fortune, who were marching with the march of mind, in a good condition for taking castles, as far as not having a groat is a qualification for such exploits. She was also a glittering bait to divers young squires expectant (whose fathers were too well acquainted with the occult signification of mortgage), and even to one or two sprigs of nobility, who thought that the lining of a civic purse would superinduce a very passable factitious nap upon a thread-bare title. The young lady had received an expensive and complicated education, complete in all the elements of superficial display. She was thus eminently qualified to be the companion of any masculine luminary who had kept due pace with the "astounding progress" of intelligence. It must be confessed, that a man who has not kept due pace with it, is not very easily found: this march being one of that "astounding" character in which it seems impossible that the rear can be behind the van. The young lady was also tolerably good looking: north of Tweed, or in Palestine, she would probable have been a beauty; but for the valleys of the Thames she was perhaps a little too much to the taste of Solomon, and had a nose which rather too prominently suggested the idea of the tower of Lebanon, which looked towards Damascus.

In a village in the vicinity of the Castle was the vicarage of the Reverend Doctor Folliott, a gentleman endowed with a tolerable stock of learning, an interminable swallow, and an indefatigable pair of lungs. His pre-eminence in the latter faculty gave occasion to some etymologists to ring changes on his name, and to decide that it was derived from Follis Optimus, softened through an Italian medium into Folle Ottimo, contracted poetically into Folleotto, and elided Anglice into Folliott, signifying a first-rate pair of bellows. He claimed to be descended lineally from the illustrious Gilbert Folliott, the eminent theologian, who was a Bishop of London in the twelfth century, whose studies were interrupted in the dead of night by the Devil, when a couple of epigrams passed between them, and the Devil, of course, proved the smaller wit of the two.

This reverend gentleman, being both learned and jolly, became by degrees an indispensable ornament to the new squire's table. Mr. Crotchet himself was eminently jolly, though by no means eminently learned. In the latter respect he took after the great majority of the sons of his father's land; had a smattering of many things, and a knowledge of none; but possessed the true northern art of making the most of his intellectual harlequin's jacket, by keeping the best patches always bright and prominent.

CHAPTER II:

THE MARCH OF MIND

Quoth Ralpho: nothing but the abuse
Of human learning you produce.—BUTLER

"God bless my soul, sir!" exclaimed the Reverend Doctor Folliott, bursting, one fine May morning, into the breakfast-room at Crotchet Castle, "I am out of all patience with this march of mind. Here has my house been nearly burned down by my cook taking it into her head to study hydrostatics in a sixpenny tract, published by the Steam Intellect Society, and written by a learned friend who is for doing all the world's business as well as his own, and is equally well qualified to handle every branch of human knowledge. I have a great abomination of this learned friend; as author, lawyer, and politician, he is triformis, like Hecate; and in every one of his three forms he is bifrons, like Janus; the true Mr. Facing-both-ways of Vanity Fair. My cook must read his rubbish in bed; and, as might naturally be expected, she dropped suddenly fast asleep, overturned the candle, and set the curtains in a blaze. Luckily, the footman went into the room at the moment, in time to tear down the curtains and throw them into the chimney, and a pitcher of water on her nightcap extinguished her wick; she is a greasy subject, and would have burned like a short mould."

The reverend gentleman exhaled his grievance without looking to the right or to the left; at length, turning on his pivot, he perceived that the room was full of company, consisting of young Crotchet, and some visitors whom he had brought from London. The Reverend Doctor Folliott was introduced to Mr. Mac Quedy, the economist; Mr. Skionar, the transcendental poet; Mr. Firedamp, the meteorologist; and Lord Bossnowl, son of the Earl of Foolincourt, and member for the borough of Rogueingrain.

The divine took his seat at the breakfast-table, and began to compose his spirits by the gentle sedative of a large cup of tea, the demulcent of a well-buttered muffin, and the tonic of a small lobster.

REV. DR. FOLLIOTT. You are a man of taste, Mr. Crotchet. A man of taste is seen at once in the array of his breakfast-table. It is the foot of Hercules, the far-shining face of the great work, according to Pindar's doctrine: [Greek text]. The breakfast is the [Greek text] of the great work of the day. Chocolate, coffee, tea, cream, eggs, ham, tongue, cold fowl, all these are good, and bespeak good knowledge in him who sets them forth: but the touchstone is fish: anchovy is the first step, prawns and shrimps the second; and I laud him who reaches even to these: potted char and lampreys are the third, and a fine stretch of progression; but lobster is, indeed, matter for a May morning, and demands a rare combination of knowledge and virtue in him who sets it forth.

MR. MAC QUEDY. Well, sir, and what say you to a fine fresh trout, hot and dry, in a napkin? or a herring out of the water into the frying-pan, on the shore of Loch Fyne?

REV. DR. FOLLIOTT. Sir, I say every nation has some eximious virtue; and your country is pre-eminent in the glory of fish for breakfast. We have much to learn from you in that line at any rate.

MR. MAC QUEDY. And in many others, sir, I believe. Morals and metaphysics, politics and political economy, the way to make the most of all the modifications of smoke; steam, gas, and paper currency; you have all these to learn from us; in short, all the arts and sciences. We are the modern Athenians.

REV. DR. FOLLIOTT. I, for one, sir, am content to learn nothing from you but the art and science of fish for breakfast. Be content, sir, to rival the Boeotians, whose redeeming virtue was in fish, touching which point you may consult Aristophanes and his scholiast in the passage of Lysistrata, [Greek text], and leave the name of Athenians to those who have a sense of the beautiful, and a perception of metrical quantity.

MR. MAC QUEDY. Then, sir, I presume you set no value on the right principles of rent, profit, wages, and currency?

REV. DR. FOLLIOTT. My principles, sir, in these things are, to take as much as I can get, and pay no more than I can help. These are every man's principles, whether they be the right principles or no. There, sir, is political economy in a nutshell.

MR. MAC QUEDY. The principles, sir, which regulate production and consumption are independent of the will of any individual as to giving or taking, and do not lie in a nutshell by any means.

REV. DR. FOLLIOTT. Sir, I will thank you for a leg of that capon.

LORD BOSSNOWL. But, sir, by-the-bye, how came your footman to be going into your cook's room? It was very providential to be sure, but-

REV. DR. FOLLIOTT. Sir, as good came of it, I shut my eyes, and ask no questions. I suppose he was going to study hydrostatics, and he found himself under the necessity of practising hydraulics.

MR. FIREDAMP. Sir, you seem to make very light of science.

REV. DR. FOLLIOTT. Yes, sir, such science as the learned friend deals in: everything for everybody, science for all, schools for all, rhetoric for all, law for all, physic for all, words for all, and sense for none. I say, sir, law for lawyers, and cookery for cooks: and I wish the learned friend, for all his life, a cook that will pass her time in studying his works; then every dinner he sits down to at home, he will sit on the stool of repentance.

LORD BOSSNOWL. Now really that would be too severe: my cook should read nothing but Ude.

REV. DR. FOLLIOTT. No, sir! let Ude and the learned friend singe fowls together; let both avaunt from my kitchen. [Greek text]. Ude says an elegant supper may be given with sandwiches. Horresco referens. An elegant supper. Di meliora piis. No Ude for me. Conviviality went out with punch and suppers. I cherish their memory. I sup when I can, but not upon sandwiches. To offer me a sandwich, when I am looking for a supper, is to add insult to injury. Let the learned friend, and the modern Athenians, sup upon sandwiches.

MR. MAC QUEDY. Nay, sir; the modern Athenians know better than that. A literary supper in sweet Edinbro' would cure you of the prejudice you seem to cherish against us.

REV. DR. FOLLIOTT. Well, sir, well; there is cogency in a good supper; a good supper in these degenerate days bespeaks a good man; but much more is wanted to make up an Athenian. Athenians, indeed! where is your theatre? who among you has written a comedy? where is your Attic salt? which of you can tell who was Jupiter's great-grandfather? or what metres will successively remain, if you take off the three first syllables, one by one, from a pure antispastic acatalectic tetrameter? Now, sir, there are three questions for you: theatrical, mythological, and metrical; to every one of which an Athenian would give an answer that would lay me prostrate in my own nothingness.

MR. MAC QUEDY. Well, sir, as to your metre and your mythology, they may e'en wait a wee. For your comedy there is the "Gentle Shepherd" of the divine Allan Ramsay.

REV. DR. FOLLIOTT. The "Gentle Shepherd"! It is just as much a comedy as the Book of Job.

MR. MAC QUEDY. Well, sir, if none of us have written a comedy, I cannot see that it is any such great matter, any more than I can conjecture what business a man can have at this time of day with Jupiter's great-grandfather.

REV. DR. FOLLIOTT. The great business is, sir, that you call yourselves Athenians, while you know nothing that the Athenians thought worth knowing, and dare not show your noses before the civilised world in the practice of any one art in which they were excellent. Modern Athens, sir! the assumption is a personal affront to every man who has a Sophocles in his library. I will thank you for an anchovy.

MR. MAC QUEDY. Metaphysics, sir; metaphysics. Logic and moral philosophy. There we are at home. The Athenians only sought the way, and we have found it; and to all this we have added political economy, the science of sciences.

REV. DR. FOLLIOTT. A hyperbarbarous technology, that no Athenian ear could have borne. Premises assumed without evidence, or in spite of it; and conclusions drawn from them so logically, that they must necessarily be erroneous.

MR. SKIONAR. I cannot agree with you, Mr. Mac Quedy, that you have found the true road of metaphysics, which the Athenians only sought. The Germans have found it, sir: the sublime Kant and his disciples.

MR. MAC QUEDY. I have read the sublime Kant, sir, with an anxious desire to understand him, and I confess I have not succeeded.

REV. DR. FOLLIOTT. He wants the two great requisites of head and tail.

MR. SKIONAR. Transcendentalism is the philosophy of intuition, the development of universal convictions; truths which are inherent in the organisation of mind, which cannot be obliterated, though they may be obscured, by superstitious prejudice on the one hand, and by the Aristotelian logic on the other.

MR. MAC QUEDY. Well, sir, I have no notion of logic obscuring a question.

MR. SKIONAR. There is only one true logic, which is the transcendental; and this can prove only the one true philosophy, which is also the transcendental. The logic of your Modern Athens can prove everything equally; and that is, in my opinion, tantamount to proving nothing at all.

MR. CROTCHET. The sentimental against the rational, the intuitive against the inductive, the ornamental against the useful, the intense against the tranquil, the romantic against the classical; these are great and interesting controversies, which I should like, before I die, to see satisfactorily settled.

MR. FIREDAMP. There is another great question, greater than all these, seeing that it is necessary to be alive in order to settle any question; and this is the question of water against human life. Wherever there is water, there is malaria, and wherever there is malaria, there are the elements of death. The great object of a wise man should be to live on a gravelly hill, without so much as a duck-pond within ten miles of him, eschewing cisterns and waterbutts, and taking care that there be no gravel-pits for lodging the rain. The sun sucks up infection from water, wherever it exists on the face of the earth.

REV. DR. FOLLIOTT. Well, sir, you have for you the authority of the ancient mystagogue, who said: [Greek text]. For my part I care not a rush (or any other aquatic and inesculent vegetable) who or what sucks up either the water or the infection. I think the proximity of wine a matter of much more importance than the longinquity of water. You are here within a quarter of a mile of the Thames, but in the cellar of my friend, Mr. Crotchet, there is the talismanic antidote of a thousand dozen of old wine; a beautiful spectacle, I assure you, and a model of arrangement.

MR. FIREDAMP. Sir, I feel the malignant influence of the river in every part of my system. Nothing but my great friendship for Mr. Crotchet would have brought me so nearly within the jaws of the lion.

REV. DR. FOLLIOTT. After dinner, sir, after dinner, I will meet you on this question. I shall then be armed for the strife. You may fight like Hercules against Achelous, but I shall flourish the Bacchic thyrsus, which changed rivers into wine: as Nonnus sweetly sings, [Greek text].

MR. CROTCHET, JUN. I hope, Mr. Firedamp, you will let your friendship carry you a little closer into the jaws of the lion. I am fitting up a flotilla of pleasure-boats, with spacious cabins, and a good cellar, to carry a choice philosophical party up the Thames and Severn, into the Ellesmere canal, where we shall be among the mountains of North Wales; which we may climb or not, as we think proper; but we will, at any rate, keep our floating hotel well provisioned, and we will try to settle all the questions over which a shadow of doubt yet hangs in the world of philosophy.

MR. FIREDAMP. Out of my great friendship for you, I will certainly go; but I do not expect to survive the experiment.

REV. DR. FOLLIOTT. Alter erit tum Tiphys, et altera quae vehat Argo Delectos Heroas. I will be of the party, though I must hire an officiating curate, and deprive poor dear Mrs. Folliott, for several weeks, of the pleasure of combing my wig.

LORD BOSSNOWL. I hope, if I am to be of the party, our ship is not to be the ship of fools: He! he!

REV. DR. FOLLIOTT. If you are one of the party, sir, it most assuredly will not: Ha! ha!

LORD BOSSNOWL. Pray sir, what do you mean by Ha! ha!?

REV. DR. FOLLIOTT. Precisely, sir, what you mean by He! he!

MR. MAC QUEDY. You need not dispute about terms; they are two modes of expressing merriment, with or without reason; reason being in no way essential to mirth. No man should ask another why he laughs, or at what, seeing that he does not always know, and that, if he does, he is not a responsible agent. Laughter is an involuntary action of certain muscles, developed in the human species by the progress of civilisation. The savage never laughs.

REV. DR. FOLLIOTT. No, sir, he has nothing to laugh at. Give him Modern Athens, the "learned friend," and the Steam Intellect Society. They will develop his muscles.

CHAPTER III:

THE ROMAN CAMP

He loved her more then seven yere,
Yet was he of her love never the nere;
He was not ryche of golde and fe,
A gentyll man forsoth was he.
The Squyr of Lowe Degre.

The Reverend Doctor Folliott having promised to return to dinner, walked back to his vicarage, meditating whether he should pass the morning in writing his next sermon, or in angling for trout, and had nearly decided in favour of the latter proposition, repeating to himself, with great unction, the lines of Chaucer:

And as for me, though that I can but lite,
On bokis for to read I me delite,
And to 'hem yeve I faithe and full credence,
And in mine herte have 'hem in reverence,
So hertily, that there is game none,
That fro my bokis makith me to gone,
But it be seldome, on the holie daie;
Save certainly whan that the month of Maie
Is cousin, and I here the foulis sing,
And that the flouris ginnin for to spring,
Farwell my boke and my devocion:

236

when his attention was attracted by a young gentleman who was sitting on a camp stool with a portfolio on his knee, taking a sketch of the Roman Camp, which, as has been already said, was within the enclosed domain of Mr. Crotchet. The young stranger, who had climbed over the fence, espying the portly divine, rose up, and hoped that he was not trespassing. "By no means, sir," said the divine, "all the arts and sciences are welcome here; music, painting, and poetry; hydrostatics and political economy; meteorology, transcendentalism, and fish for breakfast."

THE STRANGER. A pleasant association, sir, and a liberal and discriminating hospitality. This is an old British camp, I believe, sir?

REV. DR. FOLLIOTT. Roman, sir; Roman; undeniably Roman. The vallum is past controversy. It was not a camp, sir, a castrum, but a castellum, a little camp, or watch-station, to which was attached, on the peak of the adjacent hill, a beacon for transmitting alarms. You will find such here and there, all along the range of chalk hills, which traverses the country from north-east to south-west, and along the base of which runs the ancient Iknield road, whereof you may descry a portion in that long straight white line.

THE STRANGER. I beg your pardon, sir; do I understand this place to be your property?

REV. DR. FOLLIOTT. It is not mine, sir: the more is the pity; yet is it so far well, that the owner is my good friend, and a highly respectable gentleman.

THE STRANGER. Good and respectable, sir, I take it, means rich?

REV. DR. FOLLIOTT. That is their meaning, sir.

THE STRANGER. I understand the owner to be a Mr. Crotchet. He has a handsome daughter, I am told.

REV. DR. FOLLIOTT. He has, sir. Her eyes are like the fish-pools of Heshbon, by the gate of Bethrabbim; and she is to have a handsome fortune, to which divers disinterested gentlemen are paying their addresses. Perhaps you design to be one of them?

THE STRANGER. No, sir; I beg pardon if my questions seem impertinent; I have no such design. There is a son too, I believe, sir, a great and successful blower of bubbles?

REV. DR. FOLLIOTT. A hero, sir, in his line. Never did angler in September hook more gudgeons.

THE STRANGER. To say the truth, two very amiable young people, with whom I have some little acquaintance, Lord Bossnowl, and his sister, Lady Clarinda, are reported to be on the point of concluding a double marriage with Miss Crotchet and her brother; by way of putting a new varnish on old nobility. Lord Foolincourt, their father, is terribly poor for a lord who owns a borough.

REV. DR. FOLLIOTT. Well, sir, the Crotchets have plenty of money, and the old gentleman's weak point is a hankering after high blood. I saw your acquaintance, Lord Bossnowl, this morning, but I did not see his sister. She may be there, nevertheless, and doing fashionable justice to this fine May morning, by lying in bed till noon.

THE STRANGER. Young Mr. Crotchet, sir, has been, like his father, the architect of his own fortune, has he not? An illustrious example of the reward of honesty and industry?

REV. DR. FOLLIOTT. As to honesty, sir, he made his fortune in the city of London, and if that commodity be of any value there, you will find it in the price current. I believe it is below par, like the shares of young Crotchet's fifty companies. But his progress has not been exactly like his father's. It has been more rapid, and he started with more advantages. He began with a fine capital from his father. The old gentleman divided his fortune into three not exactly equal portions; one for himself, one for his daughter, and one for his son, which he handed over to him, saying, "Take it once for all, and make the most of it; if you lose it where I won it, not another stiver do you get from me during my life." But, sir, young Crotchet

238

doubled, and trebled, and quadrupled it, and is, as you say, a striking example of the reward of industry; not that I think his labour has been so great as his luck.

THE STRANGER. But, sir, is all this solid? is there no danger of reaction? no day of reckoning to cut down in an hour prosperity that has grown up like a mushroom?

REV. DR. FOLLIOTT. Nay, sir, I know not. I do not pry into these matters. I am, for my own part, very well satisfied with the young gentleman. Let those who are not so look to themselves. It is quite enough for me that he came down last night from London, and that he had the good sense to bring with him a basket of lobsters. Sir, I wish you a good morning.

The stranger having returned the reverend gentleman's good morning, resumed his sketch, and was intently employed on it when Mr. Crotchet made his appearance with Mr. Mac Quedy and Mr. Skionar, whom he was escorting round his grounds, according to his custom with new visitors; the principal pleasure of possessing an extensive domain being that of showing it to other people. Mr. Mac Quedy, according also to the laudable custom of his countrymen, had been appraising everything that fell under his observation; but, on arriving at the Roman camp, of which the value was purely imaginary, he contented himself with exclaiming: "Eh! this is just a curiosity, and very pleasant to sit in on a summer day."

MR. SKIONAR. And call up the days of old, when the Roman eagle spread its wings in the place of that beechen foliage. It gives a fine idea of duration, to think that that fine old tree must have sprung from the earth ages after this camp was formed.

MR. MAC QUEDY. How old, think you, may the tree be?

MR. CROTCHET. I have records which show it to be three hundred years old.

MR. MAC QUEDY. That is a great age for a beech in good condition. But you see the camp is some fifteen hundred years, or so, older; and three times six being eighteen, I think you get a clearer idea of duration out of the simple arithmetic, than out of your eagle and foliage.

MR. SKIONAR. That is a very unpoetical, if not unphilosophical, mode of viewing antiquities. Your philosophy is too literal for our imperfect vision. We cannot look directly into the nature of things; we can only catch glimpses of the mighty shadow in the camera obscura of transcendental intelligence. These six and eighteen are only words to which we give conventional meanings. We can reason, but we cannot feel, by help of them. The tree and the eagle, contemplated in the ideality of space and time, become subjective realities, that rise up as landmarks in the mystery of the past.

MR. MAC QUEDY. Well, sir, if you understand that, I wish you joy. But I must be excused for holding that my proposition, three times six are eighteen, is more intelligible than yours. A worthy friend of mine, who is a sort of amateur in philosophy, criticism, politics, and a wee bit of many things more, says: "Men never begin to study antiquities till they are saturated with civilisation."

MR. SKIONAR. What is civilisation?

MR. MAC QUEDY. It is just respect for property. A state in which no man takes wrongfully what belongs to another, is a perfectly civilised state.

MR. SKIONAR. Your friend's antiquaries must have lived in El Dorado, to have had an opportunity of being saturated with such a state.

MR. MAC QUEDY. It is a question of degree. There is more respect for property here than in Angola.

MR. SKIONAR. That depends on the light in which things are viewed.

Mr. Crotchet was rubbing his hands, in hopes of a fine discussion, when they came round to the side of the camp where the picturesque gentleman was sketching. The stranger was rising up, when Mr. Crotchet begged him not to disturb himself, and presently walked away with his two guests.

Shortly after, Miss Crotchet and Lady Clarinda, who had breakfasted by themselves, made their appearance at the same spot, hanging each on an arm of Lord Bossnowl, who very much preferred their company to that of the philosophers, though he would have preferred the company of the latter, or any company to his own. He thought it very singular that so agreeable a person as he held himself to be to others, should be so exceedingly tiresome to himself: he did not attempt to investigate the cause of this phenomenon, but was contented with acting on his knowledge of the fact, and giving himself as little of his own private society as possible.

The stranger rose as they approached, and was immediately recognised by the Bossnowls as an old acquaintance, and saluted with the exclamation of "Captain Fitzchrome!" The interchange of salutations between Lady Clarinda and the Captain was accompanied with an amiable confusion on both sides, in which the observant eyes of Miss Crotchet seemed to read the recollection of an affair of the heart.

Lord Bossnowl was either unconscious of any such affair, or indifferent to its existence. He introduced the Captain very cordially to Miss Crotchet; and the young lady invited him, as the friend of their guests, to partake of her father's hospitality, an offer which was readily accepted.

The Captain took his portfolio under his right arm, his camp stool in his right hand, offered his left arm to Lady Clarinda, and followed at a reasonable distance behind Miss Crotchet and Lord Bossnowl, contriving, in the most natural manner possible, to drop more and more into the rear.

LADY CLARINDA. I am glad to see you can make yourself so happy with drawing old trees and mounds of grass.

CAPTAIN FITZCHROME. Happy, Lady Clarinda! oh, no! How can I be happy when I see the idol of my heart about to be sacrificed on the shrine of Mammon?

LADY CLARINDA. Do you know, though Mammon has a sort of ill name, I really think he is a very popular character; there must be at the bottom something amiable about him. He is certainly one of those pleasant creatures whom everybody abuses, but without whom no evening party is endurable. I dare say, love in a cottage is very pleasant; but then it positively must be a cottage ornee: but would not the same love be a great deal safer in a castle, even if Mammon furnished the fortification?

CAPTAIN FITZCHROME. Oh, Lady Clarinda! there is a heartlessness in that language that chills me to the soul.

LADY CLARINDA. Heartlessness! No: my heart is on my lips. I speak just what I think. You used to like it, and say it was as delightful as it was rare.

CAPTAIN FITZCHROME. True, but you did not then talk as you do now, of love in a castle.

LADY CLARINDA. Well, but only consider: a dun is a horridly vulgar creature; it is a creature I cannot endure the thought of: and a cottage lets him in so easily. Now a castle keeps him at bay. You are a half-pay officer, and are at leisure to command the garrison: but where is the castle? and who is to furnish the commissariat?

CAPTAIN FITZCHROME. Is it come to this, that you make a jest of my poverty? Yet is my poverty only comparative. Many decent families are maintained on smaller means.

LADY CLARINDA. Decent families: ay, decent is the distinction from respectable. Respectable means rich, and decent means poor. I should die if I heard my family called decent. And then your decent family always lives in a snug little place: I hate a little place; I like large rooms and large looking-glasses, and large parties, and a fine large butler, with a tinge of smooth red in his face; an outward and visible sign that the family he serves is respectable; if not noble, highly respectable.

CAPTAIN FITZCHROME. I cannot believe that you say all this in earnest. No man is less disposed than I am to deny the importance of the substantial comforts of life. I once flattered myself that in our estimate of these things we were nearly of a mind.

LADY CLARINDA. Do you know, I think an opera-box a very substantial comfort, and a carriage. You will tell me that many decent people walk arm-in-arm through the snow, and sit in clogs and bonnets in the pit at the English theatre. No doubt it is very pleasant to those who are used to it; but it is not to my taste.

CAPTAIN FITZCHROME. You always delighted in trying to provoke me; but I cannot believe that you have not a heart.

LADY CLARINDA. You do not like to believe that I have a heart, you mean. You wish to think I have lost it, and you know to whom; and when I tell you that it is still safe in my own keeping, and that I do not mean to give it away, the unreasonable creature grows angry.

CAPTAIN FITZCHROME. Angry! far from it; I am perfectly cool.

LADY CLARINDA. Why, you are pursing your brows, biting your lips, and lifting up your foot as if you would stamp it into the earth. I must say anger becomes you; you would make a charming Hotspur. Your every-day-dining-out face is rather insipid: but I assure you my heart is in danger when you are in the heroics. It is so rare, too, in these days of smooth manners, to see anything like natural expression in a man's face. There is one set form for every man's face in female society: a sort of serious comedy walking gentleman's face: but the moment the creature falls in love he begins to give himself airs, and plays off all the varieties of his physiognomy from the Master Slender to the Petruchio; and then he is actually very amusing.

CAPTAIN FITZCHROME. Well, Lady Clarinda, I will not be angry, amusing as it may be to you: I listen more in sorrow than in anger. I half believe you in earnest: and mourn as over a fallen angel.

LADY CLARINDA. What, because I have made up my mind not to give away my heart when I can sell it? I will introduce you to my new acquaintance, Mr. Mac Quedy: he will talk to you by the hour about exchangeable value, and show you that no rational being will part with anything, except to the highest bidder.

CAPTAIN FITZCHROME. Now, I am sure you are not in earnest. You cannot adopt such sentiments in their naked deformity.

LADY CLARINDA. Naked deformity! Why, Mr. Mac Quedy will prove to you that they are the cream of the most refined philosophy. You live a very pleasant life as a bachelor, roving about the country with your portfolio under your arm. I am not fit to be a poor man's wife. I cannot take any kind of trouble, or do any one thing that is of any use. Many decent families roast a bit of mutton on a string; but if I displease my father I shall not have as much as will buy the string, to say nothing of the meat; and the bare idea of such cookery gives me the horrors.

By this time they were near the Castle, and met Miss Crotchet and her companion, who had turned back to meet them. Captain Fitzchrome was shortly after heartily welcomed by Mr. Crotchet, and the party separated to dress for dinner, the Captain being by no means in an enviable state of mind, and full of misgivings as to the extent of belief that he was bound to accord to the words of the lady of his heart.

CHAPTER IV:

THE PARTY

En quoi cognoissez-vous la folie anticque? En quoi cognoissez-vous la sagesse presente?—RABELAIS.

"If I were sketching a bandit who had just shot his last pursuer, having outrun all the rest, that is the very face I would give him," soliloquised the Captain, as he studied the features of his rival in the drawing-room, during the miserable half-hour before dinner, when dulness reigns predominant over expectant company, especially when they are waiting for some one last comer, whom they all heartily curse in their hearts, and whom, nevertheless, or indeed therefore-the-more, they welcome as a sinner, more heartily than all the just persons who had been punctual to their engagement. Some new visitors had arrived in the morning, and, as the company dropped in one by one, the Captain anxiously watched the unclosing door for the form of his beloved: but she was the last to make her appearance, and on her entry gave him a malicious glance, which he construed into a telegraphic communication that she had stayed away to torment him. Young Crotchet escorted her with marked attention to the upper end of the drawing-room, where a great portion of the company was congregated around Miss Crotchet. These being the only ladies in the company, it was evident that old Mr. Crotchet would give his arm to Lady Clarinda, an arrangement with which the Captain could not interfere. He therefore took his station near the door, studying his rival from a distance, and determined to take advantage of his present position, to secure the seat next to his charmer. He was meditating on the best mode of operation for securing this important post with due regard to bien-seance, when he was twitched by the button by Mr. Mac Quedy, who said to him: "Lady Clarinda tells me, sir, that you are anxious to talk with me on the subject of exchangeable value, from which I infer that you have studied political economy, and as a great deal depends on the definition of value, I shall be glad to set you right on that point." "I am much obliged to you, sir," said the Captain, and was about to express his utter disqualification for the proposed instruction, when Mr. Skionar walked up and said: "Lady Clarinda informs me that you wish to talk over with me the question of subjective reality. I am delighted to fall in with a gentleman who daily appreciates the transcendental philosophy." "Lady Clarinda is too good," said the Captain; and was about to protest that he had never heard the word "transcendental" before, when the butler announced dinner. Mr. Crotchet led the way with Lady Clarinda: Lord Bossnowl followed with Miss Crotchet: the economist and transcendentalist pinned in the Captain, and held him, one by each arm, as he impatiently descended the stairs in the rear of several others of the company, whom they had forced him to let pass; but the moment he entered the dining-room he broke loose from them, and at the expense of a little brusquerie, secured his position.

"Well, Captain," said Lady Clarinda, "I perceive you can still manoeuvre."

"What could possess you," said the Captain, "to send two unendurable and inconceivable bores to intercept me with rubbish about which I neither know nor care any more than the man in the moon?"

"Perhaps," said Lady Clarinda, "I saw your design, and wished to put your generalship to the test. But do not contradict anything I have said about you, and see if the learned will find you out."

"There is fine music, as Rabelais observes, in the cliquetis d'asssiettes, a refreshing shade in the ombre de salle a manger, and an elegant fragrance in the fumee de roti," said a voice at the Captain's elbow. The Captain turning round, recognised his clerical friend of the morning, who knew him again immediately, and said he was extremely glad to meet him there; more especially as Lady Clarinda had assured him that he was an enthusiastic lover of Greek poetry.

"Lady Clarinda," said the Captain, "is a very pleasant young lady."

REV. DR. FOLLIOTT. So she is, sir: and I understand she has all the wit of the family to herself, whatever that totum may be. But a glass of wine after soup is, as the French say, the verre de sante. The current of opinion sets in favour of Hock: but I am for Madeira; I do not fancy Hock till I have laid a substratum of Madeira. Will you join me?

CAPTAIN FITZCHROME. With pleasure.

REV. DR. FOLLIOTT. Here is a very fine salmon before me: and May is the very point nomme to have salmon in perfection. There is a fine turbot close by, and there is much to be said in his behalf: but salmon in May is the king of fish.

MR. CROTCHET. That salmon before you, doctor, was caught in the Thames, this morning.

REV. DR. FOLLIOTT. [Greek text]. Rarity of rarities! A Thames salmon caught this morning. Now, Mr. Mac Quedy, even in fish your Modern Athens must yield. Cedite Graii.

MR. MAC QUEDY. Eh! sir, on its own around, your Thames salmon has two virtues over all others; first, that it is fresh; and, second, that it is rare; for I understand you do not take half a dozen in a year.

REV. DR. FOLLIOTT. In some years, sir, not one. Mud, filth, gas-dregs, lock-weirs, and the march of mind, developed in the form of poaching, have ruined the fishery. But, when we do catch a salmon, happy the man to whom he falls.

MR. MAC QUEDY. I confess, sir, this is excellent: but I cannot see why it should be better than a Tweed salmon at Kelso.

REV. DR. FOLLIOTT. Sir, I will take a glass of Hock with you.

MR. MAC QUEDY. With all my heart, sir. There are several varieties of the salmon genus: but the common salmon, the salmo salar, is only one species, one and the same everywhere, just like the human mind. Locality and education make all the difference.

REV. DR. FOLLIOTT. Education! Well, sir, I have no doubt schools for all are just as fit for the species salmo salar as for the genus homo. But you must allow that the specimen before us has finished his education in a manner that does honour to his college. However, I doubt that the salmo salar is only one species, that is to say, precisely alike in all localities. I hold that every river has its own breed, with essential differences; in flavour especially. And as for the human mind, I deny that it is the same in all men. I hold that there is every variety of natural capacity from the idiot to Newton and Shakespeare; the mass of mankind, midway between these extremes, being blockheads of different degrees; education leaving them pretty nearly as it found them, with this single difference, that it gives a fixed direction to their stupidity, a sort of incurable wry neck to the thing they call their understanding. So one nose points always east, and another always west, and each is ready to swear that it points due north.

MR. CROTCHET. If that be the point of truth, very few intellectual noses point due north.

MR. MAC QUEDY. Only those that point to the Modern Athens.

REV. DR. FOLLIOTT. Where all native noses point southward.

MR. MAC QUEDY. Eh, sir, northward for wisdom, and southward for profit.

MR. CROTCHET, JUN. Champagne, doctor?

REV. DR. FOLLIOTT. Most willingly. But you will permit my drinking it while it sparkles. I hold it a heresy to let it deaden in my hand, while the glass of my compotator is being filled on the opposite side of the table. By-the-bye, Captain, you remember a passage in Athenaeus, where he cites Menander on the subject of fish-sauce:

[Greek text]. (The Captain was aghast for an answer that would satisfy both his neighbours, when he was relieved by the divine continuing.) The science of fish-sauce, Mr. Mac Quedy, is by no means brought to perfection; a fine field of discovery still lies open in that line.

MR. MAC QUEDY. Nay, sir, beyond lobster-sauce, I take it, ye cannot go.

REV. DR. FOLLIOTT. In their line, I grant you, oyster and lobster-sauce are the pillars of Hercules. But I speak of the cruet sauces, where the quintessence of the sapid is condensed in a phial. I can taste in my mind's palate a combination, which, if I could give it reality, I would christen with the name of my college, and hand it down to posterity as a seat of learning indeed.

MR. MAC QUEDY. Well, sir, I wish you success, but I cannot let slip the question we started just now. I say, cutting off idiots, who have no minds at all, all minds are by nature alike. Education (which begins from their birth) makes them what they are.

REV. DR. FOLLIOTT. No, sir, it makes their tendencies, not their power. Caesar would have been the first wrestler on the village common. Education might have made him a Nadir Shah; it might also have made him a Washington; it could not have made him a merry-andrew, for our newspapers to extol as a model of eloquence.

MR. MAC QUEDY. Now, sir, I think education would have made him just anything, and fit for any station, from the throne to the stocks; saint or sinner, aristocrat or democrat, judge, counsel, or prisoner at the bar.

REV. DR. FOLLIOTT. I will thank you for a slice of lamb, with lemon and pepper. Before I proceed with this discussion,—Vin de Grave, Mr. Skionar,—I must interpose one remark. There is a set of persons in your city, Mr. Mac Quedy, who concoct, every three or four months, a thing, which they call a review: a sort of sugar-plum manufacturers to the Whig aristocracy.

MR. MAC QUEDY. I cannot tell, sir, exactly, what you mean by that; but I hope you will speak of those gentlemen with respect, seeing that I am one of them.

REV. DR. FOLLIOTT. Sir, I must drown my inadvertence in a glass of Sauterne with you. There is a set of gentlemen in your city-

MR. MAC QUEDY. Not in our city, exactly; neither are they a set. There is an editor, who forages for articles in all quarters, from John o' Groat's house to the Land's End. It is not a board, or a society: it is a mere intellectual bazaar, where A, B, and C, bring their wares to market.

REV. DR. FOLLIOTT. Well, sir, these gentlemen among them, the present company excepted, have practised as much dishonesty as, in any other department than literature, would have brought the practitioner under the cognisance of the police. In politics, they have ran with the hare and hunted with the hound. In criticism, they have, knowingly and unblushingly, given false characters, both for good and for evil; sticking at no art of misrepresentation, to clear out of the field of literature all who stood in the way of the interests of their own clique. They have never allowed their own profound ignorance of anything (Greek for instance) to throw even an air of hesitation into their oracular decision on the matter. They set an example of profligate contempt for truth, of which the success was in proportion to the effrontery; and when their prosperity had filled the market with competitors, they cried out against their own reflected sin, as if they had never committed it, or were entitled to a monopoly of it. The latter, I rather think, was what they wanted.

MR. CROTCHET. Hermitage, doctor?

REV. DR. FOLLIOTT. Nothing better, sir. The father who first chose the solitude of that vineyard, knew well how to cultivate his spirit in retirement. Now, Mr. Mac Quedy, Achilles was distinguished above all the Greeks for his inflexible love of truth; could education have made Achilles one of your reviewers?

MR. MAC QUEDY. No doubt of it, even if your character of them were true to the letter.

REV. DR. FOLLIOTT. And I say, sir—chicken and asparagus—Titan had made him of better clay. I hold with Pindar, "All that is most excellent is so by nature." [Greek text]. Education can give purposes, but not powers; and whatever purposes had been given him, he would have gone straight forward to them; straight forward, Mr. Mac Quedy.

MR. MAC QUEDY. No, sir, education makes the man, powers, purposes, and all.

REV. DR. FOLLIOTT. There is the point, sir, on which we join issue.

Several others of the company now chimed in with their opinions, which gave the divine an opportunity to degustate one or two side dishes, and to take a glass of wine with each of the young ladies.

CHAPTER V:

CHARACTERS

Ay impute a honte plus que mediocre etre vu spectateur ocieux de tant vaillans, disertz, et chevalereux personnaiges. RABELAIS.

LADY CLARINDA (to the Captain). I declare the creature has been listening to all this rigmarole, instead of attending to me. Do you ever expect forgiveness? But now that they are all talking together, and you cannot make out a word they say, nor they hear a word that we say, I will describe the company to you. First, there is the old gentleman on my left hand, at the head of the table, who is now leaning the other way to talk to my brother. He is a good-tempered, half-informed person, very unreasonably fond of reasoning, and of reasoning people; people that talk nonsense logically: he is fond of disputation himself, when there are only one or two, but seldom does more than listen in a large company of illumines. He made a great fortune in the city, and has the comfort of a good conscience. He is very hospitable, and is generous in dinners; though nothing would induce him to give sixpence to the poor, because he holds that all misfortune is from imprudence, that none but the rich ought to marry, and that all ought to thrive by honest industry, as he did. He is ambitious of founding a family, and of allying himself with nobility; and is thus as willing as other grown children to throw away thousands for a gew-gaw, though he would not part with a penny for charity. Next to him is my brother, whom you know as well as I do. He has finished his education with credit, and as he never ventures to oppose me in anything, I have no doubt he is very sensible. He has good manners, is a model of dress, and is reckoned ornamental in all societies. Next to him is Miss Crotchet, my sister-in-law that is to be. You see she is rather pretty, and very genteel. She is tolerably accomplished, has her table always covered with new novels, thinks Mr. Mac Quedy an oracle, and is extremely desirous to be called "my lady." Next to her is Mr. Firedamp, a very absurd person, who thinks that water is the evil principle. Next to him is Mr. Eavesdrop, a man who, by dint of a certain something like smartness, has got into good society. He is a sort of bookseller's tool, and coins all his acquaintance in reminiscences and sketches of character. I am very shy of him, for fear he should print me.

CAPTAIN FITZCHROME. If he print you in your own likeness, which is that of an angel, you need not fear him. If he print you in any other, I will cut his throat. But proceed-

LADY CLARINDA. Next to him is Mr. Henbane, the toxicologist, I think he calls himself. He has passed half his life in studying poisons and antidotes. The first thing he did on his arrival here was to kill the cat; and while Miss Crotchet was crying over her, he brought her to life again. I am more shy of him than the other.

CAPTAIN FITZCHROME. They are two very dangerous fellows, and I shall take care to keep them both at a respectful distance. Let us hope that Eavesdrop will sketch off Henbane, and that Henbane will poison him for his trouble.

LADY CLARINDA. Well, next to him sits Mr. Mac Quedy, the Modern Athenian, who lays down the law about everything, and therefore may be taken to understand everything. He turns all the affairs of this world into questions of buying and selling. He is the Spirit of the Frozen Ocean to everything like romance and sentiment. He condenses their volume of steam into a drop of cold water in a moment. He has satisfied me that I am a commodity in the market, and that I ought to set myself at a high price. So you see, he who would have me must bid for me.

CAPTAIN FITZCHROME. I shall discuss that point with Mr. Mac Quedy.

LADY CLARINDA. Not a word for your life. Our flirtation is our own secret. Let it remain so.

CAPTAIN FITZCHROME. Flirtation, Clarinda! Is that all that the most ardent-

LADY CLARINDA. Now, don't be rhapsodical here. Next to Mr. Mac Quedy is Mr. Skionar, a sort of poetical philosopher, a curious compound of the intense and the mystical. He abominates all the ideas of Mr. Mac Quedy, and settles everything by sentiment and intuition.

CAPTAIN FITZCHROME. Then, I say, he is the wiser man.

LADY CLARINDA. They are two oddities, but a little of them is amusing, and I like to hear them dispute. So you see I am in training for a philosopher myself.

CAPTAIN FITZCHROME. Any philosophy, for Heaven's sake, but the pound-shilling-and-pence philosophy of Mr. Mac Quedy.

LADY CLARINDA. Why, they say that even Mr. Skionar, though he is a great dreamer, always dreams with his eyes open, or with one eye at any rate, which is an eye to his gain: but I believe that in this respect the poor man has got an ill name by keeping bad company. He has two dear friends, Mr. Wilful Wontsee, and Mr. Rumblesack Shantsee, poets of some note, who used to see visions of Utopia, and pure republics beyond the Western deep: but, finding that these El Dorados brought them no revenue, they turned their vision-seeing faculty into the more profitable channel of espying all sorts of virtues in the high and the mighty, who were able and willing to pay for the discovery.

254

CAPTAIN FITZCHROME. I do not fancy these virtue-spyers.

LADY CLARINDA. Next to Mr. Skionar sits Mr. Chainmail, a good-looking young gentleman, as you see, with very antiquated tastes. He is fond of old poetry, and is something of a poet himself. He is deep in monkish literature, and holds that the best state of society was that of the twelfth century, when nothing was going forward but fighting, feasting, and praying, which he says are the three great purposes for which man was made. He laments bitterly over the inventions of gunpowder, steam, and gas, which he says have ruined the world. He lives within two or three miles, and has a large hall, adorned with rusty pikes, shields, helmets, swords, and tattered banners, and furnished with yew-tree chairs, and two long old worm-eaten oak tables, where he dines with all his household, after the fashion of his favourite age. He wants us all to dine with him, and I believe we shall go.

CAPTAIN FITZCHROME. That will be something new, at any rate.

LADY CLARINDA. Next to him is Mr. Toogood, the co-operationist, who will have neither fighting nor praying; but wants to parcel out the world into squares like a chess-board, with a community on each, raising everything for one another, with a great steam-engine to serve them in common for tailor and hosier, kitchen and cook.

CAPTAIN FITZCHROME. He is the strangest of the set, so far.

LADY CLARINDA. This brings us to the bottom of the table, where sits my humble servant, Mr. Crotchet the younger. I ought not to describe him.

CAPTAIN FITZCHROME. I entreat you do.

LADY CLARINDA. Well, I really have very little to say in his favour.

CAPTAIN FITZCHROME. I do not wish to hear anything in his favour; and I rejoice to hear you say so, because-

LADY CLARINDA. Do not flatter yourself. If I take him, it will be to please my father, and to have a town and country house, and plenty of servants and a carriage and an opera-box, and make some of my acquaintance who have married for love, or for rank, or for anything but money, die for envy of my jewels. You do not think I would take him for himself. Why, he is very smooth and spruce as far as his dress goes; but as to his face, he looks as if he had tumbled headlong into a volcano, and been thrown up again among the cinders.

CAPTAIN FITZCHROME. I cannot believe, that, speaking thus of him, you mean to take him at all.

LADY CLARINDA. Oh! I am out of my teens. I have been very much in love; but now I am come to years of discretion, and must think, like other people, of settling myself advantageously. He was in love with a banker's daughter, and cast her off at her father's bankruptcy, and the poor girl has gone to hide herself in some wild place.

CAPTAIN FITZCHROME. She must have a strange taste, if she pines for the loss of him.

LADY CLARINDA. They say he was good-looking, till his bubble schemes, as they call them, stamped him with the physiognomy of a desperate gambler. I suspect he has still a penchant towards his first flame. If he takes me, it will be for my rank and connection, and the second seat of the borough of Rogueingrain. So we shall meet on equal terms, and shall enjoy all the blessedness of expecting nothing from each other.

CAPTAIN FITZCHROME. You can expect no security with such an adventurer.

LADY CLARINDA. I shall have the security of a good settlement, and then if andare al diavolo be his destiny, he may go, you know, by himself. He is almost always dreaming and distrait. It is very likely that some great reverse is in store for him: but that will not concern me, you perceive.

CAPTAIN FITZCHROME. You torture me, Clarinda, with the bare possibility.

LADY CLARINDA. Hush! Here is music to soothe your troubled spirit. Next to him, on this side, sits the dilettante composer, Mr. Trillo; they say his name was O'Trill, and he has taken the O from the beginning, and put it at the end. I do not know how this may be. He plays well on the violoncello, and better on the piano; sings agreeably; has a talent at versemaking, and improvises a song with some felicity. He is very agreeable company in the evening, with his instruments and music-books. He maintains that the sole end of all enlightened society is to get up a good opera, and laments that wealth, genius, and energy are squandered upon other pursuits, to the neglect of this one great matter.

CAPTAIN FITZCHROME. That is a very pleasant fancy at any rate.

LADY CLARINDA. I assure you he has a great deal to say for it. Well, next to him, again, is Dr. Morbific, who has been all over the world to prove that there is no such thing as contagion; and has inoculated himself with plague, yellow fever, and every variety of pestilence, and is still alive to tell the story. I am very shy of him, too; for I look on him as a walking phial of wrath, corked full of all infections, and not to be touched without extreme hazard.

CAPTAIN FITZCHROME. This is the strangest fellow of all.

LADY CLARINDA. Next to him sits Mr. Philpot, the geographer, who thinks of nothing but the heads and tails of rivers, and lays down the streams of Terra Incognita as accurately as if he had been there. He is a person of pleasant fancy, and makes a sort of fairy land of every country he touches, from the Frozen Ocean to the Deserts of Sahara.

CAPTAIN FITZCHROME. How does he settle matters with Mr. Firedamp?

LADY CLARINDA. You see Mr. Firedamp has got as far as possible out of his way. Next to him is Sir Simon Steeltrap, of Steeltrap Lodge, Member for Crouching-Curtown, Justice of Peace for the county, and Lord of the United Manors of Spring-gun-and-Treadmill; a great preserver of game and public morals. By administering the laws which he assists in making, he disposes, at his pleasure, of the land and its live stock, including all the two-legged varieties, with and without feathers, in a circumference of several miles round Steeltrap Lodge. He has enclosed commons and woodlands; abolished cottage gardens; taken the village cricket-ground into his own park, out of pure regard to the sanctity of Sunday; shut up footpaths and alehouses (all but those which belong to his electioneering friend, Mr. Quassia, the brewer); put down fairs and fiddlers; committed many poachers; shot a few; convicted one-third of the peasantry; suspected the rest; and passed nearly the whole of them through a wholesome course of prison discipline, which has finished their education at the expense of the county.

CAPTAIN FITZCHROME. He is somewhat out of his element here: among such a diversity of opinions he will hear some he will not like.

LADY CLARINDA. It was rather ill-judged in Mr. Crotchet to invite him to-day. But the art of assorting company is above these parvenus. They invite a certain number of persons without considering how they harmonise with each other. Between Sir Simon and you is the Reverend Doctor Folliott. He is said to be an excellent scholar, and is fonder of books than the majority of his cloth; he is very fond, also, of the good things of this world. He is of an admirable temper, and says rude things in a pleasant half-earnest manner, that nobody can take offence with. And next to him again is one Captain Fitzchrome, who is very much in love with a certain person that does not mean to have anything to say to him, because she can better her fortune by taking somebody else.

CAPTAIN FITZCHROME. And next to him again is the beautiful, the accomplished, the witty, the fascinating, the tormenting, Lady Clarinda, who traduces herself to the said Captain by assertions which it would drive him crazy to believe.

258

LADY CLARINDA. Time will show, sir. And now we have gone the round of the table.

CAPTAIN FITZCHROME. But I must say, though I know you had always a turn for sketching characters, you surprise me by your observation, and especially by your attention to opinions.

LADY CLARINDA. Well, I will tell you a secret: I am writing a novel.

CAPTAIN FITZCHROME. A novel!

LADY CLARINDA. Yes, a novel. And I shall get a little finery by it: trinkets and fal-lals, which I cannot get from papa. You must know I have been reading several fashionable novels, the fashionable this, and the fashionable that; and I thought to myself, why I can do better than any of these myself. So I wrote a chapter or two, and sent them as a specimen to Mr. Puffall, the book-seller, telling him they were to be a part of the fashionable something or other, and he offered me, I will not say how much, to finish it in three volumes, and let him pay all the newspapers for recommending it as the work of a lady of quality, who had made very free with the characters of her acquaintance.

CAPTAIN FITZCHROME. Surely you have not done so?

LADY CLARINDA. Oh, no! I leave that to Mr. Eavesdrop. But Mr. Puffall made it a condition that I should let him say so.

CAPTAIN FITZCHROME. A strange recommendation.

LADY CLARINDA. Oh, nothing else will do. And it seems you may give yourself any character you like, and the newspapers will print it as if it came from themselves. I have commended you to three of our friends here as an economist, a transcendentalist, and a classical scholar; and if you wish to be renowned through the world for these, or any other accomplishments, the newspapers will confirm you in their possession for half-a-guinea a piece.

CAPTAIN FITZCHROME. Truly, the praise of such gentry must be a feather in any one's cap.

LADY CLARINDA. So you will see, some morning, that my novel is "the most popular production of the day." This is Mr. Puffall's favourite phrase. He makes the newspapers say it of everything he publishes. But "the day," you know, is a very convenient phrase; it allows of three hundred and sixty-five "most popular productions" in a year. And in leap-year one more.

CHAPTER VI:

THEORIES

But when they came to shape the model, Not one could fit the other's noddle.—BUTLER.

Meanwhile, the last course, and the dessert, passed by. When the ladies had withdrawn, young Crotchet addressed the company.

MR. CROTCHET, JUN. There is one point in which philosophers of all classes seem to be agreed: that they only want money to regenerate the world.

MR. MAC QUEDY. No doubt of it. Nothing is so easy as to lay down the outlines of perfect society. There wants nothing but money to set it going. I will explain myself clearly and fully by reading a paper. (Producing a large scroll.) "In the infancy of society—"

REV. DR. FOLLIOTT. Pray, Mr. Mac Quedy, how is it that all gentlemen of your nation begin everything they write with the "infancy of society?"

MR. MAC QUEDY. Eh, sir, it is the simplest way to begin at the beginning. "In the infancy of society, when government was invented to save a percentage; say two and a half per cent.—"

REV. DR. FOLLIOTT. I will not say any such thing.

MR. MAC QUEDY. Well, say any percentage you please.

REV. DR. FOLLIOTT. I will not say any percentage at all.

MR. MAC QUEDY. "On the principle of the division of labour—"

REV. DR. FOLLIOTT. Government was invented to spend a percentage.

MR. MAC QUEDY. To save a percentage.

REV. DR. FOLLIOTT. No, sir, to spend a percentage; and a good deal more than two and a half percent. Two hundred and fifty per cent.: that is intelligible.

MR. MAC QUEDY.—"In the infancy of society—"

MR. TOOGOOD.—Never mind the infancy of society. The question is of society in its maturity. Here is what it should be. (Producing a paper.) I have laid it down in a diagram.

MR. SKIONAR. Before we proceed to the question of government, we must nicely discriminate the boundaries of sense, understanding, and reason. Sense is a receptivity-

MR. CROTCHET, JUN. We are proceeding too fast. Money being all that is wanted to regenerate society, I will put into the hands of this company a large sum for the purpose. Now let us see how to dispose of it.

MR. MAC QUEDY. We will begin by taking a committee-room in London, where we will dine together once a week, to deliberate.

REV. DR. FOLLIOTT. If the money is to go in deliberative dinners, you may set me down for a committee man and honorary caterer.

MR. MAC QUEDY. Next, you must all learn political economy, which I will teach you, very compendiously, in lectures over the bottle.

REV. DR. FOLLIOTT. I hate lectures over the bottle. But pray, sir, what is political economy?

MR. MAC QUEDY. Political economy is to the state what domestic economy is to the family.

REV. DR. FOLLIOTT. No such thing, sir. In the family there is a paterfamilias, who regulates the distribution, and takes care that there shall be no such thing in the household as one dying of hunger, while another dies of surfeit. In the state it is all hunger at one end, and all surfeit at the other. Matchless claret, Mr. Crotchet.

MR. CROTCHET. Vintage of fifteen, Doctor.

MR. MAC QUEDY. The family consumes, and so does the state.

REV. DR. FOLLIOTT. Consumes, air! Yes: but the mode, the proportions: there is the essential difference between the state and the family. Sir, I hate false analogies.

MR. MAC QUEDY. Well, sir, the analogy is not essential. Distribution will come under its proper head.

REV. DR. FOLLIOTT. Come where it will, the distribution of the state is in no respect analogous to the distribution of the family. The paterfamilias, sir: the paterfamilias.

MR. MAC QUEDY. Well, sir, let that pass. The family consumes, and in order to consume, it must have supply.

REV. DR. FOLLIOTT. Well, sir, Adam and Eve knew that, when they delved and span.

MR. MAC QUEDY. Very true, sir (reproducing his scroll). "In the infancy of society—"

MR. TOOGOOD. The reverend gentleman has hit the nail on the head. It is the distribution that must be looked to; it is the paterfamilias that is wanting in the State. Now here I have provided him. (Reproducing his diagram.)

MR. TRILLO. Apply the money, sir, to building and endowing an opera house, where the ancient altar of Bacchus may flourish, and justice may be done to sublime compositions. (Producing a part of a manuscript opera.)

MR. SKIONAR. No, sir, build sacella for transcendental oracles to teach the world how to see through a glass darkly. (Producing a scroll.)

MR. TRILLO. See through an opera-glass brightly.

REV. DR. FOLLIOTT. See through a wine-glass full of claret; then you see both darkly and brightly. But, gentlemen, if you are all in the humour for reading papers, I will read you the first half of my next Sunday's sermon. (Producing a paper.)

OMNES. No sermon! No sermon!

REV. DR. FOLLIOTT. Then I move that our respective papers be committed to our respective pockets.

MR. MAC QUEDY. Political economy is divided into two great branches, production and consumption.

REV. DR. FOLLIOTT. Yes, sir; there are two great classes of men: those who produce much and consume little; and those who consume much and produce nothing. The fruges consumere nati have the best of it. Eh, Captain! You remember the characteristics of a great man according to Aristophanes: [Greek text]. Ha! ha! ha! Well, Captain, even in these tight-laced days, the obscurity of a learned language allows a little pleasantry.

CAPTAIN FITZCHROME. Very true, sir; the pleasantry and the obscurity go together; they are all one, as it were—to me at any rate (aside).

MR. MAC QUEDY. Now, sir-

REV. DR. FOLLIOTT. Pray, sir, let your science alone, or you will put me under the painful necessity of demolishing it bit by bit, as I have done your exordium. I will undertake it any morning; but it is too hard exercise after dinner.

MR. MAC QUEDY. Well, sir, in the meantime I hold my science established.

REV. DR. FOLLIOTT. And I hold it demolished.

MR. CROTCHET, JUN. Pray, gentlemen, pocket your manuscripts, fill your glasses, and consider what we shall do with our money.

MR. MAC QUEDY. Build lecture-rooms, and schools for all.

MR. TRILLO. Revive the Athenian theatre; regenerate the lyrical drama.

MR. TOOGOOD. Build a grand co-operative parallelogram, with a steam-engine in the middle for a maid of all work.

MR. FIREDAMP. Drain the country, and get rid of malaria, by abolishing duck-ponds.

DR. MORBIFIC. Found a philanthropic college of anticontagionists, where all the members shall be inoculated with the virus of all known diseases. Try the experiment on a grand scale.

MR. CHAINMAIL. Build a great dining-hall; endow it with beef and ale, and hang the hall round with arms to defend the provisions.

MR. HENBANE. Found a toxicological institution for trying all poisons and antidotes. I myself have killed a frog twelve times, and brought him to life eleven; but the twelfth time he died. I have a phial of the drug, which killed him, in my pocket, and shall not rest till I have discovered its antidote.

REV. DR. FOLLIOTT. I move that the last speaker be dispossessed of his phial, and that it be forthwith thrown into the Thames.

MR. HENBANE. How, sir? my invaluable, and, in the present state of human knowledge, infallible poison?

REV. DR. FOLLIOTT. Let the frogs have all the advantage of it.

MR. CROTCHET. Consider, Doctor, the fish might participate. Think of the salmon.

REV DR. FOLLIOTT. Then let the owner's right-hand neighbour swallow it.

MR. EAVESDROP. Me, sir! What have I done, sir, that I am to be poisoned, sir?

REV. DR. FOLLIOTT. Sir, you have published a character of your facetious friend, the Reverend Doctor F., wherein you have sketched off me; me, sir, even to my nose and wig. What business have the public with my nose and wig?

MR. EAVESDROP. Sir, it is all good-humoured; all in bonhomie: all friendly and complimentary.

REV. DR. FOLLIOTT. Sir, the bottle, la Dive Bouteille, is a recondite oracle, which makes an Eleusinian temple of the circle in which it moves. He who reveals its mysteries must die. Therefore, let the dose be administered. Fiat experimentum in anima vili.

MR. EAVESDROP. Sir, you are very facetious at my expense.

REV. DR. FOLLIOTT. Sir, you have been very unfacetious, very inficete at mine. You have dished me up, like a savoury omelette, to gratify the appetite of the reading rabble for gossip. The next time, sir, I will respond with the argumentum baculinum. Print that, sir: put it on record as a promise of the Reverend Doctor F., which shall be most faithfully kept, with an exemplary bamboo.

MR. EAVESDROP. Your cloth protects you, sir.

REV. DR. FOLLIOTT. My bamboo shall protect me, sir.

MR. CROTCHET. Doctor, Doctor, you are growing too polemical.

REV. DR. FOLLIOTT. Sir, my blood boils. What business have the public with my nose and wig?

MR. CROTCHET. Doctor! Doctor!

MR. CROTCHET, JUN. Pray, gentlemen, return to the point. How shall we employ our fund?

MR. PHILPOT. Surely in no way so beneficially as in exploring rivers. Send a fleet of steamboats down the Niger, and another up the Nile. So shall you civilise Africa, and establish stocking factories in Abyssinia and Bambo.

REV. DR. FOLLIOTT. With all submission, breeches and petticoats must precede stockings. Send out a crew of tailors. Try if the King of Bambo will invest in inexpressibles.

MR. CROTCHET, JUN. Gentlemen, it is not for partial, but for general benefit, that this fund is proposed: a grand and universally applicable scheme for the amelioration of the condition of man.

SEVERAL VOICES. That is my scheme. I have not heard a scheme but my own that has a grain of common sense.

MR. TRILLO. Gentlemen, you inspire me. Your last exclamation runs itself into a chorus, and sets itself to music. Allow me to lead, and to hope for your voices in harmony.

After careful meditation,
And profound deliberation,

On the various pretty projects which have just been shown,
Not a scheme in agitation,
For the world's amelioration,
Has a grain of common sense in it, except my own.

SEVERAL VOICES. We are not disposed to join in any such chorus.

REV. DR. FOLLIOTT. Well, of all these schemes, I am for Mr. Trillo's. Regenerate the Athenian theatre. My classical friend here, the Captain, will vote with, me.

CAPTAIN FITZCHROME. I, sir? oh! of course, sir.

MR. MAC QUEDY. Surely, Captain, I rely on you to uphold political economy.

CAPTAIN FITZCHROME. Me, sir! oh, to be sure, sir.

REV. DR. FOLLIOTT. Pray, sir, will political economy uphold the Athenian theatre?

MR. MAC QUEDY. Surely not. It would be a very unproductive investment.

REV. DR. FOLLIOTT. Then the Captain votes against you. What, sir, did not the Athenians, the wisest of nations, appropriate to their theatre their most sacred and intangible fund? Did not they give to melopoeia, choregraphy, and the sundry forms of didascalics, the precedence of all other matters, civil and military? Was it not their law, that even the proposal to divert this fund to any other purpose should be punished with death? But, sir, I further propose that the Athenian theatre being resuscitated, the admission shall be free to all who can expound the Greek choruses, constructively, mythologically, and metrically, and to none others. So shall all the world learn Greek: Greek, the Alpha and Omega of all knowledge. At him who sits not in the theatre shall be pointed the finger of scorn: he shall be called in the highway of the city, "a fellow without Greek."

MR. TRILLO. But the ladies, sir, the ladies.

REV. DR. FOLLIOTT. Every man may take in a lady: and she who can construe and metricise a chorus, shall, if she so please, pass in by herself.

MR. TRILLO. But, sir, you will shut me out of my own theatre. Let there at least be a double passport, Greek and Italian.

REV. DR. FOLLIOTT. No, sir; I am inexorable. No Greek, no theatre.

MR. TRILLO. Sir, I cannot consent to be shut out from my own theatre.

REV. DR. FOLLIOTT. You see how it is, Squire Crotchet the younger; you can scarcely find two to agree on a scheme, and no two of those can agree on the details. Keep your money in your pocket. And so ends the fund for regenerating the world.

MR. MAC QUEDY. Nay, by no means. We are all agreed on deliberative dinners.

REV. DR. FOLLIOTT. Very true; we will dine and discuss. We will sing with Robin Hood, "If I drink water while this doth last;" and while it lasts we will have no adjournment, if not to the Athenian theatre.

MR. TRILLO. Well, gentlemen, I hope this chorus at least will please you:-

If I drink water while this doth last,
May I never again drink wine:
For how can a man, in his life of a span,
Do anything better than dine?
Well dine and drink, and say if we think
That anything better can be,
And when we have dined, wish all mankind
May dine as well as we.
And though a good wish will fill no dish
And brim no cup with sack,
Yet thoughts will spring as the glasses ring,
To illume our studious track.

On the brilliant dreams of our hopeful schemes
The light of the flask shall shine;
And we'll sit till day, but we'll find the way
To drench the world with wine.

The schemes for the world's regeneration evaporated in a tumult of voices.

CHAPTER VII:

THE SLEEPING VENUS

Quoth he: In all my life till now, I ne'er saw so profane a show.—BUTLER.

The library of Crotchet Castle was a large and well-furnished apartment, opening on one side into an ante-room, on the other into a music-room. It had several tables stationed at convenient distances; one consecrated to the novelties of literature, another to the novelties of embellishment; others unoccupied, and at the disposal of the company. The walls were covered with a copious collection of ancient and modern books; the ancient having been selected and arranged by the Reverend Doctor Folliott. In the ante-room were card-tables; in the music-room were various instruments, all popular operas, and all fashionable music. In this suite of apartments, and not in the drawing-room, were the evenings of Crotchet Castle usually passed.

The young ladies were in the music-room; Miss Crotchet at the piano, Lady Clarinda at the harp, playing and occasionally singing, at the suggestion of Mr. Trillo, portions of Matilde di Shabran. Lord Bossnowl was turning over the leaves for Miss Crotchet; the Captain was performing the same office for Lady Clarinda, but with so much more attention to the lady than the book, that he often made sad work with the harmony, by turnover two leaves together. On these occasions Miss Crotchet paused,

Lady Clarinda laughed, Mr. Trillo scolded, Lord Bossnowl yawned, the Captain apologised, and the performance proceeded.

In the library Mr. Mac Quedy was expounding political economy to the Reverend Doctor Folliott, who was pro more demolishing its doctrines seriatim.

Mr. Chainmail was in hot dispute with Mr. Skionar, touching the physical and moral well-being of man. Mr. Skionar was enforcing his friend Mr. Shantsee's views of moral discipline; maintaining that the sole thing needful for man in this world was loyal and pious education; the giving men good books to read, and enough of the hornbook to read them; with a judicious interspersion of the lessons of Old Restraint, which was his poetic name for the parish stocks. Mr. Chainmail, on the other hand, stood up for the exclusive necessity of beef and ale, lodging and raiment, wife and children, courage to fight for them all, and armour wherewith to do so.

Mr. Henbane had got his face scratched, and his finger bitten, by the cat, in trying to catch her for a second experiment in killing and bringing to life; and Doctor Morbific was comforting him with a disquisition to prove that there were only four animals having the power to communicate hydrophobia, of which the cat was one; and that it was not necessary that the animal should be in a rabid state, the nature of the wound being everything, and the idea of contagion a delusion. Mr. Henbane was listening very lugubriously to this dissertation.

Mr. Philpot had seized on Mr. Firedamp, and pinned him down to a map of Africa, on which he was tracing imaginary courses of mighty inland rivers, terminating in lakes and marshes, where they were finally evaporated by the heat of the sun; and Mr. Firedamp's hair was standing on end at the bare imagination of the mass of malaria that must be engendered by the operation. Mr. Toogood had begun explaining his diagrams to Sir Simon Steeltrap; but Sir Simon grew testy, and told Mr. Toogood that the promulgators of such doctrines ought to be consigned to the treadmill. The philanthropist walked off from the country gentleman, and proceeded to hold forth to young Crotchet, who stood silent, as one who listens, but in reality without hearing a syllable. Mr. Crotchet, senior, as the master of the house, was left to entertain himself with his own meditations, till the Reverend Doctor Folliott tore himself from Mr. Mac Quedy, and proceeded to expostulate with Mr. Crotchet on a delicate topic.

There was an Italian painter, who obtained the name of Il Bragatore, by the superinduction of inexpressibles on the naked Apollos and Bacchuses of his betters. The fame of this worthy remained one and indivisible, till a set of heads, which had been, by a too common mistake of Nature's journeymen, stuck upon magisterial shoulders, as the Corinthian capitals of "fair round bellies with fat capon lined," but which Nature herself had intended for the noddles of porcelain mandarins, promulgated simultaneously from the east and the west of London, an order that no plaster-of-Paris Venus should appear in the streets without petticoats. Mr. Crotchet, on reading this order in the evening paper, which, by the postman's early arrival, was always laid on his breakfast-table, determined to fill his house with Venuses of all sizes and kinds. In pursuance of this resolution, came packages by water-carriage, containing an infinite variety of Venuses. There were the Medicean Venus, and the Bathing Venus; the Uranian Venus, and the Pandemian Venus; the Crouching Venus, and the Sleeping Venus; the Venus rising from the sea, the Venus with the apple of Paris, and the Venus with the armour of Mars.

The Reverend Doctor Folliott had been very much astonished at this unexpected display. Disposed, as he was, to hold, that whatever had been in Greece, was right; he was more than doubtful of the propriety of throwing open the classical adytum to the illiterate profane. Whether, in his interior mind, he was at all influenced, either by the consideration that it would be for the credit of his cloth, with some of his vice-suppressing neighbours, to be able to say that he had expostulated; or by curiosity, to try what sort of defence his city-bred friend, who knew the classics only by translations, and whose reason was always a little ahead of his knowledge, would make for his somewhat ostentatious display of liberality in matters of taste; is a question on which the learned may differ: but, after having duly deliberated on two full-sized casts of the Uranian and Pandemian Venus, in niches on each side of the chimney, and on three alabaster figures, in glass cases, on the mantelpiece, he proceeded, peirastically, to open his fire.

REV. DR. FOLLIOTT. These little alabaster figures on the mantelpiece, Mr. Crotchet, and those large figures in the niches—may I take the liberty to ask you what they are intended to represent?

MR. CROTCHET. Venus, sir; nothing more, sir; just Venus.

REV. DR. FOLLIOTT. May I ask you, sir, why they are there?

MR. CROTCHET. To be looked at, sir; just to be looked at: the reasons for most things in a gentleman's house being in it at all; from the paper on the walls, and the drapery of the curtains, even to the books in the library, of which the most essential part is the appearance of the back.

REV. DR. FOLLIOTT. Very true, sir. As great philosophers hold that the esse of things is percipi, so a gentleman's furniture exists to be looked at. Nevertheless, sir, there are some things more fit to be looked at than others; for instance, there is nothing more fit to be looked at than the outside of a book. It is, as I may say, from repeated experience, a pure and unmixed pleasure to have a goodly volume lying before you, and to know that you may open it if you please, and need not open it unless you please. It is a resource against ennui, if ennui should come upon you. To have the resource and not to feel the ennui, to enjoy your bottle in the present, and your book in the indefinite future, is a delightful condition of human existence. There is no place, in which a man can move or sit, in which the outside of a book can be otherwise than an innocent and becoming spectacle. Touching this matter, there cannot, I think, be two opinions. But with respect to your Venuses there can be, and indeed there are, two very distinct opinions. Now, Sir, that little figure in the centre of the mantelpiece—as a grave paterfamilias, Mr. Crotchet, with a fair nubile daughter, whose eyes are like the fish-pools of Heshbon—I would ask you if you hold that figure to be altogether delicate?

MR. CROTCHET. The sleeping Venus, sir? Nothing can be more delicate than the entire contour of the figure, the flow of the hair on the shoulders and neck, the form of the feet and fingers. It is altogether a most delicate morsel.

REV. DR. FOLLIOTT. Why, in that sense, perhaps, it is as delicate as whitebait in July. But the attitude, sir, the attitude.

MR. CROTCHET. Nothing can be more natural, sir.

REV. DR. FOLLIOTT. That is the very thing, sir. It is too natural: too natural, sir: it lies for all the world like—I make no doubt, the pious cheesemonger, who recently broke its plaster facsimile over the head of the itinerant vendor, was struck by a certain similitude to the position of his own sleeping beauty, and felt his noble wrath thereby justly aroused.

MR. CROTCHET. Very likely, sir. In my opinion, the cheesemonger was a fool, and the justice who sided with him was a greater.

REV. DR. FOLLIOTT. Fool, sir, is a harsh term: call not thy brother a fool.

MR. CROTCHET. Sir, neither the cheesemonger nor the justice is a brother of mine.

REV. DR. FOLLIOTT. Sir, we are all brethren.

MR. CROTCHET. Yes, sir, as the hangman is of the thief; the squire of the poacher; the judge of the libeller; the lawyer of his client; the statesman of his colleague; the bubble-blower of the bubble-buyer; the slave-driver of the negro; as these are brethren, so am I and the worthies in question

REV. DR. FOLLIOTT. To be sure, sir, in these instances, and in many others, the term brother must be taken in its utmost latitude of interpretation: we are all brothers, nevertheless. But to return to the point. Now these two large figures, one with drapery on the lower half of the body, and the other with no drapery at all; upon my word, sir, it matters not what godfathers and godmothers may have promised and vowed for the children of this world, touching the devil and other things to be renounced, if such figures as those are to be put before their eyes.

MR. CROTCHET. Sir, the naked figure is the Pandemian Venus, and the half-draped figure is the Uranian Venus; and I say, sir, that figure realises the finest imaginings of Plato, and is the personification of the most refined and exalted feeling of which the human mind is susceptible; the love of pure, ideal, intellectual beauty.

REV. DR. FOLLIOTT. I am aware, sir, that Plato, in his Symposium, discourseth very eloquently touching the Uranian and Pandemian Venus: but you must remember that, in our universities, Plato is held to be little better than a misleader of youth; and they have shown their contempt for him, not only by never reading him (a mode of contempt in which they deal very largely), but even by never printing a complete edition of him; although they have printed many ancient books, which nobody suspects to have been ever read on the spot, except by a person attached to the press, who is, therefore, emphatically called "the reader."

MR. CROTCHET. Well, sir?

REV. DR. FOLLIOTT. Why, sir, to "the reader" aforesaid (supposing either of our universities to have printed an edition of Plato), or to any one else who can be supposed to have read Plato, or, indeed, to be ever likely to do so, I would very willingly show these figures; because to such they would, I grant you, be the outward and visible signs of poetical and philosophical ideas: but, to the multitude, the gross, carnal multitude, they are but two beautiful women, one half undressed, and the other quite so.

MR. CROTCHET. Then, sir, let the multitude look upon them and learn modesty.

REV. DR. FOLLIOTT. I must say that, if I wished my footman to learn modesty, I should not dream of sending him to school to a naked Venus.

MR. CROTCHET. Sir, ancient sculpture is the true school of modesty. But where the Greeks had modesty, we have cant; where they had poetry, we have cant; where they had patriotism, we have cant; where they had anything that exalts, delights, or adorns humanity, we have nothing but cant, cant, cant. And, sir, to show my contempt for cant in all its shapes, I have adorned my house with the Greek Venus, in all her shapes, and am ready to fight her battle against all the societies that ever were instituted for the suppression of truth and beauty.

REV. DR. FOLLIOTT. My dear sir, I am afraid you are growing warm. Pray be cool. Nothing contributes so much to good digestion as to be perfectly cool after dinner.

MR. CROTCHET. Sir, the Lacedaemonian virgins wrestled naked with young men; and they grew up, as the wise Lycurgus had foreseen, into the most modest of women, and the most exemplary of wives and mothers.

REV. DR. FOLLIOTT. Very likely, sir; but the Athenian virgins did no such thing, and they grew up into wives who stayed at home—stayed at home, sir; and looked after their husbands' dinner—his dinner, sir, you will please to observe.

MR. CROTCHET. And what was the consequence of that, sir? that they were such very insipid persons that the husband would not go home to eat his dinner, but preferred the company of some Aspasia, or Lais.

REV. DR. FOLLIOTT. Two very different persons, sir, give me leave to remark.

MR. CROTCHET. Very likely, sir; but both too good to be married in Athens.

REV. DR. FOLLIOTT. Sir, Lais was a Corinthian.

MR. CROTCHET. Od's vengeance, sir, some Aspasia and any other Athenian name of the same sort of person you like-

REV. DR. FOLLIOTT. I do not like the sort of person at all: the sort of person I like, as I have already implied, is a modest woman, who stays at home and looks after her husband's dinner.

MR. CROTCHET. Well, sir, that was not the taste of the Athenians. They preferred the society of women who would not have made any scruple about sitting as models to Praxiteles; as you know, sir, very modest women in Italy did to Canova; one of whom, an Italian countess, being asked by an English lady, "how she could bear it?" answered, "Very well; there was a good fire in the room."

REV. DR. FOLLIOTT. Sir, the English lady should have asked how the Italian lady's husband could bear it. The phials of my wrath would overflow if poor dear Mrs. Folliott-: sir, in return for your story, I will tell you a story of my ancestor, Gilbert Folliott. The devil haunted him, as he did Saint Francis, in the likeness of a beautiful damsel; but all he could get from the exemplary Gilbert was an admonition to wear a stomacher and longer petticoats.

MR. CROTCHET. Sir, your story makes for my side of the question. It proves that the devil, in the likeness of a fair damsel, with short petticoats and no stomacher, was almost too much for Gilbert Folliott. The force of the spell was in the drapery.

REV. DR. FOLLIOTT. Bless my soul, sir!

MR. CROTCHET. Give me leave, sir. Diderot-

REV. DR. FOLLIOTT. Who was he, sir?

MR. CROTCHET. Who was he, sir? the sublime philosopher, the father of the Encyclopaedia, of all the encyclopaedias that have ever been printed.

REV. DR. FOLLIOTT. Bless me, sir, a terrible progeny: they belong to the tribe of Incubi.

MR. CROTCHET. The great philosopher, Diderot-

REV. DR. FOLLIOTT. Sir, Diderot is not a man after my heart. Keep to the Greeks, if you please; albeit this Sleeping Venus is not an antique.

MR. CROTCHET. Well, sir, the Greeks: why do we call the Elgin marbles inestimable? Simply because they are true to nature. And why are they so superior in that point to all modern works, with all our greater knowledge of anatomy? Why, sir, but because the Greeks, having no cant, had better opportunities of studying models?

REV. DR. FOLLIOTT. Sir, I deny our greater knowledge of anatomy. But I shall take the liberty to employ, on this occasion, the argumentum ad hominem. Would you have allowed Miss Crotchet to sit for a model to Canova?

MR. CROTCHET. Yes, sir.

"God bless my soul, sir!" exclaimed the Reverend Doctor Folliott, throwing himself back into a chair, and flinging up his heels, with the premeditated design of giving emphasis to his exclamation; but by miscalculating his impetus, he overbalanced his chair, and laid himself on the carpet in a right angle, of which his back was the base.

CHAPTER VIII:

SCIENCE AND CHARITY

Chi sta nel mondo un par d'ore contento,
Ne gli vien tolta, ovver contaminata,
Quella sua pace in veruno momento,
Puo dir che Giove drittamente il guata.

FORTEGUERRI.

The Reverend Doctor Folliott took his departure about ten o'clock, to walk home to his vicarage. There was no moon, but the night was bright and clear, and afforded him as much light as he needed. He paused a moment by the Roman camp to listen to the nightingale; repeated to himself a passage of Sophocles; proceeded through the park gate, and entered the narrow lane that led to the village. He walked on in a very pleasant mood of the state called reverie; in which fish and wine, Greek and political economy, the Sleeping Venus he had left behind, and poor dear Mrs. Folliott, to whose fond arms he was returning, passed, as in a camera obscura, over the tablets of his imagination. Presently the image of Mr. Eavesdrop, with a printed sketch of the Reverend Doctor F., presented itself before him, and he began mechanically to flourish his bamboo. The movement was prompted by his good genius, for the uplifted bamboo received the blow of a ponderous cudgel, which was intended for his head. The reverend gentleman recoiled two or three paces, and saw before him a couple of ruffians, who were preparing to renew the attack, but whom, with two swings of his bamboo, he laid with cracked sconces on the earth, where he proceeded to deal with them like corn beneath the flail of the thresher. One of them drew a pistol, which went off in the very act of being struck aside by the bamboo, and lodged a bullet in the brain of the other. There was then only one enemy, who vainly struggled to rise, every effort being attended with a new and more signal prostration. The fellow roared for mercy. "Mercy, rascal!" cried the divine; "what mercy were you going to show me, villain? What! I warrant me, you thought it would be an easy matter, and no sin, to rob and murder a parson on his way home from dinner. You said to yourself, doubtless, "We'll waylay the fat parson (you irreverent knave), as he waddles home (you disparaging ruffian), half-seas-over, (you calumnious vagabond)." And with every dyslogistic term, which he supposed had been applied to himself, he inflicted a new bruise on his rolling and roaring antagonist. "Ah, rogue!" he proceeded, "you can roar now, marauder; you were silent enough when you devoted my brains to dispersion under your cudgel. But seeing that I cannot bind you, and that I intend you not to escape, and that it would be dangerous to let you rise, I will disable you in all your members. I will contund you as Thestylis did strong smelling herbs, in the quality whereof you do most gravely partake, as my nose beareth testimony, ill weed that you are. I will beat you to a jelly, and I will then roll you into the ditch, to lie till the constable comes for you, thief."

"Hold! hold! reverend sir," exclaimed the penitent culprit, "I am disabled already in every finger, and in every joint. I will roll myself into the ditch, reverend sir."

"Stir not, rascal," returned the divine, "stir not so much as the quietest leaf above you, or my bamboo rebounds on your body, like hail in a thunder-storm. Confess, speedily, villain; are you a simple thief, or would you have manufactured me into a subject for the benefit of science? Ay, miscreant caitiff, you would have made me a subject for science, would you? You are a school-master abroad, are you? You are marching with a detachment of the march of mind, are you? You are a member of the Steam Intellect Society, are you? You swear by the learned friend, do you?"

"Oh, no! reverend sir," answered the criminal, "I am innocent of all these offences, whatever they are, reverend sir. The only friend I had in the world is lying dead beside me, reverend sir."

The reverend gentleman paused a moment, and leaned on his bamboo. The culprit, bruised as he was, sprang on his legs, and went off in double quick time. The Doctor gave him chase, and had nearly brought him within arm's length, when the fellow turned at right angles, and sprang clean over a deep dry ditch. The divine, following with equal ardour, and less dexterity, went down over head and ears into a thicket of nettles. Emerging with much discomposure, he proceeded to the village, and roused the constable; but the constable found, on reaching the scene of action, that the dead man was gone, as well as his living accomplice.

"Oh, the monster!" exclaimed the Reverend Doctor Folliott, "he has made a subject for science of the only friend he had in the world." "Ay, my dear," he resumed, the next morning at breakfast, "if my old reading, and my early gymnastics (for, as the great Hermann says, before I was demulced by the Muses, I was ferocis ingenii puer, et ad arma quam ad literas paratior), had not imbued me indelibly with some of the holy rage of Frere Jean des Entommeures, I should be, at this moment, lying on the table of some flinty-hearted anatomist, who would have sliced and disjointed me as unscrupulously as I do these remnants of the capon and chine, wherewith you consoled yourself yesterday for my absence at dinner. Phew! I have a noble thirst upon me, which I will quench with floods of tea."

The reverend gentleman was interrupted by a messenger, who informed him that the Charity Commissioners requested his presence at the inn, where they were holding a sitting.

"The Charity Commissioners!" exclaimed the reverend gentleman, "who on earth are they?"

The messenger could not inform him, and the reverend gentleman took his hat and stick, and proceeded to the inn.

On entering the best parlour, he saw three well-dressed and bulky gentlemen sitting at a table, and a fourth officiating as clerk, with an open book before him, and a pen in his hand. The church-wardens, who had been also summoned, were already in attendance.

The chief commissioner politely requested the Reverend Doctor Folliott to be seated, and after the usual meteorological preliminaries had been settled by a resolution, nem. con., that it was a fine day but very hot, the chief commissioner stated, that in virtue of the commission of Parliament, which they had the honour to hold, they were now to inquire into the state of the public charities of this village.

REV. DR. FOLLIOTT. The state of the public charities, sir, is exceedingly simple. There are none. The charities here are all private, and so private, that I for one know nothing of them.

FIRST COMMISSIONER. We have been informed, sir, that there is an annual rent charged on the land of Hautbois, for the endowment and repair of an almshouse.

REV. DR. FOLLIOTT. Hautbois! Hautbois!

FIRST COMMISSIONER. The manorial farm of Hautbois, now occupied by Farmer Seedling, is charged with the endowment and maintenance of an almshouse.

REV. DR. FOLLIOTT (to the Churchwarden). How is this, Mr. Bluenose?

FIRST CHURCHWARDEN. I really do not know, sir. What say you, Mr. Appletwig?

MR. APPLETWIG (parish clerk and schoolmaster; an old man). I do remember, gentlemen, to have been informed, that there did stand, at the end of the village, a ruined cottage, which had once been an almshouse, which was endowed and maintained, by an annual revenue of a mark and a half, or one pound sterling, charged some centuries ago on the farm of Hautbois; but the means, by the progress of time, having become inadequate to the end, the almshouse tumbled to pieces.

FIRST COMMISSIONER. But this is a right which cannot be abrogated by desuetude, and the sum of one pound per annum is still chargeable for charitable purposes on the manorial farm of Hautbois.

REV. DR. FOLLIOTT. Very well, sir.

MR. APPLETWIG. But, sir, the one pound per annum is still received by the parish, but was long ago, by an unanimous vote in open vestry, given to the minister.

THE THREE COMMISSIONERS (una voce). The minister!

FIRST COMMISSIONER. This is an unjustifiable proceeding.

SECOND COMMISSIONER. A misappropriation of a public fund.

THIRD COMMISSIONER. A flagrant perversion of a charitable donation.

REV. DR. FOLLIOTT. God bless my soul, gentlemen! I know nothing of this matter. How is this, Mr. Bluenose? Do I receive this one pound per annum?

FIRST CHURCHWARDEN. Really, sir, I know no more about it than you do.

MR. APPLETWIG. You certainly receive it, sir. It was voted to one of your predecessors. Farmer Seedling lumps it in with his tithes.

FIRST COMMISSIONER. Lumps it in, sir! Lump in a charitable donation!

SECOND AND THIRD COMMISSIONER. Oh-oh-oh-h-h!

FIRST COMMISSIONER. Reverend sir, and gentlemen, officers of this parish, we are under the necessity of admonishing you that this is a most improper proceeding: and you are hereby duly admonished accordingly. Make a record, Mr. Milky.

MR. MILKY (writing). The clergyman and church-wardens of the village of Hm-ra-m-m-gravely admonished. Hm-m-m-m.

REV. DR. FOLLIOTT. Is that all, gentlemen?

THE COMMISSIONERS. That is all, sir; and we wish you a good morning.

REV. DR. FOLLIOTT. A very good morning to you, gentlemen.

"What in the name of all that is wonderful, Mr. Bluenose," said the Reverend Doctor Folliott, as he walked out of the inn, "what in the name of all that is wonderful, can those fellows mean? They have come here in a chaise and four, to make a fuss about a pound per annum, which, after all, they leave as it was: I wonder who pays them for their trouble, and how much."

MR. APPLETWIG. The public pay for it, sir. It is a job of the learned friend whom you admire so much. It makes away with public money in salaries, and private money in lawsuits, and does no particle of good to any living soul.

REV. DR. FOLLIOTT. Ay, ay, Mr. Appletwig; that is just the sort of public service to be looked for from the learned friend. Oh, the learned friend! the learned friend! He is the evil genius of everything that falls in his way.

The Reverend Doctor walked off to Crotchet Castle, to narrate his misadventures, and exhale his budget of grievances on Mr. Mac Quedy, whom he considered a ringleader of the march of mind.

CHAPTER IX:

THE VOYAGE

[Greek text]
Mounting the bark, they cleft the watery ways.—Homer.

Four beautiful cabined pinnaces, one for the ladies, one for the gentlemen, one for kitchen and servants, one for a dining-room and band of music, weighed anchor, on a fine July morning, from below Crotchet Castle, and were towed merrily, by strong trotting horses, against the stream of the Thames. They passed from the district of chalk, successively into the districts of clay, of sand-rock, of oolite, and so forth. Sometimes they dined in their floating dining-room, sometimes in tents, which they pitched on the dry, smooth-shaven green of a newly-mown meadow: sometimes they left their vessels to see sights in the vicinity; sometimes they passed a day or two in a comfortable inn.

At Oxford, they walked about to see the curiosities of architecture, painted windows, and undisturbed libraries. The Reverend Doctor Folliott laid a wager with Mr. Crotchet "that in all their perlustrations they would not find a man reading," and won it. "Ay," said the reverend gentleman, "this is still a seat of learning, on the principle of—once a captain, always a captain. We may well ask, in these great reservoirs of books whereof no man ever draws a sluice, Quorsum pertinuit stipere Platona Menandro? What is done here for the classics? Reprinting German editions on better paper. A great boast, verily! What for mathematics? What for metaphysics?

What for history? What for anything worth knowing? This was a seat of learning in the days of Friar Bacon. But the Friar is gone, and his learning with him. Nothing of him is left but the immortal nose, which, when his brazen head had tumbled to pieces, crying "Time's Past," was the only palpable fragment among its minutely pulverised atoms, and which is still resplendent over the portals of its cognominal college. That nose, sir, is the only thing to which I shall take off my hat, in all this Babylon of buried literature.

MR. CROTCHET. But, doctor, it is something to have a great reservoir of learning, at which some may draw if they please.

REV. DR. FOLLIOTT. But, here, good care is taken that nobody shall please. If even a small drop from the sacred fountain, [Greek text], as Callimachus has it, were carried off by any one, it would be evidence of something to hope for. But the system of dissuasion from all good learning is brought here to a pitch of perfection that baffles the keenest aspirant. I run over to myself the names of the scholars of Germany, a glorious catalogue: but ask for those of Oxford,—Where are they? The echoes of their courts, as vacant as their heads, will answer, Where are they? The tree shall be known by its fruit: and seeing that this great tree, with all its specious seeming, brings forth no fruit, I do denounce it as a barren fig.

MR. MAC QUEDY. I shall set you right on this point. We do nothing without motives. If learning get nothing but honour, and very little of that; and if the good things of this world, which ought to be the rewards of learning, become the mere gifts of self-interested patronage; you must not wonder if, in the finishing of education, the science which takes precedence of all others, should be the science of currying favour.

REV. DR. FOLLIOTT. Very true, sir. Education is well finished, for all worldly purposes, when the head is brought into the state whereinto I am accustomed to bring a marrow-bone, when it has been set before me on a toast, with a white napkin wrapped round it. Nothing trundles along the high road of preferment so trimly as a well-biassed sconce, picked clean within and polished without; totus teres atque rotundus. The perfection of the finishing lies in the bias, which keeps it trundling in the given direction. There is good and sufficient reason for the fig being barren, but it is not therefore the less a barren fig.

At Godstow, they gathered hazel on the grave of Rosamond; and, proceeding on their voyage, fell into a discussion on legendary histories.

LADY CLARINDA. History is but a tiresome thing in itself: it becomes more agreeable the more romance is mixed up with it. The great enchanter has made me learn many things which I should never have dreamed of studying, if they had not come to me in the form of amusement.

REV. DR. FOLLIOTT. What enchanter is that? There are two enchanters: he of the north, and he of the south.

MR. TRILLO. Rossini!

REV. DR. FOLLIOTT. Ay, there is another enchanter. But I mean the great enchanter of Covent Garden: he who, for more than a quarter of a century, has produced two pantomimes a year, to the delight of children of all ages; including myself at all ages. That is the enchanter for me. I am for the pantomimes. All the northern enchanter's romances put together would not furnish materials for half the Southern enchanter's pantomimes.

LADY CLARINDA. Surely you do not class literature with pantomime?

REV. DR. FOLLIOTT. In these cases, I do. They are both one, with a slight difference. The one is the literature of pantomime, the other is the pantomime of literature. There is the same variety of character, the same diversity of story, the same copiousness of incident, the same research into costume, the same display of heraldry, falconry, minstrelsy, scenery, monkery, witchery, devilry, robbery, poachery, piracy, fishery, gipsy-astrology, demonology, architecture, fortification, castrametation, navigation; the same running base of love and battle. The main difference is, that the one set of amusing fictions is told in music and action; the other in all the worst dialects of the English language. As to any sentence worth remembering, any moral or political truth, anything having a tendency, however remote, to make men wiser or better, to make them think, to make them ever think of thinking; they are both precisely alike nuspiam, nequaquam, nullibi, nullimodis.

LADY CLARINDA. Very amusing, however.

REV. DR. FOLLIOTT. Very amusing, very amusing.

MR. CHAINMAIL. My quarrel with the northern enchanter is, that he has grossly misrepresented the twelfth century.

REV. DR. FOLLIOTT. He has misrepresented everything, or he would not have been very amusing. Sober truth is but dull matter to the reading rabble. The angler, who puts not on his hook the bait that best pleases the fish, may sit all day on the bank without catching a gudgeon.

MR. MAC QUEDY. But how do you mean that he has misrepresented the twelfth century? By exhibiting some of its knights and ladies in the colours of refinement and virtue, seeing that they were all no better than ruffians, and something else that shall be nameless?

MR. CHAINMAIL. By no means. By depicting them as much worse than they were, not, as you suppose, much better. No one would infer from his pictures that theirs was a much better state of society than this which we live in.

MR. MAC QUEDY. No, nor was it. It was a period of brutality, ignorance, fanaticism, and tyranny; when the land was covered with castles, and every castle contained a gang of banditti, headed by a titled robber, who levied contributions with fire and sword; plundering, torturing, ravishing, burying his captives in loathsome dungeons, and broiling them on gridirons, to force from them the surrender of every particle of treasure which he suspected them of possessing; and fighting every now and then with the neighbouring lords, his conterminal bandits, for the right of marauding on the boundaries. This was the twelfth century, as depicted by all contemporary historians and poets.

MR. CHAINMAIL. No, sir. Weigh the evidence of specific facts; you will find more good than evil. Who was England's greatest hero—the mirror of chivalry, the pattern of honour, the fountain of generosity, the model to all succeeding ages of military glory? Richard the First. There is a king of the twelfth century. What was the first step of liberty? Magna Charta. That was the best thing ever done by lords. There are lords of the twelfth century. You must remember, too, that these lords were petty princes, and made war on each other as legitimately as the heads of larger communities did or do. For their system of revenue, it was, to be sure, more rough and summary than that which has succeeded it, but it was certainly less searching and less productive. And as to the people, I content myself with these great points: that every man was armed, every man was a good archer, every man could and would fight effectively, with sword or pike, or even with oaken cudgel; no man would live quietly without beef and ale if he had them not; he fought till he either got them, or was put out of condition to want them. They were not, and could not be, subjected to that powerful pressure of all the other classes of society, combined by gunpowder, steam, and fiscality, which has brought them to that dismal degradation in which we see them now. And there are the people of the twelfth century.

MR. MAC QUEDY. As to your king, the enchanter has done him ample justice, even in your own view. As to your lords and their ladies, he has drawn them too favourably, given them too many of the false colours of chivalry, thrown too attractive a light on their abominable doings. As to the people, he keeps them so much in the background, that he can hardly be said to have represented them at all, much less misrepresented them, which indeed he could scarcely do, seeing that, by your own showing, they were all thieves, ready to knock down any man for what they could not come by honestly.

MR. CHAINMAIL. No, sir. They could come honestly by beef and ale, while they were left to their simple industry. When oppression interfered with them in that, then they stood on the defensive, and fought for what they were not permitted to come by quietly.

MR. MAC QUEDY. If A., being aggrieved by B., knocks down C., do you call that standing on the defensive?

MR. CHAINMAIL. That depends on who or what C. is.

REV. DR. FOLLIOTT. Gentlemen, you will never settle this controversy till you have first settled what is good for man in this world; the great question, de finibus, which has puzzled all philosophers. If the enchanter has represented the twelfth century too brightly for one, and too darkly for the other of you, I should say, as an impartial man, he has represented it fairly. My quarrel with him is, that his works contain nothing worth quoting; and a book that furnishes no quotations, is me judice, no book—it is a plaything. There is no question about the amusement,—amusement of multitudes; but if he who amuses us most is to be our enchanter [Greek text], then my enchanter is the enchanter of Covent Garden.

CHAPTER X:

THE VOYAGE, CONTINUED

Continuant nostre routte, navigasmes par trois jours sans rien descouvrir.—RABELAIS.

"There is a beautiful structure," said Mr. Chainmail, as they glided by Lechlade church; "a subject for the pencil, Captain. It is a question worth asking, Mr. Mac Quedy, whether the religious spirit which reared these edifices, and connected with them everywhere an asylum for misfortune, and a provision for poverty, was not better than the commercial spirit, which has turned all the business of modern life into schemes of profit and processes of fraud and extortion. I do not see, in all your boasted improvements, any compensation for the religious charity of the twelfth century. I do not see any compensation for that kindly feeling which, within their own little communities, bound the several classes of society together, while full scope was left for the development of natural character, wherein individuals differed as conspicuously as in costume. Now, we all wear one conventional dress, one conventional face; we have no bond of union but pecuniary interest; we talk anything that comes uppermost for talking's sake, and without expecting to be believed; we have no nature, no simplicity, no picturesqueness: everything about us is as artificial and as complicated as our steam-machinery: our poetry is a kaleidoscope of false imagery, expressing no real feeling, portraying no real existence. I do not see any compensation for the poetry of the twelfth century."

MR. MAC QUEDY. I wonder to hear you, Mr. Chainmail, talking of the religious charity of a set of lazy monks and beggarly friars, who were much more occupied with taking than giving; of whom those who were in earnest did nothing but make themselves and everybody about them miserable with fastings and penances, and other such trash; and those who were not, did nothing but guzzle and royster, and, having no wives of their own, took very unbecoming liberties with those of honester men. And as to your poetry of the twelfth century, it is not good for much.

MR. CHAINMAIL. It has, at any rate, what ours wants, truth to nature and simplicity of diction.

The poetry, which was addressed to the people of the dark ages, pleased in proportion to the truth with which it depicted familiar images, and to their natural connection with the time and place to which they were assigned. In the poetry of our enlightened times, the characteristics of all seasons, soils, and climates may be blended together with much benefit to the author's fame as an original genius. The cowslip of a civic poet is always in blossom, his fern is always in full feather; he gathers the celandine, the primrose, the heath-flower, the jasmine, and the chrysanthemum all on the same day and from the same spot; his nightingale sings all the year round, his moon is always full, his cygnet is as white as his swan, his cedar is as tremulous as his aspen, and his poplar as embowering as his beech. Thus all nature marches with the march of mind; but among barbarians, instead of mead and wine, and the best seat by the fire, the reward of such a genius would have been to be summarily turned out of doors in the snow, to meditate on the difference between day and night and between December and July. It is an age of liberality, indeed, when not to know an oak from a burdock is no disqualification for sylvan minstrelsy. I am for truth and simplicity.

292

REV. DR. FOLLIOTT.—Let him who loves them read Greek: Greek, Greek, Greek.

MR. MAC QUEDY.—If he can, sir.

REV. DR. FOLLIOTT.—Very true, sir; if he can. Here is the Captain who can. But I think he must have finished his education at some very rigid college, where a quotation or any other overt act showing acquaintance with classical literature was visited with a severe penalty. For my part, I make it my boast that I was not to be so subdued. I could not be abated of a single quotation by all the bumpers in which I was fined.

In this manner they glided over the face of the waters, discussing everything and settling nothing. Mr. Mac Quedy and the Reverend Doctor Folliott had many digladiations on political economy: wherein, each in his own view, Doctor Folliott demolished Mr. Mac Quedy's science, and Mr. Mac Quedy demolished Dr. Folliott's objections.

We would print these dialogues if we thought anyone would read them; but the world is not yet ripe for this haute sagesse Pantagrueline. We must therefore content ourselves with an echantillon of one of the Reverend Doctor's perorations.

"You have given the name of a science to what is yet an imperfect inquiry, and the upshot of your so-called science is this: that you increase the wealth of a nation by increasing in it the quantity of things which are produced by labour: no matter what they are, no matter how produced, no matter how distributed. The greater the quantity of labour that has gone to the production of the quantity of things in a community, the richer is the community. That is your doctrine. Now, I say, if this be so, riches are not the object for a community to aim at. I say the nation is best off, in relation to other nations, which has the greatest quantity of the common necessaries of life distributed among the greatest number of persons; which has the greatest number of honest hearts and stout arms united in a common interest, willing to offend no one, but ready to fight in defence of their own community against all the rest of the world, because they have something in it worth fighting for. The moment you admit that one class of things, without any reference to what they respectively cost, is better worth having than another; that a smaller commercial value, with one mode of distribution, is better than a greater commercial value, with another mode of distribution; the whole of that curious fabric of postulates and dogmas, which you call the science of political economy, and which I call politicae aeconomiae inscientia, tumbles to pieces."

Mr. Toogood agreed with Mr. Chainmail against Mr. Mac Quedy, that the existing state of society was worse than that of the twelfth century; but he agreed with Mr. Mac Quedy against Mr. Chainmail, that it was in progress to something much better than either—to which "something much better" Mr. Toogood and Mr. Mac Quedy attached two very different meanings.

Mr. Chainmail fought with Doctor Folliott, the battle of the romantic against the classical in poetry; and Mr. Skionar contended with Mr. Mac Quedy for intuition and synthesis, against analysis and induction in philosophy.

Mr. Philpot would lie along for hours, listening to the gurgling of the water round the prow, and would occasionally edify the company with speculations on the great changes that would be effected in the world by the steam-navigation of rivers: sketching the course of a steamboat up and down some mighty stream which civilisation had either never visited, or long since deserted; the Missouri and the Columbia, the Oroonoko and the Amazon, the Nile and the Niger, the Euphrates and the Tigris, the Oxus and the Indus, the Ganges and the Hoangho; under the over canopying forests of the new, or by the long-silent ruins of the ancient, world; through the shapeless mounds of Babylon, or the gigantic temples of Thebes.

Mr. Trillo went on with the composition of his opera, and took the opinions of the young ladies on every step in its progress; occasionally regaling the company with specimens; and wondering at the blindness of Mr. Mac Quedy, who could not, or would not, see that an opera in perfection, being the union of all the beautiful arts—music, painting, dancing, poetry—exhibiting female beauty in its most attractive aspects, and in its most becoming costume—was, according to the well-known precept, Ingenuas didicisse, etc., the most efficient instrument of civilisation, and ought to take precedence of all other pursuits in the minds of true philanthropists. The Reverend Doctor Folliott, on these occasions, never failed to say a word or two on Mr. Trillo's side, derived from the practice of the Athenians, and from the combination, in their theatre, of all the beautiful arts, in a degree of perfection unknown to the modern world.

Leaving Lechlade, they entered the canal that connects the Thames with the Severn; ascended by many locks; passed by a tunnel, three miles long, through the bowels of Sapperton Hill; agreed unanimously that the greatest pleasure derivable from visiting a cavern of any sort was that of getting out of it; descended by many locks again through the valley of Stroud into the Severn; continued their navigation into the Ellesmere canal; moored their pinnaces in the Vale of Llangollen by the aqueduct of Pontycysyllty; and determined to pass some days in inspecting the scenery, before commencing their homeward voyage.

The Captain omitted no opportunity of pressing his suit on Lady Clarinda, but could never draw from her any reply but the same doctrines of worldly wisdom, delivered in a tone of badinage, mixed with a certain kindness of manner that induced him to hope she was not in earnest.

But the morning after they had anchored under the hills of the Dee— whether the lady had reflected more seriously than usual, or was somewhat less in good humour than usual, or the Captain was more pressing than usual—she said to him: "It must not be, Captain Fitzchrome; 'the course of true love never did run smooth:' my father must keep his borough, and I must have a town house and a country house, and an opera box, and a carriage. It is not well for either of us that we should flirt any longer: 'I must be cruel only to be kind.' Be satisfied with the assurance that you alone, of all men, have ever broken my rest. To be sure, it was only for about three nights in all; but that is too much."

The Captain had le coeur navre. He took his portfolio under his arm, made up the little valise of a pedestrian, and, without saying a word to anyone, wandered off at random among the mountains.

After the lapse of a day or two, the Captain was missed, and everyone marvelled what was become of him. Mr. Philpot thought he must have been exploring a river, and fallen in and got drowned in the process. Mr. Firedamp had no doubt he had been crossing a mountain bog, and had been suddenly deprived of life by the exhalations of marsh miasmata. Mr. Henbane deemed it probable that he had been tempted in some wood by the large black brilliant berries of the Atropa Belladonna, or Deadly Nightshade; and lamented that he had not been by, to administer an infallible antidote. Mr. Eavesdrop hoped the particulars of his fate would be ascertained; and asked if anyone present could help him to any authentic anecdotes of their departed friend. The Reverend Doctor Folliott proposed that an inquiry should be instituted as to whether the march of intellect had reached that neighbourhood, as, if so, the Captain had probably been made a subject for science. Mr. Mac Quedy said it was no such great matter to ascertain the precise mode in which the surplus population was diminished by one. Mr. Toogood asseverated that there was no such thing as surplus population, and that the land, properly managed, would maintain twenty times its present inhabitants; and hereupon they fell into a disputation.

Lady Clarinda did not doubt that the Captain had gone away designedly; she missed him more than she could have anticipated, and wished she had at least postponed her last piece of cruelty till the completion of their homeward voyage.

CHAPTER XI:

CORRESPONDENCE

"Base is the slave that pays."—ANCIENT PISTOL.

The Captain was neither drowned nor poisoned, neither miasmatised nor anatomised. But, before we proceed to account for him, we must look back to a young lady, of whom some little notice was taken in the first chapter; and who, though she has since been out of sight, has never with us been out of mind: Miss Susannah Touchandgo, the forsaken of the junior Crotchet, whom we left an inmate of a solitary farm, in one of the deep valleys under the cloud-capt summits of Meirion, comforting her wounded spirit with air and exercise, rustic cheer, music, painting, and poetry, and the prattle of the little Ap Llymrys.

One evening, after an interval of anxious expectation, the farmer, returning from market brought for her two letters, of which the contents were these:

"Dotandcarryonetown, State of Apodidraskiana.
"April 1, 18..

My Dear Child,

"I am anxious to learn what are your present position, intention, and prospects. The fairies who dropped gold in your shoe, on the morning when I ceased to be a respectable man in London, will soon find a talismanic channel for transmitting you a stocking full of dollars, which will fit the shoe as well as the foot of Cinderella fitted her slipper. I am happy to say I am again become a respectable man. It was always my ambition to be a respectable man, and I am a very respectable man here, in this new township of a new state, where I have purchased five thousand acres of land, at two dollars an acre, hard cash, and established a very flourishing bank. The notes of Touchandgo and Company, soft cash, are now the exclusive currency of all this vicinity. This is the land in which all men flourish; but there are three classes of men who flourish especially,— methodist preachers, slave-drivers, and paper-money manufacturers; and as one of the latter, I have just painted the word BANK on a fine slab of maple, which was green and growing when I arrived, and have discounted for the settlers, in my own currency, sundry bills, which are to be paid when the proceeds of the crop they have just sown shall return from New Orleans; so that my notes are the representatives of vegetation that is to be, and I am accordingly a capitalist of the first magnitude. The people here know very well that I ran away from London; but the most of them have run away from some place or other; and they have a great respect for me, because they think I ran away with something worth taking, which few of them had the luck or the wit to do. This gives them confidence in my resources, at the same time that, as there is nothing portable in the settlement except my own notes, they have no fear that I shall run away with them. They know I am thoroughly conversant with the principles of banking, and as they have plenty of industry, no lack of sharpness, and abundance of land, they wanted nothing but capital to organise a flourishing settlement; and this capital I have manufactured to the extent required, at the expense of a small importation of pens, ink, and paper, and two or three inimitable copper plates. I have abundance here of all good things, a good conscience included; for I really cannot see that I have done any wrong. This was my position: I owed half a million of money; and I had a trifle in my pocket. It was clear that this trifle could never find its way to the right owner. The question was, whether I should keep it, and live like a gentleman; or hand it over to lawyers and commissioners of bankruptcy, and die like a dog on a dunghill. If I could have thought that the said lawyers, etc., had a better title to it than myself, I might have hesitated; but, as such title was not apparent to my satisfaction, I decided the question in my own favour, the right owners, as I have already said, being out of the question altogether. I have always taken scientific views of morals and politics, a habit from which I derive much comfort under existing circumstances.

"I hope you adhere to your music, though I cannot hope again to accompany your harp with my flute. My last andante movement was too forte for those whom it took by surprise. Let not your allegro vivace be damped by young Crotchet's desertion, which, though I have not heard it, I take for granted. He is, like myself, a scientific politician, and has an eye as keen as a needle to his own interest. He has had good luck so far, and is gorgeous in the spoils of many gulls; but I think the Polar Basin and Walrus Company will be too much for him yet. There has been a splendid outlay on credit, and he is the only man, of the original parties concerned, of whom his Majesty's sheriffs could give any account.

"I will not ask you to come here. There is no husband for you. The men smoke, drink, and fight, and break more of their own heads than of girls' hearts. Those among them who are musical, sing nothing but psalms. They are excellent fellows in their way, but you would not like them.

"Au reste, here are no rents, no taxes, no poor-rates, no tithes, no church establishment, no routs, no clubs, no rotten boroughs, no operas, no concerts, no theatres, no beggars, no thieves, no king, no lords, no ladies, and only one gentleman, videlicet, your loving father,

Timothy Touchandgo."

P.S.—I send you one of my notes; I can afford to part with it. If you are accused of receiving money from me, you may pay it over to my assignees. Robthetill continues to be my factotum; I say no more of him in this place: he will give you an account of himself."

"Dotandcarryonetown, etc.

"Dear Miss,

"Mr. Touchandgo will have told you of our arrival here, of our setting up a bank, and so forth. We came here in a tilted waggon, which served us for parlour, kitchen, and all. We soon got up a log-house; and, unluckily, we as soon got it down again, for the first fire we made in it burned down house and all. However, our second experiment was more fortunate; and we are pretty well lodged in a house of three rooms on a floor; I should say the floor, for there is but one.

"This new state is free to hold slaves; all the new states have not this privilege: Mr. Touchandgo has bought some, and they are building him a villa. Mr. Touchandgo is in a thriving way, but he is not happy here: he longs for parties and concerts, and a seat in Congress. He thinks it very hard that he cannot buy one with his own coinage, as he used to do in England. Besides, he is afraid of the Regulators, who, if they do not like a man's character, wait upon him and flog him, doubling the dose at stated intervals, till he takes himself off. He does not like this system of administering justice: though I think he has nothing to fear from it. He has the character of having money, which is the best of all characters here, as at home. He lets his old English prejudices influence his opinions of his new neighbours; but, I assure you, they have many virtues. Though they do keep slaves, they are all ready to fight for their own liberty; and I should not like to be an enemy within reach of one of their rifles. When I say enemy, I include bailiff in the term. One was shot not long ago. There was a trial; the jury gave two dollars damages;

the judge said they must find guilty or not guilty; but the counsel for the defendant (they would not call him prisoner) offered to fight the judge upon the point: and as this was said literally, not metaphorically, and the counsel was a stout fellow, the judge gave in. The two dollars damages were not paid after all; for the defendant challenged the foreman to box for double or quits, and the foreman was beaten. The folks in New York made a great outcry about it, but here it was considered all as it should be. So you see, Miss, justice, liberty, and everything else of that kind, are different in different places, just as suits the convenience of those who have the sword in their own hands. Hoping to hear of your health and happiness, I remain,

> "Dear Miss, your dutiful servant,
> "Roderick Robthetill."

Miss Touchandgo replied as follows to the first of these letters:

"My Dear Father,

"I am sure you have the best of hearts, and I have no doubt you have acted with the best intentions. My lover, or, I should rather say, my fortune's lover, has indeed forsaken me. I cannot say I did not feel it; indeed, I cried very much; and the altered looks of people who used to be so delighted to see me, really annoyed me so, that I determined to change the scene altogether. I have come into Wales, and am boarding with a farmer and his wife. Their stock of English is very small; but I managed to agree with them, and they have four of the sweetest children I ever saw, to whom I teach all I know, and I manage to pick up some Welsh. I have puzzled out a little song, which I think very pretty; I have translated it into English, and I send it you, with the original air. You shall play it on your flute at eight o'clock every Saturday evening, and I will

301

play and sing it at the same time, and I will fancy that I hear my dear papa accompanying me.

"The people in London said very unkind things of you: they hurt me very much at the time; but now I am out of their way, I do not seem to think their opinion of much consequence. I am sure, when I recollect, at leisure, everything I have seen and heard among them, I cannot make out what they do that is so virtuous, as to set them up for judges of morals. And I am sure they never speak the truth about anything, and there is no sincerity in either their love or their friendship. An old Welsh bard here, who wears a waistcoat embroidered with leeks, and is called the Green Bard of Cadeir Idris, says the Scotch would be the best people in the world, if there was nobody but themselves to give them a character: and so I think would the Londoners. I hate the very thought of them, for I do believe they would have broken my heart, if I had not got out of their way. Now I shall write you another letter very soon, and describe to you the country, and the people, and the children, and how I amuse myself, and everything that I think you will like to hear about: and when I seal this letter, I shall drop a kiss on the cover.

"Your loving daughter,
"Susannah Touchandgo.

P.S.—Tell Mr. Robthetill I will write to him in a day or two. This is the little song I spoke of:

"Beyond the sea, beyond the sea,
My heart is gone, far, far from me;
And ever on its track will flee
My thoughts, my dreams, beyond the sea.

"Beyond the sea, beyond the sea,
The swallow wanders fast and free;

Oh, happy bird! were I like thee,
I, too, would fly beyond the sea.

"Beyond the sea, beyond the sea,
Are kindly hearts and social glee:
But here for me they may not be;
My heart is gone beyond the sea."

CHAPTER XII:

THE MOUNTAIN INN

[Greek text]
How sweet to minds that love not sordid ways
Is solitude!—MENANDER.

The Captain wandered despondingly up and down hill for several days, passing many hours of each in sitting on rocks; making, almost mechanically, sketches of waterfalls, and mountain pools; taking care, nevertheless, to be always before nightfall in a comfortable inn, where, being a temperate man, he whiled away the evening with making a bottle of sherry into negus. His rambles brought him at length into the interior of Merionethshire, the land of all that is beautiful in nature, and all that is lovely in woman.

Here, in a secluded village, he found a little inn, of small pretension and much comfort. He felt so satisfied with his quarters, and discovered every day so much variety in the scenes of the surrounding mountains, that his inclination to proceed farther diminished progressively.

It is one thing to follow the high road through a country, with every principally remarkable object carefully noted down in a book, taking, as therein directed, a guide, at particular points, to the more recondite sights: it is another to sit down on one chosen spot, especially when the choice is unpremeditated, and from thence, by a series of explorations, to come day by day on unanticipated scenes. The latter process has many advantages over the former; it is free from the disappointment which attends excited expectation, when imagination has outstripped reality, and from the accidents that mar the scheme of the tourist's single day, when the valleys may be drenched with rain, or the mountains shrouded with mist.

The Captain was one morning preparing to sally forth on his usual exploration, when he heard a voice without, inquiring for a guide to the ruined castle. The voice seemed familiar to him, and going forth into the gateway, he recognised Mr. Chainmail. After greetings and inquiries for the absent: "You vanished very abruptly, Captain," said Mr. Chainmail, "from our party on the canal."

CAPTAIN FITZCHROME. To tell you the truth, I had a particular reason for trying the effect of absence from a part of that party.

MR. CHAINMAIL. I surmised as much: at the same time, the unusual melancholy of an in general most vivacious young lady made me wonder at your having acted so precipitately. The lady's heart is yours, if there be truth in signs.

CAPTAIN FITZCHROME. Hearts are not now what they were in the days of the old song: "Will love be controlled by advice?"

MR. CHAINMAIL. Very true; hearts, heads, and arms have all degenerated, most sadly. We can no more feel the high impassioned love of the ages, which some people have the impudence to call dark, than we can wield King Richard's battleaxe, bend Robin Hood's bow, or flourish the oaken graft of the Pindar of Wakefield. Still we have our tastes and feelings, though they deserve not the name of passions; and some of us may pluck up spirit to try to carry a point, when we reflect that we have to contend with men no better than ourselves.

CAPTAIN FITZCHROME. We do not now break lances for ladies.

MR. CHAINMAIL. No; nor even bulrushes. We jingle purses for them, flourish paper-money banners, and tilt with scrolls of parchment.

CAPTAIN FITZCHROME. In which sort of tilting I have been thrown from the saddle. I presume it was not love that led you from the flotilla?

MR. CHAINMAIL. By no means. I was tempted by the sight of an old tower, not to leave this land of ruined castles, without having collected a few hints for the adornment of my baronial hall.

CAPTAIN FITZCHROME. I understand you live en famille with your domestics. You will have more difficulty in finding a lady who would adopt your fashion of living, than one who would prefer you to a richer man.

MR. CHAINMAIL. Very true. I have tried the experiment on several as guests; but once was enough for them: so, I suppose, I shall die a bachelor.

CAPTAIN FITZCHROME. I see, like some others of my friends, you will give up anything except your hobby.

MR. CHAINMAIL. I will give up anything but my baronial hall.

CAPTAIN FITZCHROME. You will never find a wife for your purpose, unless in the daughter of some old-fashioned farmer.

MR. CHAINMAIL. No, I thank you. I must have a lady of gentle blood; I shall not marry below my own condition: I am too much of a herald; I have too much of the twelfth century in me for that.

CAPTAIN FITZCHROME. Why, then your chance is not much better than mine. A well-born beauty would scarcely be better pleased with your baronial hall than with my more humble offer of love in a cottage. She must have a town-house, and an opera-box, and roll about the streets in a carriage; especially if her father has a rotten borough, for the sake of which he sells his daughter, that he may continue to sell his country. But you were inquiring for a guide to the ruined castle in this vicinity; I know the way and will conduct you.

The proposal pleased Mr. Chainmail, and they set forth on their expedition

CHAPTER XIII:

THE LAKE—THE RUIN

Or vieni, Amore, e qua meco t'assetta.
ORLANDO INNAMORATO.

MR. CHAINMAIL. Would it not be a fine thing, Captain, you being picturesque, and I poetical; you being for the lights and shadows of the present, and I for those of the past; if we were to go together over the ground which was travelled in the twelfth century by Giraldus de Barri, when he accompanied Archbishop Baldwin to preach the crusade?

CAPTAIN FITZCHROME. Nothing, in my present frame of mind, could be more agreeable to me.

MR. CHAINMAIL. We would provide ourselves with his Itinerarium; compare what has been, with what is; contemplate in their decay the castles and abbeys, which he saw in their strength and splendour; and, while you were sketching their remains, I would dispassionately inquire what has been gained by the change.

CAPTAIN FITZCHROME. Be it so.

But the scheme was no sooner arranged, than the Captain was summoned to London by a letter on business, which he did not expect to detain him long. Mr. Chainmail, who, like the Captain, was fascinated with the inn and the scenery, determined to await his companion's return;

and, having furnished him with a list of books, which he was to bring with him from London, took leave of him, and began to pass his days like the heroes of Ariosto, who

-tutto il giorno, al bel oprar intenti,
Saliron balze, e traversar torrenti.

One day Mr. Chainmail traced upwards the course of a mountain stream to a spot where a small waterfall threw itself over a slab of perpendicular rock, which seemed to bar his farther progress. On a nearer view, he discovered a flight of steps, roughly hewn in the rock, on one side of the fall. Ascending these steps, he entered a narrow winding pass, between high and naked rocks, that afforded only space for a rough footpath, carved on one side, at some height above the torrent.

The pass opened on a lake, from which the stream issued, and which lay like a dark mirror, set in a gigantic frame of mountain precipices. Fragments of rock lay scattered on the edge of the lake, some half-buried in the water: Mr. Chainmail scrambled some way over these fragments, till the base of a rock sinking abruptly in the water, effectually barred his progress. He sat down on a large smooth stone; the faint murmur of the stream he had quitted, the occasional flapping of the wings of the heron, and at long intervals, the solitary springing of a trout, were the only sounds that came to his ear. The sun shone brightly half-way down the opposite rocks, presenting, on their irregular faces, strong masses of light and shade. Suddenly he heard the dash of a paddle, and, turning his eyes, saw a solitary and beautiful girl gliding over the lake in a coracle: she was proceeding from the vicinity of the point he had quitted, towards the upper end of the lake. Her apparel was rustic, but there was in its style something more recherchee, in its arrangement something more of elegance and precision, than was common to the mountain peasant girl. It had more of the contadina of the opera, than of the genuine mountaineer; so at least thought Mr. Chainmail; but she passed so rapidly, and took him so much by surprise, that he had little opportunity for accurate observation. He saw her land, at the farther extremity, and disappear among the rocks: he rose from his seat, returned to the mouth of the pass, stepped from stone to stone across the stream, and attempted to pass round by the other side of the lake; but there again the abruptly sinking precipice closed his way.

Day after day he haunted the spot, but never saw again either the damsel or the coracle. At length, marvelling at himself for being so solicitous about the apparition of a peasant girl in a coracle, who could not, by any possibility, be anything to him, he resumed his explorations in another direction.

One day he wandered to the ruined castle, on the sea-shore, which was not very distant from his inn; and sitting on the rock, near the base of the ruin, was calling up the forms of past ages on the wall of an ivied tower, when on its summit appeared a female figure, whom he recognised in an instant for his nymph of the coracle. The folds of the blue gown pressed by the sea-breeze against one of the most symmetrical of figures, the black feather of the black hat, and the ringleted hair beneath it fluttering in the wind; the apparent peril of her position, on the edge of the mouldering wall, from whose immediate base the rock went down perpendicularly to the sea, presented a singularly interesting combination to the eye of the young antiquary.

Mr. Chainmail had to pass half round the castle, on the land side, before he could reach the entrance: he coasted the dry and bramble-grown moat, crossed the unguarded bridge, passed the unportcullised arch of the gateway, entered the castle court, ascertained the tower, ascended the broken stairs, and stood on the ivied wall. But the nymph of the place was gone. He searched the ruins within and without, but he found not what he sought: he haunted the castle day after day, as he had done the lake, but the damsel appeared no more.

CHAPTER XIV:

THE DINGLE

The stars of midnight shall be dear
To her, and she shall lean her ear
In many a secret place,
Where rivulets dance their wayward round,
And beauty, born of murmuring sound,
Shall pass into her face.—WORDSWORTH.

Miss Susannah Touchandgo had read the four great poets of Italy, and many of the best writers of France. About the time of her father's downfall, accident threw into her way Les Reveries du Promeneur Solitaire; and from the impression which these made on her, she carried with her into retirement all the works of Rousseau. In the midst of that startling light, which the conduct of old friends on a sudden reverse of fortune throws on a young and inexperienced mind, the doctrines of the philosopher of Geneva struck with double force upon her sympathies: she imbibed the sweet poison, as somebody calls it, of his writings, even to a love of truth; which, every wise man knows, ought to be left to those who can get anything by it. The society of children, the beauties of nature, the solitude of the mountains, became her consolation, and, by degrees, her delight. The gay society from which she had been excluded, remained on her memory only as a disagreeable dream. She imbibed her new monitor's ideas of simplicity of dress, assimilating her own with that of the peasant-girls in the neighbourhood: the black hat, the blue gown, the black stockings, the shoes, tied on the instep.

Pride was, perhaps, at the bottom of the change: she was willing to impose in some measure on herself, by marking a contemptuous indifference to the characteristics of the class of society from which she had fallen.

And with the food of pride sustained her soul
In solitude.

It is true that she somewhat modified the forms of her rustic dress: to the black hat she added a black feather, to the blue gown she added a tippet, and a waistband fastened in front with a silver buckle; she wore her black stockings very smooth and tight on her ankles, and tied her shoes in tasteful bows, with the nicest possible ribbon. In this apparel, to which, in winter, she added a scarlet cloak, she made dreadful havoc among the rustic mountaineers, many of whom proposed to "keep company" with her in the Cambrian fashion, an honour which, to their great surprise, she always declined. Among these, Harry Ap-Heather, whose father rented an extensive sheepwalk, and had a thousand she-lambs wandering in the mountains, was the most strenuous in his suit, and the most pathetic in his lamentations for her cruelty.

Miss Susannah often wandered among the mountains alone, even to some distance from the farmhouse. Sometimes she descended into the bottom of the dingles, to the black rocky beds of the torrents, and dreamed away hours at the feet of the cataracts. One spot in particular, from which she had at first shrunk with terror, became by degrees her favourite haunt. A path turning and returning at acute angles, led down a steep wood-covered slope to the edge of a chasm, where a pool, or resting-place of a torrent, lay far below. A cataract fell in a single sheet into the pool; the pool boiled and bubbled at the base of the fall, but through the greater part of its extent, lay calm, deep, and black, as if the cataract had plunged through it to an unimaginable depth, without disturbing its eternal repose. At the opposite extremity of the pool, the rocks almost met at their summits, the trees of the opposite banks intermingled their leaves, and another cataract plunged from the pool into a chasm, on which the sunbeams never gleamed. High above, on both sides, the steep woody slopes of the dingle soared into the sky; and from a fissure in the rock, on which the little path terminated, a single gnarled and twisted oak stretched itself over the pool, forming a fork with its boughs at a short distance from the rock. Miss Susannah often sat on the rock, with her feet resting on this tree; in time, she made her seat on the tree itself, with her feet hanging over the abyss; and at length, she accustomed herself to lie along upon its trunk, with her side on the mossy bole of the fork, and an arm round one of the branches. From this position a portion of the sky and the woods was reflected in the pool, which, from its bank, was but a mass of darkness. The first time she reclined in this manner, her heart beat audibly; in time she lay down as calmly as on the mountain heather; the perception of the sublime was probably heightened by an intermingled sense of danger; and perhaps that indifference to life, which early disappointment forces upon sensitive minds, was necessary to the first experiment. There was, in the novelty and strangeness of the position, an excitement which never wholly passed away, but which became gradually subordinate to the influence, at once tranquillising and elevating, of the mingled eternity of motion, sound, and solitude.

One sultry noon, she descended into this retreat with a mind more than usually disturbed by reflections on the past. She lay in her favourite position, sometimes gazing on the cataract; looking sometimes up the steep sylvan acclivities, into the narrow space of the cloudless ether; sometimes down into the abyss of the pool, and the deep bright-blue reflections that opened another immensity below her. The distressing recollections of the morning, the world and all its littlenesses, faded from her thoughts like a dream; but her wounded and wearied spirit drank in too deeply the tranquillising power of the place, and she dropped asleep upon the tree like a ship-boy on the mast.

At this moment Mr. Chainmail emerged into daylight, on a projection of the opposite rock, having struck down through the woods in search of unsophisticated scenery. The scene he discovered filled him with delight: he seated himself on the rock, and fell into one of his romantic reveries; when suddenly the semblance of a black hat and feather caught his eye among the foliage of the projecting oak. He started up, shifted his position, and got a glimpse of a blue gown. It was his lady of the lake, his enchantress of the ruined castle, divided from him by a barrier which, at a few yards below, he could almost overleap, yet unapproachable but by a circuit perhaps of many hours. He watched with intense anxiety. To listen if she breathed was out of the question: the noses of a dean and chapter would have been soundless in the roar of the torrent. From her extreme stillness, she appeared to sleep: yet what creature, not desperate, would go wilfully to sleep in such a place? Was she asleep, then? Nay, was she alive? She was as motionless as death. Had she been murdered, thrown from above, and caught in the tree? She lay too regularly and too composedly for such a supposition. She was asleep, then, and, in all probability, her waking would be fatal. He shifted his position. Below the pool two beetle-browed rocks nearly overarched the chasm, leaving just such a space at the summit as was within the possibility of a leap; the torrent roared below in a fearful gulf. He paused some time on the brink, measuring the practicability and the danger, and casting every now and then an anxious glance to his sleeping beauty. In one of these glances he saw a slight movement of the blue gown, and, in a moment after, the black hat and feather dropped into the pool. Reflection was lost for a moment, and, by a sudden impulse, he bounded over the chasm.

He stood above the projecting oak; the unknown beauty lay like the nymph of the scene; her long black hair, which the fall of her hat had disengaged from its fastenings, drooping through the boughs: he saw that the first thing to be done, was to prevent her throwing her feet off the trunk, in the first movements of waking. He sat down on the rock, and placed his feet on the stem, securing her ankles between his own: one of her arms was round a branch of the fork, the other lay loosely on her side. The hand of this arm he endeavoured to reach, by leaning forward from his seat; he approximated, but could not touch it: after several tantalising efforts, he gave up the point in despair. He did not attempt to wake her, because he feared it might have bad consequences, and he resigned himself to expect the moment of her natural waking, determined not to stir from his post, if she should sleep till midnight.

In this period of forced inaction, he could contemplate at leisure the features and form of his charmer. She was not one of the slender beauties of romance; she was as plump as a partridge; her cheeks were two roses, not absolutely damask, yet verging thereupon; her lips twin-cherries, of equal size; her nose regular, and almost Grecian; her forehead high, and delicately fair; her eyebrows symmetrically arched; her eyelashes, long, black, and silky, fitly corresponding with the beautiful tresses that hung among the leaves of the oak, like clusters of wandering grapes. Her eyes were yet to be seen; but how could he doubt that their opening would be the rising of the sun, when all that surrounded their fringy portals was radiant as "the forehead of the morning sky?"

CHAPTER XV:

THE FARM

Da ydyw'r gwaith, rhaid d'we'yd y gwir,
Ar fryniau Sir Meirionydd;
Golwg oer o'r gwaela gawn
Mae hi etto yn llawn llawenydd.

Though Meirion's rocks, and hills of heath,
Repel the distant sight,
Yet where, than those bleak hills beneath,
Is found more true delight?

At length the young lady awoke. She was startled at the sudden sight of the stranger, and somewhat terrified at the first perception of her position. But she soon recovered her self-possession, and, extending her hand to the offered hand of Mr. Chainmail, she raised herself up on the tree, and stepped on the rocky bank.

Mr. Chainmail solicited permission to attend her to her home, which the young lady graciously conceded. They emerged from the woody dingle, traversed an open heath, wound along a mountain road by the shore of a lake, descended to the deep bed of another stream, crossed it by a series of stepping-stones, ascended to some height on the opposite side, and followed upwards the line of the stream, till the banks opened into a spacious amphitheatre, where stood, in its fields and meadows, the farmhouse of Ap-Llymry.

During this walk, they had kept up a pretty animated conversation. The lady had lost her hat, and, as she turned towards Mr. Chainmail, in speaking to him, there was no envious projection of brim to intercept the beams of those radiant eyes he had been so anxious to see unclosed. There was in them a mixture of softness and brilliancy, the perfection of the beauty of female eyes, such as some men have passed through life without seeing, and such as no man ever saw, in any pair of eyes, but once; such as can never be seen and forgotten. Young Crotchet had seen it; he had not forgotten it; but he had trampled on its memory, as the renegade tramples on the emblems of a faith which his interest only, and not his heart or his reason, has rejected.

Her hair streamed over her shoulders; the loss of the black feather had left nothing but the rustic costume, the blue gown, the black stockings, and the ribbon-tied shoes. Her voice had that full soft volume of melody which gives to common speech the fascination of music. Mr. Chainmail could not reconcile the dress of the damsel with her conversation and manners. He threw out a remote question or two, with the hope of solving the riddle, but, receiving no reply, he became satisfied that she was not disposed to be communicative respecting herself, and, fearing to offend her, fell upon other topics. They talked of the scenes of the mountains, of the dingle, the ruined castle, the solitary lake. She told him, that lake lay under the mountains behind her home, and the coracle and the pass at the extremity, saved a long circuit to the nearest village, whither she sometimes went to inquire for letters.

Mr. Chainmail felt curious to know from whom these letters might be; and he again threw out two or three fishing questions, to which, as before, he obtained no answer.

The only living biped they met in their walk was the unfortunate Harry Ap-Heather, with whom they fell in by the stepping-stones, who, seeing the girl of his heart hanging on another man's arm, and, concluding at once that they were "keeping company," fixed on her a mingled look of surprise, reproach, and tribulation; and, unable to control his feelings under the sudden shock, burst into a flood of tears, and blubbered till the rocks re-echoed.

They left him mingling his tears with the stream, and his lamentations with its murmurs. Mr. Chainmail inquired who that strange creature might be, and what was the matter with him. The young lady answered, that he was a very worthy young man, to whom she had been the innocent cause of much unhappiness.

"I pity him sincerely," said Mr. Chainmail and, nevertheless, he could scarcely restrain his laughter at the exceedingly original figure which the unfortunate rustic lover had presented by the stepping-stones.

The children ran out to meet their dear Miss Susan, jumped all round her, and asked what was become of her hat. Ap-Llymry came out in great haste, and invited Mr. Chainmail to walk in and dine: Mr. Chainmail did not wait to be asked twice. In a few minutes the whole party, Miss Susan and Mr. Chainmail, Mr. and Mrs. Ap-Llymry, and progeny, were seated over a clean homespun table cloth, ornamented with fowls and bacon, a pyramid of potatoes, another of cabbage, which Ap-Llymry said "was poiled with the pacon, and as coot as marrow," a bowl of milk for the children, and an immense brown jug of foaming ale, with which Ap-Llymry seemed to delight in filling the horn of his new guest.

Shall we describe the spacious apartment, which was at once kitchen, hall, and dining-room,—the large dark rafters, the pendent bacon and onions, the strong old oaken furniture, the bright and trimly-arranged utensils? Shall we describe the cut of Ap-Llymry's coat, the colour and tie of his neckcloth, the number of buttons at his knees,—the structure of Mrs. Ap-Llymry's cap, having lappets over the ears, which were united under the chin, setting forth especially whether the bond of union were a pin or a ribbon? We shall leave this tempting field of interesting expatiation to those whose brains are high-pressure steam-engines for spinning prose by the furlong, to be trumpeted in paid-for paragraphs in the quack's corner of newspapers: modern literature having attained the honourable distinction of sharing, with blacking and Macassar oil, the space which used to be monopolised by razor-strops and the lottery; whereby that very enlightened community, the reading public, is tricked into the perusal of much exemplary nonsense; though the few who see through the trickery have no reason to complain, since as "good wine needs no bush," so, ex vi oppositi, these bushes of venal panegyric point out very clearly that the things they celebrate are not worth reading.

The party dined very comfortably in a corner most remote from the fire: and Mr. Chainmail very soon found his head swimming with two or three horns of ale, of a potency to which even he was unaccustomed. After dinner Ap-Llymry made him finish a bottle of mead, which he willingly accepted, both as an excuse to remain and as a drink of the dark ages, which he had no doubt was a genuine brewage from uncorrupted tradition.

In the meantime, as soon as the cloth was removed, the children had brought out Miss Susannah's harp. She began, without affectation, to play and sing to the children, as was her custom of an afternoon, first in their own language, and their national melodies, then in English; but she was soon interrupted by a general call of little voices for "Ouf! di giorno." She complied with the request, and sang the ballad from Paer's Camilla: "Un di carco il mulinaro." The children were very familiar with every syllable of this ballad, which had been often fully explained to them. They danced in a circle with the burden of every verse, shouting out the chorus with good articulation and joyous energy; and at the end of the second stanza, where the traveller has his nose pinched by his grandmother's ghost, every nose in the party was nipped by a pair of little fingers. Mr. Chainmail, who was not prepared for the process, came in for a very energetic tweak from a chubby girl that sprang suddenly on his knees for the purpose, and made the roof ring with her laughter.

So passed the time till evening, when Mr. Chainmail moved to depart. But it turned out on inquiry that he was some miles from his inn, that the way was intricate, and that he must not make any difficulty about accepting the farmer's hospitality till morning. The evening set in with rain: the fire was found agreeable; they drew around it. The young lady made tea; and afterwards, from time to time, at Mr. Chainmail's special request, delighted his ear with passages of ancient music. Then came a supper of lake trout, fried on the spot, and thrown, smoking hot, from the pan to the plate. Then came a brewage, which the farmer called his nightcap, of which he insisted on Mr. Chainmail's taking his full share. After which the gentleman remembered nothing till he awoke, the next morning, to the pleasant consciousness that he was under the same roof with one of the most fascinating creatures under the canopy of heaven.

CHAPTER XVI:

THE NEWSPAPER

[Greek text]
Sprung from what line, adorns the maid
These, valleys deep in mountain-shade?
PIND. Pyth. IX

Mr. Chainmail forgot the Captain and the route of Giraldus de Barri. He became suddenly satisfied that the ruined castle in his present neighbourhood was the best possible specimen of its class, and that it was needless to carry his researches further.

He visited the farm daily: found himself always welcome; flattered himself that the young lady saw him with pleasure, and dragged a heavier chain at every new parting from Miss Susan, as the children called his nymph of the mountains. What might be her second name, he had vainly endeavoured to discover.

Mr. Chainmail was in love: but the determination he had long before formed and fixed in his mind, to marry only a lady of gentle blood, without a blot in her escutcheon, repressed the declarations of passion which were often rising to his lips. In the meantime he left no means untried to pluck out the heart of her mystery.

The young lady soon divined his passion, and penetrated his prejudices. She began to look on him with favourable eyes; but she feared her name and parentage would present an insuperable barrier to his feudal pride.

Things were in this state when the Captain returned, and unpacked his maps and books in the parlour of the inn.

MR. CHAINMAIL. Really, Captain, I find so many objects of attraction in this neighbourhood, that I would gladly postpone our purpose.

CAPTAIN FITZCHROME. Undoubtedly this neighbourhood has many attractions; but there is something very inviting in the scheme you laid down.

MR. CHAINMAIL. No doubt there is something very tempting in the route of Giraldus de Barri. But there are better things in this vicinity even than that. To tell you the truth, Captain, I have fallen in love.

CAPTAIN FITZCHROME. What! while I have been away?

MR. CHAINMAIL. Even so.

CAPTAIN FITZCHROME. The plunge must have been very sudden, if you are already over head and ears.

MR. CHAINMAIL. As deep as Llyn-y-dreiddiad-vrawd.

CAPTAIN FITZCHROME. And what may that be?

MR. CHAINMAIL. A pool not far off: a resting-place of a mountain stream which is said to have no bottom. There is a tradition connected with it; and here is a ballad on it, at your service.

LLYN-Y-DREIDDIAD-VRAWD.
THE POOL OF THE DIVING FRIAR.

Gwenwynwyn withdrew from the feasts of his hall:
He slept very little, he prayed not at all:
He pondered, and wandered, and studied alone;
And sought, night and day, the philosopher's stone.

He found it at length, and he made its first proof
By turning to gold all the lead of his roof:

Then he bought some magnanimous heroes, all fire,
Who lived but to smite and be smitten for hire.

With these on the plains like a torrent he broke;
He filled the whole country with flame and with smoke;
He killed all the swine, and he broached all the wine;
He drove off the sheep, and the beeves, and the kine;

He took castles and towns; he cut short limbs and lives;
He made orphans and widows of children and wives:
This course many years he triumphantly ran,
And did mischief enough to be called a great man.

When, at last, he had gained all for which he held striven,
He bethought him of buying a passport to heaven;
Good and great as he was, yet he did not well know,
How soon, or which way, his great spirit might go.

He sought the grey friars, who beside a wild stream,
Refected their frames on a primitive scheme;
The gravest and wisest Gwenwynwyn found out,
All lonely and ghostly, and angling for trout.

Below the white dash of a mighty cascade,
Where a pool of the stream a deep resting-place made,
And rock-rooted oaks stretched their branches on high,
The friar stood musing, and throwing his fly.

To him said Gwenwynwyn, "Hold, father, here's store,
For the good of the church, and the good of the poor;"
Then he gave him the stone; but, ere more he could speak,
Wrath came on the friar, so holy and meek.

He had stretched forth his hand to receive the red gold,
And he thought himself mocked by Gwenwynwyn the Bold;
And in scorn of the gift, and in rage at the giver,
He jerked it immediately into the river.

Gwenwynwyn, aghast, not a syllable spake;
The philosopher's stone made a duck and a drake;
Two systems of circles a moment were seen,
And the stream smoothed them off, as they never had been.

Gwenwynwyn regained, and uplifted his voice,
"Oh friar, grey friar, full rash was thy choice;
The stone, the good stone, which away thou hast thrown,
Was the stone of all stones, the philosopher's stone."

The friar looked pale, when his error he knew;
The friar looked red, and the friar looked blue;
And heels over head, from the point of a rock,
He plunged, without stopping to pull off his frock.

He dived very deep, but he dived all in vain,
The prize he had slighted he found not again;
Many times did the friar his diving renew,
And deeper and deeper the river still grew.

Gwenwynwyn gazed long, of his senses in doubt,
To see the grey friar a diver so stout;
Then sadly and slowly his castle he sought,
And left the friar diving, like dabchick distraught.

Gwenwynwyn fell sick with alarm and despite,
Died, and went to the devil, the very same night;

The magnanimous heroes he held in his pay
Sacked his castle, and marched with the plunder away.

No knell on the silence of midnight was rolled
For the flight of the soul of Gwenwynwyn the Bold.
The brethren, unfeed, let the mighty ghost pass,
Without praying a prayer, or intoning a mass.

The friar haunted ever beside the dark stream;
The philosopher's stone was his thought and his dream:
And day after day, ever head under heels
He dived all the time he could spare from his meals.

He dived, and he dived, to the end of his days,
As the peasants oft witnessed with fear and amaze.
The mad friar's diving-place long was their theme,
And no plummet can fathom that pool of the stream.

And still, when light clouds on the midnight winds ride,
If by moonlight you stray on the lone river-side,
The ghost of the friar may be seen diving there,
With head in the water, and heels in the air.

CAPTAIN FITZCHROME. Well, your ballad is very pleasant: you shall show me the scene, and I will sketch it; but just now I am more interested about your love. What heroine of the twelfth century has risen from the ruins of the old castle, and looked down on you from the ivied battlements?

MR. CHAINMAIL. You are nearer the mark than you suppose. Even from those battlements a heroine of the twelfth century has looked down on me.

CAPTAIN FITZCHROME. Oh! some vision of an ideal beauty. I suppose the whole will end in another tradition and a ballad.

MR. CHAINMAIL. Genuine flesh and blood; as genuine as Lady Clarinda. I will tell you the story.

Mr. Chainmail narrated his adventures.

CAPTAIN FITZCHROME. Then you seem to have found what you wished. Chance has thrown in your way what none of the gods would have ventured to promise you.

MR. CHAINMAIL. Yes, but I know nothing of her birth and parentage. She tells me nothing of herself, and I have no right to question her directly.

CAPTAIN FITZCHROME. She appears to be expressly destined for the light of your baronial hall. Introduce me in this case, two heads are better than one.

MR. CHAINMAIL. No, I thank you. Leave me to manage my chance of a prize, and keep you to your own chance of a-

CAPTAIN FITZCHROME. Blank. As you please. Well, I will pitch my tent here, till I have filled my portfolio, and shall be glad of as much of your company as you can spare from more attractive society.

Matters went on pretty smoothly for several days, when an unlucky newspaper threw all into confusion. Mr. Chainmail received newspapers by the post, which came in three times a week. One morning, over their half-finished breakfast, the Captain had read half a newspaper very complacently, when suddenly he started up in a frenzy, hurled over the breakfast table, and, bouncing from the apartment, knocked down Harry Ap Heather, who was coming in at the door to challenge his supposed rival to a boxing-match.

Harry sprang up, in a double rage, and intercepted Mr. Chainmail's pursuit of the Captain, placing himself in the doorway, in a pugilistic attitude. Mr. Chainmail, not being disposed for this mode of combat, stepped back into the parlour, took the poker in his right hand, and displacing the loose bottom of a large elbow chair, threw it over his left arm as a shield. Harry, not liking the aspect of the enemy in this imposing attitude, retreated with backward steps into the kitchen, and tumbled over a cur, which immediately fastened on his rear.

Mr. Chainmail, half-laughing, half-vexed, anxious to overtake the Captain, and curious to know what was the matter with him, pocketed the newspaper, and sallied forth, leaving Harry roaring for a doctor and tailor, to repair the lacerations of his outward man.

Mr. Chainmail could find no trace of the Captain. Indeed, he sought him but in one direction, which was that leading to the farm; where he arrived in due time, and found Miss Susan alone. He laid the newspaper on the table, as was his custom, and proceeded to converse with the young lady: a conversation of many pauses, as much of signs as of words. The young lady took up the paper, and turned it over and over, while she listened to Mr. Chainmail, whom she found every day more and more agreeable, when suddenly her eye glanced on something which made her change colour, and dropping the paper on the ground, she rose from her seat, exclaiming: "Miserable must she be who trusts any of your faithless sex! never, never, never, will I endure such misery twice." And she vanished up the stairs. Mr. Chainmail was petrified. At length, he cried aloud: "Cornelius Agrippa must have laid a spell on this accursed newspaper;" and was turning it over, to look for the source of the mischief, when Mrs. Ap Llymry made her appearance.

MRS. AP LLYMRY. What have you done to poor dear Miss Susan? she is crying ready to break her heart.
MR. CHAINMAIL. So help me the memory of Richard Coeur-de-Lion, I have not the most distant notion of what is the matter.
MRS. AP LLYMRY. Oh, don't tell me, sir; you must have ill-used her. I know how it is. You have been keeping company with her, as if you wanted to marry her; and now, all at once, you have been insulting

her. I have seen such tricks more than once, and you ought to be ashamed of yourself.

MR. CHAINMAIL. My dear madam, you wrong me utterly. I have none but the kindest feelings and the most honourable purposes towards her. She has been disturbed by something she has seen in this rascally paper.

MRS. AP LLYMRY. Why, then, the best thing you can do is to go away, and come again tomorrow.

MR. CHAINMAIL. Not I, indeed, madam. Out of this house I stir not, till I have seen the young lady, and obtained a full explanation.

MRS. AP LLYMRY. I will tell Miss Susan what you say. Perhaps she will come down.

Mr. Chainmail sat with as much patience as he could command, running over the paper, from column to column. At length he lighted on an announcement of the approaching marriage of Lady Clarinda Bossnowl with Mr. Crotchet the younger. This explained the Captain's discomposure, but the cause of Miss Susan's was still to be sought: he could not know that it was one and the same.

Presently, the sound of the longed-for step was heard on the stairs; the young lady reappeared, and resumed her seat: her eyes showed that she had been weeping. The gentleman was now exceedingly puzzled how to begin, but the young lady relieved him by asking, with great simplicity: "What do you wish to have explained, sir?"

MR. CHAINMAIL. I wish, if I may be permitted, to explain myself to you. Yet could I first wish to know what it was that disturbed you in this unlucky paper. Happy should I be if I could remove the cause of your inquietude!

MISS SUSANNAH. The cause is already removed. I saw something that excited painful recollections; nothing that I could now wish otherwise than as it is.

327

MR. CHAINMAIL. Yet, may I ask why it is that I find one so accomplished living in this obscurity, and passing only by the name of Miss Susan?

MISS SUSANNAH. The world and my name are not friends. I have left the world, and wish to remain for ever a stranger to all whom I once knew in it.

MR. CHAINMAIL. You can have done nothing to dishonour your name.

MISS SUSANNAH. No, sir. My father has done that of which the world disapproves, in matters of which I pretend not to judge. I have suffered for it as I will never suffer again. My name is my own secret: I have no other, and that is one not worth knowing. You see what I am, and all I am. I live according to the condition of my present fortune, and here, so living, I have found tranquillity.

MR. CHAINMAIL. Yet, I entreat you, tell me your name.

MISS SUSANNAH. Why, sir?

MR. CHAINMAIL. Why, but to throw my hand, my heart, my fortune, at your feet, if-.

MISS SUSANNAH. If my name be worthy of them.

MR. CHAINMAIL. Nay, nay, not so; if your hand and heart are free.

MISS SUSANNAH. My hand and heart are free; but they must be sought from myself, and not from my name.

She fixed her eyes on him, with a mingled expression of mistrust, of kindness, and of fixed resolution, which the far-gone inamorato found irresistible.

MR. CHAINMAIL. Then from yourself alone I seek them.

MISS SUSANNAH. Reflect. You have prejudices on the score of parentage. I have not conversed with you so often without knowing what they are. Choose between them and me. I too have my own prejudices on the score of personal pride.

MR. CHAINMAIL. I would choose you from all the world, were you even the daughter of the executeur des hautes oeuvres, as the heroine of a romantic story I once read turned out to be.

MISS SUSANNAH. I am satisfied. You have now a right to know my history, and if you repent, I absolve you from all obligations.

She told him her history; but he was out of the reach of repentance. "It is true," as at a subsequent period he said to the captain, "she is the daughter of a money-changer: one who, in the days of Richard the First, would have been plucked by the beard in the streets: but she is, according to modern notions, a lady of gentle blood. As to her father's running away, that is a minor consideration: I have always understood, from Mr. Mac Quedy, who is a great oracle in this way, that promises to pay ought not to be kept; the essence of a safe and economical currency being an interminable series of broken promises. There seems to be a difference among the learned as to the way in which the promises ought to be broken; but I am not deep enough in this casuistry to enter into such nice distinctions."

In a few days there was a wedding, a pathetic leave-taking of the farmer's family, a hundred kisses from the bride to the children, and promises twenty times reclaimed and renewed, to visit them in the ensuing year.

CHAPTER XVII:

THE INVITATION

A cup of wine, that's brisk and fine,
And drink unto the lemon mine.
Master Silence.

This veridicous history began in May, and the occurrences already narrated have carried it on to the middle of autumn. Stepping over the interval to Christmas, we find ourselves in our first locality, among the chalk hills of the Thames; and we discover our old friend, Mr. Crotchet, in the act of accepting an invitation, for himself, and any friends who might be with him, to pass their Christmas Day at Chainmail Hall, after the fashion of the twelfth century. Mr. Crochet had assembled about him, for his own Christmas festivities, nearly the same party which was introduced to the reader in the spring. Three of that party were wanting. Dr. Morbific, by inoculating himself once too often with non-contagious matter, had explained himself out of the world. Mr. Henbane had also departed, on the wings of an infallible antidote. Mr. Eavesdrop, having printed in a magazine some of the after-dinner conversations of the castle, had had sentence of exclusion passed upon him, on the motion of the Reverend Doctor Folliott, as a flagitious violator of the confidences of private life.

Miss Crotchet had become Lady Bossnowl, but Lady Clarinda had not yet changed her name to Crotchet. She had, on one pretence and another, procrastinated the happy event, and the gentleman had not been very pressing; she had, however, accompanied her brother and sister-in-law, to pass Christmas at Crotchet Castle. With these, Mr. Mac Quedy, Mr. Philpot, Mr. Trillo, Mr. Skionar, Mr. Toogood, and Mr. Firedamp were sitting at breakfast, when the Reverend Doctor Folliott entered and took his seat at the table.

REV. DR. FOLLIOTT. Well, Mr. Mac Quedy, it is now some weeks since we have met: how goes on the march of mind?

MR. MAC QUEDY. Nay, sir; I think you may see that with your own eyes.

REV. DR. FOLLIOTT. Sir, I have seen it, much to my discomfiture. It has marched into my rickyard, and set my stacks on fire, with chemical materials, most scientifically compounded. It has marched up to the door of my vicarage, a hundred and fifty strong; ordered me to surrender half my tithes; consumed all the provisions I had provided for my audit feast, and drunk up my old October. It has marched in through my back-parlour shutters, and out again with my silver spoons, in the dead of the night. The policeman who has been down to examine says my house has been broken open on the most scientific principles. All this comes of education.

MR. MAC QUEDY. I rather think it comes of poverty.

REV. DR. FOLLIOTT. No, sir. Robbery, perhaps, comes of poverty, but scientific principles of robbery come of education. I suppose the learned friend has written a sixpenny treatise on mechanics, and the rascals who robbed me have been reading it.

MR. CROTCHET. Your house would have been very safe, Doctor, if they had had no better science than the learned friend's to work with.

REV. DR. FOLLIOTT. Well, sir, that may be. Excellent potted char. The Lord deliver me from the learned friend.

MR. CROTCHET. Well, Doctor, for your comfort, here is a declaration of the learned friend's that he will never take office.

REV. DR. FOLLIOTT. Then, sir, he will be in office next week. Peace be with him. Sugar and cream.

MR. CROTCHET. But, Doctor, are you for Chainmail Hall on Christmas Day?

REV. DR. FOLLIOTT. That am I, for there will be an excellent dinner, though, peradventure, grotesquely served.

MR. CROTCHET. I have not seen my neighbour since he left us on the canal.

REV. DR. FOLLIOTT. He has married a wife, and brought her home.

LADY CLARINDA. Indeed! If she suits him, she must be an oddity: it will be amusing to see them together.

LORD BOSSNOWL. Very amusing. He! He! Mr. Firedamp. Is there any water about Chainmail Hall?

REV. DR. FOLLIOTT. An old moat.

MR. FIREDAMP. I shall die of malaria.

MR. TRILLO. Shall we have any music?

REV. DR. FOLLIOTT. An old harper.

MR. TRILLO. Those fellows are always horridly out of tune. What will he play?

REV. DR. FOLLIOTT. Old songs and marches.

MR. SKIONAR. Among so many old things, I hope we shall find Old Philosophy.

REV. DR. FOLLIOTT. An old woman.

MR. PHILPOT. Perhaps an old map of the river in the twelfth century.

REV. DR. FOLLIOTT. No doubt.

MR. MAC QUEDY. How many more old things?

REV. DR. FOLLIOTT. Old hospitality; old wine; old ale; all the images of old England; an old butler.

MR. TOOGOOD. Shall we all be welcome?

REV. DR. FOLLIOTT. Heartily; you will be slapped on the shoulder, and called Old Boy.

LORD BOSSNOWL. I think we should all go in our old clothes. He! He!

REV. DR. FOLLIOTT. You will sit on old chairs, round an old table, by the light of old lamps, suspended from pointed arches, which, Mr. Chainmail says, first came into use in the twelfth century, with old armour on the pillars and old banners in the roof.

LADY CLARINDA. And what curious piece of antiquity is the lady of the mansion?

REV. DR. FOLLIOTT. No antiquity there; none.

LADY CLARINDA. Who was she?

REV. DR. FOLLIOTT. That I know not.

LADY CLARINDA. Have you seen her?

REV. DR. FOLLIOTT. I have.

LADY CLARINDA. Is she pretty?

REV. DR. FOLLIOTT. More,—beautiful. A subject for the pen of Nonnus or the pencil of Zeuxis. Features of all loveliness, radiant with all virtue and intelligence. A face for Antigone. A form at once plump and symmetrical, that, if it be decorous to divine it by externals, would have been a model for the Venus of Cnidos. Never was anything so goodly to look on, the present company excepted; and poor dear Mrs. Folliott. She reads moral philosophy, Mr. Mac Quedy, which indeed she might as well let alone; she reads Italian poetry, Mr. Skionar; she sings Italian music, Mr. Trillo; but, with all this, she has the greatest of female virtues, for she superintends the household and looks after her husband's dinner. I believe she was a mountaineer: [Greek text][1] as Nonnus sweetly sings.

CHAPTER XVIII:

CHAINMAIL HALL

Vous autres dictes que ignorance est mere de tous maulx, et dictes vray: mais toutesfoys vous ne la bannissez mye de vos entendemens, et vivez en elle, avecques elle, et par elle. C'est pourquoy tant de maulx vous meshaignent de jour en jour.— RABELIAS, 1. 5. c. 7.

The party which was assembled on Christmas Day in Chainmail Hall comprised all the guests of Crotchet Castle, some of Mr. Chainmail's other neighbours, all his tenants and domestics, and Captain Fitzchrome. The hall was spacious and lofty; and with its tall fluted pillars and pointed arches, its windows of stained glass, its display of arms and banners intermingled with holly and mistletoe, its blazing cressets and torches, and a stupendous fire in the centre, on which blocks of pine were flaming and crackling, had a striking effect on eyes unaccustomed to such a dining-room. The fire was open on all sides, and the smoke was caught and carried back under a funnel-formed canopy into a hollow central pillar. This fire was the line of demarcation between gentle and simple on days of high festival. Tables extended from it on two sides to nearly the end of the hall.

Mrs. Chainmail was introduced to the company. Young Crotchet felt some revulsion of feeling at the unexpected sight of one whom he had forsaken, but not forgotten, in a condition apparently so much happier than his own. The lady held out her hand to him with a cordial look of more than forgiveness; it seemed to say that she had much to thank him for. She was the picture of a happy bride, rayonnante de joie et d'amour.

Mr. Crotchet told the Reverend Doctor Folliott the news of the morning. "As you predicted," he said, "your friend, the learned friend, is in office; he has also a title; he is now Sir Guy de Vaux."

REV. DR. FOLLIOTT. Thank heaven for that! he is disarmed from further mischief. It is something, at any rate, to have that hollow and wind-shaken reed rooted up for ever from the field of public delusion.

MR. CROTCHET. I suppose, Doctor, you do not like to see a great reformer in office; you are afraid for your vested interests.

REV. DR. FOLLIOTT. Not I, indeed, sir; my vested interests are very safe from all such reformers as the learned friend. I vaticinate what will be the upshot of all his schemes of reform. He will make a speech of seven hours' duration, and this will be its quintessence: that, seeing the exceeding difficulty of putting salt on the bird's tail, it will be expedient to consider the best method of throwing dust in the bird's eyes. All the rest will be

[Greek text in verse] as Aristophanes has it; and so I leave him, in Nephelococcygia.

Mr. Mac Quedy came up to the divine as Mr. Crotchet left him, and said: "There is one piece of news which the old gentleman has not told you. The great firm of Catchflat and Company, in which young Crotchet is a partner, has stopped payment."

REV. DR. FOLLIOTT. Bless me! that accounts for the young gentleman's melancholy. I thought they would overreach themselves with their own tricks. The day of reckoning, Mr. Mac Quedy, is the point which your paper-money science always leaves out of view.

MR. MAC QUEDY. I do not see, sir, that the failure of Catchflat and Company has anything to do with my science.

REV. DR. FOLLIOTT. It has this to do with it, sir, that you would turn the whole nation into a great paper-money shop, and take no thought of the day of reckoning. But the dinner is coming. I think you, who are so fond of paper promises, should dine on the bill of fare.

The harper at the head of the hall struck up an ancient march, and the dishes were brought in, in grand procession.

The boar's head, garnished with rosemary, with a citron in its mouth, led the van. Then came tureens of plum-porridge; then a series of turkeys, and in the midst of them an enormous sausage, which it required two men to carry. Then came geese and capons, tongues and hams, the ancient glory of the Christmas pie, a gigantic plum pudding, a pyramid of mince pies, and a baron of beef bringing up the rear.

"It is something new under the sun," said the divine, as he sat down, "to see a great dinner without fish."

MR. CHAINMAIL. Fish was for fasts in the twelfth century.

REV. DR. FOLLIOTT. Well, sir, I prefer our reformed system of putting fasts and feasts together. Not but here is ample indemnity.

Ale and wine flowed in abundance. The dinner passed off merrily: the old harper playing all the while the oldest music in his repertory. The tables being cleared, he indemnified himself for lost time at the lower end of the hall, in company with the old butler and the other domestics, whose attendance on the banquet had been indispensable.

The scheme of Christmas gambols, which Mr. Chainmail had laid for the evening, was interrupted by a tremendous clamour without.

REV. DR. FOLLIOTT. What have we here? Mummers?

MR. CHAINMAIL. Nay, I know not. I expect none.

"Who is there?" he added, approaching the door of the hall.

"Who is there?" vociferated the divine, with the voice of Stentor.

"Captain Swing," replied a chorus of discordant voices.

REV. DR. FOLLIOTT. Ho, ho! here is a piece of the dark ages we did not bargain for. Here is the Jacquerie. Here is the march of mind with a witness.

MR. MAC QUEDY. Do you not see that you have brought disparates together? the Jacquerie and the march of mind.

REV. DR. FOLLIOTT. Not at all, sir. They are the same thing, under different names. [Greek text]. What was Jacquerie in the dark ages is the march of mind in this very enlightened one—very enlightened one.

MR. CHAINMAIL. The cause is the same in both; poverty in despair.

MR. MAC QUEDY. Very likely; but the effect is extremely disagreeable.

REV. DR. FOLLIOTT. It is the natural result, Mr. Mac Quedy, of that system of state seamanship which your science upholds. Putting the crew on short allowance, and doubling the rations of the officers, is the sure way to make a mutiny on board a ship in distress, Mr. Mac Quedy.

MR. MAC QUEDY. Eh! sir, I uphold no such system as that. I shall set you right as to cause and effect. Discontent arises with the increase of information. That is all.

REV. DR. FOLLIOTT. I said it was the march of mind. But we have not time for discussing cause and effect now. Let us get rid of the enemy.

And he vociferated at the top of his voice, "What do you want here?"

"Arms, arms," replied a hundred voices, "Give us the arms."

REV. DR. FOLLIOTT. You see, Mr. Chainmail, this is the inconvenience of keeping an armoury not fortified with sand bags, green bags, and old bags of all kinds.

MR. MAC QUEDY. Just give them the old spits and toasting irons, and they will go away quietly.

MR. CHAINMAIL. My spears and swords! not without my life. These assailants are all aliens to my land and house. My men will fight for me, one and all. This is the fortress of beef and ale.

MR. MAC QUEDY. Eh! sir, when the rabble is up, it is very indiscriminating. You are e'en suffering for the sins of Sir Simon Steeltrap and the like, who have pushed the principle of accumulation a little too far.

MR. CHAINMAIL. The way to keep the people down is kind and liberal usage.

MR. MAC QUEDY. That is very well (where it can be afforded) in the way of prevention; but in the way of cure the operation must be more drastic. (Taking down a battle-axe.) I would fain have a good blunderbuss charged with slugs.

MR. CHAINMAIL. When I suspended these arms for ornament, I never dreamed of their being called into use.

MR. SKIONAR. Let me address them. I never failed to convince an audience that the best thing they could do was to go away.

MR. MAC QUEDY. Eh! sir, I can bring them to that conclusion in less time than you.

MR. CROTCHET. I have no fancy for fighting. It is a very hard case upon a guest, when the latter end of a feast is the beginning of a fray.

MR. MAC QUEDY. Give them the old iron.

REV. DR. FOLLIOTT. Give them the weapons! Pessimo, medius fidius, exemplo. Forbid it the spirit of Frere Jean des Entommeures! No! let us see what the church militant, in the armour of the twelfth century, will do against the march of mind. Follow me who will,

338

and stay who list. Here goes: Pro aris et focis! that is, for tithe pigs and fires to roast them.

He clapped a helmet on his head, seized a long lance, threw open the gates, and tilted out on the rabble, side by side with Mr. Chainmail, followed by the greater portion of the male inmates of the hall, who had armed themselves at random.

The rabble-rout, being unprepared for such a sortie, fled in all directions, over hedge and ditch.

Mr. Trillo stayed in the hall, playing a march on the harp, to inspirit the rest to sally out. The water-loving Mr. Philpot had diluted himself with so much wine as to be quite hors de combat. Mr. Toogood, intending to equip himself in purely defensive armour, contrived to slip a ponderous coat of mail over his shoulders, which pinioned his arms to his sides; and in this condition, like a chicken trussed for roasting, he was thrown down behind a pillar in the first rush of the sortie. Mr. Crotchet seized the occurrence as a pretext for staying with him, and passed the whole time of the action in picking him out of his shell.

"Phew!" said the divine, returning; "an inglorious victory; but it deserves a devil and a bowl of punch."

MR. CHAINMAIL. A wassail-bowl.

REV. DR. FOLLIOTT. No, sir. No more of the twelfth century for me.

MR. CHAINMAIL. Nay, Doctor. The twelfth century has backed you well. Its manners and habits, its community of kind feelings between master and man, are the true remedy for these ebullitions.

MR. TOOGOOD. Something like it: improved by my diagram: arts for arms.

REV. DR. FOLLIOTT. No wassail-bowl for me. Give me an unsophisticated bowl of punch, which belongs to that blissful middle period, after the Jacquerie was down, and before the march of mind was up. But, see, who is floundering in the water?

Proceeding to the edge of the moat, they fished up Mr. Firedamp, who had missed his way back, and tumbled in. He was drawn out, exclaiming, "that he had taken his last dose of malaria in this world."

REV. DR. FOLLIOTT. Tut, man; dry clothes, a turkey's leg and rump, well devilled, and a quart of strong punch, will set all to rights.

"Wood embers," said Mr. Firedamp, when he had been accommodated with a change of clothes, "there is no antidote to malaria like the smoke of wood embers; pine embers." And he placed himself, with his mouth open, close by the fire.

REV. DR. FOLLIOTT. Punch, sir, punch: there is no antidote like punch.

MR. CHAINMAIL. Well, Doctor, you shall be indulged. But I shall have my wassail-bowl, nevertheless.

An immense bowl of spiced wine, with roasted apples hissing on its surface, was borne into the hall by four men, followed by an empty bowl of the same dimensions, with all the materials of arrack punch, for the divine's especial brewage. He accinged himself to the task with his usual heroism, and having finished it to his entire satisfaction, reminded his host to order in the devil

REV. DR. FOLLIOTT. I think, Mr. Chainmail, we can amuse ourselves very well here all night. The enemy may be still excubant: and we had better not disperse till daylight. I am perfectly satisfied with my quarters. Let the young folk go on with their gambols; let them dance to your old harper's minstrelsy; and if they please to kiss under the mistletoe, whereof I espy a goodly bunch suspended at the end of the hall, let those who like it not leave it to those

340

who do. Moreover, if among the more sedate portion of the assembly, which, I foresee, will keep me company, there were any to revive the good old custom of singing after supper, so to fill up the intervals of the dances, the steps of night would move more lightly.

MR. CHAINMAIL. My Susan will set the example, after she has set that of joining in the rustic dance, according to good customs long departed.

After the first dance, in which all classes of the company mingled, the young lady of the mansion took her harp, and following the reverend gentleman's suggestion, sang a song of the twelfth century.

FLORENCE AND BLANCHFLOR.

Florence and Blanchflor, loveliest maids,
Within a summer grove,
Amid the flower-enamelled shades
Together talked of love.

A clerk sweet Blanchflor's heart had gain'd;
Fair Florence loved a knight:
And each with ardent voice maintained
She loved the worthiest wight.

Sweet Blanchflor praised her scholar dear,
As courteous, kind, and true!
Fair Florence said her chevalier
Could every foe subdue.

And Florence scorned the bookworm vain,
Who sword nor spear could raise;

And Blanchflor scorned the unlettered brain
Could sing no lady's praise.

From dearest love, the maidens bright
To deadly hatred fell,
Each turned to shun the other's sight,
And neither said farewell.

The king of birds, who held his court
Within that flowery grove,
Sang loudly: "'Twill be rare disport
To judge this suit of love."

Before him came the maidens bright,
With all his birds around,
To judge the cause, if clerk or knight
In love be worthiest found.

The falcon and the sparrow-hawk
Stood forward for the fight:
Ready to do, and not to talk,
They voted for the knight.

And Blanchflor's heart began to fail,
Till rose the strong-voiced lark,
And, after him, the nightingale,
And pleaded for the clerk.

The nightingale prevailed at length,
Her pleading had such charms;
So eloquence can conquer strength,
And arts can conquer arms.

The lovely Florence tore her hair,
And died upon the place;
And all the birds assembled there
Bewailed the mournful case.

They piled up leaves and flowerets rare
Above the maiden bright,
And sang: "Farewell to Florence fair,
Who too well loved her knight."

Several others of the party sang in the intervals of the dances. Mr.
Chainmail handed to Mr. Trillo another ballad of the twelfth century, of
a merrier character than the former. Mr. Trillo readily accommodated it
with an air, and sang:

THE PRIEST AND THE MULBERRY TREE.

Did you hear of the curate who mounted his mare,
And merrily trotted along to the fair?
Of creature more tractable none ever heard;
In the height of her speed she would stop at a word,
And again with a word, when the curate said Hey,
She put forth her mettle, and galloped away.

As near to the gates of the city he rode,
While the sun of September all brilliantly glowed,
The good priest discovered, with eyes of desire,
A mulberry tree in a hedge of wild briar,
On boughs long and lofty, in many a green shoot,
Hung large, black, and glossy, the beautiful fruit.

The curate was hungry, and thirsty to boot;
He shrunk from the thorns, though he longed for the fruit;
With a word he arrested his courser's keen speed,
And he stood up erect on the back of his steed;
On the saddle he stood, while the creature stood still,
And he gathered the fruit, till he took his good fill.

"Sure never," he thought, "was a creature so rare,
So docile, so true, as my excellent mare.
Lo, here, how I stand" (and he gazed all around),
"As safe and as steady as if on the ground,
Yet how had it been, if some traveller this way,
Had, dreaming no mischief, but chanced to cry Hey?"

He stood with his head in the mulberry tree,
And he spoke out aloud in his fond reverie.
At the sound of the word, the good mare made a push,
And down went the priest in the wild-briar bush.
He remembered too late, on his thorny green bed,
Much that well may be thought cannot wisely be said.

Lady Clarinda, being prevailed on to take the harp in her turn, sang
the following stanzas.

In the days of old,
Lovers felt true passion,
Deeming years of sorrow
By a smile repaid.
Now the charms of gold,
Spells of pride and fashion,
Bid them say good morrow
To the best-loved maid.

Through the forests wild,
O'er the mountains lonely,
They were never weary
Honour to pursue.
If the damsel smiled
Once in seven years only,
All their wanderings dreary
Ample guerdon knew.

Now one day's caprice
Weighs down years of smiling,
Youthful hearts are rovers,
Love is bought and sold:
Fortune's gifts may cease,
Love is less beguiling;
Wisest were the lovers
In the days of old.

The glance which she threw at the captain, as she sang the last verse, awakened his dormant hopes. Looking round for his rival, he saw that he was not in the hall; and, approaching the lady of his heart, he received one of the sweetest smiles of their earlier days.

After a time, the ladies, and all the females of the party, retired. The males remained on duty with punch and wassail, and dropped off one by one into sweet forgetfulness; so that when the rising sun of December looked through the painted windows on mouldering embers and flickering lamps, the vaulted roof was echoing to a mellifluous concert of noses, from the clarionet of the waiting-boy at one end of the hall, to the double bass of the Reverend Doctor, ringing over the empty punch-bowl, at the other.

CONCLUSION

From this eventful night, young Crotchet was seen no more on English mould. Whither he had vanished was a question that could no more be answered in his case than in that of King Arthur after the battle of Camlan. The great firm of Catchflat and Company figured in the Gazette, and paid sixpence in the pound; and it was clear that he had shrunk from exhibiting himself on the scene of his former greatness, shorn of the beams of his paper prosperity. Some supposed him to be sleeping among the undiscoverable secrets of some barbel-pool in the Thames; but those who knew him best were more inclined to the opinion that he had gone across the Atlantic, with his pockets full of surplus capital, to join his old acquaintance, Mr. Touchandgo, in the bank of Dotandcarryonetown.

Lady Clarinda was more sorry for her father's disappointment than her own; but she had too much pride to allow herself to be put up a second time in the money-market; and when the Captain renewed his assiduities, her old partiality for him, combining with a sense of gratitude for a degree of constancy which she knew she scarcely deserved, induced her, with Lord Foolincourt's hard-wrung consent, to share with him a more humble, but less precarious fortune, than that to which she had been destined as the price of a rotten borough.

Footnotes:

1   A mountain-wandering maid,
     Twin-nourished with the solitary wood.